Puddles of Love

Netty Morgan

This book is a work of fiction. The names and characters, are products of the writer's imagination or have been used fictitiously and are not to be construed as real. Any resemblance to persons, living or dead, is entirely coincidental.

Copyright © 2016 Netty Morgan

All rights reserved.

ISBN-13 978-1530398560:

For Mark, my husband who has supported me loved me and been by my side through the good and the bad for thirty years. I love you.

For my wonderful Dad whom I miss so much. He always said that dogs and children are the best judge of character.

For my beautiful "Big Fella" Foley. When we said goodbye at Christmas, it was one of the hardest days of my life.   I miss you every single day.

CONTENTS

	Acknowledgments	viii
	Prologue	Pg 1
1	Helen's Heroes	Pg 3
2	Percival Boston Junior	Pg 12
3	G is for…?	Pg 26
4	1st May 2015 – Zakynthos	Pg 34
5	Conversations with a cat	Pg 42
6	Eggs and Bacon	Pg 52
7	Puppy Love	Pg 62
8	A Whirlwind of a Woman	Pg 75
9	Revelations	Pg 86
10	Ela, ela	Pg 96
11	Knickers or not?	Pg 106
12	The Kalvos Cup	Pg 116
13	A Veiled Muse	Pg 130
14	I Spy with My Snotty Eye	Pg 143
15	You Can't Con Nora	Pg 155
16	A Party in the Pool	Pg 168

17	Sweet Nothings	Pg 179
18	Wine and Roses	Pg 189
19	A Geo What?	Pg 200
20	Let's Fly, Let's Fly Away	Pg 209
21	By Land, By Air, By Sea	Pg 218
22	And the Winner is…	Pg 224
23	September 15th, 2013	Pg 234
24	A Sting in the Tale	Pg 236
25	The Logic of a Child	Pg 245
	Epilogue	Pg 251
	About the Author	Pg 254

PUDDLES OF LOVE

ACKNOWLEDGMENTS

Although this book is a work of fiction, the stray dogs and cats on Zakynthos are very real. There are also many groups and individuals that dedicate themselves to rescuing, fostering and re-homing the strays. On top of this, they organise the feeding stations, fundraise and do numerous other selfless things, far too many to mention here. I have listed these groups at the end.

To write a book I needed to invent a couple of not so nice characters and a rivalry between three different groups. If there are any "not so nice" characters amongst the animal lovers in Zakynthos, I'm yet to find them. Everyone is amazing and how they manage to dedicate so much time to what they do is beyond me. There is also no rivalry between the different groups, in fact, it's the total opposite. They all work to support each other and help whenever they can. This novel is very much a figment of my imagination and far from what really happens in Zakynthos.

I owe so many thanks to so many people, and if I miss anyone out, I apologise profusely. To Gemma Smith, my main reader, motivator and mistake spotter. Thank you for believing in me, you are a star. As is your wonderful husband Danny Smith, who spent many hours formatting my complete mess of a manuscript. To my coffee buddy Jenni Fuller, who cried when she read the prologue, I'm sorry I made you cry.

To two wonderful people, Bob and Lorna Croft, who introduced me to their world and taught me so much about rescuing, fostering and rehoming the dogs and in the process became such special friends. To the real cat lady of Zakynthos, Marilyn Williams who far from being a crazy cat lady is a wise and intelligent woman. Her knowledge of cats is endless as is the constant stream of cats that she rescues, fosters and rehomes.

To Sheryl Voultsou and her wonderful family who run Callinica Hotel in Tsilivi. Lily's hotel is very much based on Callinica and for our family is a home from home. We truly cherish every holiday we spend with you.

Some of the restaurants mentioned are real too. Kaliva, Two

Brothers, Menir and of course the wonderful Wine and Roses run by friends Osiada and George. These restaurants are all in Tsilivi and are all amazing. I can't mention Tsilivi and restaurants without thanking the wonderful Edison Sonni Salobeai known to many as Sonni for the years of friendship. We have watched Sonni grow from a young waiter in a chip shop to jointly running his own restaurant M-eating. We are so very proud of all he has achieved.

To Bobby Goertz and Penny Draper. Island FM played merrily in the background as I typed each day and your wonderful chatter about Zakynthos always kept me smiling.

To Chrissie Parker, author of the wonderful "Among the Olive Groves." who gave me such valuable advice on the minefield of Self-publishing.

To the many wonderful volunteers throughout the UK who fundraise and home check for all the relevant groups. You are all stars.

I can't forget Brooke, my Granddaughter, who insisted at the last minute that she needed to be a character in my book. I duly obliged as Grandmothers always do.

To Daniel, Hayley, Poppy, Hannah, Stef, Joey, Jack, Terry and Steph. My beautiful family.

Last, but most certainly not least, to Puddles, who had the cheek to find me, follow me and make me cry my eyes out. Puddles started it all.

If you would like to support the stray cats and dogs of Zakynthos please take a look at the following groups:

Zakynthos Animal Welfare Fund: www.zawf.gr
Zante Strays: www.zantestrays.gr
Sue Deeth: http://www.healingpawsdogrescue.com
Toni Kaplanis:
https://www.facebook.com/groups/730580320342220/?fref=ts

PROLOGUE
22ND FEBRUARY 2015

Madeline Kalvos gazed through her rheumy blue eyes at the wonderful view stretched out below. The crystal blue Ionian Sea lapped gently over the golden sands of an empty Gerakas beach. To the left the majestic cliffs loomed over the beach; a chunk of them missing as if a mythical creature had flown down and taken a bite. To the right the smaller Pelouzo Islet was dwarfed by the larger island of Marathonisi.

Madeline gazed down at the beautiful dog whose head rested in her lap. As she fondled his silky red ears and felt the lump of a shotgun pellet wedged firmly under the skin, she recalled the day she had found him four years ago. She had been heading into Zante Town when at the side of the road she'd spotted a bundle of red fur. Screeching to a halt, she'd climbed out of her pick-up truck with a heavy heart, expecting to find yet another poisoned dog. Walking towards the dog her pulse had raced when he'd lifted a weary head and trembled with fear and cold. Reaching his side, the tears had flown freely down her cheeks. The dog was lying in a puddle of muddy rainwater. Carefully lifting his skinny, flea-ridden body she'd carried him to the truck and placed him carefully on the passenger seat. Continuing on her journey, she'd reached out and stroked his bony head trying to calm the quivering fear.

"If you make it through the night I shall call you Puddles." Madeline had whispered to the dog.

Puddles had not only made it through the night, but he had also made it through the next four years and blossomed into a healthy Springer Setter cross. Puddles had been Madeline's constant companion and source of comfort through the last difficult years.

Puddles suddenly pricked his ears and wagged his tail. Madeline turned her head to see a bright blue Jeep struggling up the steep and crumbly chalk road towards her villa.

"Oh my darling Puddles, It's time for me to go." Madeline's throat constricted as she buried her face into the dog's soft neck and whispered her goodbyes, knowing that she would never see him or her beautiful home again.

Markos Kalvos parked the jeep and walked round the side of the villa. He stood silently. Fighting back his own tears as he watched the heartbreaking scene in front of him. His late Uncle's wife Madeline was now sobbing as she clutched at Puddles, who was whimpering and trying to lick the salty tears from her face. Up until two years ago when cancer had started to ravage her body Madeline Kalvos had remained active and sprightly with a strength of mind and body that belied her near on eighty years of age. Now she barely had the strength to stand up, and he knew it would only be a matter of weeks or even days before he would also be saying goodbye. Madeline could no longer cope with the pain and Markos was here to take her to the hospital. They both knew she would not be returning home.

Markos gently carried Madeline to his jeep and felt Puddles tugging at his trouser leg, when he closed the passenger door he watched as the dog jumped up and clawed at the window, desperate to get to his beloved owner.

Markos' son Christos walked out of the villa wiping his reddened eyes and lifted Puddles into his arms.

"Just go." He said gruffly to his father and Markos jumped into the jeep and started the engine.

They drove off down through the olive groves and Madeline glanced in the mirror. She broke down as she saw Puddles barking and straining to get out of Christos' arms.

Composing herself, she reached out a shaky hand and clutched at Markos' strong, tanned arm.

"Promise me Markos, when Helen arrives, you will welcome her and help her," she begged.

Markos grunted his reassurance but silently raged against Madeline's long lost family who had so viciously cut all ties with her nearly forty years ago.

CHAPTER 1
HELEN'S HEROES

Helen leant against the toilet door and sighed as Dotty ripped off the mohair jumper.

"I told you to get a cardigan; it's all about the layers." Helen teased then laughed as Dotty knelt under the ancient hand dryer and switched it on. The thin stream of cool air that stuttered from the vent did little to combat the hot flush Dotty was having.

"I need a doctor Helen." Dotty gasped, flapping the top of her silk blouse back and forth as the red flush crept over her enormous breasts.

"Dotty, you've seen a doctor and had every blood test possible, you are going through the menopause, and it's about time you faced up to it." Dotty shook her head in denial and her blonde extensions stuck to the sweat that had formed on her hot cheeks. A tapping sounded on the door, and Helen eased it open.

"Is everything okay?" asked their friend Molly "Ron's just about to start."

"Another hot flush," whispered Helen "I'll be right out." Molly giggled "Thank God you got her in here, I don't think Ron could cope with a repeat of last week." Helen rolled her eyes and thought back to the week before.

In the middle of round five Dotty had suffered her first ever hot flush, convinced she was having a heart attack she'd ripped off her jumper and t-shirt and grabbed the gastropub menu to fan herself. With her surgically enhanced breasts not always needing a bra she had sat there topless and totally unaware of the chaos she was causing as Merv the Perv and the Boys at the Bar cheered ecstatically and launched into *"You've got a lovely bunch of coconuts."* Merv's wife had whacked him round the head with her handbag and stormed out. Things had only calmed down when Ron the landlord had rung the bar bell and threatened to cancel the quiz.

Dotty started to undo her blouse and Helen gave her a stern look

"Don't you dare take that off, sort yourself out and you better redo your make-up."

The very vain Dotty gasped and raced to the mirrors, screeching as she spotted one of her false eyelashes perched prettily on the end of her nose. Helen rejoined her team and found Ian, Molly's husband and Gerald laughing as Molly described the scene in the ladies' toilets. Helen joined in the laughter and silently thanked them all for being such kind and caring friends.

Helen and her husband William had been doing the weekly quiz at their local pub for eight long years. It was the highlight of their week and always such a good laugh. With their twins Jamie and Annabelle growing up and heading off to university they had settled into middle age with a sense of calm tranquillity. Their love for each other had moved from the passionate throes of new love, through the bonding years of parenthood to a deep, mutual respect for each other. Although both independent, Helens favourite time of day had always been supper time. When William wasn't away on one of his boring business trips, they would sit down together with a glass of wine and discuss their day, ask each other for advice and sometimes Skype one or both of the twins. Helen missed suppertime, more than anything else, when suppertime came around each day Helen would shed a few silent tears and remember William with love and sadness.

Helen would never, ever forget the start of that dreadful day eighteen months ago. She had been sitting in her classroom waiting for her Year 11 group to finish their lunch. Marion, the school secretary, had popped her head round the door.

"Helen, there's an urgent phone call for you from the hospital."

"Oh for goodness sake," said Helen "What's Papa done now?" Her Father-in-law was forever getting himself into minor scrapes and falls. He was too proud to go into a nursing home and insisted on cooking, shopping and doing everything himself despite it often ending up in a trip to A&E. Helen knew every nurse, Doctor and Consultant by name now and was surprised that Papa didn't have his own reserved bed.

"Do me a favour Marion and ask Viv if she will take the register and hand back the homework, I shouldn't be too long." Marion had smiled and nodded her consent, and Helen had raced off down the corridor to the main office and picked up the phone.

"Hello is that Mrs. Hardy?" a serious sounding voice had said.

"Yes, speaking." Helen had heard the background beeps, clatters, clangs and murmurs of a busy A&E department.

"Mrs. Hardy." The voice had said, "This is Staff Nurse Johnson, I'm so sorry, but Mr. Hardy has been involved in a car accident, it's quite serious, could you come at once?"

With a sinking feeling Helen had organised cover for the rest of the day, grabbed her car keys and set off.

Helen had started the car, plugged her phone into the hands-free and quickly dialled Williams's number.

"I am currently unavailable." Williams's voice had echoed around the car "Please leave a message and I will return your call as soon as possible."

"William, it's me, Papa is at St James and it doesn't sound good, I'll meet you there." Helen knew William checked his phone regularly and had hoped that he wouldn't be too long.

Helen had walked into the A&E department and spotted their good friend Gerald stood at reception. He was a consultant at the hospital and had been best friends with William and Helen since their university days.

"Hello Gerald." Helen had said "What are you doing down in A&E? Have you seen Papa? Is he badly hurt?"

Gerald had grabbed both of Helens hands; she'd noticed the grim look on his face and the tears swimming in his eyes and a cold shiver had started to creep from the pits of her stomach up to her throat.

"What is it?" she'd whispered.

"Helen, I'm so, so sorry, it's not Papa, it's William."

And that, thankfully, is where the memories of that day stopped. Helen had no recall of the next few hours. She did not remember being led to Williams's bedside or the discussions with the doctors about turning his life support off. She certainly didn't recall giving permission for his organs to be donated although she knew that's what he would have wanted. It was almost as if her mind had deliberately switched itself off, although Gerald, many months later had told her she had held herself together and acted with a strength and dignity she should be proud of.

She only had vague recollections of the next few days which had seemed to blur into one long horrible nightmare. She remembered Papa sobbing as he cuddled the twins and Dotty undressing her and putting her to bed. She was pretty sure that her wonderful neighbours Ian and Molly had been popping in and out with food and comforting hugs. Sympathy cards by the dozens had appeared on the shelves and bookcases, but she didn't think she had read any of the kind words that friends, relatives, and colleagues had written.

Helen remembered the funeral though, oh how she remembered that awful day; it was the one memory that would steal into her dreams, night after lonely night. No matter how hard she tried to summon up the happy times they had spent together, the sight of her beloved husband's coffin, adorned with the beautiful white roses, invaded every happy memory and left her weeping deeply into her pillows.

Helen felt herself descending back into a pit of gloom, she mentally shook herself and glanced around the table. These wonderful friends had been her source of strength and comfort over the past few months. Her best friend Dotty had gradually brought her out of her despair and reeled her back into the strong arms of the people closest to her. She'd not thought it would ever be possible to find herself laughing again, but here she was, laughing, giggling and starting to enjoy life. Going back to Quiz Night had been perhaps the hardest thing to do but the right thing to do. She loved the friendly rivalry between the teams. She laughed at the overly competitive Boys at the Bar team who sulked like babies when they lost. She even managed to chuckle at Merv the Perv calling her honey and offering to keep her warm at night. She was eternally grateful to Gerald, who had been by her side, helping to sort the nightmare of paperwork involved in any death, the will, probate, inheritance tax and insurances. So here she was, eighteen months a widow and now, thanks to Williams foresightedness, quite a wealthy widow. Helen was financially secure and the twins, although absolutely devastated at their father's death, were both young enough and strong enough to move on with their lives. They had both completed their degrees and were now, with Helen's blessing, using some of their inheritance to travel the world on a gap year.

Helen looked over at the empty seat opposite her. There had been plenty of offers to fill Williams place on the team but each and every team member politely refused and left the empty seat there. As Ron, the landlord, yelled for quiet Helen raised her glass of wine and blew a kiss to the empty chair.

Helen turned her thoughts back to the quiz as she felt Gerald nudging her knee under the table. Looking up, she saw Dotty waltzing back to the table, underneath her blouse had been hidden the most exotic black and gold, *Moulin Rouge*, type garment that Helen had ever seen. Dotty's incredibly large boobs spilled out over the top and as she sat back down Ian spluttered his mouthful of beer over the quiz sheet.

"Wow," said Molly as she grabbed a pile of serviettes and started mopping up the spilt beer. "Is that one of your creations Dotty?" Dotty had her own very successful lingerie company and loved showing off her latest designs.

"Yes, it will be online for sale next week, do you want me to put one aside for you?"

"Er…I'm not sure it's my type of thing." Stammered Molly "but it looks amazing on you Dotty."

Helen straightened her back, folded her arms and in her best teacher's voice addressed Dotty.

"I know what you're doing Dorothy Amanda Boothroyd."

"I'm not doing anything." Grinned Dotty

"Oh yes you are, and it's not going to work."

"Well, you two may know what's going on." Declared Gerald, who was trying hard to look anywhere but at Dotty's boobs "We, on the other hand, don't have a clue, would you care to enlighten us?"

"Well." Said Helen "Last week we won by a massive 58 points, Dotty has this theory that Merv's team, the Boys at the Bar team and the Quiztastics were so distracted by her boobs that they couldn't concentrate. I do believe that she is trying to repeat that this week."

"Rubbish." Declared Dotty, tossing her glorious mane of blonde and honey brown extensions and sticking her boobs out a bit more. Helen slowly reached under the table and pulled out a dark green Marks and Spencer carrier bag and slid it over the table towards Dotty.

"I will probably never speak to you again Helen Hardy." Muttered Dotty as she pulled a beautiful blue cashmere cardigan out of the bag and slung it over her shoulders.

"Put it on correctly and button it up." Said Helen "or shall I start with the summer of 1979."

"Don't you dare." Cried Dotty as she hurriedly shoved her arms into the cardigan and started buttoning "What happened in 79 stays in 79."

"Right you horrible lot." Yelled Ron. "First round is on The Simpsons." As a collective groan went round the older members of the pub team, Dotty turned to the Boys at the Bar, who were high-fiving each other, smiled seductively and slowly undid her top two buttons.

Helen grinned to herself and as Molly and Ian were the only team members who had ever watched The Simpsons she turned to Gerald to ask how his week had been.

"Oh busy as usual." Answered Gerald. "That reminds me I bought two tickets for the annual fundraising ball; I know you couldn't manage it last year, but I was hoping you would consider coming as my guest this year?"

"Oh." Said Helen "Would you mind if I don't give you an answer now Gerald, I'd like to think about it."

"Of course Helen, I fully understand but…you know William would have wanted you to carry on living your life."

Helen took a deep breath and battled down the flash of anger she could feel building inside her. How dare Gerald tell her what William would have wanted. She was living her life in the best way she could. Yes, of course, there were days when she shut herself away and ignored all phone calls and visitors, but these were few and far between now. She had taken early retirement from teaching but spent two days a week volunteering in the hospitals W.R.V.S shop. She filled the rest of her time with baking, knitting, and reading. She would often take her elderly neighbour's dog out for long walks and enjoyed days out with Dotty at least twice a month. Gerald's constant over protection of her was starting to grate on her nerves. Although she would be eternally grateful for his support in the days and weeks following Williams's death, she had a niggling concern that there was an ulterior motive behind all the attention he paid her. They had been out a few times for meals and theatre trips, and while Helen saw these as merely friends getting together, she was fearful that Gerald was starting to see them as dates that would eventually lead to something else. He didn't want a wife; she knew that but she feared the lonely man was seeking her permanent companionship, and that was never going to happen.

Helen jumped as Ron's voice shattered her thoughts.

"Round two. General Knowledge. Question number one. Who were the Four Horseman of the Apocalypse?"

"Oh, I know." Said Dotty "D'Artagnan, Athos, Porthos and Aramis." As Helen and Gerald burst out laughing Dotty glared at them "What?" she said.

"They're the Musketeers." Laughed Helen. "And there's only three of them not four; D'Artagnan wasn't a Musketeer."

"Of course he was." Said Dotty, pulling out her phone to Google D'Artagnan.

"Oi Ron." Shouted Angie, Merv's wife "Dotty's got her phone out." "That's not the only thing she's got out." Said Merv the Perv and ducked to avoid Angie's handbag.

"I am not cheating; I am looking up D'Artagnan." Declared Dotty as the pub erupted in laughter.

"Sorry Dotty." Said Ron "You know the rules, Sin Bin for ten minutes." As the rest of the pub chanted "Sin Bin, Sin Bin." Dotty wiggled her way over to the Sin Bin. Anyone caught with their phone out would have to spend ten minutes in the Sin Bin, which was a bar stool placed next to Walter, the pubs resident drunk. Walter was the loveliest man with a heart of gold but after every pint of Guinness he drank, his thick Glaswegian accent would become more and more difficult to understand. Walter did the quiz by himself every week, and nearly always came last, except when Helen or Molly would sneak over to help him.

"Well," Gerald said. "Can't see that Dotty will give him much help."

"No." Giggled Molly. "But Walters certainly going to enjoy ogling her boobs, good job there's a cardiologist in the pub."

"Pestilence, War, Famine and hmm…I can't remember the last one." Said Helen bringing the team back to the question.

"It's Death." whispered Molly with tears swimming in her eyes.

As Gerald quickly wrote down the answers, Helen reached over to Molly and clasped her hands.

"Its ok Molly, I'm not going to break down every time someone mentions the word death." She said kindly. Molly blushed and excused herself, running to the toilets. The death of her good friend's husband had been hard on them all.

Helen threw herself into the next four rounds as the teams battled, debated and attempted unsuccessfully to challenge Ron's answers. At the end of the penultimate round, Ron announced the current positions. Walter, of course, was coming last with the Boys at the Bar only a few points ahead of him. Dotty winked at Helen as her distraction tactics had obviously worked. In third place was Merv the

Perv's rowdy table and there was only one point between the Quiztastics and Helen's Heroes at the top. As Ron announced the final "Killer" round, a hush settled over the teams. The final round was evil; each question was worth 10 points but if you put a wrong answer you lost all the points for that round. Helen's team answered the first two questions easily, missed out the third and fourth and high-fived Dotty as she cleverly answered question number five about Victoria Beckham.

"Question Number Six." Said Ron "Who was the wife of Leofric, Earl of Mercia?"

"Lady Chatterley." Said Gerald confidently, writing it down.

"I thought it was Lady Godiva." Said Helen.

"No Helen." Said Gerald pompously "It was definitely Lady Chatterley; I saw this question in my quiz book a couple of weeks ago."

"Well, I think you are wrong." Said Helen pursing her lips and glaring at Dotty, who was snorting into her cardigan.

"Helen, I appreciate that you have a wonderful knowledge of literature, but I am a hundred percent sure that I am right."

Helen turned her head to hide the blush of embarrassment she felt at Gerald's pompous and condescending attitude. Lady Godiva wouldn't even come under literature she thought angrily. The legend was based on a real historical figure. Ian and Molly rolled their eyes at each other not wanting to get involved and Dotty glared at Gerald, disliking this nasty side of him. Helen sat quietly as the round finished and waited expectantly for Ron to give the answers.

"Number six." Said Ron "The wife of Leofric, Earl of Mercia was Lady Godiva."

"Yes," thought Helen silently, as the team groaned and looked accusingly at Gerald in disgust.

"Well." Retaliated Gerald, "The quiz book must be wrong; I shall certainly be writing to the editor."

"Well done Gerald." Said Dotty, who was never quite as reticent as Helen or the others "We've bummed out now."

As the winning Quiztastic team cheered themselves and counted their winnings, Helen gathered her coat and bag.

"May I give you a lift home Helen?" asked Gerald, looking quite sheepish.

"No thank you Gerald, Dotty is stopping at mine tonight and has her car."

"Oh! Do you think she should be driving? She has had quite a few."

" Gerald." Interrupted Dotty, who had been earwigging. "I may be Dotty by name and Dotty by nature, but I'm not daft enough to drink and drive, if you didn't have your head shoved so far up your arse you might have noticed that I've been drinking Mocktails all night."

Helen watched as Gerald puffed up his shoulders and stuck his neck out in indignation, she grabbed Dotty's arm and dragged her out of the pub shouting a cheery "Goodnight" to everyone.

Outside the pub, Helen and Dotty grabbed each other and collapsed in hysterical laughter.

"Oh Dotty, he's never going to speak to you again." Gasped Helen.

"That was the idea." Screeched Dotty struggling to contain herself "I think I may have just wet myself. Come on, let's go home, we can snuggle up with a hot chocolate and a dose of Patrick Swayze."

"Great minds think alike." Said Helen wrapping her arms around her best friend as they snorted and giggled their way over the car park to Dotty's bright pink Volkswagen Beetle.

Later that night as Helen and Dotty sat on the sofa watching Patrick Swayze wiggling his hips and running his hands across his exquisite chest Helen suddenly remembered the strange letter she had opened that morning.

"Oh Dotty, what do you think of this?" She asked as she handed Dotty the letter. It was from a firm of solicitors asking her to contact them urgently regarding the estate of a Madeline Kalvos.

"I've never heard of a Madeline Kalvos," said Helen "It must be meant for someone else."

"Kalvos," said Dotty, "I think Kalvos is a Greek name, how very odd, maybe it was someone William knew."

"I don't think so," said Helen. "He never mentioned any Greek friends and we didn't ever go to Greece, remind me to give them a ring in the morning and tell them they have the wrong Helen Hardy."

CHAPTER 2
PERCIVAL BOSTON JUNIOR

    Helen awoke to the glimmer of April sunshine peeping through her bedroom curtains and the pleasant smell of freshly brewed coffee wafting up the stairs. As she stretched and glanced at the clock displaying 8:20am she realised that she had slept the whole night through. Wow, she thought, that didn't happen very often. She nearly always woke in the early, lonely hours of the morning and in the drowsy moments between sleep and full alertness would stretch her arm over to a sleeping William only to realise once more that he wasn't there. Suddenly she heard the sound of a lawn mower starting up and looked out the window to see Dotty pushing the mower up the garden. Helen laughed out loud at the sight of Dotty dressed in a hot pink velour tracksuit with SEXY written in large gold letters across her pert bottom. She had teamed her outfit with pale pink fluffy boots which Helen could see were getting damper with each step across the dewy grass. Helen knew that Dotty would only cut half the lawn and leave the rest for Helen.
    This time last year she had confided in Dotty that some of her worst moments came when she was faced with the jobs that William had always done. Changing the oil in the car, going into the loft and other jobs that Helen's generation liked to leave for the men.
    Her biggest fear was mowing the lawn. It was a job that William had made look so easy but the first time Helen had dragged the old petrol driven mower out of the shed she had been completely stumped. There were levers and buttons that she had never noticed before. She had worked out that the little pictures of a hare and tortoise were meant to indicate fast and slow but didn't have a clue what the other knobs and levers were for. She had been sat gloomily staring with hatred at the long straggly grass and redundant lawn mower when Dotty had turned up.
    Taking the situation in at a glance Dotty had dragged Helen out to the local garden centre and flirting outrageously with the handsome young sales assistant had purchased a brand new, female-friendly mower along with a generous discount. Back at Helens she had

confidently started the machine and wiggled her way up and down the garden leaving a trail of wavy light and dark green stripes. Helen had smiled, William would have been so cross at the crooked lines weaving up and down his beloved lawn. Helen had disappeared into the kitchen to make coffee and when she'd heard the whirring of the engine stop she'd peered out the back door to see Dotty relaxed in one of the rattan garden chairs with her feet up on the old table. Helen had carried their coffees out and as she'd placed them on the table and shooed Dotty's feet off she had spotted the gleam in Dotty's eyes.

"What?" she'd asked knowing she wasn't going to like the answer.

"Well I've done half the lawn" Dotty had replied "You can do the rest" and with that Dotty had winked, taken a quick gulp of her coffee and hugged Helen goodbye.

Watching Dotty now, Helen recalled how she had spent the next two hours finding other chores to do and thinking evil thoughts about her devious best friend. Concealed beneath Dotty's ditzy exterior was actually a very quick mind and she'd known that Helen would get more and more frustrated with the sight of a half cut, uneven lawn. William's obsession with orderliness and cleanliness had rubbed off on Helen over the years and eventually unable to stand it anymore Helen had jumped up, pulled on her garden shoes and following the instruction manual had started the mower. She had been so immensely proud of herself as she'd breathed in the glorious smell of newly cut grass and regarded the straight even stripes that she had created. That had been the start of Dotty's therapy, and whenever Helen came across a job she couldn't do Dotty would start it and leave Helen to finish it. Dotty would half wire a plug, half wallpaper a wall, half drill a hole and leave Helen to do the rest. Over the course of a few months, Helen had become more and more confident and discovering that absolutely everything could be Googled or You Tubed had excelled in being her own "Man about the House" Last Christmas Eve she had laughed with glee and excitement when Dotty had presented her with a flowery pink toolkit.

As Helen wandered down the stairs and into the kitchen, she heard the lawn mower switch off and poured herself and Dotty a mug of coffee each. While she was reaching into the cupboard for the packet of croissants she'd bought the day before she heard Dotty opening the back door.

"For goodness sake" moaned Dotty "look at my boots" Helen glanced around and laughed as she saw Dotty holding up her once fluffy pink boots which were now an excellent shade of green as hundreds of grass clippings clung to the damp fur.

"You idiot," said Helen "you should have put my wellies on."

"Not on your Nelly" exclaimed Dotty "Hilda's hunky Grandson is doing her garden next door; I couldn't possibly wear your ugly wellies with this tracksuit."

As Jamie, her elderly neighbour's Grandson was at least thirty years younger than Dotty and was also absolutely smitten with Ian and Molly's daughter Libby; Helen smiled at Dotty's futile attempts to snare a toy boy. To be honest, Helen thought if any of the twenty to thirty-year-olds that Dotty flirted with, ever returned the attention she would probably run a mile.

"Right," said Dotty pulling out a chair and picking up her coffee. "Let's have another look at this letter of yours."

Helen buttered the warmed up croissants while Dotty re-read the letter and suggested Helen ring them after breakfast.

"It's Saturday." Helen said, "no one will be there."

"Well you don't know that for sure," said Dotty "some of these London firms work all weekend" and with that she grabbed her mobile and dialled the number on the top of the letter.

"Dotty I'll ring them Mon…" Helen began to say but was cut off by the prim and proper voice coming through Dotty's speakerphone

"Good Morning, Boston, Boston, and Merriweather, this is Daphne speaking; how may I assist you today."

"Oh, Good Morning" replied Helen frantically waving at Dotty, who was pulling faces at the posh tone of Daphne's voice. "This is Helen Hardy I've had a letter from you about the estate of a Madeline Kalvos but I'm afraid you have the wrong person as…"

"Please hold the line" interrupted Daphne "I will transfer your call to Mr. Boston Junior."

"How rude" declared Dotty and they both winced as the tinny sound of Amazing Grace screeched from the phone.

Five minutes of holding later as Helen was just about to hang up in disgust they both jumped as an even posher, privately schooled voice boomed around the kitchen.

"Mrs. Hardy, Percival Boston Jr here. How absolutely wonderful.

We have been searching for you for a couple of months; this is just marvellous in fact it's absolutely spiffing."

"Mr. Boston, I was just trying to explain to someone called Daphne that I think you have the wrong Helen Hardy" replied Helen glaring at Dotty who had stood up and had one hand clapped over her mouth, and the other clamped between her crossed legs, once again on the verge of wetting herself with laughter.

"Oh no," said Percival Boston Jr "We do our research very thoroughly, very thoroughly indeed. Can you confirm that you are indeed Helen Hardy, previously Helen Chambers, born on 23 May 1965 in Battle Hospital, Reading?"

"Err mm well yes" confirmed Helen amazed at the information they had.

"Oh Goody gumdrops," said Percival" Helen shoved a tea towel into a convulsing Dotty's mouth.

"I would love you to pop into our office with some proof of your identification; then we can discuss the late Mrs. Kalvos' estate" continued Percival.

Helen was getting more confused by the minute as she tried to explain once again that she did not know a Madeline Kalvos.

"Well Madeline Kalvos was formerly Madeline Chambers, and I believe through our research that she was your paternal Aunt, your father's sister?" queried Percival "I'm getting awfully confused myself Mrs. Hardy" he continued "Surely you must have been aware that your Aunt Madeline passed away in February? I am so awfully, terribly sorry if I'm the bearer of bad news."

"But that's ridiculous" exclaimed Helen "I don't have an Aunt Madeline" Suddenly Helen spotted Dotty frantically waving the letter on which she had scribbled in large capital letters AUNT MADDIE

"Oh" exclaimed Helen "I did have an Aunt Maddie but no… no… that's all too silly; Aunt Maddie died years and years ago."

"Well like I said," replied Percival if you could just pop into the office…"

Dotty grabbed the phone off Helen and in a voice posher than Daphne's announced

"Good Morning Mr. Boston, my name is Dorothy Boothroyd. I am Mrs. Hardy's personal assistant. Mrs. Hardy has an appointment in Knightsbridge at three o'clock this afternoon, could you please transfer me back to Daphne so we can arrange a suitable time to pop in today."

As Helen mouthed her annoyance at Dotty they both suddenly chuckled as they heard Percival Boston Junior shouting for Daphne and swearing his frustration at "This abominable machine."

When Dotty finally switched her phone off after agreeing a two o'clock appointment, they stared at each other in complete and utter disbelief.

"I don't get it," said Helen "Aunt Maddie died years ago, there is something very strange about all of this."

"Well, how do you know she died?" asked Dotty "Did you go to her funeral? Did you visit a grave? How do you know she died?"

Thinking it was a very astute question for Dotty, Helen wracked her brains trying to remember what must have been almost forty years ago.

"Well, I can remember I was supposed to be going to the premiere of Escape to Witch Mountain with Aunt Maddie or was it somewhere else? Argh" moaned Helen as she put her head in both hands and clutched her hair as she tried to work out which were real memories and which were just recollections of the wonderful imagination she'd had as a child.

"Just sit down and breathe" soothed Dotty "What were you wearing?" she asked as she hoped gentle questioning would evoke Helen's memories.

"OK" sighed Helen "I was sat in my bedroom, and I had on my brand new long yellow dress, do you remember it Dotty, it was trimmed with lace and had a wide silk sash round the waist."

"Ugh yes" replied Dotty shuddering at the hideous long dresses they had worn in the seventies. "Carry on"

"I can remember being excited and it must have been either just before or just after my ninth or tenth birthday as the trip was a present from Aunt Maddie" Helen silently thought some more and Dotty asked if she remembered the trip.

"No" said Helen "That's the thing I remember most, Aunt Maddie never turned up, and I think I must have cried myself to sleep" As the memories started flooding back Helen continued "I woke up and could hear my parents whispering downstairs, but it was an angry whispering as if they were arguing but trying not to wake me. I went downstairs, and my father sat me down and told me that Aunt Maddie had gone away and wouldn't ever be coming back."

"So he never actually said she had died?" asked Dotty

"No," said Helen "but the next day at school I remember I was crying and…Do you remember that lovely dinner lady we had; she was a big black lady with a lovely smile, she was always giving us cuddles and extra helpings?"

"Yes" recalled Dotty "Mrs. Swainson."

"That's right," said Helen smiling fondly at the memory "Well she found me round by the boiler house crying and when I told her what was wrong she told me that Aunt Maddie must have died and told me all about heaven. I guess I assumed she was right and… do you know what Dotty? I don't think anyone ever mentioned Aunt Maddie again."

"Wow," said Dotty "This just gets weirder and weirder."

"Hmm" pondered Helen "and talking of weird, since when were you my PA? And what the hell was all that about an appointment in Knightsbridge?"

"Cap the dayum" exclaimed Dotty "Seize the Day."

"I think you mean Carpe Diem" laughed Helen

"All right you snotty know it all" laughed Dotty "last time I was this intrigued was waiting for the final Harry Potter book to be published. Let's go and find some suitable outfits for our meeting with the fabulous Percival Boston Jr" They both laughed as Dotty grabbed Helens hand and pulled her up the stairs.

An hour later, while they waited for the taxi to arrive. Helen and Dotty gazed up and down at each other's outfits and didn't know whether to laugh or cry. Dotty had raided Helens daughter's cupboards and had teamed a long mid-calf pencil skirt with a tight fitted black jacket which was straining over her large boobs. Her black court shoes and the fashionable black glasses she was wearing gave her the look of the ultimate professional PA. She had rolled her long hair into a neat French plait and carried her laptop in a bag over her shoulder. Helen had rummaged through her wardrobe and found a pale blue linen shift dress. She had casually slung Dotty's M&S cashmere cardigan over her shoulders and added a matching pearl earrings and necklace set.

"Right let's do this Mrs. Hardy," said Dotty as the taxi pulled up. Helen jumped in the back after Dotty and shivered as she felt a thrill of both excitement and fear shudder through her body.

Once they were settled on the train to Waterloo, Dotty pulled out her laptop explaining that she had some emails to answer and phone calls to make. Helen gazed round the first class carriage and marvelled, for perhaps the thousandth time, how Dotty could switch in an instant from the ditzy, blonde lifelong friend to the steely businesswoman who owned a chain of lingerie shops across the UK and kept a constant strict eye on her hundreds of employees.

Watching the fields rush past the window Helen allowed herself to remember her Aunt Maddie. They had spent so much time together all those years ago and Helen's favourite holidays had been the ones spent near Weymouth with her parents and her Aunt. After a week or two, her parents would head home and leave Dotty in Maddie's care. Helen could still picture the endless sunny hours they spent wandering along the beach collecting shells and twisted bits of driftwood. The older couple staying in the cottage next door would let them take their two border collies with them and they would race alongside, splashing in and out of the sea and digging frantically in the sand. Helen chuckled silently to herself as she remembered one of the collies yelping as it buried its nose in the sand and came back out with a large crab attached to its face.

When they returned to the rented cottage each evening Helen would watch her Aunt Drill tiny holes into the shells and string them together to make wonderful bracelets. She would help her Aunt lay the pieces of driftwood along the windowsills to dry and some evenings they would amble slowly down to the seaside café and order the chips which came wrapped in newspaper. They would take their chips and sit on the quayside watching the fishing boats gliding gently back into their overnight docks. At the end of the summer, they would pile their luggage, the elderly neighbours and their dogs along with copious amounts of shells and driftwood into Maddie's old green Morris Minor and sing their way home.

"Penny for them?" said Dotty as the train pulled up at the signals outside Waterloo Station.

"I was just thinking about Aunt Maddie and the fun we used to have" replied Helen "how strange that I'd completely forgotten that she ever existed."

"I remember her," said Dotty "she always looked so happy and carefree and seemed to float everywhere; I wonder how old she was when she died... well vanished".

"I think she must have been about forty" replied Helen "That's if

I was ten when she went."

"She always seemed much younger than that…like a teenager," reminisced Dotty as the train finally pulled into the station.

Once they had pushed and shoved their way off the train and through the ticket barriers, Helen automatically turned to her left and started heading towards the underground.

"Where are you going?" said Dotty grabbing her arm and pulling her the other way.

"To get the tube of course, do you know which line we need? Is it Bakerloo?"

"Tube" exclaimed Dotty, raising her eyes in disgust "I'm not going down into that grubby underground, ugh! Just the thought of those sweaty bodies crammed together makes me feel sick. Follow me I've arranged for the company limo to meet us outside" and as Dotty dragged her through the station and down the stairs to the exit Helen wasn't sure whether to be disgusted at Dotty's snobbery or impressed with her organisation.

Outside the station, Helen spotted a uniformed chauffer standing next to a shiny, dark blue Mercedes Sedan. Hmm, not quite a Limo she thought.

"Good afternoon Michael," said Dotty handing him a piece of paper with the address written down.

"When did you copy that down?" exclaimed Helen, staggered at Dotty's efficiency.

"Ah I'm not just a pretty face Mrs. Hardy" replied Dotty winking at Helen

As Helen followed Dotty onto the luxurious cream leather seats she groaned as the sound of Irving Berlin's *"Anything You Can Do; I Can Do Better"* rang out from the smartphone in her pocket.

"Oh no, that's Gerald" she groaned quickly grabbing the phone and pressing the decline button.

"How did you know that was Gerald?" Dotty asked, "You knew it was him before you even looked at the display."

"It's his ringtone" she explained, "I have different ringtones for different people, the twins showed me how to programme it last Christmas."

"Oh that's clever, oh that's very clever" laughed Dotty as the wickedness of the song choice dawned on her "That's so fitting for that pompous idiot," she said slapping her thighs in delight. Helen pretended to fiddle with her phone and glanced sideways at Dotty, waiting for the inevitable question.

"So…What's my ringtone then?" Dotty eventually asked.

"Not telling" Helen mumbled as she tried to suppress the giggles erupting from deep within her belly.

"Tell me" pleaded Dotty

"Nope" spluttered Helen

"Oh no don't" Helen squealed, clutching her stomach as Dotty whipped out her phone and speed dialled Helen's number. The loud shriek of laughter finally burst out of Helen as the sound of Freddy Mercury singing "*Fat Bottomed Girls*" rang round the car.

"Oh God, I can't breathe" gasped Helen laughing even harder at the complete disbelief and indignation on a speechless Dotty's face.

"It's irony" Helen tried to explain "You're always saying *does my bum look big in this?*" As Helen howled even louder, Dotty tried to hide her grin, secretly thrilled that for the first time in months her friend was laughing so freely.

Five minutes later with Helen's make up repaired they stood outside a huge black door looking for a bell to ring. Dotty pointed out a small brass plaque announcing that Boston, Boston, and Merriweather resided on the second floor, and as no bell could be found Helen turned the doorknob and pushed open the heavy door. Another sign at the bottom of an imposing staircase signalled the way to go. At the top of the second flight of stairs, they found Daphne's office and opened the door composing themselves as they remembered her ultra-posh voice.

"Ah Good Afternoon, you must be Mrs. Hardy" assumed Daphne "and your assistant Ms. Booth…Oh…My…God" Daphne stuttered as she stared at Dotty. "Oh goodness me, you're Dorothy Boothroyd. How absolutely exquisite to meet you, you won't believe this, but I'm actually wearing a pair of your knickers right now."

"Daphne. How Dare You" thundered the deep booming voice of Percival Boston Jr making Helen and Dotty jump so much that they grabbed each other's hands in shock.

Helen slowly turned and stared at the portly man standing in the doorway. He must have been only just five feet tall and not far off five feet round. Over a dark blue shirt, he wore a bright yellow waistcoat with matching bow tie and had teamed these with pinstripe trousers. The overall effect was more that of a clown than a solicitor.

"It's fine… Mr. Boston, I presume" said Helen "Shall we go to your office?" and taking Percival by the elbow she swung him round and with her free hand signalled to Dotty to sort out the now snivelling Daphne.

Helen followed the waddling man down an ornately decorated corridor and explained who Dotty was.

"It's all very well you sticking up for that girl," puffed Percival as he took out a large white handkerchief and mopped the sweat off his forehead. "But I can guarantee that within minutes of you leaving; Daphne will have updated her Facebook status to "Just met the woman whose knickers I'm wearing" and added some of those despicable little smiley faces with tears sprouting out the cheeks. It's simply not good enough."

Helen murmured her understanding as she walked into his office and perched on the edge of a beautiful red chesterfield armchair.

"So tell me about my Aunt Madeline?" she said, changing the subject, and smiled as Percival reverted to the jovial man she'd heard over the phone.

"Ah yes, of course," he said picking up a file. "Your Aunt wrote to us back in August last year asking us to draw up her will and naming us as the executors. It was all very complicated as she resided in Greece so there was an awful lot of paperwork involved and it took us a couple of months before we had the Will and Codicil all legally binding. In February, we received a letter from a Markos Kalvos informing us that she had died and enclosing a Greek death certificate. As I said on the phone earlier, it took us a while to find you."

Helen breathed deeply and relaxed back into the chair thinking about what he had said.

"Are you sure that Madeline Kalvos was my Aunt?" questioned Helen as she handed over her passport, birth and marriage certificate and explained how she'd been so sure her Aunt had died long ago.

"Oh golly gosh, absolutely my dear. We have a top notch team of researchers here, now let me see…Ah yes, here it is" said Percival pulling a piece of paper out of the pile in front of him. "Your father was Harold Chambers born August 14th, 1933 and your mother, whom he married in June 1963, was Ruth Granger born December 2nd, 1937. Is that correct?"

Helen nodded and thought back to 2001 and 2003 when her

father then mother had passed away. On both occasions, her, William and the twins had gone through all the family albums and she couldn't recall seeing any pictures of Aunt Maddie it was almost as if her parents had wanted her to forget her existence.

"Right" continued Percival "Madeline named you as the sole inheritor of her entire estate which consists of roughly £60,000 after we have deducted our expenses of course and her property in Zakynthos, Greece."

"Oh My," said Helen "Gosh... Zakynthos, what a pretty name, I've never heard of it" Helen was struggling to take all the information in and was still very puzzled by the disappearance of her Aunt for forty years.

"Just a couple more things before we start signing paperwork," said Percival "In October your Aunt added a codicil to the first will and if you don't mind me saying, quite a mysterious one at that. In simple terms, she stated that for you to inherit this property, you must spend exactly thirty days on the Island of Zakynthos…and…" Percival paused dramatically "On or before the final day you will have to decide whether you wish to move permanently to the island."

"What on earth" interrupted Helen, flabbergasted "That's ridiculous."

"And…" continued Percival, mopping his brow again "If you choose not to live in Zakynthos then you will forfeit all rights to the property, and it will revert to…"

"Who?" queried Helen frustrated at Percival's theatrics

"I don't know" squeaked the solicitor, his voice rising with excitement "This is why it's all so dreadfully exciting."

Helen felt more exasperated than excited as she begged Percival to explain.

"Well my dear, Madeline left two sealed envelopes with us, one is a letter for you to take away with you today and the other came with very strict instructions that it is only to be opened after you had carried out the instructions in the codicil" Helen looked at the two envelopes that Percival was waving in front of her and felt grateful to Daphne for keeping Dotty busy, knowing full well that Dotty would have snatched the envelope and torn it open.

"Oh there's more, there's more" Percival exclaimed, clapping his hands like an excited little boy. "Inside the second envelope there is a further letter for you and a piece of paper with the name of who it reverts to written on it; if you can predict who is named, on that piece of paper, then the codicil will become null and void and you get to do whatever you wish with the property"

Helen felt as if she had been transported to another crazy dimension. Her head was spinning with all the information and the bizarreness of it all. As Percival waited expectantly for her to respond she held out her hand for the letter addressed to her. She peered at the spidery writing that just said Helen and hoped that its contents would give her the answers to the numerous questions whirling around her head. She decided to tuck the envelope in her handbag for now. She wasn't sure that she wanted Dotty to see it and she had a very strong feeling that she needed to be alone when she read it.

"Can we leave the paperwork, for now, Mr. Boston?" Helen asked, "I'll make another appointment for next week; I just need to get my head around all this before I sign anything."

"Oh… Absolutely! Of course" agreed Percival "Here take this" and he handed Helen a blue folder. "I had Daphne put together all the information you will need, it has lots of details about Zakynthos and also contact information for Markos Kalvos who is dealing with your Aunts estate out there."

"Thank you," said Helen as she shook his hand and turned towards the door just wanting to get out in the fresh air and clear her head.

Dotty took one look at Helen's face, calmly said her goodbyes and followed her downstairs and back into the waiting car. She tapped the waiting chauffer on the shoulder and asked him to drop them at her apartment, guessing correctly that Helen needed to be somewhere quiet.

As the car weaved its way through the London traffic, Dotty watched silently as Helen turned on her phone and sighed at the six missed calls and two voicemails from Gerald.

"Give it here," she said taking the phone and quickly tapped out a message to Gerald.

Hi Gerald, sorry had phone on silent I'm in the theatre with Dotty, can't answer, will ring later.

Helen mouthed her thanks and put the phone back in her handbag spotting the blue folder Percival had given her.

"Have you heard of Zakynthos?" she asked Dotty

"Yes" replied Dotty "it's one of the Greek Islands, a lot of people call it Zante but I've never been there…Why?" Dotty watched as a slow grin formed on Helens face and a glimmer of excitement started to shine in her eyes.

"Fancy a holiday?" grinned Helen who was starting to see the funny side of it all "What was it you said earlier…Cap the Dayum"

"Seize the day" yelled Dotty high-fiving Helens outstretched palm despite not having a clue what Helen was talking about.

Much, much later Helen snuggled herself down into Dotty's spare bed and reflected back on the strange day. She and Dotty had spent the rest of the afternoon and late into the evening pouring over the information Percival had provided and Googling Zakynthos. They even Googled "Madeline Kalvos" and finding nothing had tried "Madeline Chambers" but couldn't find a single piece of information that would solve the mystery of her disappearance. They had puzzled over the mysterious codicil to her will and with Dotty coming up with more and more bizarre scenarios they had giggled late into the night.

Helen suddenly remembered the letter hidden away in her handbag and realised that she might have had the answer in there all along. Mentally kicking herself for being so forgetful she reached over to the bedside table and grabbed her bag. Helen pulled out the envelope and ran her fingers slowly over the faded ink, she turned the envelope over and felt the slim bumpy ridge of something hidden inside. Taking a deep breath, she peeled back the flap and gasped as a beautiful shell bracelet fell into her hands. Feeling the tears welling, she slowly slid the bracelet onto her wrist and drew out the folded piece of paper.

My Darling Helen

We had such fun making these bracelets, do you remember? I live above a beautiful beach now and every time I gaze down at the golden sand, I think of you and the wonderful summers we had together. I'm so deeply saddened that I know nothing of your life. Are you a wife? A mother? I wonder what you look like now; you were such a beautiful child.

After the big fall out with your father I gathered my savings, sold my car and threw some clothes in a rucksack and set off on an amazing adventure backpacking through Europe, Oh Helen it was such fun. I met so many people, I picked grapes, milked cows, worked in bars and cafes in many different countries and a stranger on a train one day was a best friend the next. I sent you so many postcards from so many places. Did you keep them? I wonder.

And so it was that in the summer of 1977, after nearly a year of travel I found Zakynthos, it took me thirty days to fall in love with this beautiful island and that was the end of my journey, I never left. I met and fell in love with a wonderful man and I've been happy, so very happy.

When I wrote to you on your 18th birthday and invited you to stay, I was so excited. I imagined us walking along the beach and sitting in the local taverna, sharing a carafe of the village wine. When I received the letter from your father saying you were spending the summer with a friend and had no wish to see me ever again, I was heartbroken.

I am old now and with age comes wisdom, and I realise that your loyalty was to your father. I had no right to expect you to see me; it would have put you in an awful position and I'm so sorry if it caused you any anguish.

Please forgive my strange request attached to the will but although my body is failing me, my spirit is strong and I must ensure that my life's work is continued. You may or may not be the one to do this; only time will tell but as a child, I saw in you the same compassion and strength of mind that has seen me through the last forty years.

I am tired now so must say goodbye.
With love
Aunt Maddie
P.S. Please love my Puddles

Helen clutched the letter to her chest sobbing with frustration, rage and anger at the years that had been denied to her and her Aunt. She had never received a single postcard and certainly hadn't received a letter on her 18th birthday. She felt an unbearable fury at her father who'd not even allowed her a choice. As she laid her exhausted head onto the pillow, Helen vowed to repay her Aunt and put right the wrongs of the past.

CHAPTER 3
G IS FOR...?

Helen rolled over the next morning and winced through her swollen and bloodshot eyes at Dotty twirling around at the end of the bed.

"What do you think?" said Dotty, who was wrapped in a stunning, black, silk and satin negligee.

"Gorgeous" croaked Helen, her throat still on fire from a night of crying.

"Oh, darling" exclaimed Dotty suddenly noticing what a state Helen was in. "You look dreadful...bad night?"

"Guess you could say that" smiled Helen ruefully, handing Dotty the letter and watching her friends body language shift from shock to disbelief.

"Good Grief, you must be devastated."

"Hmm" agreed Helen, I was, and then I was angry...then sad...then I suppose resigned to the fact that it's happened...there's nothing I can do to change the past...but" she said sitting up and throwing off the bed covers. "Maybe I can change the future; maybe I can continue Aunt Maddie's work, whatever it is...or was" she laughed "right now I need to get up, sort my face out and start planning. Can you sort me out some paper and a pen while I have a quick shower?"

Ten minutes later and feeling much fresher Helen wrapped herself in the soft fluffy dressing gown and started towelling her hair dry. Hearing the vacuum cleaner start, she wandered out of the bedroom, feeling amused as she didn't think Dotty even knew what a vacuum cleaner was for. She walked into the lounge and stopped, gobsmacked at the naked male bottom swaying in front of her as the man attached to it hoovered round the furniture. Clamping a hand over her mouth to stop the squeak of shocking emerging, she sidestepped the gyrating, actually quite cute she thought, bum and dashed into the kitchen.

"What...who...is that?" she asked Dotty, who was rummaging through a drawer looking for a pen.

"Oh that's Christian, my man that does," replied Dotty with a casual wave as if it was perfectly normal to have a naked man cleaning her lounge.

"And what exactly is it that Christian *does*?" demanded Helen, still blushing with embarrassment.

"Well sadly he just cleans…it would be rather nice if he did more" Dotty smirked "but his boyfriend Luke is currently cleaning my bathroom."

"Good Morning Mam," said a deep, sexy voice behind Helen.

"Oh…err…good morning Christian" replied Helen, trying to avert her eyes but desperately wanting to steal a glance at the hunk of a man behind her. Giving in to temptation she sneaked a peek over her shoulder and sighed with relief when she spotted the apron tied around Christian's waist.

"We are just about finished here Ms. Boothroyd," said Christian "Same time next week?"

"Yes please," said Dotty shoving a pile of cash in his apron pocket, kissing his cheek and slapping his bare bum "If I'm not here you know where the key is"

"You are incorrigible" declared Helen "Where did you find him? Actually don't answer that, I don't think I want to know, just give me that pen and paper."

Dotty handed Helen pen, paper and a mug of coffee and sat down opposite her. She watched as Helen stuck one end of the pen in her mouth and tapped her fingers on the table thinking.

"Right," said Helen, putting pen to paper and starting to write "Here's the plan."

1: Book flights to Zakynthos.
2: Book a hotel.
3: Email the twins.
4: Cancel paper, milk and anything else.
5: Ask Molly and Ian to keep an eye on the house.
6: Clean out Williams…

Suddenly the sound of Gerald's ringtone startled them both and Dotty reached over to the kitchen side and grabbed Helen's phone.

"Oh god I forgot to ring him back last night" Helen groaned taking the phone and hitting the accept button.

"Hi Gerald, I'm so sorry I didn't return your calls, I was so exhausted last night I decided to stop at Dotty's" Helen lied and spotting Dotty mouthing "Don't tell him" switched the phone to speaker and laid it on the table between them.

"Helen, I was very concerned" scolded Gerald "We were supposed to be going to the garden centre yesterday and when I couldn't contact you I was extremely worried."

"Oh…gosh Gerald, I'm so sorry I completely forgot…something came up and…" Helen gabbled, trying rapidly to think of a good excuse.

"Hi Gerald" Dotty interrupted, winking at Helen "It's completely my fault, I got myself into a bit of a pickle, and Helen came to the rescue…women's problems you know?"

"Right…ho-hum…OK" stuttered Gerald, always embarrassed by any mention of "Women's problems" "Well how about this afternoon Helen, I can pick you up about two o'clock, and we can have a bite to eat after we've got your plants."

"Gerald that's really kind," said Helen, glancing at the list she had been writing "but I've decided I'm going to make a start on clearing out Williams study this afternoon."

"Oh," said Gerald, obviously taken aback "Well I'll come over and help you, glad to see you're moving on Helen, life goes on, and all that" Gerald said in a stiff upper lipped tone.

"To be honest, Gerald it's something I want to do alone, but I will ring you if I need any help," Helen said very firmly, murmuring her goodbyes and turning off her phone.

Helen looked over at Dotty, who had a strange expression on her face as she contemplated whether to say what was on her mind.

"Spit it out," said Helen, picking up her mug of coffee, quite sure that nothing Dotty said could shock her anymore.

"Don't you think Gerald is getting a bit obsessed with you? And a bit controlling, I think he wants to take Williams place" suggested Dotty gently.

"What?" Helen spluttered, swiping at the mouthful of coffee dribbling down her chin.

"That's utterly ridiculous Dotty, Gerald is just a friend and he was William's best friend" exclaimed Helen staggered that Dotty was putting into words what she had secretly been wondering for a while. She was well aware of Gerald's feelings but was also well aware that Dotty didn't know Gerald as well as she did.

"Hmm," said Dotty reaching forward and clasping Helens hands

"Just go careful Helen, I don't trust that man and I think a month away will do you a world of good, now where were we?"

Much later that afternoon Helen picked up the key to Williams study and headed towards the solid oak door. She had got to this point so many times before but had always stopped, unable to carry on.

Earlier in the day Helen and Dotty had ticked off the first couple of items on the list. When Dotty had realised she was due to meet a potential fabric supplier in Rome, the following week, they had agreed that Helen would go by herself to Zakynthos and Dotty would fly over from Italy a few days later. Having no idea where, in Zakynthos, the property was located they had settled on a hotel in a resort called Tsilivi and booked initially for one week, unsure what they were going to find. With the decisions made and plans in place, Helen was feeling a new determination to move on with her life and an inner strength she'd not felt for a long while.

Twisting the key in the lock, she was surprised at how easily it turned. It was well over a year since anybody had been in William's study, the police had had a quick look as part of their investigation into the crash, though Helen didn't have a clue what they could possibly find that would help and Gerald had collected some paperwork from William's desk to help with the probate but since then Helen had not allowed anyone in. As the door swung open, Helen gulped and put her hand over her mouth at the musty smell of the airless room.

Moving to the side of the room, she pulled apart the curtains and opened the windows wide, tutting as a gust of wind rushed in and scattered a pile of paperwork over the floor. Picking the paper up Helen placed it back on the desk and idly ran her finger through the dust accumulated on the surface. She walked around the desk and settled into Williams's leather chair trying to identify the feelings and emotions rushing through her. There was none of the devastating anguish that could leave her holed up in the house for weeks. She felt sad, but it was a sad she was coping with. As she struggled to analyse exactly how she was feeling she suddenly realised that it was guilt. Yesterday when she had started to write number six on her list, she had done so after an unexpected realisation that she hadn't thought about William for twenty-four hours. Now the guilt of that realisation was slowly dawning on her. Did that mean she no longer loved him?

She asked herself or had the excitement of the Aunt Maddie situation blown away the final cobwebs of grief? Rationalising her thoughts and knowing the latter to be true Helen shook herself and started to clear the desk.

Spotting Williams desktop planner, she allowed her eyes to drift to September 15^{th,} 2013, the day he had died. Seeing a red ring marked around the date she looked around for Williams's diary, intrigued to know what he had been doing that day. Opening a desk drawer, she spotted the Filofax and pulled it out. Thumbing through it for the right date, Helen frowned as she saw a small yellow Post-it Note *"9:00am Meeting with G… ask about loan"* was written in Williams clear, neat handwriting. How odd she thought frowning, G must be Gerald, and she was sure he had never mentioned seeing William that morning and what did *"ask about loan"* mean? Helen was sure that William wouldn't need to take a loan out. How very strange she said to herself, pulling out her phone to ring Gerald. As Helen heard a monotone voice inviting her to leave a message she put the phone down and mentally reminded herself to ring him later. Helen opened a bin bag and methodically started clearing the piles of paper.

Opening another drawer, she spotted Williams spare Epipen and remembered the frightening day ten years ago when he had gone into anaphylactic shock after being stung by a bee. She recalled her sheer terror as his face had swelled and he had grabbed at his throat gasping for breath. Thankfully Gerald had been there and recognised the signs. It had been a scary wait for the ambulance but once the paramedics had administered a hefty shot of epinephrine and Williams breathing had steadied. Helen had calmed down. Since then William had carried his Epipen everywhere and kept a spare one in his desk.

Glancing at the clock and realising she still had to go and ask Molly and Ian about looking after the house, Helen spent the next hour filling bags and boxes with rubbish and recycling. She marked two boxes of books to go to the charity shop then dusted, polished and hoovered until the study was empty but sparkling clean. Wiping a grubby hand over her sweaty forehead Helen felt a sense of accomplishment and grinned to herself. Looking at the now sparse shelves, she wondered if she should change the room into a craft room for herself. One step at a time she thought laughing.

Later that evening, curled up in one of Molly's comfortable

armchairs, she stroked the head of the huge fat chocolate Labrador, who was determined to share the chair with her, despite his size.

"I've always wanted a dog," she told Molly "I had so many pets as a child and grew up with dogs and cats snuggled on my bed every night but William never really liked animals or the mess that came with them. Maybe I could look at getting a rescue dog when I get back from Greece."

"That's if you come back from Greece" Molly laughed "You might decide after the thirty days to stay."

Molly and Ian had been so excited when she'd told them the news earlier and immediately offered to run her to the airport and promised to look after her house.

"Oh goodness," Helen said. "What a thought, and besides, for all I know this "*property*" could be a crumbling wooden shack. My Aunt Maddie was always a bit eccentric."

Molly laughed, and Helen took a sip of the delicious home-made dandelion wine and snuggled the dog, feeling more excited than she had in years.

Early Friday evening Helen strolled slowly down the country lanes savoring the sights and smells of the last days of April. Being such a beautifully warm day and with daylight starting to stretch longer into the evenings, she had declined Molly and Ian's offer of a lift and chosen instead to walk the mile and a half to the local pub and quiz night. Since Monday morning, she had worked manically, organizing and packing for what could, potentially, be a whole month away.

She smiled as she thought of the brief email she'd had back from the twins who had told her she was "Awesome" and promised to love her whatever she did as long as she updated them weekly. Helen had laughed at the short response, she'd learnt a while ago that emails would be few and far between as the twins scaled mountains and waded through rainforests and rivers, both adventure junkies they knew better than to tell their mum what they were doing next as they knew it only caused untold worry for Helen.

Nearing the pub, Helen spotted Gerald's green Jaguar parked outside and inwardly groaned. She'd been hoping he would not be here as she hadn't yet told him of her plans. It was not through want of trying, since last Sunday she had rang him at least five times but it had kept on going to his voicemail, and he hadn't returned any of her calls. He's probably still sulking about the Garden Centre she thought as she opened the pub door.

Helen ignored Gerald, who was stood at the bar chatting to Ron and weaved her way through the tables to where Molly and Ian had saved her seat and already bought her a large glass of lime and soda. As she shook off her coat and settled down, she noticed Gerald sliding sheepishly into the seat next to her.

"Evening Helen" he muttered "Did you get Williams study sorted? No problems I hope?"

"Not really," said Helen "there was one thing though…I've been trying to call you, but you didn't return my calls?"

"Ah yes…sorry, dratted phone broke, I've been meaning to call you to give you my new number…but…hectic week, you know" said Gerald with a guilty look on his face.

"Oh," said Helen confused, normally barely a day would go by between Gerald's constant calls "I just wanted to ask you about the day William died?"

As Helen explained the strange note jotted in Williams diary, she watched a deep blush rise up Gerald's face.

"Oh no," Gerald declared, obviously lying "I certainly didn't have any meetings arranged that day, I was working."

"Hmm" pondered Helen, wondering why he was lying "Must have been a different G, guess I'll never know."

As Helen took a sip of her drink silently promising to get to the bottom of it, Molly, blushing bright red and obviously embarrassed by the strange atmosphere, interrupted and quickly changed the subject.

"Finished Packing Helen?" she asked

"Yes" said Helen excitedly "All ready to go, Dotty flew to Rome yesterday and is meeting me in Zakynthos next weekend. Are you sure you don't mind running me to the airport so early…"

"What?" thundered Gerald, interrupting "You're going on holiday, and you haven't bothered to tell me?"

"I have been trying to ring you Gerald" replied Helen, hurt at Gerald's angry tone.

As Helen explained the whole situation, starting with the letter, telling him about the strange codicil and finishing with the fact that in thirty-six hours, she would be on a flight to Zakynthos, she watched, with a sense of trepidation as Gerald went redder and redder, his chest puffing up and his fingers clenching the edge of the table as he tried to control his temper.

"Well" exploded Gerald "That's preposterous Helen. You should have given me the letter and let me deal with it all. What a ridiculous notion that you should have to go all the way to Zakynthos to sort this nonsense out. I blame that stupid Dotty, putting silly ideas into your head and to think you have spent the whole week planning these shenanigans without even having the decency to consult me. First thing tomorrow we will call this Percival person and try and sort this mess out."

Gerald took a deep breath and shook his head in disgust and Helen bit her lip, mulling over his complete belittling of her. She picked up her lime and soda and swirled the pint glass round, watching the ice cubes clink together. Slowly Helen stood and poured the whole, icy pint over Gerald's head. With the whole pub erupting in cheers she placed both hands on the table, leant down and gazed into his stunned eyes.

"Gerald," she said slowly and calmly "I am very grateful for all the support you have given me, but I am a grown woman, and I do have the intelligence and the capability to make my own decisions. On Sunday morning, I am going to Zakynthos and if you wish to remain friends with me; I suggest you stop interfering in my life and stop trying to control everything I do."

Helen stood upright and casually put her coat back on. Inwardly she was wanting to scream with laughter at the lime and soda dripping down Gerald's face.

"I'll see you Sunday," she said to a convulsing Molly and Ian and spotting one of the Boys at the Bar filming the whole thing, winked and said, "Make sure you send that to Dotty."

CHAPTER 4
1ST MAY 2015 - ZAKYNTHOS

Markos Kalvos leaned casually against his old, dusty pick-up truck and surveyed the scene in front of him. To the right of the small kiosk selling coffee and snacks, a few people were sat at metal tables having a last cigarette before heading to the check-in desks. Others were waving a sad goodbye to friends and family and trudging dejectedly through the large glass doors. He watched the silver taxis drop passengers at one end then glide past the kiosk to join the queue on the left. The airport was still quiet, in a few weeks it would be a hustling and bustling hive of activity as thousands of tourists flew in and out of his beautiful island.

Dionysios Solomos Airport was the last place Markos wanted to be; he was still stunned that the English woman had the audacity to come over to try and claim an inheritance she didn't deserve.

Over the last four decades, he had seen the pain and anguish etched on Madeline's face whenever she reminisced about her long lost family. Markos had been a young, grieving boy of 13 when Madeline had arrived on the island. His mother had died the year before, and Markos had been heading into a downward spiral of angst and misery. Regularly skipping school, he would spend hours roaming the Islands Mountains and dusty tracks and would only stop to cuddle and play with the many stray dogs and cats that roamed freely on the land. So many times he would bring back an injured or lonely pup only for his father to chase it away or dump it back up in the mountains. When Madeline had met his Uncle she had taken Markos under her wing and become a surrogate mother. She'd helped him tend the wounded dogs and shown him how to bottle-feed the tiny abandoned puppies and kittens. When his father had demanded he leave school early and join him working the land, she had encouraged him to follow his dreams and even funded his studies in England. Finally returning from England a few years later, as a qualified vet, she had already purchased and equipped a property in the centre of Zakynthos Town. When he'd seen his name **Markos Kalvos Vet and Veterinary Clinic** stretched across the front of the shop, he'd promised to repay every penny. Madeline, however, had refused, asking only that he continue to help the islands strays. Markos was grateful that Madeline had had the foresight to add the codicil to her will. He didn't have a clue whose name was written in the mysterious envelope but he trusted that Madeline had done the right thing. Although he had promised the dying Madeline that he would look after Helen when she arrived, he certainly had no intentions of making life easy for her.

Hearing a cheery "Yasou Markos," he turned to his right and smiled at the short, tubby man trying to lift a large dog crate out of the boot of a dusty old car. Jogging over to help, he lifted the crate with the ease of a man twenty years younger and placed it carefully on the ground. Bending down he gently put his fingers through the wire cage door and petted the quivering spaniel inside. As a warm, soft tongue licked his outstretched fingers, Markos murmured words of comfort trying to sooth the terrified pup. Hearing a yapping from inside the car he jumped back up and helped the man lift the second crate from the back seat. He placed the crate in front of the first one so that the almost identical dogs could see each other, hoping it would calm them both.

"Kalimera Alf," said Markos, "They look wonderful, you and Peggy have done a great job."

"Thank you, Markos," said the man breathing heavily. "Peggy won't get out the car, it's the same thing, every bleeding time, she insists on coming to the airport to say goodbye then blubs all the way here and all the way back."

Seeing the tears swimming in Alf's own eyes Markos smiled fondly knowing that the man's heart was breaking just as much as his wife's. The couple were just two of the many people on the island who picked up the strays, fostered them and sent them on their way to new families overseas. Knowing that Alf and Peggy had bottle-fed, weaned, then nurtured these two for the past five months, he understood the gut-wrenching loss they felt every time they sent their babies off into the unknown. The fact that they had done this over and over again for many, many years was a testament to their absolute love of the dogs.

"What are you doing here anyway Markos?" asked Alf "Not often we see you at the airport."

"I'm waiting for Madeline's niece to arrive" he explained "Her planes due in twenty minutes."

"Oh" said an excited Peggy, whose tears miraculously dried up as she jumped out of the car. "I saw on Facebook that she was arriving today, how exciting."

The Islands rumour mill had been going wild for the past week as news of Helen's discovery had spread through the ex-pat community. Markos' clinic had been filled with people popping in and out trying to catch up with all the latest gossip. Madeline had been the islands heroine, despite her hatred of any recognition, fuss or praise for the work she did, the community had adored her and was devastated when she finally passed away. Her funeral had been huge. Buried only two days after she died, people had come from all across the island to say their goodbyes. Now the islanders were very firmly divided in their opinions of Helen, some, like Markos, had already made their minds up that she was a conniving bitch. Others like Alf and Peggy were eager to meet her and judge for themselves what sort of person she was.

As Markos saw the large orange and white EasyJet plane glide slowly down to earth, he said his goodbyes and strode back to his truck. He debated whether to take the cardboard sign that read "Helen Hardy" in large black letters, into the airport or to wait by his truck and see if he could spot her as she arrived. Deciding he didn't want to join the throng of tourist reps and car hire agents that gathered outside the arrivals doors, he leaned back against his truck and watched. As he'd thought earlier, he wasn't going to make life easy for Helen Hardy.

Helen jolted awake, hearing the captain announce that they would shortly start making their descent into Zakynthos, she rubbed her eyes and stretched, surprised that she had managed to fall asleep. The last thing she remembered was gazing down in awe at the sunrise glistening on the snowy white peaks of the Alps as they peeped through the fluffy clouds below.

The last thirty-six hours, since she'd emptied her drink over Gerald's head, had been manic. It had only taken ten minutes for Dotty, in another country, to view the film the Boys at the Bar had uploaded to Twitter, Instagram, and Facebook and tagged her in. Dotty had rung her, ecstatic at what Helen had dared to do and declaring she was going to make the film go viral. After an hour of general chat about Rome, Zakynthos and of course the pompous Gerald, Helen had switched off her phone. Far too excited to sleep, she had spent most of the night spring-cleaning the whole house and writing lists for Molly and Ian, instructing them how often to water the plants and where to find the cat food that she left out every night for the big black fluffy stray cat that wandered into her garden each evening.

On Saturday, she had dashed up to London and spent another amusing hour in the company of the strange Percival Boston Jr, who she was starting to like immensely. After signing countless pieces of paperwork, he had informed her that Markos Kalvos would be meeting her at the airport.

When she'd hugged Molly goodbye in the early hours of Sunday morning and looked up at the large sign welcoming her to Gatwick North Terminal she'd suddenly realised that this was the first time she had ever flown on her own. Heaving her luggage onto the weighing scales at the check-in desk she contemplated how much she must have taken William and the little things he'd done for granted. Even hoisting her hand luggage into the overhead lockers on the plane was something William had always done.

With her ears starting to pop Helen heard the Captain instruct the crew to "Prepare the cabin for landing" and reached down to shove her handbag under the seat in front of her. Gazing out of the window she gasped as she saw a perfect little Island that looked just like a large turtle rearing its head out of the vivid turquoise seas. How beautiful she thought. Once the plane had shuddered to a halt and taxied to a final stop, Helen undid her safety belt and reached down to retrieve her handbag. Never having liked being pushed and shoved in crowds, she decided to stay in her seat until the eager sun-seekers had made their way down the planes narrow aisle. Gathering her hand luggage, she was one of the last to exit the plane and as she stood at the top of the steps she squinted in the bright sunshine and felt a surprisingly strong gust of warm wind blowing on her face. At the bottom of the steps stood a bus and seeing the impatience etched on some of the passengers faces, she rushed across the tarmac and jumped on. Clinging uncomfortably to one of the central poles, as the bus lurched forwards, Helen hoped they didn't have far to go, then laughed as the bus travelled a few short yards and shuddered to a stop. Helen found herself in a small arrivals hall with two passport control desks at the far end. She joined the left-hand queue and shuffled forwards watching as a very bored man in a smart security uniform scarcely glanced at people's passports before waving them through. Expecting the same treatment, Helen held up her passport and felt a stab of irrational fear as the guard shouted "Wait" she turned and saw the man holding out his hand for her passport. Wondering why she had been singled out and hearing the tuts of frustration from the few stragglers behind her Helen handed her passport over and watched as the man looked slowly at the picture and then back at her.

"Your Aunt…she is Madeline Kalvos…Yes?" He asked in broken English

Helen, startled, nodded her agreement, not wanting to correct his use of the present tense.

"She good woman…she help me many times…welcome to Zakynthos."

The man smiled and handed the passport back to Helen and as he beckoned the next person forward Helen could have sworn he had tears in his eyes. Helen turned right and found herself in a larger baggage reclaim area surprised to see cases already trundling around the moving carousel. Waiting for her old suitcase to appear she wondered how the man knew her Aunt and how he had recognised her name. Oh well, she thought, this whole situation is extraordinary, it was just over a week since she'd opened the letter from Boston, Boston, and Merriweather and now, here she was about to discover why her Aunt had spent half her life on this island.

Markos was starting to get impatient, half an hour after the plane had landed he still hadn't spotted anyone he thought could be Helen Hardy. He had watched smiling families, loaded with luggage, stream out of the airport and pile into taxis. Others came out of the automatic glass doors and rummaged in their bags for the cigarettes they desperately needed. The car hire reps had come out smiling and leading holidaymakers towards the cars parked at the far end of the airport. Assuming she must be sat inside, he snatched up the cardboard sign and strode across the two narrow roads towards arrivals. Suddenly he spotted a lady, on her own, walking out of the double glass doors and gazing around. Markos stood still and reached out his hand to a nearby post to steady himself. The jolt of recognition had taken his breath away and almost knocked him off his feet. Helen was the spitting image of the younger Madeline that he had first met so many years ago. Placing his hand on his chest, Markos stared at the woman. With her strawberry blonde hair tied in a messy bun on the top of her head and the floaty green and turquoise skirt billowing around her slim legs she could almost be Madeline he thought. Feeling his heart still racing at her beauty, he reminded himself that the beauty was probably only skin deep and hid the selfishness inside this woman who had ignored his beloved Madeline for so long.

Helen jumped as she felt someone grab the handle of her suitcase, looking round she saw a tall, handsome man take hold of the handle.

"I am Markos Kalvos," he said, "You come with me now."

Helen, taken aback by this man's gruff and abrupt manner, snatched her suitcase back and informed him she could manage it herself. Shrugging his shoulders Markos marched off back over the road and Helen unsure whether she was doing the right thing, decided to follow him. He led her to a light blue pick-up truck and taking the case from her threw it in the back and opened the passenger door for her.

"Where you stay?" Markos asked with a thick Greek accent. Markos had no intentions of engaging in any conversations with Helen so despite the fact that he could speak beautiful English, fluently, and already knew where she was staying, he had strengthened his accent and missed a few words deliberately hoping she would assume his English was poor.

"Here," said Helen holding out the booking form which had the address written at the top.

Helen went to climb into the truck and quickly realised that he hadn't opened the door for her at all. Seeing the steering wheel, she blushed with embarrassment as she realised that they drove on the other side of the road in Zakynthos. Walking around to the passenger side Helen climbed in and stared stonily ahead.

"Markos reached over to the cubby hole in front of her and pulled out an envelope and threw it on her lap. Helen recognised her Aunts handwriting and clutched the envelope unsure whether to open it now or wait till she was alone. She looked out of the window and watched as they manoeuvred out of the airport and onto a small main road. Soon they turned right, and Helen studied the beauty of the land they were driving past. The gnarled ancient trunks of the many olive trees stood proud and strong as their white blossom and tiny green leaves swayed in the wind. Purple thistles edged the narrow winding roads and open fields full of grape vines appeared and disappeared in the gaps in the overgrown hedges.

Helen chose to open the letter. Markos obviously didn't speak much English, and she hated uncomfortable silences.

My Darling Helen

If you are reading this letter, then it must mean you have arrived on my beautiful island. Oh, I am so excited to think of you seeing it for the very first time. Isn't it stunning?

You must excuse Markos if he is grumpy and rude. He does not understand the English way even though he spent many years there studying. Yes, he studied to become a vet in England. I often wondered if you had gone to university, I thought of asking him to look for you while he was there but decided it wouldn't be fair on him…or you. Maybe you became an author Helen. I used to love reading the stories you wrote about the mermaids in Weymouth, do you remember? Anyway I am rambling, something that sadly comes with age. Markos is very Greek, they argue and shout and scream at each other, sometimes so fast I cannot keep up, and my grasp of the Greek language is rather good after nearly forty years, they air all their views quite openly and yet remain fiercely loyal to each other. We English can be far more reserved and bottle up our emotions which can lead to family rifts that last forever. Markos does not understand why we have not spoken for many years.

Soon Markos will take you up to my Villa, oh you will love it. Did you fly in over the island that looks like a giant turtle? That is Marathonisi; you can see it from my Villa.

When you feel brave enough, hire a car and spend some time driving around and over the island, don't be a tourist, please don't go where the reps encourage you to go. Follow the island with your heart and feel the way. Get to know my friends; there are many, both English and Greek. Don't expect people to turn up on time; we have our GMT zone here, but it stands for Greek Maybe Time! Maybe now; maybe later, you will see that to embrace fully the Zakynthian way you must accept their friendship and relish their company.

Over the next thirty days, you will discover what my life was all about. I hope and pray that you make the decisions that are right for you and not just right for me.

Have fun Helen
With all my love

Aunt Maddie
P.S. Have you found my Puddles?

Markos glanced sideways and watched Helen fold up the letter and wipe a tear from her eye, tears of guilt; he thought angrily even though he had no idea what the letter contained.

"So you studied in England?" Helen asked although it was a rhetorical question as she already knew the answer.

"Yes," said Markos at least having the grace to look ashamed "I started at the Royal Veterinary College in 1983, I was there for six years."

"Really," said Helen, interested "I was at the University of Greenwich for four years, I started in 1984, how strange that we both studied in London at the same time."

Markos grunted and pulled the car over at the bottom of a steep hill.

"We are here," he said, jumping out of the car and hauling her suitcase from the back of the truck. Good job there was nothing breakable in there Helen thought as he dropped it roughly at her feet.

"I will pick you up here at about ten o'clock tomorrow" Markos said in a suddenly much improved English as he jumped back in the truck and screeched off down the road.

Well thought Helen, that didn't go too well, I suppose things can only get better from here on. Dragging her suitcase behind her, she walked through a beautiful brick arch that was covered in creeping vines. Oh how pretty, she thought as she stared at the beautiful bar built around one of the ancient Olive trees.

"Kalimera," said a friendly man, walking round from behind the bar to meet her. "I am Elias, Welcome to Tsilivi."

CHAPTER 5
CONVERSATIONS WITH A CAT

Helen was so busy taking in her surroundings; she didn't notice Elias dashing off with her suitcase. She looked across the large pool to the gorgeous, pinky peach buildings that stood above a crazy paving wall. Beneath the wall were a line of sunbeds and umbrellas. Only two of the sunbeds were occupied and spotting Helen, a woman sat up and waved. Shouting a cheery "Good Morning," Helen waved back then dodged out of the way as a tiny dark-haired woman, with a pile of soft white towels in her arms, tried to sidle past. The woman nodded her head to the right, and Helen looked over to see Elias disappearing up a set of steps, lined each side with lush green fir trees.

Helen raced after him and reaching the top of the steps found herself halfway up a short but steep hill, feeling grateful for the long walks she took, that kept her fit, she set off up the hill. She breathed in the wonderful smells of the pretty flowers that sprung from every nook and cranny and smiled at the lemon, pomegranate and apricot trees that lined the hill. Tiny lizards darted in and out of the stone walls, and she heard the occasional chirp of a cicada. Stopping at the top, to catch her breath, she saw a second smaller set of rooms, painted in the same colour as the ones below and each surrounded by a white balcony. She counted five on the bottom and five on the top. Walking round the corner, looking for Elias and her suitcase she let out a squeal of delight at the sight in front of her.

Five little kittens were playing on a stretch of grass at the back of the rooms. A few larger cats were lazing in the sun, and a group of chickens were pecking at the grass. Two of the cats ambled over and started rubbing themselves around the bottom of her legs, purring contentedly. Helen bent down to stroke them and watched as one of the little kittens bravely started to bounce towards her. She laughed as the kitten got within two feet of her outstretched hand then turned and raced back to the safety of his brothers and sisters.

Looking for Elias, Helen saw that door number five was open and strolled towards it feeling the stress of the flight and the journey with Markos easing out of her tense body. Listening intently to Elias' rapid instructions about the air con and the safe, she stood in the doorway of the small but charmingly quaint room.

"Is okay?" asked Elias, staring at her.

"Yes, lovely" replied Helen "Oh Elias, is there Wi-Fi?" she asked as he backed out the door.

"Ah…the Wi-Fi…yes" Elias said and with palms out in front of him and a heavy shrug of the shoulders he continued "Sometimes is good; Sometimes is bad" Helen laughed at the forlorn look on his face and felt an overwhelming urge to pat him on the head and reassure him that "Yes, is Okay"

Helen closed the door behind Elias and stood in the tiny kitchenette. There was a fridge tucked under a small worktop which housed a sink, kettle and a weird rectangular table-top stove with two electric rings. She peered through a door on the left and found a tiny bathroom with a toilet, sink and shower. Seeing a picture of a toilet roll with a large red cross through it, she bent down and read the small, handwritten note that said "Please put all toilet tissue in the bin provided and not in the toilet" Oh crikey she thought, Dotty will go mental when she sees that. Helen walked through the pretty bedroom and out through the already open balcony doors.

"Oh wow," she said out loud "Look at that view" Over the roof of the building in front she could see many more, smaller rooftops nestling amongst olive groves. Further on the sea stretched out as far as the horizon and little white sailing boats and yachts bobbed along the gentle waves that rippled over the surface. Helen could hear the squeals and shouts of children having fun and grabbing the balcony and raising on her toes she could just make out the slides and flumes of the waterpark opposite. Hearing a meow, she peeked over the balcony railing and saw a scraggy white cat sat on the grass just below. With a quick leap, the cat landed next to her and started rubbing its head over her hands. Amused, Helen tickled the cat under its chin. The cat lifted its head in delight, and Helen saw the twisted mouth and the protruding tooth. Running her hands along its back, she felt the bare patches of fur and ridges of many scars.

"Oh dear, you have been in the wars," she said gently to the cat. "Right I need a shower I must stink after that flight" not at all concerned that she was having a conversation with a cat, Helen headed to the bathroom.

Feeling refreshed from the deliciously hot shower, Helen quickly unpacked, hanging her summer dresses up and piling the rest in the bottom of the small wardrobe. She opened her small hand-luggage case and pulled out her little blue laptop. Damn it! She thought I didn't ask Elias what the Wi-Fi password was. Quickly dressing in a pair of cropped trousers and a plain t-shirt she picked up the key and headed out of the room. She carefully worked her way down the steep hill and steps and found herself back by the swimming pool. Walking over to the bar looking for Elias, she heard a chirpy "Hello" and a pretty woman a few years younger than her stepped out from behind the bar.

"Afternoon love, I'm Lilian, but everyone calls me Lily and Elias calls me Silly Lily" she laughed holding out her hand.

"Oh you're English," said Helen, shaking the outstretched hand. I was looking for Elias I need the Wi-Fi password."

"Ah that husband of mine, he'll be off somewhere, fixing a tap or replacing a lock, we only opened yesterday, and it's always a mad rush getting everything sorted and working out what's stopped working over the winter. Here take a seat and I'll write the password down for you, want a coffee, tea, cold drink?" she asked, wiping her hands on the pinny tied round her waist.

"Coffee sounds wonderful, thank you," said Helen realising she'd had nothing to eat or drink since the flight. "Is there somewhere nearby I can get some milk and coffee for my room?"

"There's a little shop just next door" Lily pointed to the archway "But you watch the old bag doesn't diddle you, she can be an evil old cow."

Helen settled back into the wicker chair feeling totally relaxed and liking these friendly people.

Lily, meanwhile, trotted through the bar and into the little kitchen at the back. Switching the noisy coffee machine on and gently closing the door behind her, she pulled her mobile from her pocket and quickly tapped out a number,

"She's here" she whispered into the phone. "She's very pretty, looks a lot like Madeline…Oh yes, seems very polite…Yes, of course…I've got to go…making her coffee…bye Peggy, bye". Lily shoved the phone back in her pocket and finished making the coffee. Switching the machine off, she headed back into the bar and saw Helen's shoulders shuddering with silent laughter.

"Oh Lord," she said, following Helen's gaze to the commotion on the far side of the pool. Putting the coffee on the table, she laughed out loud at the sight of the rather large lady trying to get up off the sun lounger.

"One- two- three- heave" the woman was saying as she rocked back and forth on the edge of the lounger, trying to get some momentum going. "Come on George, put some welly into it" she shouted at the poor man behind her who was valiantly trying to lift her ample curves. "Oi Lily" she shouted across the pool "Stop your bleeding giggling and get over here and help."

Helen clamped both hands over her mouth as she watched Lily and the man take an arm each and haul the woman up. Seeing the woman wrap herself in a sarong and start waddling around the pool towards her, she stifled her giggles and tried to compose herself.

"Hello love," said the woman to Helen, flopping herself down in a chair. "I'm Maggie, Lily's Mum, and that's her Dad, George" pointing at the man who had settled back on his sun lounger and picked up a book.

"Hi, I'm Helen, I'm so sorry I laughed," Helen said holding out her hand.

"Oh Lordy, you laugh all you want" Maggie reached over and patted Helen's hands reassuringly "life's too bloody short to care about people laughing at me."

Lily brought out two more coffees and giving one to her mum, cupped her hands around the other and perched on one of the barstools.

"So what's a lovely thing like you doing over here all by yourself?" asked Maggie, never backwards in coming forwards.

Helen blushed at the compliment, turning fifty in a few weeks she was flattered to be called "Young."

"My friend Dotty will be joining me in a few days, so I won't be on my own for long" she reassured Maggie "I'm quite used to my own company."

"Hubby not joining you then?" Lily asked, spotting Helen's wedding ring. Helen picked up her coffee and took a quick gulp waiting for the lump to form in her throat, surprisingly it never came, and she answered quite calmly.

"My husband passed away eighteen months ago…its fine," she said as Lily's face fell, embarrassed she'd asked such an obtrusive question. "You weren't to know."

Maggie, who was at an age when the death of loved ones and old friends was fast becoming a regular fact of life, smiled kindly and offered her condolences.

"Are you and your friend stopping long then?" asked Maggie

"Err…I'm not sure really" replied Helen, wondering what all the questions were about and catching Lily glaring at her mum. "I've come over to sort my Aunt's estate out; it depends on how long it takes I suppose."

"Right Mum!" said Lily jumping up to stop her asking any more questions. "What do you and Dad want for lunch?" hearing Maggie request a Cheese roll, Helen realised how hungry she was and asked Lily if she could see the menu. Lily passed her a hand-written laminated list and pulled a notebook and pen out of her apron pocket.

"Can I have an omelette please Lily, I'll just run back to my room and get my purse."

"No problem," said Lily "Don't worry about paying straight away, I keep a note of everything, you can pay later, if you need some bits from the shop though, she'll want her money straight away, won't she Mum" she laughed rolling her eyes at her Mum.

"Oh Lordy me," said Maggie "She frightens the living daylights out of me."

Helen laughed thinking the poor woman couldn't be that bad and finishing her coffee headed back up the steps to get her purse. Looking back through the fir trees she frowned at the sight of Lily and her Mum sat head to head at the table frantically whispering to each other.

"Well I like her," said Maggie "I've told you before Lilian, you shouldn't judge a book by its cover."

"I like her too!" exclaimed Lily getting out her phone and dialling Peggy again "And Elias said she was thrilled with the cats and chickens and when he walked back down the hill he saw her stroking Scraggy cat, and that old battle-cat hates people normally."

"Your old Grandad always said kids and animals were the best judge of character" answered Maggie as they both heard a heavy panting coming from Lily's phone.

"Oh dear me" breathed Peggy's voice "I've just run down the garden, Alf would give me a right telling off if he knew I was gossiping with you, what have you found out then?"

"Not much really" said Lily "but she seems really nice and friendly, oh and she's a widow, which is sad."

"Well don't you go telling anyone else that" puffed a still out of breath Peggy "That Snotty Selena will have half the Island believing she killed her husband off before the weeks out."

"Got to go," said Lily as her mum grabbed her hand and nodded towards Helen coming back down the steps.

Lily waved at Helen and moved back behind the bar and into the kitchen to make the lunch and Maggie heaved herself out of the wicker chair and set off back round the pool to wake George, who had fallen asleep with his book over his face.

Helen, guessing they had been talking about her, shrugged it off as normal inquisitive behaviour and wandered through the archway to find the shop. She almost gagged as she went through the little shops door, the musty, mouldy smell was worse than Williams office had been. Trying to take shallow breaths through her mouth she squeezed between the shelves that were piled high with dusty old tins, packets, and bottles and grabbed a newer looking box of tea bags and a small jar of coffee.

Hunting round for milk she spied a set of fridges at the far end of the shop and carefully stepped her way over the mass of toys littered across the floor. Casting her eyes over the items crammed into the fridges she tried to work out which cartons were milk. Eliminating all the cartons that had pictures of fruit on she settled on a green carton with Noy Noy written above a picture of a cow and a smiling milkmaid. Clambering back over the toys, she looked up as she heard the shops door bell clang. Nearing the counter she froze as a screaming torrent of abuse suddenly came from behind it.

Ducking behind one of the shelves she peered round the edge and watched as a tiny old woman dressed all in black came charging round from behind the counter. The woman was waving a withered old hand angrily at the man who had just walked in and hurling and spitting abuse in his face. Helen, glad she couldn't understand a word of the Greek that was emanating from the woman's mouth, felt herself shaking and not sure if she was shaking with fear or laughter, shuffled herself further back. As it all went silent, she took another peek and was gobsmacked to see the old woman lift up a walking stick and stark whacking the man as he beat a hasty retreat out of the shop. While the woman slowly manoeuvred her way back round the counter, Helen edged towards the front of it and placed the items carefully on the top. The old woman picked up the coffee and brought it close to her eyes, peering at the faded price ticket, with a grunt she rang the price into an old fashioned till. When she'd repeated the process, very slowly, with the other two items she ripped off a till receipt and handed it to Helen.

"You pay huh" she rasped at Helen, who handed over a ten Euro note, squeaked "Keep the change" and ran out of the shop.

Pale-faced and still shaking, Helen walked back to the bar and found a Maggie and her now wide awake husband, sat at one of the tables with a yummy looking cheese roll each and a plate of golden chips placed in the middle between them. Telling them what she'd just witnessed, they both chortled with laughter and invited her to sit with them.

"So do you live here too?" Helen asked the lovely couple, grateful for their company.

"Oh no love," said George, we come over every May and every September, too bloody hot for us in the summer.

"Our Lily came over in 1986" Maggie explained "she was just going to work the summer season as a rep, but then the silly sausage went and fell in love with Elias and never came home."

"That must have been hard for you?" said Helen, who missed her twins on a daily basis and couldn't imagine them moving away permanently.

"Oh it broke my heart, didn't it George? The first few years were terrible and so expensive to ring her up, we'd only spend five minutes on the phone, then when the grandchildren came along, it was even harder. We used to come over for two weeks in the summer and Lily would come home for a couple of weeks at Christmas..." Maggie's voice trailed off as she remembered back to those days and felt herself welling up.

"It's all good now though" interrupted George, patting his wife's hand "We've both retired and can spend much longer out here now and even when we go home we can skype every day if we want to. That blooming internets a wonderful thing."

"Yes" agreed Maggie "and now the Grandchildren are older they all come over for three weeks at Christmas and Lilian's even got me one of them Facebook thingies," she said proudly.

"You talking about me again Mum?" Lily called from behind the bar "Don't you believe a word of it Helen" She winked bringing over a plate, piled high with a fluffy omelette and a fresh looking salad "Now do you want any chips to go with that?"

"Goodness no, thank you," said Helen wondering how she was going to eat the huge amount of food. "Your Mum and Dad said you have children?" Helen asked, picking up the salt.

"Yes, twin boys aged 14, Georgios and Dimitri, driving me up the bloody wall at the moment."

"Oh I have twins," said Helen. "Girl and boy though and a bit older…22…I still worry myself stupid over them" explaining how they were travelling the world on a gap year and agreeing with Maggie and George about the benefits of the internet and Skype. Picking up her knife and fork to start eating the delicious food she didn't notice Lily surreptitiously take out her mobile. "*She has twins*" she messaged to Peggy and smiled as the little picture of a "*thumbs up*" came straight back.

Feeling stuffed Helen sat back and wondered if she should go for a sleep or try and see the day out. Leaving home in the early hours of the morning and putting her watch two hours ahead was playing havoc with her internal body clock. Deciding to allow herself an hour's nap she asked Lily for the passwords. Lily handed her a piece of paper explaining that the top password "Georgios1" was for the bar area and "Dimitri1" was for the rooms.

"Can't guarantee it'll work though" she laughed "Internets bloody useless here. The one up in the rooms does seem to work a bit better though."

Helen smiled her thanks and braced herself for the steep hill, guessing correctly it would seem steeper with such a full stomach.

Propping herself up on the pillows, Helen stretched out on the bed and opened her laptop. Typing in the password she waited patiently for the Wi-Fi to connect and cheered when the little icon in the corner flashed green, confirming that she was connected. She clicked onto her Facebook and felt a delicious sense of guilty pleasure upon seeing that the film of Gerald, had indeed, gone viral. The little square speech bubble at the top indicated that she had two messages and opening them saw a lovely message from her son James "Love you Mum, have fun xxx" and another from Dotty "Will be there Tuesday, not Wednesday, finished early Ciao!" Brilliant thought Helen, mentally reminding herself to let Lily know. Closing Facebook and opening her emails Helen browsed through the usual Spam and adverts and spotted an email from Gerald, oh dear she thought, glad there were plenty of miles between them.

Helen
I feel I must apologise for my appalling behaviour. You are absolutely correct; I have no right to interfere in your life and of course, you have the intelligence to make your own decisions. I have only been trying to help you and as William helped me so much throughout our years of friendship, I felt and still feel duty bound to support and help you. I do hope we can move past this argument and continue to be friends. Have a wonderful time in Zakynthos and let me know if you need any help of advice.
Yours
Gerald

Good grief, that was a turn up for the books. Helen had opened the email expecting a verbal tirade of abuse. Gerald must be feeling guilty thought Helen, he never apologised for anything because he never believed he was in the wrong. She decided to reply later when she'd had time to think about what to say. Scrolling through, she saw an email from Percival Boston Jr and double clicked to open it.

Good Morning Helen
I hope this email finds you in fine form. Now then, regarding that little matter you asked me to look into I need you to sign the attached forms, an electronic signature will be fine if you have one or, if not maybe you could print them off and fax or scan them back to me. Make sure nobody sees you though! Can't be trusting anyone these days. Anyway if you could give me a ring at some point, that would be spiffing. Hope you are having a super time over there. Our little adventure reminds me of all those marvellous Famous Five books I read as a child.
Anyway I look forward to hearing all about your escapades.
Tootle Pip for now
Percival Boston Jr

Helen laughed out loud at the email and opening the attachments, she added her electronic signature and sent them straight back. All of the last week, the note she'd found in Williams diary had been bugging her and despite searching the whole house she hadn't managed to locate Williams bank statements to see if he'd taken out any secret loans. At her meeting with Percival yesterday she'd asked his advice and was astonished when he'd jumped up, clapped his hands and asked her if he could investigate it for her. Confessing a love for Sherlock Holmes and declaring he'd always wanted to be a private investigator he'd put an imaginary pipe in his mouth and declared "Elementary, my dear Helen, elementary."

Helen closed the laptop and settled back against the comfy pillows, loving the rush of warm air coming through the open patio doors and feeling strangely contented she closed her eyes and drifted off to sleep.

CHAPTER 6
EGGS AND BACON

The loud screeching of a cockerel crowing startled Helen awake. Disorientated, she fumbled around for a light switch, confused as to why it was so dark. Rubbing her eyes, she reached over for her phone and peered at the time. What? She thought, sitting up and staring at the display reading 05:38 am, that can't be right. Needing a wee, she dashed to the bathroom, relieved herself and splashed cold water on her face.

"Have I been asleep for nearly fourteen hours?" she said aloud and seeing the closed patio doors and closed curtains racked her brains trying to remember when she'd woken up and closed them. Must be going mad she thought, switching the kettle on. Waiting for it to boil she went over to the doors and pulling the curtains apart, saw a beautiful pale pink-tinged sky. Quickly sliding open the glass doors, she stepped out onto the patio and shivered, despite the 26 degrees of yesterday's sun it was a lot chillier this morning. Going back inside, Helen made herself a coffee and grabbed a cardigan.

With her feet tucked under her, on the white plastic chair, Helen let her eyes graze over the dawning horizon. On the far right, over the top of a small hill, she spotted the sun rising, turning the sky a vivid pink and purple. Sighing contentedly, she mulled over the fact she had slept for so long, deciding her body and mind must have needed it after the chaotic last week of sleepless nights. She pondered over the day ahead and shuddered at the thought of another journey with the rude Markos.

Picking up her coffee she wrapped both hands around the mug and sensing movement below, looked down to see the scraggy cat squeezing through the balcony rails.

"Good Morning Scraggy," she said as the cat jumped in her lap and started pawing her legs trying to get comfy.

"Maybe I'll get a cat as well as a dog when I get back home," she said to the purring cat. She thought about her Aunt's second letter, the cryptic P.S.s about Puddles was still puzzling her.

"Maybe Puddles is a cat like you Scraggy, what do you think?"

Not realising how close she'd come to the truth Helen gently shooed the cat off her and headed for the bathroom to get washed and dressed.

Assuming that nobody would be about yet, Helen wondered what to do with herself, at home she would have gone for an early morning walk or picked up her knitting. Her rumbling stomach reminded her that she'd slept right through dinner last night, but she doubted anyone would be serving breakfast this early in the morning.

"Right Scraggy, I suppose I'd better email Gerald back" Fetching her laptop she opened Gerald's apology and mulled over her response. She didn't want to appear too friendly but at the same time didn't want to come across as rude. "Ok, how does this sound Scraggy?"

Hi Gerald

Thank you for the apology. I would also like to apologise for my actions - it was unforgivable of me. Zakynthos is a very beautiful island, and so far, the people I have met are all very friendly. I will let you know if I need any help. Dotty will be arriving tomorrow so I'm sure we will have fun.
Speak Soon
Helen

She read back through her reply a couple of times and satisfied that it set the right tone of friendliness, hit the send button.

The scraggy cat's ears perked up at the same time as Helen heard the voices drifting up from somewhere below her. She moved over to the balcony and looked down at the back of the rooms below. The same tiny, dark-haired woman, who had been carrying the towels yesterday, was mopping the patio area and chatting to Elias, who had a screwdriver in one hand and was scratching the back of his head with the other.

"Morning, err- Kalimera" she called out. Elias and the woman both waved up at her, then continued with their conversation. Hearing a voice shouting "Ela, ela" from behind her, Helen walked back through her room and opened the front door.

"Ah, how cute is that," she said, watching the little kittens pounce and leap across the grass towards Lily, who was emptying cat food into a variety of different dishes. Three or four older cats were rubbing around her legs, and as Lily bent down to fill another dish, the scraggy cat came running round the side of the building and leapt on her back.

"Ouch, get off me, you daft old bugger" squealed Lily as the cat clawed her shoulders. Helen laughed and went over to help, lifting the cat off Lily's back and putting him on the floor next to one of the dishes.

"You've certainly got a lot of cats, Lily" Helen declared, stroking one of the kittens.

"None of them are mine, they're all strays, and I'm just the mug that feeds them all" Lily laughed as she replaced the lid on the large bucket of food. "Now then Helen, how are you feeling this morning?" she asked, "I hope you don't mind, but I sneaked in to check on you last night, we were getting a bit worried when you didn't come back down to the bar."

"I'm so sorry," Helen said, "I think I must have been exhausted, I've not slept like that for years" Helen laughed, feeling a bit embarrassed and hoping Lily didn't think she was always that lazy.

"Oh, never you mind, you're not the first and you certainly won't be the last" Lily reassured her. "When I saw that you were dead to the world I shut your patio doors and pulled your curtains, we get a lot of mosquitos at this time of year, and I didn't want you getting bitten or getting cold."

"Thank you" Helen wondered if she should be feeling annoyed by the thought of someone coming in the room while she was asleep but genuinely believed that these kind people were just looking out for her. "You're up and about very early Lily."

"It's always the same Monday's, the Danish arrive about 8:30 am and half of them will want breakfast, so it's all hands on deck, my mum, bless her, is already down at the bar getting ready for the mad rush. You must be hungry?"

"Starving" agreed Helen, rubbing her rumbling stomach.

"Well pop on down to the bar, I've just got to get those lazy sons of mine out of bed and then I'll be down to rustle you up a nice bacon sarnie or something."

After grabbing her mobile and locking her door, Helen made her way down to the bar to find George wiping clean the tables which were covered in a mass of fallen olive tree blossom. She could hear a clattering of pots and pans coming from the little kitchen and assumed it was Maggie.

"Morning George" Helen waved "It's good of you and Maggie to help out like this."

"Oh it's only for this week, Elias' brother, Yannis, will be back on Saturday. His Mother-in-law is in the hospital, on the mainland, so he's taken his wife over to visit her. To be honest, it's only Monday that's a bit manic at this time of year, because of the Danish."

"Lily mentioned the Danish," said Helen "are there a lot of them, then?"

"They fill those eight rooms on the top row" George pointed to the block of rooms above the pool."

"You get a mixture of couples and families" interrupted Maggie, coming out of the kitchen "Lovely people the Danish, they do love their trips."

"What trips do they go on?" asked Helen, interested.

"Oh, all over the place, The Shipwreck, Blue Caves, Turtle spotting…here you go," said Maggie handing her a pile of tourist leaflets that were placed neatly on the bar. Helen flicked through the leaflets and seeing that one was a map started to unfold it then looked up when she heard a car pull up on the road outside the archway. Not quite believing her eyes, she watched a young boy jumped out from behind the driver's seat. George and Maggie seeing her startled expression started laughing.

"Meet out Grandson Dimitri," said George. The young, smiling and very handsome boy came over and shook Helens hand quite formally.

"Hello," said Helen "You don't look old enough to drive."

"My father, he teach me when I thirteen," Dimitri said proudly, walking behind the bar and helping himself to a bottle of water from the fridge "I drive good…yes?" he asked Helen.

"Yes," said Helen laughing "Is it legal?" she asked George.

"Oh no, not at all" he chortled "Look out, here comes the other one" Helen looked around to see a lad, identical to Dimitri, running down the steep slope, the boy disappeared behind the fir trees and re-emerged half way down the steps. In front of him on a long chain, lead wiggled a little brown dog. Helen laughed, delighted, as the dog tugged the boy towards them.

"Fudge, stop" shouted the lad as the dog jumped up at a beaming Helen.

"It's ok" Helen reassured him, stroking the chocolatey brown and velvety soft fur which had been shaved short. She laughed as the dog wriggled his whole body excitedly and barked "Hello" at her. "Hello Boy," she said pulling aside the lighter, sandy coloured fringe that covered a pair of shining hazel eyes. "I guess that you're Georgios," she asked the boy, holding out her hand to the lad who gave it a quick shake and nodded shyly. "And you must be Fudge," she said, thinking the dog looked a bit like a Bichon Frise.

"Papoose, can you take us to school?" Georgios asked his Grandfather as he tied the dog's chain to one of the heavy parasol bases. "My father is trying to fix the door on room fourteen" he explained, and Helen was very impressed with his English, guessing that both boys were bi-lingual.

"Lovely boys," she said to Maggie who had ushered George and the twins through the archway and picked up the damp cloth to finish wiping the tables "Very polite."

"Hmm" agreed Maggie "different as chalk and cheese, though, Dimitri has no fear, Elias got him a moped last summer and he races it up and down that slope, scares me stupid, he does" Maggie stopped to wipe her sweating forehead with the back of her arm then continued "Georgios is the quiet one, he loves his books and all the animals, spends hours cuddling that dog" She gazed down fondly at Fudge who had settled under the table with his head resting on Helen's feet.

The sound of a van pulling up on the road halted their conversation, and Helen watched as a young man with a bag full of assorted rolls and bread, ran through the archway and dropped it on the counter, with a quick "Yasou" he dashed back through the arch and into his van.

"All we need now is Lily to bring the eggs down and we can have a nice egg and bacon roll in peace before the Danes get here," said Maggie, walking over to pick up the rolls.

Remembering the chickens roaming freely up the back Helen's mouth watered at the thought of fresh eggs and bacon, a treat she rarely allowed herself back home. Seeing the map, half unfolded on the table, she opened it fully and spread it over the table. Taking a quick look underneath, she realised that one side was a map of Tsilivi, with various adverts for restaurants and trips dotted around the edges. The other side was a map of the whole Island with little icons indicating the areas of interest. Looking first at the Tsilivi side Helen was amazed at the amount of restaurants and bars that were situated within the small area. She ran her finger along what looked like the main road until she found the hotel she was in and saw that they were at the far end of the resort which explained why it was quiet. Turning the map over she felt Fudge stir and giggled as he crept out from under the table and started wagging his tail and running around in circles, barking excitedly. Looking up she saw Lily walking towards them with a wicker basket in her hands.

"Get down, you silly sausage" Lily said to the dog, holding the basket away from the sniffing Fudge's nose. "Here you go Mum" she handed the basket to Maggie and flopped down into the chair opposite Helen.

"He's gorgeous," Helen said to Lily as Fudge settle back under the table.

"He turned up about four years ago" explained Lily. "He followed me everywhere for three weeks until I couldn't cope with those sad eyes staring at me anymore" she laughed "So I took him in."

"Are there many strays in Zakynthos?" asked Helen thinking of all the cats up the back.

"Oh you'll soon know all about the strays," said Maggie putting two mugs off coffee down in front of her and Lily.

"Mum," said Lily quickly interrupting and turning to Helen "Mum means that you will soon spot all the strays as you start looking around the Island, they wander up and down the roads and on the beaches" As a flustered Maggie disappeared back behind the bar Helen felt as if she'd missed something.

"Oh you're looking at one of our maps" Lily changed the subject and started to point out places that Helen should visit. Maggie, coming back out with her mug of coffee, sat down and showed her where the Blue Caves and The Shipwreck were located nearer the top of the Island.

"I wonder where my Aunt lived" mused Helen, not realising she was speaking out loud.

"Oh down there in Vassilikos," said Maggie, then looking horror-struck, clamped her hand over her mouth. Helen looked up slowly at Maggie then at Lily, who was glaring daggers at her Mum.

"Oh…no…oh…" moaned Maggie into her hand "I'm sorry Lily, I didn't think, me and my bloody big mouth."

"You know where my Aunt lived?" gasped Helen

"No…wait…how do you even know who my Aunt was? None of this makes any sense…" Helen stared at Maggie then Lily, then remembered the security guard at the passport desk who'd known who she was. "I'm not sure what's going on here," Helen said "but I'd be very grateful if you could explain before I start thinking I'm losing my mind."

Lily looked at Helen's confusion and battled with her loyalty to Markos and her feelings for this poor woman.

"Okay Helen, I'll be straight with you, but you've got to promise me you won't say a word to Markos" Lily looked beseechingly at Helen until Helen nodded her agreement, unsure what Markos had to do with anything.

"Your Aunt" Lily began "Was very much loved and respected by many people on Zakynthos and when she died…" Lily sniffed and took a deep breath "There was a lot of speculation about her estate and who would inherit everything. Most people assumed Markos would, as he was like a son to her" Lily saw that this piece of information startled Helen, who raised her eyebrows in surprise. "Anyway Madeline had often talked about a niece called Helen, so when Markos closed up the villa people started to assume that her niece…you…had inherited everything.

"Some people were very angry" interrupted Maggie and when Helen asked "Why" Lily went on to explain.

"Nobody had ever seen you and Madeline had never had any visitors from the UK so "some people," thought…well…that it was very unfair that a complete stranger, who'd never bothered to visit her Aunt, would walk in and just…well…take everything."

"Markos being one of those people," Helen said, suddenly understanding his rudeness.

"Markos is just very loyal to your Aunt's memory," said Lily not wanting to get into a discussion about Markos. "Anyway, Markos has this receptionist…"

"Vile girl" interrupted Maggie, then blushed as her daughter shushed her.

"This receptionist" Lily repeated "She likes to listen in on Markos' phone calls and overheard him talking to someone in the UK about a "Helen Hardy" Well she put two and two together and it took about two hours for the gossip to spread through the community and for everyone to start looking you up on Facebook but there were so many Helen Hardy's that nobody could work out which one you were" Lily stopped to take a breath and Helen smiled as, being a former secondary school teacher, her Facebook was disguised under the name "Hellie Castle" a combination of her childhood nickname and her Mother-in-law's maiden name.

"So when the booking form came through last week, with your name on it well I guess we knew who you were but..." reaching over to give Helen a reassuring pat on the arm "We haven't told a soul that you're staying here, have we Mum."

"Well," said Maggie "Only Alf and Peggy, they were your Aunt's best friends...and...well, we trust them, don't we Lily?"

"Wow" breathed Helen "That explains the guy at the airport," She told them what had happened to her as she went through the passport control.

"Oh no," said Lily "That means everyone will know you are on the island" pulling her phone from her pocket she opened her Facebook and groaned at all the posts. "I bet he put it on Facebook the minute everyone was through security," she said showing Helen the speculation and gossip that had been whizzing over the internet since yesterday.

"Thank goodness he didn't take a picture of you," said Maggie "mind you, you look so much like your Aunt, it won't be long before someone recognises you.

Helen, quickly scanning all the posts and seeing words such as *'Gold Digger" "Harlot" and "Bitch'* slid the phone back to Lily and put her head in her hands thinking she might just hole up in her room until she could get on the next flight back to Gatwick.

"Helen, I know this looks bad," Lily said holding up the phone "but honestly, there's a lot of people on your side. As I said people respected your Aunt and respected her decisions."

"So..." said Helen slowly "Do you know what my aunts will said?"

"Oh yes," said Maggie "Well sort of...that nasty girl at the vets waited until Markos went out and rifled through his desk and emails. We know all about the Will and the Codicil but the girls English is not that good, so we got her version of it. There's a lot of people around here who think it should be their name inside that secret envelope."

"Markos was so angry when he found out who'd spread the

gossip, that he sacked her on the spot" continued Lily.

Lily and Maggie looked at each other as Helen sat there silently taking it all in. She had so many questions she didn't know where to start. Maggie, upset by the uncomfortable silence and feeling guilty for opening her big mouth, picked up the empty mugs and asked if anyone wanted breakfast.

"Yes, thank you, Maggie, could I have an egg and bacon roll" Helen replied, no longer feeling remotely hungry but wanting Maggie out of the way. "Lily," she said quietly once Maggie was busy in the kitchen "Why don't you want me to tell Markos about this conversation?"

"Oh," said Lily, "Markos felt that if you knew how well we knew your Aunt, then you might…well…oh…" Lily struggled to find the right words "please don't be offended by this, but he thought you might just pretend to be a lovely, sweet person to try and get information from us" Helen thought Lily was going to cry, she looked so upset. "But even though I've only just met you, I already think that you are a lovely person Helen, even Scraggy cat has taken a liking to you, and he hates everyone normally."

Helen smiled, realising she'd stumbled across the cat's name by chance.

"So…let me get this straight," she said, half to herself and half to Lily. "There's some people on this island who think I'm a scheming, conniving bitch and others who are prepared to judge me for themselves?"

"In a nutshell yes" agreed Lily "but there are a few people you need to be careful of Helen, some will pretend to be your best friend, they're the real conniving ones but…I've said too much already…"

"It's okay Lily; I'm not going to pump you or anyone else for information…and…thank you for being honest with me" giving herself time to compose her words Helen folded the map back up and slipped it into her handbag feeling Lily's questioning eyes still on her. "There are reasons I never visited my Aunt" she went on "but I'm not going to try and justify myself to Markos or anyone else, I'm here to fulfil my Aunt Maddie's wishes and in the same way, you didn't prejudge me, I don't intend to prejudice anyone else" she smiled at Lily "Now I think your Danish may have arrived a bit early" she pointed at the large coach pulling up on the road.

"Oh Lordy," said Lily, sounding just like her mum.

Helen watched as Lily greeted the smiling but weary-looking families as they piled off the coach and collected their luggage. A stunning blonde-haired rep, dressed in a crisp white shirt and navy skirt shook Lily's hand and then led the travellers around the side of the pool and up to the rooms.

"Watch the top row of balconies," said Maggie, putting Helen's breakfast in front of her. "It's like one of them Mexican waves" Helen looked up, not understanding what Maggie meant, then laughed as one by one each set of patio doors opened, and the Danish walked out onto the balconies and took in the view.

"Probably got about half an hour to eat our breakfasts before they start descending on us" laughed Lily, sitting back down and picking up her bacon and egg roll.

Just before 10 am Helen was perched on one of the bar stools waiting nervously for Markos to pick her up. Leaving Maggie and Lily to dish up breakfast to their hungry Danish guests, she'd gone back up to her room and sent a long email to Dotty bringing her up-to-date on the events of the past two days. Finding a pen and paper, she'd looked over the map and jotted down a list of places she'd like to visit while she was here, wondering if the Shipwreck was as beautiful in reality as it was on the stunning pictures the leaflets portrayed.

Hearing her phone ping, she glanced at the message from Dotty, which simply said "OMW."

"Any idea what OMW means?" she asked Lily, who was collecting up empty plates and mugs from a nearby table.

"On My Way" replied Lily, who having teenagers, was used to the lazy acronyms used to relay a message. "Is that from Markos? I wouldn't have thought he'd send a message like that."

"No" said Helen "It's my friend Dotty, she was supposed to arrive on Wednesday, then she sent me a message saying it would be Tuesday and now, apparently, she's "On her way." knowing Dotty that could mean anytime between now and tomorrow morning" Helen said "Will it be a problem Lily, if she arrives early?"

"Goodness no," said Lily, picking up a large diary placed next to the phone behind the bar. "We're not expecting anyone else for a couple of weeks and the rooms all prepared, is it Dorothy Boothroyd?" She asked looking at the week's bookings. "I'm sure

I've heard that name before, can't think where though."

Helen bit her lip and looked away, remembering that the beautiful sarong that Maggie had wrapped around her curves the day before was one of Dotty's biggest sellers of the previous year.

CHAPTER 7
PUPPY LOVE

Markos drove quickly down the back roads into Tsilivi, annoyed that he had to run the English woman around the island. He had been up most of the night saving the life of yet another stray dog that had been hit by a car on the busy road near the airport. The little tan and white mongrel's back leg and hip had been broken badly and during a lengthy operation, he'd pinned the bones back together. Thankfully the dog had come round safely, and he'd left his new receptionist ringing round the already overflowing foster carers trying to secure a safe home for the dog to recuperate.

Pulling up outside the hotel, he saw Helen sat at the bar and felt a hot surge of sudden lust low down in his stomach, angry at himself he thumped his fist on the trucks horn and felt better when he saw Helen jump, and nearly topple off her stool at the loud noise. He watched her wave goodbye to Lily and realising he was being childish and feeling a bit guilty leant over and opened the door for her.

"Kalimera," he said, and once Helen was buckled in, swung the truck around and started back up the hill.

"Wait, stop" shouted Helen, who glancing behind, had spotted a frantically waving Lily trying to stop them. Markos quickly reversed back down the hill and screeched to a halt next to Lily.

"Peggy's on the phone," she told Markos "She's been trying to get hold of you, says it's urgent" She handed Markos the phone and shrugged her shoulders at Helen who was watching Markos listening intently to the woman on the other end of the phone.

"Okay, I'll go and look," said Markos into the phone before ending the conversation and handing the mobile back to Lily. Driving off for the second time he explained to Helen. "There is an emergency up near Kalipado, a small village just up the road. Someone has reported a dog lying injured on the side of the road, I must stop there first before we go to the villa."

"Of course," said Helen "no problem" and looking at Markos saw the tiredness etched on his unshaven face. "Markos, you look exhausted, if you would rather leave the visit to the Villa today I would understand."

Markos looked across at Helen, trying to decide if the concern on her face and the empathy in her eyes were real.

"Thank you but today is my only free time this week" Crossing a junction at the end of the road he slowed the truck down and crept along slowly, peering from side to side amongst the olive groves that seemed to go on forever. "There," he said pointing to a lifeless black and white dog laying under one of the trees.

"Oh no" exclaimed Helen, undoing her seatbelt and opening the door. Not waiting for Markos, she ran to the dog's side and sighed as she realised there was no hope. She gently stroked the dog's head and with her fingertips, closed its staring, motionless eyes. "You poor thing" she whispered as Markos reached her side and knelt down to look at the dog.

"Poisoned, maybe," he said, checking the dog over and seeing no obvious injuries. He felt under the dog's stomach and sighed heavily "She has not long given birth, there may be pups nearby, I must look."

"We will both look," said Helen firmly, her heart constricting at the thought there could be some scared, hungry puppies lying helpless. Agreeing to look on opposite sides of the road Helen crossed over and walked slowly and carefully between the trees and shrubs that swathed the land. Keeping her eyes and ears peeled. Thinking she'd heard a whimper, she stood still and listened carefully. Yes, there it was again she thought and crouched down low peering under a thick clump of gorse bushes. As another louder squeak came from beneath Helen laid down and squinted through the spikey branches.

"There you are," she said softly as she spotted a tiny pink nose sniffing the air. "Markos, over here" she shouted and started to ease herself under the gorse, not caring that the vicious thorns were scratching her bare arms. Inching forward slowly, she eventually got within reach of a hollowed out dip and counted three tiny puppies, all with their eyes still fused shut. Stretching her arms out she scooped them up and started to edge backwards. She barely felt the gorse ripping at her hair, skin and clothes as she tried desperately to shield the puppies from the spikes.

Markos, hearing Helen shout, ran to the other side of the road and gazed around, trying to work out where her yell had come from.

Hearing a rustling, he moved further into the grove and stared, amazed, at the sight of Helen pulling herself out from under an evil looking shrub. As Helen finally removed herself and sat up with the pups in her arms. He slowly ran his eyes over her dishevelled state and instantly fell in love.

"You're bleeding," he said gruffly looking at Helens ripped and scratched arms and legs. Her pretty summer dress was torn in a dozen places, and her hair was littered with twigs and leaves. She was clutching onto the three tiny puppies and gazing up at him with unshed tears in her eyes.

"Can you save them?" she asked, trying hard not to burst into tears.

"I'll try" he promised and walking over to her, gently took her by the elbow and helped her up, realising that she was not going to let go of the puppies he led her to the truck and helped her into the passenger seat. As he lifted the pups mother into the back of his truck and covered the body with a blanket he tried to stop the rush of emotions flooding through his body, he had only ever fallen in love once before, and that had ended badly. He certainly didn't want to go down that road again.

Steeling himself, Markos climbed back into the driver's seat and pulled out his phone. Ignoring all the earlier missed calls and messages he dialled Alf and Peggy's number. Starting the engine, he drove off one-handed and hearing Alf's cheery "Hello" asked him to get some bottles prepared for the three newborns, seeing Helens bleeding arms still clutching the puppies he suggested Alf get a first aid kit ready as well and switched the phone off before Alf could ask why.

"That was a stupid thing to do," he said to Helen "You should have waited for me."

"Well, it's not as if you were going to fit under that bush" retorted Helen, stunned at his angry tone after the gentle way he'd lifted her and helped her into the truck. She hugged the puppies tighter to her and turned her head away, looking out the window and making it clear she didn't want to talk to him.

Fifteen minutes later Markos pulled up outside a small house in a pretty little village. A short, tubby man, waiting outside the house, opened Helens door and gawped at the sight of her.

"Bleeding hell," he said, "Who's cage did you rattle, Peggy quick" he shouted over his shoulder and Helen saw a friendly, smiling woman come out of their front door.

"Oh my goodness" she cried "you poor thing" realising the woman was talking to her and not the puppies she noticed for the first time how badly cut and grazed she was. Glimpsing in the wing mirror, she spotted the cuts on her face and the twigs in her hair.

"Oh, I'm sorry," Helen said, trying to pull the twigs out and wincing as her fingers got caught by a thorn. "I don't normally look like this" Sliding off the seat she felt something running down her leg, looking down she saw the long deep gash on her thigh and the blood pooling on the pavement below and started swaying. She felt a strong pair of arms wrap around her waist and scoop her up under her knees as she drifted into a swirling blackness.

"Oh Christ, she's fainted" yelled Alf, quickly grabbing the puppies as they slipped out of Helens arms. "Get the kettle on Peggy" he instructed and ushered Markos inside.

Markos carried Helen over to a large comfy sofa and laid her down gently, he slid up her blood soaked dress and looked at the horrendous cut.

"I didn't realise she was so badly hurt," he said to Peggy, who was coming out of the kitchen with a large first aid kit in her arms. "She just dived straight under a horrible gorse bush to get to the pups, instead of waiting for me."

"Well she's certainly her Aunt's niece then isn't she" Peggy replied, thinking that Helen resembled Madeline Kalvos in more than just her looks and seeing the stricken look on Markos' face shooed him out of the room. "Helen, Helen," she said gently shaking her shoulder.

Helen, feeling fuzzy and hearing her name as if from a distance, shook her dizzy head in confusion, opening her eyes she looked up at the kindly face looking down on her.

"Oh…what happened," she said, putting her hand on her head and trying to sit up "The puppies" she exclaimed looking down as if they should still be in her arms.

"The puppies are fine love, Alf and Markos are sorting them out, I'm more concerned about you at the moment" Peggy reassured her "You fainted."

"I never faint," said Helen even more confused "Oh gosh, I'm bleeding all over your lovely sofa, oh no, I'm so sorry" Helen tried again to sit up, shocked at the amount of blood that had poured from her leg.

"Now you just lay there," said Peggy firmly, pushing Helen back against the cushions "don't you go worrying about the blood, it'll wash out" Peggy pulled a large dressing from the first aid kid and held it firmly over the wound to stem the bleeding. "You've lost quite a lot of blood, and that's probably why you fainted, and I think you are going to have to get some stitches in that cut" Peggy looked at Helen, glad to see the colour returning to her pale face. "I'm Peggy, I was your Aunt's best friend, me and Alf were going to pop over to Tsilivi in a couple of days to say hello to you" Taking a quick peek under the dressing she sighed with relief that the bleeding seemed to have stopped. "Right if you could just keep that pressed against the wound I'll go and get some warm water, and we'll see if we can sort you out."

Helen shuffled herself upright a bit more and felt hugely embarrassed that she'd fainted. Vaguely remembering the strong arms that had caught her, she blushed even more at the thought of Markos carrying her in. She looked up as Peggy came back in carrying a mug in one hand and a small bowl in the other.

"Here you go love, a nice cup of Yorkshire tea, my son sends a box of teabags over every month" She put the mug on a small coffee table and opened up the first aid box. "Now then, this is going to sting a bit."

Alf sat at a table in their large garden listening to Markos describe how Helen had got into such a state. In his lap two of the puppies were slurping on the small bottles of special puppy formula, he was holding in their mouths. Markos was checking over the other Puppy and seeming pleased with its health, he picked up a third bottle and placed it in its tiny mouth.

"Two boys and a girl," he told Alf "Probably three days old, they all seem ok; I guess their mum had gone off to feed herself" He frowned at the thought of the poisoned piece of meat that had probably been left out deliberately to kill the dog that was stealing the chickens. "There were no injuries, Alf; I'm going to do a post-mortem to see if it was poison."

"Wouldn't surprise me, I'd love to get my hands on the evil bastards that poison them. I'd shove the bleeding poison down their own bleeding throats" swore Alf "at least Helen managed to save these little ones" as one of the tiny pups stopped suckling, Alf with surprisingly gentle fingers massaged its little stomach. He picked up a damp cotton wool ball and wiped the tiny puppy's bottom doing the job its mother would normally do with her tongue, to stimulate it to toilet. Repeating the process with the second little boy, he looked up at Markos, who had gone very quiet. "You Okay?" he asked.

"Hmm," said Markos "Helen was amazing; do you think I have been wrong about her?" He looked at Alf with such a guilty expression on his face that Alf wanted to laugh out loud.

"Oh Markos, my friend, you probably need to spend some more time with her and work that one out for yourself" he laughed and placing the two little puppies in a cardboard box lined with blankets he stood up. "I'm going to pop along to our friendly doctor to see if he'll come and sort that cut out, might save you a trip to the hospital."

"Tell him it's Madeline's niece," Markos said wryly "I'm sure he'll come at once, but tell him quietly, or you will have half the village on your doorstep wanting a peek at the famous Helen."

Markos finished feeding the little girl and placed her with her brothers. He picked up the box and carried it carefully through the kitchen and into the living room. Helen was still laying on the sofa but was now propped up with cushions and, thankfully he thought, looking a lot better. Peggy had cleaned most of the cuts and grazes and put a few dressings on some of the deeper ones. While Helen was holding a large dressing against her thigh; Peggy was teasing the twigs and leaves out of her tangled hair.

"Are the puppies okay?" she asked Markos, straining to see in the box.

"Sit still" scolded Peggy, "I need to get this wretched stick untangled, Markos bring them closer" she instructed and smiled as Markos carefully lifted the puppies out and placed them gently on Helens stomach.

"Oh" breathed Helen "They are beautiful" she smiled up at Markos, who was thinking the same thing about her.

"Two boys and a girl Peggy, have you got enough milk?" he asked "I can always get Christos to bring some over this evening...my son" he explained to Helen, who felt an unexpected lurch of disappointment that he was married.

"I'll get Alf to check what we've got, there" she said to Helen

"That's all of them out but your hairs going to need a good wash to get all the leaves and dirt out" she laughed" Now what are you going to call these precious little babies?"

"Me?" exclaimed Helen "Oh no, whoever ends up owning them should name them."

"We give all our babies foster names" Peggy explained "They need a name to go on their health books at the vets" She reached over and stroked the little pups looking at their still closed eyes and pink noses. The little girl was nearly all white with two small black patches on her back, and the two boys were almost identical to each other, both black with four white socks, but one boy had a white patch over his left eye, the other a white patch over his right eye. "Would you look at that" exclaimed Peggy "Give them a couple of days, then we'll get some pictures up on Facebook, see if we can find them homes."

The front door banged open, and Alf came in followed by a tall, grey-haired, bespectacled man carrying an old-fashioned doctor's bag.

"This is Doctor Marouda" he explained to Helen "his English is about as good as my Greek" he chortled "So Markos here will have to translate."

As the two men discussed Helen and her leg in a language she didn't think she'd ever understand, Helen petted the puppies trying to think of some names. The pretty white girl reminded her of the Jasmine that blossomed in her garden at home, yes Jasmine, that's a pretty name, she thought.

"Helen," said Markos "Doctor Marouda will look at your leg, and as long as there are no complications he will be able to stitch it for you; he needs to know when you had your last tetanus injection?"

"Just last year" said Helen, "I caught my thumb on a rusty nail" Markos nodded and translated her words for the doctor, who smiled at Helen and said something in Greek back to Markos, who laughed and explained that he needed to take the puppies off her so the doctor could examine her leg.

Markos gathered up the puppies and put them back in the box. Moving over to an armchair he watched Helen grit her teeth as the doctor removed the dressing and prodded and poked her leg. Dr. Marouda tutted and sighed and placed the dressing back over the wound. He rifled through Peggy's first aid kit and finding a bandage, carefully wrapped it round Helens leg and secured it with a bit of tape. He turned to Markos and said something, seeing Markos' angry retort Helen guessed they were disagreeing about her and feeling embarrassed, wished the sofa would swallow her up. After a few minutes of the two men almost shouting at each other accompanied by a lot of wild hand gesticulation, Markos finally nodded, stood up and shook the doctor's hand. He showed the Doctor out of the door and called for Peggy and Alf.

"Doctor Marouda will not stitch the wound here" he explained to them all "he wanted Helen to go to the hospital but has agreed that if we get Helen over to his clinic, he will do it there, it is more sterile."

"Is he saying my house is dirty?" said Peggy, offended.

"No, Peggy" Markos walked over to Peggy and put his arm around her "Doctor Marouda was very impressed with your first aid skills" he assured her "but the wound needs to be thoroughly cleaned before he can stitch it and Helen will need quite a lot of local anaesthetic and antibiotics. It is better he does it there."

"Look," said Helen "You have all been so kind, but I don't want to put anyone out anymore if you can just call me a taxi I will be fine getting myself to the hospital."

Peggy, Alf and Markos all shouted "No" at the same time and looked aghast at Helen's idea. Peggy seeing the bewilderment on Helen's face perched carefully next to her and took one of Helens hands in both of her own.

"The hospital here is not what you are used to at home," she told Helen kindly "The new hospital is quite lovely, but chances are they will get you in one of their beds and have you hooked up to a drip before the day's out, and they won't be letting you home anytime soon."

"And they don't have the nursing staff to look after you here," continued Alf "You have to hire a private nurse, or a family member is expected to stay with you to do the general nursing care, right?" He looked at Markos for confirmation and as Helen saw Markos nodding his agreement she mentally kicked herself for getting in such a predicament and causing all this bother to these kind strangers.

"Peggy, could I use your bathroom," Helen asked, realising she was desperate for a wee and shuffling her legs around, so she was sitting up with her feet on the floor. As she went to push herself up, she felt a sharp pain shoot down her leg and sat back down with a grimace. Markos was next to her in an instance and helped her into an upright position, keeping tight hold of her in case she fainted again. Assuring him she was fine and taking Peggy's arm; Helen hopped to the bathroom. As they reached the bathroom, Helen could hear an excited yapping coming from behind the closed door.

"Oh bugger," swore Peggy "I forgot we'd shut the little sods in there. Here lean up against the door frame or they'll knock you flying when I open the door," slowly pushing the door open she revealed five more little black and tan puppies who were tumbling over each other in their excitement to get out of the open door. Shouting for Alf to come and help she shooed the pups towards the kitchen and helped Helen into the bathroom.

"Right, I'll leave you to sort yourself out, give us a shout when you've finished."

Helen, supporting herself with one hand on the wall, hopped over to the loo and easing her knickers carefully over the large bandage, sank down gratefully. Holding her head in both hands, she tried not to burst into tears at the pain in her leg and the soreness of all the other cuts and grazes that she was now starting to feel. Pulling herself together she looked round for the bin to put her toilet tissue into. Gripping the edge of the sink, she pulled herself upright and eased herself in front of a large mirror above it. "Oh dear," she thought looking at the state of herself. Balancing on one leg, she filled the sink and splashed the warm water over her face. Hearing Peggy tapping on the door, she shouted for her to come in and smiled as Peggy came round the door carrying a chair.

"We can do better than a quick splash of water," she said and putting the chair in front of the sink, she emptied the dirty water and told Helen to sit down and lay her head back over the sink.

As Helen gratefully laid her head back, she could hear Peggy chattering away but with the running water and the delicious feeling you get when someone else is massaging your head she closed her eyes, relaxed and drifted off into a daydream. *Walking along a sandy beach, holding tightly onto a masculine hand she laughed at the puppies bouncing along beside them. With the hot sun beaming down on her bare shoulders, she smiled and gazed up at…"*

"There you go," said Peggy "Wrapping a towel around her head and startling her out of her daydream. "That's better, now it's probably not the sort of thing you normally wear but your very welcome to borrow this" Peggy handed Helen a simple cotton sundress that was covered in tiny blue rosebuds, thanking her, Helen said it was exactly her sort of thing and Peggy trotted out of the bathroom leaving Helen sat in the chair towelling dry her hair.

Remembering the strange daydream, Helen tried to work out whose hand it was that she had been gripping so tightly, it wasn't Williams, his hand had been pale and covered with a light dusting of freckles. This hand was much larger and deeply tanned, with a smattering of dark hair. Feeling horribly guilty at betraying Williams's memory Helen put down the towel and started to pull off her blood-soaked dress, eyeing the ripped material she scrunched it up and put it in a bin next to the sink. Thinking that her pink, plastic flip-flops could be washed, she placed them in the sink and turned on the taps. Peggy had done a brilliant job cleaning up her arms and legs; she thought looking at the clean skin around the various dressings and uncovered scratches. Pulling Peggy's sundress over her head and feeling much better she turned her hands to the job of cleaning up her flip-flops.

Alf, Peggy, and Markos sat around the large table in the garden watching the various dogs of all shapes and sizes playing in the sunshine. The black and tan puppies, excited to be out it the garden, yapped and danced around their legs and pounced at the bigger dogs with tiny little growls. Markos laughed as the biggest of the pups leapt over to a large black and white spotted dog who was laying contentedly in the sunshine. The brave puppy tugged at the bigger dog's ears then squealed as the dog lazily lifted his leg and flopped it on top of the pup, trapping him underneath. Alf laughing too, ambled over and rescued the little puppy, snuggling it up under his chin. The three of them were trying to work out how to get Helen over to the doctors without being spotted by the nosy villagers who would probably break the internet if they realised Helen was in their village.

"Doctor Marouda suggested we bring her over at three o'clock when he closes for lunch," said Markos looking at his watch and seeing it was just gone midday. "Our biggest problem will be Mavra," he said.

"She's already sent me three messages, asking why you're here," Peggy said to Markos, laughing when he rolled his eyes and groaned. "It's okay, I've told her you're doing the health check on the three adoptees" she reassured him. "Luckily she didn't spot you and Helen turning up."

Mavra was one of their Greek neighbours who doted on the dogs she saved and put her heart and soul into raising money and awareness for the strays. Unfortunately, she had a tendency to interfere in everyone else's business, believing her way was the only way to do things. She was also one of the biggest gossips and was often the root cause of many of the arguments that happened in the community. The biggest problem though was her massive crush on Markos. She called into the vets on almost a daily basis with a variety of different excuses, and if they spotted her in time, Markos' staff would be forced to lie to her and say he was out on a call while he hid in the operating theatre. The fact that she lived opposite the doctor's clinic and was more than likely ensconced in her front garden keeping her eyes peeled on Markos' car was worrying them.

"Goodness. I've never seen so many dogs in one garden," said Helen's voice and seeing her standing on one foot in the doorway, with her damp curls hanging loosely around her pretty face, Markos felt his throat constrict at her beauty. He found it difficult to believe she would soon be fifty. Her figure and looks were that of a woman in her mid-thirties. Peggy, spotting the way Markos was looking at Helen felt sorry for Mavra, if there had ever been the slightest chance of Markos returning her advances it was long gone now. Alf, concerned the dogs were going to jump up to greet Helen, walked down the garden whistling and opened a gate that led to a large enclosed grassy area. Watching seven of the dog's race after Alf and go happily through the gate she asked Peggy if they were all theirs.

"Goodness, no" replied Peggy "four of them are ours" she pointed out four of the dogs, naming them. "The other three only got here a couple of days ago from other fosterers, they're just here so we can organise their final health checks and passports and drop them at the airport on Thursday, they've all got homes to go to in the UK, lucky things."

"And these?" asked Helen, who had hopped over to an empty chair and was now fussing the five little puppies jumping up at her.

"These are the bin babies," said Peggy, they were found chucked in a bin in Kalamaki, still with their umbilical cords attached, there were seven, tied up in a bin bag but two of the little darlings had already died before we got there." Peggy wiped a tear from her eye as she remembered the rescue. "Anyway," she continued "They're coming up eight weeks old now and doing fine."

"Thanks to you and Alf," said Markos standing up. "I need to go and check on a dog back at the clinic," he said "I don't think we will make it up to your Aunt's villa today," he said wryly to Helen, who seemed to be staring at his large tanned hands.

"Oh, no, I don't think so" Helen smiled. "Don't worry I'm sure the villa can wait another day or two. Thank you for looking after me" she said shyly lifting up one of the puppies and holding it to her blushing face.

Peggy waved Markos off and brought out a stool for Helen to put her leg up on, a small amount of blood was starting to seep through the bandage round her leg and Peggy wondered if they should just go over to the Doctors now rather than wait. Asking Alf's advice, he suggested they have lunch first and keep an eye on the amount of blood coming through. Peggy scuttled into the kitchen to rustle up a nice Greek salad while Alf told Helen more about all the dogs they had been rescuing for so many years.

CHAPTER 8
A WHIRLWIND OF A WOMAN

Two tiny cups of the strong Greek coffee, which Lily had made in the small traditional Briki pot, sat on the bar in front of Markos and his best friend of many years Elias who were deep in conversation. Markos had sped back to his clinic in Zante Town and finding the stray dog happily eating some chicken and rice and wagging her tail, was content to leave his two junior partners in charge. He had headed over to the hotel to let Lily and Elias know what had happened. Lily, shocked and upset had rushed off to Helen's room to pack her an overnight bag, thinking that Helen would be better off stopping at Peggy's overnight once her leg had been stitched. The two men were trying to devise a plan to get Mavra out of the way.

"She needs to be gone for at least an hour," said Markos "That will give us enough time to get Helen into the clinic, have her treatment and get her back out again."

"Can we invent a lost dog for her to go looking for?" suggested Elias

"Hmm, not sure she'd fall for that one, Oh, wait I have an idea we…" Markos and Elias turned at the sound of a car screeching to a halt and beeping its horn frantically; they watched as an irate taxi driver opened the back door and started piling luggage up on the pavement.

"Cooee" waved a petite blonde woman with rather large breasts "Could you lovely boys help me please" she shouted over the wall, then turned and smacked at the taxi driver who was throwing even more, very expensive looking, luggage onto the ground. "Could someone please tell this man that this is Louis Vuitton luggage" the woman squealed.

Markos turned backed to the bar, hiding his laughter while the laid-back Elias walked towards her. George who was behind the bar chose to go and hose around the edge of the pool rather than get involved and Maggie was snoring on a sun lounger oblivious to the woman's arrival

"Is okay" Elias shrugged to the woman, "I help, no problem"

picking up some of the luggage he said something in rapid Greek to the taxi driver who threw his hands in the air in disgust and climbed back in the car.

"That man was so rude to me," said the woman "He tried to charge me fifty Euros because I had so much luggage, stupid man," The woman, eyeing Elias up and rather liking what she saw stuck out her hand "Dorothy Boothroyd, I believe my friend Helen is staying here."

Markos, listening, coughed and spluttered the coffee he'd just taken a swig of over the bar. Lily having returned from Helen's room to all the commotion, took charge and told Elias to load the luggage into his car and take it up to the room. Eyeing all the gorgeous luggage enviously, she did wonder how this woman was going to fit it all in the little room.

"Oh not that," said Dotty, grabbing a very long cardboard tube from Elias "that's my samples, can't risk those getting damaged." Dotty carried the tube through the archway and placed it carefully on the bar "Now then where's Helen?" she said, looking round "She's been ignoring my calls and texts all morning."

Lily, realising that Markos was not going to say anything, led Dotty to a table.

"I'm afraid Helen is a bit...er...indisposed at the moment," she told Dotty "Let me get you a drink, and I'll tell you all about it." Taking Dotty's order of a "Frappe, milk, no sugar," she went back behind the bar and glared at Markos, who seemed to be finding the arrival of Helen's friend highly amusing.

"Right, here you go" Lily put the Frappe down in front of Dotty and sat down to explain what had happened that morning. Expecting Dotty to be alarmed and upset she was surprised to see a grin spreading over the woman's face. As she continued, Dotty started to giggle and by the time Lily had finished explaining that Helen was currently waiting to be taken to the local doctors to be stitched up Dotty was in fits of laughter and wiping the tears from her eyes.

"Oh the silly cow," she laughed "She'll never learn," seeing Lily's confused face and noticing that the rather handsome man at the bar had turned around to listen, she continued. "It's not the first time she's done this sort of thing; I doubt it will be the last," thinking hard, she remembered "1978, thirteen years old, she broke her arm in two places falling out of a tree while trying to rescue a cat. 1982, seventeen years old, she crashed her first car into a ditch rather than run a rabbit over. 1991, she nearly drowned rescuing a dog that had slipped through the ice on a lake." Seeing the pairs shocked faces she laughed out loud "Oh there's so much more, just last year she cut her thumb badly on a rusty nail while she was trying to free a little Muntjac deer that was trapped in a fence." Taking a sip of her frappe, Dotty licked her lips at the yummy taste. "I'm usually the ditzy one," Dotty laughed, "but when it comes to animals Helen just jumps straight in and doesn't think of the consequences." Seeing Lily and Markos raising their eyes at each other she wondered what the look was all about.

Looking around, Dotty liked what she saw, living a high maintenance lifestyle she loved going back to the simple life. Lily also liked what she saw. The woman sat opposite her was beautiful, her perfect makeup, beautifully manicured nails, and expensive designer clothes hid a down-to-earth woman who, finding her best friend's predicament so funny, obviously had a wicked sense of humour. Markos meanwhile was mulling over the things Dotty had said about Helen. His heart which had decided to flip somersaults every time he saw her was battling with his head which still couldn't understand why she had ignored her Aunt for so many years.

Lily cleared the table and offered to take Dotty up to her room, reminding her to pick up the tube of sample materials she'd left on the bar. With the tube stuck safely under her arm, Dotty followed Lily, smiling at the man hosing leaves and blossom away from the edge of the pool.

"That's my dad George," said Lily "and my mum Maggie" pointing out a curvy woman, snoozing on a nearby sun lounger.

"Hello," said Dotty, walking over to shake George's hand. Hearing Markos calling that she'd forgotten her handbag, Dotty swung round and caught George right between the legs with the cardboard tube. Clutching his manhood and squealing like a baby, he toppled into the pool with an almighty splash that splattered up and over the sleeping Maggie. Startled she sat up and seeing her husband floundering in the pool grabbed the parasol pole to pull herself up and toppled off the side of the sun lounger.

"Oh my gawd, what's happening" Maggie screeched loudly as she scrabbled to heave herself up off the wet tiles.

Markos and Elias laughing loudly, ran over to pick up the sopping wet Maggie and Lily, overcome with laughter reached down to help her dad out of the pool.

"Oh crumbs, I'm so sorry," said Dotty and bent down to help George as well, who catching an eyeful of her huge bosom, spluttered and gasped even more.

Sorting her mum and dad out and assuring Dotty that she didn't need to keep apologising Lily hoped that this whirlwind of a woman would be staying for a while, she hadn't had so much fun in years. As she pointed the way up the steps, Dotty turned back to Maggie and said "Nice sarong, by the way."

Seeing it was already 2:30 pm, Markos, remembering the idea he'd had to lure Mavra away from her house waved a cheery goodbye and set off back to Macherado, the village that Peggy and Alf lived in. Reaching the beautiful church of Agia Mavra, that his stalker had been named after, he tucked his truck out of sight behind one of the tourist coaches parked in the car park. Picking up his mobile he rang Mavra's phone.

"Yasou Mavra," he said and asked her if there was any chance she could drive up to the feeding station behind Madeline's villa and fill up the food dishes. "I've been so busy today; I haven't had a chance to get up there and I've just been called out to an emergency."

"Of course Markos" replied a sultry voice "anything for you and of course Madeline was my best friend, I helped her many times with the feeds; I will go straight away."

Thanking her, Markos slipped out of his truck and waited until he saw Mavra's car whizz by, ridiculously pleased that his plan had worked he ran round the corner and slipped inside Peggy and Alf's back gate. Coming across Peggy, Alf and Helen, each with a puppy and bottle in hands he smirked as he told them what he had done.

"I've hidden my truck" he explained to Helen "so we will help you up the road to the doctors," Markos said, wishing he didn't feel so excited at the thought of holding her again. "Oh, and your friend has arrived."

"My friend?" Helen asked, confused "Oh Dotty, oh good grief I forgot all about her" seeing Markos biting his lip and trying not to laugh and knowing her friend so well, she grimaced and asked, "What's she done now?"

Markos sat down and told them all about Dotty's arrival with the angry taxi driver, and as Peggy and Alf started to laugh, he described perfectly how George and Maggie both ended up sopping wet. Peggy and Alf roared with laughter and Helen sat there with her head in her hand appalled at her best friend's antics.

"It's okay Helen, everyone found it very amusing, even George and Maggie" he laughed. "Now we must get you over to the doctors" seeing the amount of blood that had seeped through the bandage on Helens leg and how pale she was looking he was concerned that it wouldn't be long before she fainted again.

Hopping out of the door with Alf one side and Markos the other, Helen felt the blood starting to trickle down her leg again. Feeling slightly dizzy she grabbed the door frame and took a deep breath, she clutched the men's arms and hopped a few feet forward. Markos also spotting the blood bent down and lifting her into his arms marched quickly down the road with Alf puffing behind. Kicking the doctor's door open he walked straight through to the doctor's office and laid Helen on the long black surgical couch. Doctor Marouda, seeing all the blood and the panic on Markos's face pushed him out of the door murmuring his reassurances and turned quickly back to Helen.

Mavra, thrilled to be helping her beloved Markos, drove happily down the road. All of a sudden she slammed on her brakes and slapping herself on the head, swore as she remembered the cakes she'd left baking in the oven. Turning her car round she sped back up the road, terrified that she'd arrive home to see her little house burning with the dogs and cats trapped inside. Reaching the church, she turned the corner and braked at the sight in front of her. Moving her face closer to the windscreen, she saw Markos striding up the road with a very pretty woman clutched tightly in his arms and a waddling Alf following behind. She watched as they turned into the doctors and disappeared behind the closed door. Driving slowly up the road, she pulled into her driveway and quickly ran in to turn off the oven. "Hmm, some emergency," she thought, feeling a hot, angry flash of jealousy course through her. Taking a seat in front of her little window, she picked up a small pair of binoculars and sat waiting for them to emerge wanting to get a good look at the woman Markos had been carrying.

Markos was pacing round and round the small waiting room with Alf, sat in a chair, watching him. Seeing a packet of cigarettes left on the receptionist's desk, he took one out and lit it inhaling deeply.

"Since when did you smoke," said Alf, helping himself to one and settling back to enjoy it.

"Since I was 14, growled Markos, but only when I'm stressed" he started pacing again then looking at Alf said "The doctor can't speak English, I should be in there" guessing that nothing he said would make any difference Alf remained quiet.

The doctor patted Helen's arm, respecting how brave she had been as he'd injected a lot of local anaesthetics, flushed out and cleaned the large wound and closed it with more than thirty stitches. Taping a bandage over the large dressing he walked to a cupboard and pulled out an old pair of crutches.

"Two days, no walk," he said in stilted English, shaking his head and wagging his finger "then one week, these" he held up the crutches. "I give you…" unsure of the correct words he opened the door and called Markos.

Explaining in Greek that he would give Helen a prescription for antibiotics and painkillers that she must start today Markos nodded and translated to Helen, who had sat herself up, relieved that the local anaesthetic had taken away the horrible pain. The doctor repeated his instructions about no walking at all for two days and handed Markos the crutches and prescription, he, in turn, handed them to Alf, who was hovering by the office door. Markos pulled out his wallet and started to give the doctor some money, the doctor shook his head and waved the money away saying something in Greek, hearing "Madeline" mentioned Helen frowned, wondering what that was all about.

"Your Aunt, helped Doctor Marouda in many ways" Markos explained, seeing Helen's frown "He wishes to repay her, by helping her niece" Helen smiled and asked Markos how to say thank you in Greek.

"Efharisto para poli" Helen tried out the words Markos suggested and seeing the doctor's smile and nod, felt pleased with herself. Markos picked Helen back up and with Alf leading the way and holding open the door he carried her back out into the sunshine.

"Bleeding hell," said Alf "That's all we bloody need" seeing Mavra stood in her doorway with her arms folded and a scowl on her face.

Helen heard Markos groan and felt him clutch her a bit tighter. She looked across at the woman walking towards them. Mavra, she saw was, dressed in a pair of scruffy jeans, a pink t-shirt, and a long black cardigan, her long, straggly, black hair was streaked with grey and tied in a loose plait with a large flowery scrunchy. She looked very angry as she stopped in front of Markos and started shouting at him in Greek. Markos just stood still, holding Helen tightly and smiled kindly at Mavra.

"Yasou Mavra," he said, and switched to English for Helen and Alf's benefit. "This is Helen Hardy, Madeline's niece, she was badly hurt today, rescuing some puppies. I am helping her back to Peggy and Alf's as the doctor has banned her from walking." Helen could not believe how quickly Mavra's whole demeanor changed from an angry whirling dervish to a sweet angelic lady.

"Helen, I am Mavra, I am so very, very pleased to meet you," she gushed "Madeline was my very best friend, we spent so many hours together." Helen bit her lip as she heard Alf cough "bloody liar," into his hand. "I think you must come to my house, I can make you special drink from my plants, it is better than your English tea." She pointed to her little house opposite and instructed Markos to take Helen there.

"Thank you Mavra," interrupted Alf "but Peggy's already made up the spare bed and Helen's just had thirty stitches put in her poor leg so isn't up to visiting anyone yet." Alf put his hand on Markos' shoulder and gently shoved him in the right direction. "Once she is rested we will be taking her back to her hotel in Keri." As they walked off Helen glanced over Markos' shoulder and smiled at the dumbstruck Mavra, who just stood staring at them. What a strange woman she thought. Peggy, who was stood in her doorway watching, dropped her head into her hands and groaned.

Putting Helen carefully on the sofa, Markos stood back up and stared at Peggy and Alf, who were staring at each other. Abruptly, almost as if they'd had a telepathic conversation, Alf raced to the wall and yanked out the phone line while Peggy ran and pulled the curtains shut. Helen yawned, feeling the same light-headed tiredness she got after a couple of glasses of wine, no longer caring what was going on she nestled back against the cushions and closed her eyes. Thinking she was already dreaming, she snuggled into the warm arms that lifted and carried her down the corridor and into the spare bedroom. Markos lay Helen down onto Peggy's spare bed and pulling the sheet over her fought an overwhelming urge to sweep the damp tendrils of hair from her face and kiss her.

"Dr. Marouda gave her a strong injection of painkiller," he

explained to a concerned Peggy. "As soon as the local anesthetic wears off she's going to feel every stitch; best she sleeps through the first couple of hours."

"What do we do now?" said Peggy wringing her hands together "Mavra will be ringing everyone as we speak, we'll be bombarded with visitors."

"I think Alf's quick thinking may have given us a couple of hours," said Markos, telling Peggy what Alf had said to Mavra. "I'm guessing all the hotels in Keri will have their phones ringing off the hook right about now" he laughed. "Lily packed an overnight case for Helen; it's in the truck. I'll go and get it now and see if Mavra's car is still in her drive."

Mavra's car was indeed still in her drive, and Mavra was sat inside her little house busy updating her Facebook status in both Greek and English

"Just met Helen Hardy, she's in Macherado, apparently injured!!! How exciting!!!"

She wrote the same on her Twitter account adding the hashtag *#helenhardyinjured*, knowing it would generate a lot of interest on their small island. She sat back smiling evilly; she had seen the way Markos was holding the English woman so tightly, and if Helen Hardy thought she was going to waltz into their lives and steal her man, then she had better be prepared for a fight. Needing to keep on Markos' good side she made sure everything was turned off, this time, shut in the dogs, and got back into her car. Pulling out her phone, she sent Markos a quick text letting him know she was heading off to the feeding station and that she hoped Helen was okay.

Peggy's mobile phone started vibrating again, after the non-stop unanswered calls over the last half hour, she had given in and turned it to silent mode. Taking a quick look and seeing Lily's name lit up on the display she hit the accept button and switched it to the speaker so that Markos and Alf could hear.

"Have you seen Facebook?" cried Lily's voice "They're crucifying her" as Peggy told her they hadn't dared look at the internet yet, Lily went on "listen to this," she said, imitating a posh voice that they all recognised as Snotty Selena's and read out:

"So H.H arrives on our Island and instantly fakes an injury to try and make us all feel sorry for her!!! Not falling for that one LOL" and here's another

Lily continued.

"*H.H. seems to have set her sights on our lovely local vet!!!* Peggy smiled as she saw Markos blush and hide his head in his hands. "We need to stop this; poor Helen only got here yesterday." Peggy and Alf nodded into the silence as they realised that despite it seeming like they'd known Helen forever, she had in fact only arrived yesterday and only met them that morning."

"We need a distraction of some sort," said Markos "We need to give them all something else to talk about."

"Oh" came a voice over the phone that Peggy and Alf didn't recognise. "Dotty here, I have an idea, if you don't mind me coming over to yours I think between us we can plan the perfect distraction." Hearing Lily offer to drive Dotty over, Markos suggested they make it quick as Mavra had set off to the feeding station and would be out the way for at least an hour.

"Hello," said Dotty smiling warmly at Peggy and Alf "I'm Dorothy Boothroyd, but please call me Dotty, oh how adorable," Dotty squealed excitedly, as she scooped up two of the black and tan puppies that were jumping up at her legs. Peggy, seeing Alf ogling Dotty's large breasts, smacked him round the head and sent him off to put the kettle on.

"Goodness," said Peggy, realisation dawning "You're that Dorothy Boothroyd" and reaching forward gave Dotty a huge hug "My daughter-in-law manages one of your shops, how lovely to meet you."

"Oh which one?" asked Dotty, genuinely interested and when Peggy mentioned the Reading branch Dotty clasped both her hands "That's Suzanne's, that means you're going to become Grandparents in November, how lovely." Peggy smiled and nodded, chuffed to bits that Dotty knew their daughter-in-law.

"Have I missed something?" said Lily looking blankly at Peggy and Dotty. As Peggy explained who Dotty really was Lily's face lit up with recognition. "Ha, wait till I tell mum, oh, her sarong, oh," recalling Dotty's earlier throw-away comment she grinned at Dotty "Helen didn't say a word about who you are." Markos and a returning Alf, who knew as much about women's underwear as they did about women's hair and make-up shrugged their shoulders at each other and went to check on the newborns.

An hour later, all five of them were sat round the table, which was littered with bits of scribbled on paper. They had taken it in turns to check on a sleeping Helen, who was still blissfully unaware of the most recent gossip flying through cyberspace or any of the manic planning that Dotty was overseeing in the garden. Markos had been to the pharmacy and seeing the strength of the antibiotics and painkillers Dr. Marouda had prescribed assured them all that Helen would probably sleep a lot of the next few days away and was best left safely secreted at Peggy and Alf's. He'd spotted Mavra's car parked back in her driveway and suggested Dotty wait till the cover of darkness before she left. Lily secure in the knowledge that her mum and dad were covering the bar back at the hotel was happy to stay and enjoy a few exciting hours off.

"Right," said Dotty, who had spent the past hour emailing and phoning various people in her company, including Suzanne, Peggy's daughter-in-law. "Stage one, Markos posts an update on his clinic's Facebook page in Greek and English, let's hear it, Markos?"

"Having seen a lot of false information on Facebook today," Markos read out loud "I would like to set the record straight. This morning I picked Helen Hardy up to take her up to her Aunt's villa. On route, I was redirected to an emergency and found a dog, possibly poisoned, on the side of the road. Seeing that she had recently given birth Helen and I hunted for the puppies which were located under a thick gorse bush. In a selfless act, Helen rescued the puppies during which she received a severe injury to her leg, which has now been treated. Helen is recovering in a hotel in Keri and does not wish to be disturbed for the next couple of days."

"Perfect," said Dotty. Now Stage two, fifteen minutes later Maggie will update her status and tag Lily in it." Knowing that Lily was not the sort to gossip they'd roped in Maggie, who was completely over excited and couldn't wait to start spreading the news "read it out Lily," Dotty instructed.

"Can't believe the famous lingerie designer Dorothy Boothroyd is staying at my daughter's little hotel! And to think I'm wearing one of her sarongs!"

"Wonderful," said Dotty, clicking refresh on her emails "Ah here it comes," she opened an email from her Public Relations Manager and quickly scanned the message and attached document. "So stage three, in a couple of hours my company will release this statement to the press, and hopefully it won't take long for the eyes of your

Zakynthos local media to pick it up." She read the attachment out loud to her grinning partners in crime.

"Lingerie designer, Dorothy Boothroyd, has recently arrived on the beautiful Island of Zakynthos, Greece, home of the famous Shipwreck at Navagio Beach. Ms. Boothroyd, famed for her preference of using authentic members of the public as opposed to professional models, is looking for females of all age, shapes and sizes to feature in her next catalogue, which will be shot in a variety of different locations in Zakynthos. Only women who currently reside in Zakynthos may apply. Please contact…" not bothering to read out all the contact details Dotty looked at the smiling faces and said, "Okay, I think we're just about sorted."

"I can't believe that you're doing all this," breathed Peggy "and you're really bringing our Suzanne over to help out?" Dotty nodded.

"My managers know better than anyone what sells and which items to advertise," she was thrilled to be helping these lovely strangers who had opened their home and arms to Helen and for a couple of months, she had been searching for the ideal location for her photo shoot. It was a win, win all round as far as she was concerned.

"Hi," said a voice from the kitchen "What have I missed."

CHAPTER 9
REVELATIONS

Early Thursday morning, Lily turned on the tap and picked up the hose, the olive tree blossom was falling thick and fast and as well as the tiled floor, covered the tables, chairs, and bar. Hosing everything down and out towards the road she heard the sound of flip-flops splashing through the water and moved the hose out of the way to let a small woman get past. The woman, dressed in cut-off jeans and a creased over-sized t-shirt was carrying an "I LOVE ZANTE" beach bag and sporting a pair of the cheap, fake Ray Ban sunglasses found in many of the local souvenir shops. Her short, black, shiny bob was mostly hidden by a trilby style straw sunhat. Lily watched her cross the road and turn right, heading for the large hotel across the road. How rude, thought Lily, she didn't even bother to say "good morning" or "thank you."

The woman carried on along the boardwalk and slipping into the hotel through a small metal gate walked around a large L-shaped pool and into a busy reception area. Ignoring everyone, she went out through the Hotels glass doors and crossed the road to Stamnes restaurant. Finding a table, she ordered a coffee and took out her mobile phone.

Helen, hearing "*Fat Bottomed Girls*" grabbed her phone off Peggy's kitchen side and pressing accept asked "Did it work?"

"Yes, yes, yes," squealed Dotty's excited voice "Lily didn't have a clue it was me, this wigs bloody itchy though." Hearing Helen laughing she told her she'd see her later and ended the phone call.

Lily coiled the hose back up and took a look around. It had taken a good twenty minutes to clean the bar area but, finally, they were ready. The bar was fully stocked, and they had tripled their alcohol and food orders for the next three weeks. All eight rooms up the back, plus the two larger apartments were spick and span, ready for their guests to arrive at the weekend. It was many years since they had been fully booked so early in the season but Dotty had insisted that the members of her staff, who were flying over on Saturday, would stay there. Elias had pulled in some of his younger male cousins to help run the bar at night and they had employed two of the local women to help with the cleaning and cooking. For the rest of today and tomorrow Lily, exhausted, intended to relax. Wandering into the little kitchen to switch on the coffee machine she heard the sound of a chair scraping across the floor and looked out to see the woman, who had been so rude earlier, sat at one of the tables.

"Won't be a moment," she said, and finding her notepad and pencil, walked over to take the woman's order "What can I get you love?" she asked politely then frowned as the woman's shoulders started heaving up and down and a strange gurgling sound came from her mouth. "Are you okay?" she asked, concerned.

"Wonderful Darling!" exclaimed Dotty, pulling off her wig and screaming with laughter at Lily's shocked face. "I'm sick to death of hiding up in my room," ever since Maggie had updated her Facebook status, poor Lily and Elias had been inundated with locals, eager to catch a glimpse of the famous Dorothy Boothroyd. Poor Dotty had been holed up in her room for two days and was starting to feel like a prisoner.

"Fantastic," screeched Lily "Quick put it back on before Mum and Dad get here, see if you can catch them out."

Helen, still giggling at the thought of Dotty in disguise, put down her phone and limped into the garden to see if she could help with anything. Peggy and Alf were crating up the three dogs who were heading off to the airport. Peggy had been tearful since she'd woken up but Alf reassured Helen it was always the same. As soon as they heard that the dogs had arrived safely, Peggy would be fine. Seeing that no help was needed, Helen sat at the garden table and switched on her laptop.

The last two days had been a bit of a blur. During her more lucid moments, she'd been brought up-to-date with Dotty's ingenious plan. The rest of the time she had spent in a drug induced sleep, swinging between the sweetest dreams of running along a beach holding a strong, tanned hand to the horrific nightmares of clutching Williams hand as he lay dying at the side of a road. Hating the feeling of being so out of control, she had stopped taking the painkillers the night before and certainly felt better for it.

Opening her emails, she deleted the obvious spam and junk and opened the one from Molly.

Hi Helen
Dotty told us about your accident! Typical! Hope you get better soon, everything fine here.
Love Molly and Ian xxxx

Helen smiled and moved onto the next email which was from Gerald.

Dearest Helen, I ran into Ian yesterday, and he told me of your accident. I do hope you are recovering well and let me know if I can do anything to help. I am a little concerned as Percival Boston contacted me on Monday, requesting copies of Williams's financial affairs. He claims that you gave him permission. I shredded all the copies many months ago and I must confess to feeling somewhat hurt Helen as I worked endlessly to sort Williams's finances. In future, please ask me for anything you need. There really is no need to involve solicitors.
Regards
Gerald

Helen sighed, feeling guilty. Gerald had indeed spent many hours sorting all Williams's affairs out. That little post-it note she had found in the diary probably meant nothing, and she'd stupidly let the emotions of that crazy week rule her head. Gerald was completely right of course, she thought. She picked up her mobile and sent him a quick text apologising and reassuring him she was fine and would let him know if she needed any help.

Seeing an email from Percival, that was flagged as urgent, she clicked it open, already mentally trying to phrase a reply that would call off his investigation without offending him.

My Dear Helen
I have some rather exciting news. We have received all the copies of your late husband's bank statements, and it seems you were right, there are some discrepancies. William had a high-interest savings account that had a considerable sum of money in it. Were you aware of this? Anyway I digress. Approximately three years ago he withdrew £45,000 in cash. Following this withdrawal, regular monthly payments of between one and three thousand were paid into the account, predominantly in cash but there were a couple of cheque deposits. Over the course of a year, £15,000 was put back in. The next couple of months there were a couple of smaller payments between one and two hundred and then, for the few

months preceding his death nothing was paid in. Now then my dear, I would deduce from all this, that rather than William taking out a loan, as you initially suspected, he had, in fact, given out a loan to someone. Maybe the mysterious "G" the note referred to. Of course, you may be fully aware of all this but if not, and if you wish me to continue on our exciting adventure together, please do let me know. I quite relish hunting down who the cheques came from.
I await your reply with anticipation.
Yours
Percival Boston Junior.

Helen sat back, surprised at how calmly she had taken this latest revelation. Of course, she'd known about the savings account. William had received a large inheritance following the death of his mother. Using some of it to pay off their mortgage, he had put the rest into savings. The extra monthly income they had, from not having to pay the mortgage anymore, had gone into the savings account. Their plans to retire early, rent out their house and use their savings to travel the world, had been shattered by Williams's death.

She hadn't known anything about money being taken out of this account though, and the thought of William keeping secrets shocked her to the core. Apart from his Papa or the twins, Helen couldn't imagine William lending anyone that amount of money. She thought back to the "G" William had been meeting the morning of his death. Racking her brain, she still couldn't think of anyone, apart from Gerald, who's first or surname began with the letter G. The idea that Gerald would borrow money was ridiculous. As a successful cardiologist, he earned much more than William and Helen put together. He also led quite a simple life, definitely not prone to extravagant spending. In hindsight, she thought, she should have paid more attention when Gerald had gone over Williams finances with her. Her state of mind at the time though, was so far removed from reality that she probably wouldn't have noticed anything wrong. Maybe, she thought, William had spent the missing £45,000 himself. Shaking her head, she doubted this, and determined to get to the bottom of it all, instructed Percival to continue the hunt.

Hearing a chug, chug of a moped pulling up outside the house, Helen closed the laptop and prepared to hide in the spare bedroom. Despite most of the attention now on Dotty and her fashion shoot, a few dedicated locals were still trying to hunt her down.

"It's okay Helen; it's just Christos" called Alf. "He's going to help me with the dogs so Peggy can stay here with you.

Helen heard the side gate open and looking up, saw a young man push his moped through the gates. He flipped down the stand, took off his helmet and walked towards Helen with an outstretched hand and a wide grin on his face.

"Hello," he said "I'm Markos' son, It's great to meet you, I hope your legs a bit better" Helen was completely taken aback by the young man's blonde hair, blue eyes and very English sounding voice.

"Hello," she replied, shaking his hand "It's very refreshing to see a young man wearing a helmet" thinking of all the youngsters she'd seen flying about on mopeds and quads with no regard for their safety.

"Oh, I'm afraid the English rules of the road are ingrained in me" he laughed, and seeing her confused look went on "I moved to England with my mother when I was four, I only moved back here permanently last year when I qualified as a vet."

"Really," said Helen "I didn't know that, where in England did you live?"

"Our house was in Henley, but to be honest, most of my childhood was spent between boarding school and holidays here on Zakynthos. My mother and stepfather liked to travel a lot" he smiled wryly as if he was glad his childhood days were over.

"Now then young Christos, are you ready?" said Alf walking over to them "We need to get going."

"Yep, ready as ever." Christos laughed, "Oh Helen, my father said if you think you can manage it, he will take you up to the villa today, he has to go to the mainland for a few days so won't be around next week."

"Oh, okay, I have the crutches if I need them, that would be wonderful; please thank your father. Helen wasn't sure if she was more excited at seeing the villa or seeing Markos again. "Oh Peggy, come and have a cup of tea," she said, seeing Peggy mopping her eyes yet again as she said goodbye to the dogs.

"I'm a silly mare," said Peggy a while later "It's not as if I've even fostered those three, I just worry about them stuck in those crates, on the plane, probably scared stiff…"

Seeing that Peggy was about to break down into further sobs Helen asked her how long she'd been fostering dogs.

"Oh, dearie me love, ever since we moved here twenty-five years ago," Peggy laughed "and it was that Aunt of yours that got us started, hang on a sec…" Peggy got up and walked into the kitchen; Helen could hear cupboards and drawers being opened and shut and wondered what Peggy was looking for. "Here we go," said Peggy" coming back out, her arms full of old photo albums.

Peggy put them on the table and invited Helen to look through them while she sorted the new-born puppies out. Helen picked up the oldest looking album and started turning over the pages. A younger looking Peggy and Alf, posing with a toddler smiled out of the pages. Moving on Helen saw the toddler growing into a young boy. The album was full of the usual happy family events that people snapped with their cameras, days at the beach, birthdays, Christmas. Nearing the end Helen stopped and stared at a photo of a smiling woman, holding the boy on her shoulders. Squinting and moving the album a bit closer, she opened her eyes wide in shock. Pulling back the plastic covering that protected the pictures, she picked up the photo and ran her fingers over the face of her Aunt Maddie. In the same way that a certain smell or the sound of a song evoked a long lost memory the photo sent Helen reeling back into a moment in her past.

She recalled her Aunt Maddie swinging her onto her back and cantering down the beach, neighing and pretended to be a horse. Helen could almost taste the salty sea breeze blowing in her face and feel her Aunt Maddie's damp, strawberry blonde hair tickling her chin. As the memory faded, she looked more closely at the photo and realised how much she looked like her Aunt.

"Helen, Helen, quick, look, the babies have opened their eyes," Peggy placed the box on the table and Helen saw three pairs of vivid blue eyes twinkling up at her. "Oh my darling girl, whatever's wrong?" said Peggy, spotting the tears swimming in Helen's own bright blue eyes.

Helen handed Peggy the photo. Smiling through the tears, she described the wonderful moment in her past that she'd just remembered.

"Oh that's my Jacob, Maddie did love him, and she spoilt him rotten," she laughed "She talked about you a lot you know…she missed you so much." Peggy handed Helen the little girl pup and picked up the two boys. "Do you know, she told me once that she wouldn't marry her Kostas, Markos' uncle, until you could come over and be a bridesmaid." Hearing Helen gasp she continued. "She said she wrote to you on your eighteenth birthday, but…well, I guess you were young and busy…"

"I didn't know," breathed Helen, so quietly that Peggy could barely hear her "I honestly didn't know," Helen repeated, fighting back the tears. "I never got the letter," Helen snuggled the tiny puppy under her chin and tried to compose herself. "My parents led me to believe that Maddie had died, they took away every photo and every memory until in my young mind; she had never existed." Helen gulped and went on. "My father never gave me the letter; he never gave me a choice…" Helens voice broke as she thought of her poor Aunt, who must have felt so rejected, for so many years. "It's the only reason I came to Zakynthos, Peggy, to try and put right my father's wrongs."

Peggy was stunned into silence, what a cruel man Helen's father must have been. She felt utterly devastated for both her best friend, who had died without knowing the truth and this kind, compassionate woman in front of her, who had missed out on a loving relationship with her Aunt.

Maggie placed a large dish of Moussaka in the centre of the table and told everyone to help themselves. Dotty helped herself to a decent sized portion, grateful for the steep hill that was keeping her fit and picked up a piece of the delicious garlic bread that Maggie had just pulled out of the oven. With the continuing stream of nosy visitors starting to annoy them, Elias and Markos had carried a large table and some chairs up the hill and placed them on the sunny patch of grass behind the rooms and away from prying eyes. Enjoying a relaxed lunch and a glass of the village wine, Dotty was describing Percival Boston Junior to a laughing Lily and Maggie. Markos and Elias were chatting away in Greek, and George, quiet as always was tucking into his wife's cooking.

"Must have been quite a shock for Helen, finding out about the Will?" said Maggie, already on her second glass of the potent wine.

"Oh, I think she was more shocked to find out that her Aunt hadn't died years ago!" declared Dotty, pushing her fork into the Moussaka. Hearing the table fall silent and seeing their questioning faces, Dotty put the fork down and told them how Helen's father had seemingly obliterated Madeline from their lives. Enjoying, as always, being the centre of attention Dotty went on to tell them of the postcards and letter he'd not given Helen and the dreadful state Helen was in when she'd read Madeline's first letter.

"I don't mind telling you," Dotty said to the appalled faces round the table. "I was really quite worried for a while, all this landing on her only eighteen months after her husband died but in a strange way it was probably the best thing that could have happened to Helen, once she'd got over the shock, it gave her something new to focus on and she's bloody determined to do the right thing by her Aunt. She doesn't give a damn about the inheritance." Realising that she'd probably said far too much, Dotty shovelled the forkful of Moussaka into her mouth and stopped talking.

The sudden, deafening silence lasted all of thirty seconds before everyone started talking at once. Maggie and George bombarded Dotty with a barrage of questions and Lily tried to translate what Dotty had said to a confused Elias. Markos quietly pushed back his chair and thanked Maggie for the lunch. He slipped into his truck and started the engine. As he drove away from the hotel, he allowed the tears to fall. Unable to see, he pulled up under the olive groves and let out all the anguish and anger he'd bottled up since his beloved Madeline had died. He punched both fists on the steering wheel and flinging open the door jumped out and started kicking his tyres. How cruel and callous he thought. With no-one left to direct his anger at, Markos finally grieved for the loss of his surrogate mother and the years of hurt she'd felt, thinking that Helen wanted nothing to do with her. Calming himself he got back in the truck. Terrified of the feelings he'd had towards Helen; he'd deliberately kept away for the last two days. Now with an urgency and lust, he'd not allowed himself to feel for many, many years, he needed to be by her side.

Helen and Peggy were giggling over the silly names they were coming up with for the puppies. Both in agreement that Jasmine suited the little girl they were struggling to name the two boys. The bigger of the boys was in Helens hands, struggling to hold the bottle himself between his tiny paws, his independence reminded Helen of her stubborn father-in-law.

"Papa," she suggested "You remind me of Papa."

"Oh that's perfect," giggled Peggy "Now what about this little one?" The other boy was the runt of the litter and much smaller than his brother and sister.

"Smudge," suggested Helen, and Peggy nodded slowly, as she mulled the name over "Jasmine, Papa and Smudge," Helen tested out the names and liking them, made her decision, chuffed that she'd been allowed to name them.

They both heard the side gate swing open and looked up to see Markos striding towards them, wearing sunglasses to hide his red-rimmed eyes and dressed in a pair of chinos and a white, short-sleeved shirt. He waved a cheery "Yasou" to the ladies and took a seat at the table. Hearing another voice echoing Markos' greeting they all looked up to see Mavra coming through the gate, followed by a large woman who was totally overdressed for the warm weather. As Helen openly stared at the woman she heard Markos mutter sorry under his breath as he realised he'd parked his truck in full sight of Mavra's beady eyes. Mavra sidled over to Helen and almost curtseyed, gushing her admiration for her bravery in rescuing the pups and patted her heavily bandaged leg.

"Move over Mavra," boomed the other woman who was dressed in an immaculate, pale yellow pleated skirt and matching 1950's style twin-set and the obligatory pearls. "Good Afternoon Helen. I'm Selena Warrington-Smyth," shoving a white, gloved hand almost in Helens face. "Now then, my dear girl, I'm sure Peggy here has done a wonderful job of looking after you, and I must admit that it was very clever of Alf to send everyone on a wild goose chase around the Keri hotels." Selena paused and shot Peggy a pointed look. "However," she exclaimed pompously "We have held a meeting and decided the best thing would be for you to move in with me for the next couple of weeks so that you can recuperate properly with the very best of care." Helen looked up at Selena and Mavra, who was nodding like one of those little dogs you saw in the back of cars, she bit back the rude retort she wanted to shout and instead smiled graciously and shook Selena's hand.

"That's very kind of you Selena, but I am quite alright, in fact, I will be moving back to my hotel this evening, and Markos here has very kindly offered to drive me," she replied, childishly knowing it would annoy the smitten Mavra.

"Oh, nonsense, my dear," insisted Selena "I was such close friends with the darling Madeline, she would never forgive me if I didn't take care of you and…well…to be honest, my house is a far more sterile place to be, not so many dog hairs you know." As she said this, Selena stared snottily around at the various dogs and puppies and brushed some imaginary dog hairs off her skirt. Peggy, quivering with rage, started to rise out of her seat but was stopped by Markos, who gripped her shoulder gently and eased her back down.

"Selena, Mavra," he said, looking at each woman in turn and in such a stern voice that even Peggy and Helen felt scared. "I fully understand that you are all very excited to meet Helen, however," he said very loudly "She has been through a very traumatic experience and is only just starting to get better, I suggest very strongly that you leave her alone for a few more days and…" He stood up and put his palm almost in Selena's face to stop her interrupting. "And" he repeated, "If Helen is feeling well enough, Peggy and Alf will bring her along to the Fundraising walk tomorrow night, now if you don't mind we are about to have lunch, goodbye." Selena, insulted, tossed her head, spun around and grabbing Mavra's arm stormed out of the garden.

"What's the Fundraising walk" Helen whispered to a convulsing Peggy

"Oh just you wait and see" giggled Peggy "Just you wait and see."

CHAPTER 10
ELA, ELA

Climbing the steep, crumbly chalk road, Helens breath was taken away by the beautiful views. The part of the journey from Zante town to Vassilikos had been charming. The smooth road had meandered along the coastline, taking them first through Argassi and then up and around the sharp bends, one minute, high above the sea, the next, back down between rows of tall pine trees. Markos had pointed out various beaches along the route. Porto Zorro, St Nicholas, and Banana Beach just a few of the ones she remembered. As the road got even steeper, Helen gripped the side of her seat, desperately wanting to shut her eyes tight but not wanting to miss a minute of the stunning views.

Reaching the top, a picturesque, stone clad villa came into view. A vibrant pink Bougainvillea swept across the front of the villa and was trimmed neatly around each pretty shutter framed window. Pots of all sizes and shapes were scattered around the edges, each one overflowing with trailing flowers. A railed veranda ran the whole way around the villa, and a pretty rustic arch surrounded a welcoming front door. Markos stopped the truck close to the door and came around to help Helen down.

"Oh wow, how pretty," said Helen and seeing the large heap of driftwood piled artistically in front of the arch, she limped over and crouched down running her hands over the smooth pale wood. "I used to help Aunt Maddie collect driftwood," she told Markos, who nodded as he fondly remembered doing the same. Spotting some words carved into the wood, she traced her fingers around them spelling out Villa Elena "Oh!" she breathed, looking up at Markos, a question in her eyes.

"Elena," he said, "It is the Greek version of Helen." His feelings of love for this woman doubled as he watched her crouched in front of the old pile of wood, not concerned at all with the interior of the gorgeous villa.

A loud, excited barking came from the olive grove situated on the hill behind them. Helen stood up and shielding her eyes against the bright sunlight looked to see where the barking came from. A striking dog, with a rich, red silky coat came bounding out of the woods. With his tail wagging and his ears perked up he looked expectantly down towards them.

"Ela, ela" shouted Markos in vain "he won't come," he said to Helen "He's still waiting for Madeline to come back, I tried taking him home with me, but he just escaped and found his way back up here. We haven't been able to catch him since. We leave food and water out for him, and he has a place to shelter in but…" He shrugged his shoulders.

"Ela, is that his name?" asked Helen, then laughed as Markos explained that "Ela" meant come on or come here. Helen watched the dog's head drop and his tail curl between his legs. He slowly turned and padded back between the trees. "Oh bless him," Helen said "How sad."

"Yes" agreed Markos "poor Puddles."

Helen stared at Markos, so this was Puddles she thought. Oh the poor thing, she knew only too well how much it hurt when the person you loved so much disappeared forever. Asking Markos for her crutches she limped over to the bottom of the grassy slope that led up to the olive grove and spotted Puddles curled up in the twisted roots of one of the trees. Placing her crutches on the ground, she sat herself down and started softly whistling a tune. Every now and again she said "Puddles" softly but in a high sing-song voice. Markos leant against his truck and watched as each time she sang out "Puddles" the dog pricked up his ears. Helen laid herself back in the sunshine with one hand behind her head and the other down by her side, gently tugging at tufts of grass. Every so often she continued to call the dog. Markos, getting bored and knowing it was a lost cause, went over to unlock the large front door. He went into Madeline's huge open plan kitchen and pulled some bottled water from the fridge. Taking a sip, he looked out of the kitchen window to see if Helen had given up yet.

Helen, far from giving up, he saw, had rolled onto her stomach and was lazily watching Puddles who had lifted his head and moved a bit closer. Markos watched in amazement as each time Helen called his name softly, the dog crawled forward a few inches on his belly, stopped and lay with his head between his paws. Helen and Puddles repeated this process a few more times until he was only a few feet away from her.

Hah, thought Markos, he won't come any closer and picking up the bottle of water he walked back outside and leant back up against his truck.

Helen, realising he wasn't ready to trust her yet, gently rolled onto her back and slowly sat up with her back to the dog. Very quietly she started to murmur "who's a good boy then" Picking up a blade of grass she placed it between her thumbs and brought it to her mouth, blowing gently. Puddles pricked up his ears at the strange high pitched whistling and cocked his head to one side. Helen, without looking around, called his name again "Puddles" and tried out the Greek "Ela, ela" Slowly Puddles crept forward again and came within a foot of Helens back. Sensing he was close, Helen reached one arm out to her side and laid her hand palm upwards on the grass.

Markos held his breath as the dog inched forward and sniffed at the hand. Helen continued to talk to him softly and keeping very still allowed Puddles to move around her, sniffing. He watched, not quite believing what he was seeing as the dog laid down next to Helen and placed his head gently in her lap.

"Hello Boy," said Helen, fondling his velvety soft head and running her fingers through his soft, silky ears. "Aren't you beauty" she ran her hand down his handsome back and scratched him gently just above his tail. Puddles arched his back in delight and slowly wagged his tail. Not quite convinced that the dog fully trusted her, Helen lay back down with both hands behind her head and waited to see what Puddles would do. Puddles wanting his back scratched again stood over Helen and wagging his tail faster shoved his nose against her head. When Helen ignored him, he let out a high pitched "play with me" bark and nuzzled her head again. Laughing Helen sat up and cuddled the dog into her body, scratching his back and rubbing his head. Remembering her Aunts plea to *"please love my Puddles"* she wondered how anyone could not love the gorgeous dog.

Gently shoving the soppy dog to the side Helen tried to push herself up but feeling a sharp pain in her leg, plopped back down again laughing. Puddles licked her face and shoved his nose under her chin. Helen laughed out loud at the tickling sensation and tried, unsuccessfully again to get up. Laughing, Markos put the bottle of water on the roof of the truck and walked over. Helen, still giggling at her predicament, grabbed hold of Markos' outstretched hands and as he pulled her up, quicker than she expected, the momentum overbalanced her, and she fell against his chest. Markos instinctively wrapped his arms around her and Helen, just for a moment, allowed herself to melt into his strong arms, feeling sensations she'd not felt for many, many years. Puddles, barking up at them both, broke the moment and Helen, embarrassed wriggled herself out of Markos' arms and bent to pick up her crutches.

Entering the villa, Helen looked around at the simple, rustic and cool interior. Her Aunt's pieces of driftwood littered the windowsills and watercolours of both Dorset and Zakynthos landscapes hung on the walls. The furniture was covered with dustsheets, but the rays of sunlight streaming through the window emphasised the dust that covered the tables and sideboards. Helen hopped over to one of the sideboards and looked at the many photos in frames decorated with the tiny shells her Aunt had loved so much.

"Helen," said Markos from the doorway. "I need to take some food up to the feeding station, will you be ok for fifteen minutes?"

"Yes, fine," said Helen, looking at Puddles, who had not yet left her side "I'm sure Puddles will look after me" she laughed.

Helen picked up each photo in turn and wiped the dust from the glass. The pictures told the story of her Aunt's life on this lovely island. From older black and white photos of Madeline sitting on a beach surrounded by smiling people and dogs to more up-to-date ones of a much older Madeline with Puddles by her side. Helen looked at the aged face that smiled out of one of the photos and wondered if that's what she would look like if she ever reached her Aunt's grand old age. Smiling at the thought, she wandered into the kitchen and instantly loved the dark oak cupboards and worktops cluttered with signs of a woman who loved cooking. Noticing last year's calendar still on the wall she took a look and wondered what all the different scribbled reminders meant. The words "Dozy" "Crazy" and "Lazy appeared regularly and were ringed with a red circle as if to highlight their importance. She saw Percival's name written and gulped as she imagined her Aunt sat in this very kitchen, planning her will and the crazy codicil. Feeling thirsty, Helen wondered if there were any cold drinks in the fridge and limped towards it. Staring her in the face, attached to the fridge by two Caretta, Caretta turtle magnets was another of the envelopes with her name penned on the front. Forgetting her thirst, she tucked the envelope down her top and looked for a place to sit and read it. Noticing the patio doors leading outside, she hopped over and balancing on one crutch, eased back the heavy bolts and pushed open the doors. "Wow," she thought. The view from her Aunt's balcony made the other views she'd seen pale into insignificance. Settling herself into a large, white wicker rocking chair she took a moment to gaze out over the turquoise Ionian waters and marvel again at the imposing island that resembled one of the turtles the island was famous for.

Helen, feeling Puddles settle himself at her feet opened the envelope and started to read the now familiar writing.

> *My Dear Helen*
>
> *You've reached my wonderful Villa, what do you think? Beautiful isn't it, and such a beautiful view.*
>
> *Now back to my life's work. I need to start at the beginning, those heady, lazy days of a hot summer, when I fell in love with my husband-to-be Kostas. We would travel around the island with me perched on the back of his rusty old motorbike. Whenever and wherever we stopped, I would see dogs, some chained up, guarding goats or chickens, some running loose, so skinny and frail, and the puppies, how I cried over the dumped babies I found.*
>
> *Now don't get me wrong. There are some Greeks who adore their dogs and cats and treat them as pets, the way we do. Others can be very cruel; they will poison or shoot the strays that invade their land. Most though, just simply don't see their dogs as pets. In their eyes they are there to do a job, to guard the house or, like Puddles, to become a hunting dog. Sadly, once they are no longer useful, they are often just dumped. If they become sick or pregnant, they are dumped. Helen, you mustn't blame or attack the Greeks for this, though, it is their way of life, it is what their parents and grandparents did…*

Helen noticed the writing seemed to trail off as if her Aunt had fallen asleep, then started again.

> *When I made the decision to stay on the island I searched high and low for the perfect place to live that would enable me to help the many strays. Oh, Helen, I fell in love with this spot the moment I set eyes on the beautiful views. Over the next year, while I waited for the villa to be built I started bringing the strays up to the olive grove behind. They were safe there, no risk of poison and plenty of food and water. Over the last many years Kostas and I have watched the island grow. As more tourists came to soak up our sun, more hotels and restaurants sprung up. Over the years we watched something wonderful happen, holidaymakers fell in love with the strays and started to offer them homes. Others fell in love with Zakynthos and chose to retire here. The*

English community grew, and grew, and others from other countries joined too. Amongst these were many, many animal lovers and groups were set up all dedicated to helping the strays.

I chose to continue to do my own thing. I had no interest in aligning myself with any of these groups, but I supported them all and offered advice, if wanted, for they all had the same common goal as me, to save the animals.

I'm tired now Helen, so very tired. There is so much more I want to tell you but no time left. Markos will come soon to take me to the hospital. I want to spend my last moments in my beautiful villa saying goodbye to my Puddles. I have no fear of dying but my heart is breaking for my most loyal and faithful dog. How do I explain to him that I won't be coming back...?

The letter ended suddenly and Helens own heart broke as she imagined her Aunt's final goodbye to her dog. Helen gazed down at the beautiful dog and admired the blonde fluffy tail feathers that were fanned out on the floor. The same coloured feathers peeped out between each of his pads and under his belly and contrasted beautifully with his rich red coat.

"Are you okay Helen?" came Markos' voice from the kitchen. He walked to the patio doors and for a few seconds thought he'd been transported back in time as he saw Helen sat in the old rocking chair with Puddles at her feet.

"Yes," said Helen slowly, "I think I've just read the final letter from my Aunt." She waited for Markos to sit in an identical rocking chair next to her and told him about the letter.

"She died a few hours later," said Markos "almost as soon as we'd got her into the hospital bed, she slipped into a coma and went peacefully." He didn't tell Helen that he'd sat holding her Aunt's hand and wept as she'd passed quietly away. "She made me promise to look after you Helen," he looked into Helen's sad face and apologised "I'm sorry, I was so angry with you and your family. Dotty explained what happened; she said you didn't know..." His voice trailed off as he stared out at the sea, feeling horribly guilty.

"Markos, it's fine," said Helen "I would have jumped to the same conclusion, shall we start again, friends?" she asked smiling and holding out her hand. As Markos took the offered hand, he hoped they would soon be far more than friends.

"There is coffee, and fresh milk in the fridge," Markos said, "I can make you one if you want to look around more?" Helen, remembering her earlier thirst, nodded and pushed herself out of the chair. Puddles stretched and stood as well, not wanting to let the lovely woman out of his sight.

Leaning against the kitchen side, with coffee in hand, Helen asked Markos what the strange names on the old calendar meant.

"Hah," he laughed "Your Aunt had a wicked sense of humour, they are the three main groups on the island that fundraise, care for and foster the dogs and cats and other animals. They are just your Aunts nicknames for them," he smiled and suggested she ask Peggy and Lily to fill her in "You will meet a few of them tomorrow when they start their quest to win the Kalvos cup." Markos laughed and rolled his eyes at Helens raised, questioning eyebrows "Ask Peggy," he repeated.

"Thank you for bringing me," Helen said to Markos, an hour later as they locked the villa up and headed back to his truck. She was genuinely grateful that he had given up his afternoon to drive her up and show her around.

"No problem," he said, opening the passenger door and helping her in. Before he could shut the door, Puddles leapt in and settled at her feet. "I think he's coming with us" Markos laughed, still astonished at the way Helen had worked her magic on the dog "Is that okay?"

"Oh, it's more than okay" laughed Helen "as long as nobody else minds."

Markos was still laughing as they reached the bottom of the steep chalky hill but this time at Helen, who, terrified, had shut her eyes tight and held her breath all the way down.

"You'll soon get used to it," he said, enjoying this new comfortable friendship they had eased into. Hearing his phone ring he handed it to Helen and asked her to switch on the speaker phone.

"Hello, Markos, it's Lily," her voice echoing around the truck. "We are having a big dinner this evening before the hoards descend on us Saturday," she laughed "Do you want to bring Helen straight here, Peggy and Alf are working their way around the feeding stations so it'll save them having to drive back to pick her up."

"No problem" replied Markos, and winking at Helen said "but expect three of us for dinner, not two," giggling, Helen switched off the phone and settled back to enjoy the views. With plenty of time before dinner, they planned to stop off at Markos' clinic and collect a new, lead, collar and bed for Puddles and give him some much-needed flea and worm treatment.

"Well, If I wasn't bleeding seeing it, with me own bleeding eyes, I wouldn't bleeding believe it," said Alf as he watched the shiny, freshly bathed Puddles leap out of the truck and bound towards his old friend Fudge. The two dogs barked in excitement and wiggled and tumbled over each other, wagging their tails and licking each other delightedly

"What?" asked Dotty, confused by the dumbstruck, gawping faces around the table.

"Every single one of us, including the twins." Lily pointed to the pair at the end of the table whose heads were bent over their mobile phones, "and half the bloody island, have spent hours trying to catch that bloody dog." Lily shook her head in disbelief as Puddles proudly strutted around the table, greeting everyone like long lost friends before heading back to a smiling Helens side.

A few hours later with stomachs full and copious amounts of wine and beer consumed Elias fired up a couple of patio heaters and lit the candles that were spread out on the table. Helen had filled them all in on Madeline's last letter, and Markos had described how Helen had coaxed down the now besotted Puddles. Remembering the calendar Helen turned to Peggy.

"So Peggy," she said, enjoying the warm glow the village wine had given her "Tell me about Dozy, Crazy and Lazy?" Alf and Lily burst out laughing and encouraged Peggy to spill the beans.

"Right," said Peggy, who loved to tell a good story "If you are all sitting comfortably, I shall begin."

Helen and Dotty, with their arms on the table and their chins nestled in their hands were both, indeed, sitting comfortably and listening very carefully.

"Well, when me and Alf first came to the island twenty-five years ago, we came across a poor, skinny little dog and rushed him to the vets. A much younger and newly qualified Markos here helped us out and introduced us to his uncle's wife, Madeline. Well me and Madeline liked each other straight away and became firm friends, working together to help out the dogs. Over the next few years, more and more people started to help, and a group of people led by Cynthia and her husband Don decided to set up Dogs of Zakynthos. Now these were wonderful people, who did a lot of good. They worked out ways to get the dogs abroad and set about fundraising; trouble is they are all a lot older now, and a few including Cynthia are starting to lose their marbles, so Madeline called them the Dozies" Peggy stopped to take a sip of her wine.

"A few years later," she continued "a beautiful young lady, Bethany, arrived in Zakynthos. Now she was a youngster with pots of inherited money and not a clue what to do with it all. Seeing all the stray cats hanging about and coming across a box of newborn kittens dumped in a skip, she set up her Cat Haven and recruited a group of ladies to help. Your Aunt, nicknamed them the Crazies as in the crazy cat ladies." Peggy stopped again and looked around at the enthralled faces. Grabbing Elias' cigarettes she lit one and continued with her story.

"Now, let me think, it must have been fifteen years ago, that Snotty Selena turned up. Oh boy, did that woman rattle a few cages. She turned up on this island, thinking she was better than the rest of us. She started holding her snotty coffee mornings and then she thought she was Hyacinth-Bleeding-Bucket and started holding bloody candlelit suppers" as the whole table burst into laughter, Peggy smiled and stubbed out the cigarette. "Well Snotty Selena, tried to join and take over every committee going, including the Dozies and the Crazies. When year, after year nobody voted her in she decided she could do better and started up the Lovers of all Animals in Zakynthos. Well Selena Warrington-Smyth does absolutely nothing at all, just bosses everyone else about so it didn't take long for your Aunt to name them the Lazies."

Everyone roared with laughter as Peggy wagged her finger at Dotty and Helen and told them they were secret nicknames and they mustn't ever tell.

"So what's the Kalvos cup then" she smiled across at Markos, who winked in return.

"Oh," screamed Lily, who'd had more than a few wines "Madeline started that up a few years ago. The three groups were so hell bent on trying to outdo each other with the amount of money they raised that Madeline decided to make it official and offered an annual prize and a cup to the group that raised the most each year."

"Ah," said Alf "your Aunt was a wise old bird, they all doubled and even tripled their efforts to win that bleeding cup."

"But they're all raising money for the same thing," said Dotty, confused

"Exactly" chorused everyone around the table and burst out laughing.

Markos, realising he had an early start to the mainland the next morning stood up and stretched. He worked his way round the table saying goodnight. Reaching Helen and Dotty, he overheard Helen say quietly to Dotty "William would have loved it here," seeing the unshed tears, swimming in Helens eyes, his heart sank as he realised she was still very much in love with her dead husband.

CHAPTER 11
KNICKERS OR NOT?

"I've still got so many unanswered questions," said Helen, frustrated. Lazing by the pool, next to Dotty, she had been mulling things over and over in her head and was getting nowhere.

"Try me," said Dotty, pulling the sun lounger into the upright position. "Give me a question and I'll try and answer it."

"And me," said Maggie, who was sat the other side of Dotty towelling herself dry after a quick but chilly dip in the pool.

"Okay," said Helen, sitting up as well "Why did my parents and Aunt Maddie fall out? It must have been something pretty huge to cause a rift like that."

"Hmm." Dotty tapped her finger on her pursed lips, thinking hard "Maybe your mum was a closet lesbian and had a secret affair with your Aunt." Dotty grinned, "One day, your dad came home from work early and found them cavorting, naked, in the bedroom and banished Madeline for life."

"Hah" laughed Helen, thinking of her strict, prudish mum "You're in the wrong career Dotty, you should be writing for Mills and Boon."

"It'll be money," said Maggie "Root of all evil, I bet it had something to do with money." Helen nodded, she'd been thinking along the same lines.

"Well you may never know the answer to that one," said Dotty "next question?"

"Ok, said Helen "In my Aunt's first letter, she mentioned her "life's work" and questioned whether I was the right person to continue it. I don't get it" Helen paused, trying to put into words what she was thinking "From what I've gathered there are plenty of people on this island who help out the strays, what did she do that others can't?"

"Oh she did far more than that," said Maggie "She helped people too, if she heard of any families struggling financially, she'd leave a box of groceries on their doorstep or a bag of clothes for their kids, she'd sit with the elderly in hospital to give their families a break,"

Maggie continued, "but you're right Helen, others here do the same thing."

"Do you know what I think?" said Lily, who was sat on the edge of the pool with her legs dangling in the cool water. "Madeline Kalvos was the lynchpin of the community, she held everything together, and kept everything running smoothly."

"I'm not sure what you mean?" said Helen confused, "I thought my Aunt kept out of all the different groups and did her own thing."

"Yes, and that's my point," said Lily, pulling her feet from the pool and twisting round to face Helen. "Because she kept out of it all, she was friends with everyone. If there were ever any arguments or silly spats, Madeline would sort it all out."

"That's true" interrupted Maggie "remember those poor little Laganas pups, lordy me, what a palaver that was," she said, rolling her eyes at the memory.

"What happened?" asked both Dotty and Helen at the same time.

"Oh crikey, yes," said Lily, who'd forgotten all about it. "Madeline was here, having coffee with mum and me, when she got a message saying six little pups had been found, dumped in a box, down in Laganas. Well, I offered to drive your Aunt over there and mum jumped in - to be nosey -" laughing at Maggie's offended face and shushing her denials, Lily carried on "It was utter chaos when we got there, Cynthia and Don from the Dozies had hold of one side of the box and Selena and Mavra from the Lazies had hold of the other. They were tugging the box so bloody hard that the poor pups were terrified."

"Don't forget the tourists," interrupted Maggie, who wanted to tell the story herself. "Lordy me, the poor tourists who had first found the pups were Italian and couldn't speak much English or Greek, they were shouting and hollering at a hotel manager who was yelling back in a mix of Greek and English that if the pups weren't taken off his land he would shoot the lot of them," seeing Helen and Dotty's shocked faces, Lily took up the story.

"Madeline pulled a whistle out of her pocket and blew it so hard that everyone, including mum and me, jumped and put their hands over their ears, the cardboard box dropped on the floor, and Madeline scooped it up and carried it over to my car." Lily stopped to take a breath. "We took the pups to Markos, got them checked over, then delivered three of them to Cynthia and the other three to

Mavra." Lily smiled as she remembered how pleased Cynthia and Mavra had been to get the pups "That's what Madeline did, she sorted problems and solved disputes, and I can't think of a single person on this Island who could take her place."

"What about your gorgeous vet Markos?" asked Dotty "Gosh, he's so scrummy I wouldn't mind him solving my little or big problems." Dotty stuck out her boobs and jiggled them from side to side, laughing and ducking to avoid the slap that Helen was aiming her way.

"Nor would half the woman on the Island," squealed Maggie "Poor Markos spends most of his time hiding away from all the women that fancy him."

"Mavra is the worst" laughed Lily "but the rest of them give her a bloody good run for her money."

"Did someone mention my name" The four women jumped and collectively groaned as Mavra came walking over to the pool, followed by Snotty Selena, who was wearing what could only be described as a pair of tweed plus fours, which she had teemed with a matching tweed jacket and a flat cap. In her hands, she carried a pair of the Nordic walking poles that had become so popular over the last few years.

"Good Morning Ladies," boomed Selena "Ah, you must be Ms. Boothroyd?" she said to Dotty, sticking out her hand "Now then, I'm sure someone of your class would be much more comfortable staying with me, I would imagine this little hotel is a bit basic for someone used to the finer things in life." Selena noticed Helen and pursed her lips. "Lily how nice of you to invite Helen over and introduce her to Ms. Boothroyd. You're certainly making yourself indispensable aren't you dear." Oh Christ, thought Helen, knowing that Dotty was going to make mincemeat of this stuck-up cow.

"Ah, Selena Warrington-Smyth I presume," said Dotty, putting on a very posh voice "I've heard so much about you" winking at an annoyed Lily, Dotty stood up and shook Selena's hand. "Now then Selena, just between you and me, I was chatting to my dear friends Victoria and David just last week, and they recommended this sweet little hotel. They managed to spend ten days here last year without being recognised once. Can you imagine?" Dotty let out a high, tinkling and very fake peel of laughter "Now then dear ladies, are you interested in becoming models for my next catalogue?" Dotty walked towards Maggie and picked up the sarong that Maggie had draped on the back of the sun lounger "let's try this" she said, starting to wrap the material around Selena's rather large frame and securing it with a deftly tied knot. The Sarong, which fit Maggie's size 16 frame beautifully and enhanced her ample curves, barely fit around Selena's large waist. Dotty placed a finger to her lips and walked around Selena, running her eyes up and down the length of her body. "Perfect!" she declared "Absolutely perfect darling!" she repeated to a smug looking Selena "I've been thinking of designing a plus-sized range for the more mature woman, and you, my dear, will be the perfect model."

The speechless hugely insulted Selena, huffed and puffed as she ripped off the sarong and once again, tossing her head, turned and stormed off through the archway, Mavra, perplexed as she tried to translate the term plus-sized chased after her muttering about the Beckhams.

"Oh blimey, she's ripped me Sarong," Maggie screeched with laughter, clutching her stomach and Lily, with tears pouring down her face grabbed the side of the sun lounger to stop her mum toppling off.

"Your friends, Victoria and David huh?" Helen raised her eyebrows at Dotty who was dipping her toes into the pool with a smirk on her face

"Hmm, yes," said Dotty airily, blowing on her fingers "Didn't I tell you, my accountant David and his wife Vicky stayed here last year, didn't run into anyone they knew the whole ten days they were here."

"Oh for Gawd's sake, get me off this sun lounger before I wet myself," Maggie snorted.

Helen picked up her book and tried to concentrate on the words but finding herself reading the same paragraph, over and over, she gave up. Reaching down, she patted the snoozing Puddles and looked around at the empty sun loungers. Earlier that morning the Danish guests had all trooped out through the archway and onto a waiting coach for a day trip to Athens. Maggie and Lily had gone to rustle up some lunch and Dotty had picked up Maggie's ripped sarong and tapping the side of her nose and winking, had gone off up the steps to her room. Helen was bored; she'd always found it incredibly difficult to sit and do nothing and never understood how people could lay for hours in the sun. She was also in a lot more pain than she'd let on to anyone. Trying to do without the strong painkillers was harder than she thought. Her stitches had started to tighten and felt hot and itchy. Thinking she'd be better off in the shade, she reached for the crutches and tried to work out how to get up. Damn it; she thought as she tried to heave herself forward; now I know how Maggie feels.

"Here, let me help you," said a voice, and Helen turned to see one of the most beautiful women she'd ever seen bending down to help her. Tall and willowy, with a mass of curly, red hair and striking green eyes the woman was dressed simply in frayed denim shorts and a pretty, white gypsy top.

"Helen, this is Bethany," said Lily, carrying a large bowl of salad over to the nearby table. "Hang on; I'll give you a hand" taking a hand each Bethany and Lily pulled Helen up and helped her over to the table.

"You poor thing," said Bethany "What did you do to your leg?"

"She had a fight with a gorse bush and lost," laughed Lily "Bethany, this is Helen Hardy. Madeline's niece."

"Oh, hello, I didn't know Madeline had a niece, how lovely to meet you," Bethany said, genuinely not knowing who Helen was "Where do I start looking for the kitten Lily?"

"He was up the back this morning, but could be anywhere, feel free to hunt around. A cute little kitten turned up this morning," Lily explained to Helen "but that scraggy cat's not having it and keeps attacking the poor little thing, Bethany's come to collect it."

"Oh, if it's a grey and white one, he was curled up under one of the lemon trees behind my room," said Helen "pretty little thing."

Helen watched Bethany pick up a cat basket and leisurely walk off, stopping to look under every bush and tree she passed.

"Away with the fairies, that one," said Maggie bringing out a large jug of homemade lemonade. "Knows everything there is to know about cats, but ask her what day it is and she wouldn't have a clue."

"She seems lovely" murmured Helen, distracted by the sight of Dotty dragging a very large Louis Vuitton suitcase down the steps.

"Who is that ravishing creature?" asked Dotty when she finally reached the table "I don't think I've ever seen such a gorgeous bum."

"You sure you're not a secret closet lesbian," asked Lily winking at Helen.

"Oh I'd never be a closet lesbian, I'd make sure the whole world knew it" laughed Dotty "but in my line of work, I know a good bum when I see one, and that one would sell a hell of a lot of knickers."

"What's with the suitcase Dotty?" asked Helen, then reached for her mobile as the message tone pinged. "Oh, it's from Molly. "Ring, Skype or Facetime me ASAP, got some serious gossip"" Helen read the message out loud "That's odd, Molly doesn't do gossip."

"I'll ring her from my phone," said Dotty "put it on expenses," finding Molly's name in her huge contact list, she set the phone to the loudspeaker and placed it between her and Helen.

"Hello," said a breathless Molly, as if she'd ran to answer the phone "Dotty, is that you? Is Helen with you?"

"Yes, we're both here," said Helen "What's the matter, it's not Papa again is it?" suddenly dawning on her that Papa could have got into another scrape.

"No, Papas fine, it's Gerald we're worried about, I think he's been suspended from work."

"What?" exclaimed Helen and Dotty at the same time, looking at each other in disbelief.

"Oh, Helen, it's all a bit odd. He came round here a couple of days ago, and he looked awful; he hadn't shaved, and he had a coffee stain all down the front of his shirt, he looked really haggard." Dotty and Helen raised their eyes at each other; Gerald never looked anything but immaculate.

"Anyway," continued Molly. "He told us that he'd been working long hours for months and was owed a lot of leave so he'd decided to take some time off and go away for a couple of weeks." Helen nodded, knowing that Gerald hadn't taken any time off since before William had died. "He asked Ian if he'd mind keeping an eye on the house, and then offered to pay me to go and give his house a good spring clean, while he went away."

"Really? said Dotty, "I thought he had a daily housekeeper that cooked and cleaned for him."

"Well, so did we" Molly went on "anyhow, yesterday I took Papa up to the hospital to see his diabetes nurse, and we popped into the WRVS shop, your friend Helen, the one everyone calls a mighty mouth?"

"Jane," said Helen, knowing straight away that Molly was describing the hospitals queen of gossip.

"Yes, Jane, well she told us that Gerald was the talk of the hospital, apparently he's been suspended and is under investigation."

"Whatever for?" gasped Helen, not quite believing what she was hearing

"Oh, we don't know for sure, apparently there're two different stories doing the rounds, some are saying he made a mistake in the operating theatre and a patient nearly died; others are saying he was caught stealing drugs, but whatever he's done, he's disappeared, Ian went round his house last night, and there's no sign of him."

"Did he tell you where he was going on holiday?" asked Dotty, looking at Helen's worried face.

"Not really, just said he was going to travel around Europe and see where he ended up, I don't think he'd made any real plans, anyway I've got to go I'm running late for work. It could all be a load of rubbish, but he's definitely gone. I'll let you know if I hear anything else."

Dotty and Helen stared at each other, utterly stunned by the news.

"Don't get me wrong Helen," Dotty said, "You know me and Gerald aren't the best of friends, but I wouldn't wish that on anyone, especially Gerald, the thought of people gossiping about him would crucify him."

"You're right Dotty," said Helen, knowing that Gerald's pompous and sometimes snobbish attitude hid a huge inferiority complex. "I'll try ringing him," waving away Dotty's offer of her phone Helen grimaced "He's not going to answer if he sees your name come up."

Gerald wasn't answering Helen either, after trying unsuccessfully three times she'd ended up leaving him a chatty voicemail, telling him all about Zakynthos and hoping he wouldn't realise she'd heard from Molly.

"Don't worry," said Maggie patting her hand, Dotty here tells me your friend can look after himself. Helen nodded, but over the last thirty years she and William had secretly supported Gerald through some pretty serious bouts of depression, realising there was absolutely nothing else she could do, she tried to focus her thoughts back on Dotty, who was opening her large Louis Vuitton suitcase.

Helen, Maggie, and Lily oohed and ahhed over the beautiful swathes of material that were piled up in one-half of the suitcase, unzipping another section Dotty revealed a very expensive sewing machine and reels of pretty coloured cotton.

"I couldn't repair your sarong Maggie, but I can certainly make you some more, and I would love it if you could model them in my catalogue" she looked at Maggie who held both hands to her rapidly blushing cheeks.

"Me" Maggie whispered "Really? Who would want to look at my fat blubber spread across your lovely catalogue pages?" she said, not sure whether Dotty was kidding or not.

"Maggie, your curves are very sexy and you make my sarongs look beautifully exotic, now have a look through this material and choose your favourites."

"Oh my, our Lily, can you imagine their faces down at the bingo hall when I tell them I'm a Dorothy Boothroyd model," she grinned, "Oh Hello Bethany, you're back."

"Hello," said Bethany, who had returned with a kitten safely enclosed in the cat basket "I'm Bethany" she stretched her hand out to Helen,

"Yes," Helen shook the hand, confused "I'm Helen, Madeline's niece" she reminded her.

"Oh, I didn't know Madeline had a niece, what did you do to your poor leg?" seeing Lily raising her eyebrows and twirling her fingers around her head Helen smiled.

"This is my friend Dotty" introduced Helen, putting her hand on Dotty's arm

"Oh, hello Dotty, that's pretty material," said Bethany "Look, Lily, I found the kitten."

"Brilliant," said Lily "Do you want to stop for lunch?"

"Yes please, I don't think I had breakfast this morning, I'll just put the kitten in the car." Bethany disappeared through the arch, carrying the loudly protesting kitten and Helen shook her head and laughed at the peculiar woman.

"Told you," said Maggie "Our crazy cat lady lives in cloud cuckoo land; we all love her to bits, but she's best in small doses."

Half an hour later the ladies had finished the delicious Greek Pastichio that Lily had made. Helen and Dotty had loved the macaroni, and meat dish and both asked for the recipe. Dotty, determined to sign Bethany up as a model steered the conversation back to the photo shoot and asked Bethany if she'd ever done any modelling.

"Oh Mummy was a model," said Bethany. "Well, I think that's

what she used to do. I remember coming home from boarding school one day, and she was laying on the sofa naked and our gardener was sketching her." Three of the ladies around the table snorted while Dotty managed to keep a straight face.

"Right," said Dotty, so would you be interested in modelling for my little catalogue, I have a gorgeous bra and knicker set that would look amazing on you.

"Oh, I don't wear knickers" exclaimed Bethany and Maggie praised the Lord that the men were nowhere near to hear this revelation.

"You don't?" said Dotty who was still managing to control her urge to laugh "Why's that then?"

"Oh, Mummy lost her knickers once, it was okay though, because Daddy found them in the gardeners shed but he was ever so cross with Mummy for losing them."

"I'm not surprised!" Maggie blurted out.

"Cook said that if Mummy didn't keep dropping her knickers, she wouldn't keep losing them," Bethany continued "I didn't want Daddy to be cross with me, so I thought it best just to stop wearing knickers, well I couldn't lose them then, could I?"

Maggie grabbed a pile of plates and shuffled, bent double into the kitchen and Lily quickly followed suit, their screeches of laughter could be heard clearly by the three ladies left round the table, but Bethany didn't bat an eyelid she was so totally oblivious to the hilarity she'd caused. Lily, having finally composed herself, came back out with a damp cloth and started wiping the table.

"Will you be at the fundraising walk tonight?" she asked Bethany, who was rummaging through Dotty's material.

"Oh yes, where is it?

"Same place as always, down at the Two Brothers Bar."

"Oh okay, a strange name that, isn't it?"

"Not really," said Lily "seeing as its two brothers that run it."

"Oh, are they brothers, I didn't know that," said Bethany, standing up, "anyway, I must go, bye Lily," she reached over and gave Lily a hug "bye Hilary, bye Dorcas," she said to Helen and Dotty, who not trusting themselves to speak, just waved.

"Oh my god, I love her," squealed Dotty "Will she even remember to turn up tonight?"

"She'll be there," assured Maggie "One of her long-suffering

Crazy gang will go and hunt her down and bring her along."

CHAPTER 12
THE KALVOS CUP

Markos sat at the back of the large hall completely oblivious to the PowerPoint the guest speaker was talking through. His laptop, which he'd switched on to take notes, was instead displaying the results of a Google search for William Hardy, sighing at the fifty or more million results Markos realised his search was as pointless as his visit to Athens. He had been looking forward to the seminar for many months, but thoughts of Helen and her dead husband continued to flood his mind, and any hope of concentrating on the lecture was long gone. He closed the laptop and shuffled passed the seated guests, apologising as he trod on toes and banged against knees.

Walking out into the bright sunshine, he looked at his watch and debated whether to head to the hotel he had booked or make the long drive to Killini and catch the Ferry back to Zakynthos. He had left home early that morning, and the ninety-minute Ferry crossing added to the long drive to Athens had mentally and physically exhausted him. He stopped at a nearby café and ordered a strong Greek coffee. With the small cup of coffee in front of him, he gathered his thoughts, re-opened his laptop and typed "William and Helen Hardy" and when over twelve million results appeared, he sighed and moved the cursor to the images icon. Quickly scrolling through the hundreds of pictures that appeared he stopped when a picture of Helen and Dotty in glamorous evening dresses emerged at the bottom of the screen. Further clicking led him to an album of photos under the title "St James Hospital Fundraising Ball 2012" Amongst the hundred or more images were a series of ten photos containing Helen. Markos felt a stirring below as he studied a picture of Helen, stood alone and looking beautiful in a long silver dress that wrapped around her body like liquid. He moved on, embarrassed by the effect she was having on his nether regions. He felt a hot stab of jealousy at the next image. Helen was gazing lovingly up into the eyes of a tall and distinguished-looking man. The man's sandy coloured hair flopped across his face as he looked lovingly back at his wife and caressed her cheek. Markos felt physically sick at the image. He rubbed his tired eyes and ran his fingers through his thick hair. For only the second time in his life, he was in love, so totally and completely in love that it was impacting on every aspect of his life, and he didn't know what to do.

Feeling a light touch on his shoulder he turned his head expecting to see the waitress offering a top-up, but the space behind him was empty, confused he looked around but the waitress was nowhere in sight, and the nearby chairs and tables were empty and silent. Markos smiled ironically as not for the first time a tiny little voice in his usually sceptical mind questioned if Madeline was still around, hovering beside him and comforting him. He wondered what Madeline's advice would be if she were still around to offer it and clear as day he heard her voice "Follow your heart lad, it can't hurt any more than it does right now."

Helen liked what she saw, Tsilivi at night was buzzing. An eclectic mix of pop, rock, Irish and traditional Greek music hummed out of the restaurants and bars and welcoming hosts stood at the entrances enticing the tourists in with promises of free drinks and wonderful food. Lily had advised Helen and Dotty to get to the bar early, and they were settled on comfortable cream sofas waiting for the fun to begin. Dotty was once again disguised in the black wig, and oversized clothes and the ladies had earlier decided that, if asked, she was an old friend of Lily's.

"Kalispera, lovely ladies, what can I get you?" said a handsome young waiter.

"A Multiple Orgasm please," said a brazen Dotty, licking her lips and flirting outrageously

"Bleeding hell," said Maggie "You're not backwards in coming forwards are you? I'll have a Black Russian please young man." Lily and Helen decided to share a carafe of the local village wine, and George ordered a pint of his favourite, Mythos.

"Kalispera everyone," said Christos, walking towards their table with a large silver cup in his hand. "I've been lumbered with doing the honours this year unless any of you want to volunteer" he laughed.

"Volunteer for what?" asked Helen and Dotty, admiring the beautiful cup that had a dog and cat engraved on the side and a list of names and dates etched on the black base.

"Oh you poor sod!" declared Lily "Christos has to do the annual speech," she explained "Madeline always got up and delivered a rousing speech to set the fundraisers off. Markos was dreading having to replace her this year; crafty sod probably organised to be away deliberately," she laughed

"What the hell?" exclaimed Dotty, as the waiter placed a large cocktail in front of her. The very large glass was overflowing with grapes, bananas, cocktail umbrellas and a lit sparkler which was threatening to set alight a two-foot long straw. "I'll have to stand on the table to reach the end of that straw," she giggled.

"Yamas!" declared George, lifting up his Mythos and clinking glasses. "Here Christos, shuffle in next to us," he invited "Looks like the fun's about to start."

Helen glanced around and saw an elderly couple with a scruffy white dog heading towards them.

"Evening Cynthia, evening Don!" chorused George, Maggie, and Lily "This is Madeline's niece Helen," introduced Lily. Helen remembered that these were the unofficial leaders of the Dozies and smiled a hello.

"Hello," said Don "pleased to meet you, I'm Don, this is my wife Cynthia, and this is one of our rescues Rufus" Don picked up the little dog and held him up proudly for Helen to admire.

"That's not Rufus," said Cynthia "That's my little Digby, the best Poodle I've ever had." Helen looked at the scruffy little dog that was so clearly not a Poodle and smiled kindly at the elderly pair.

"Oh Don, this bar looks just like the one we used to go to when we lived in Zante, it's even got the same football shirts on the ceiling."

"Yes dear," agreed Don, patting her hand kindly and rolling his eyes. "Shall we go and save a table for our friends?" Don mouthed "sorry!" at Helen and clutching his wife's hand tightly, led her over to a table in the corner where a large group of people and an array of dogs were gathered.

"How sad," said Maggie, if I ever get like that you make sure you put me in a bleeding good home George, oh look here come the Crazies."

Hearing Dotty snort, Helen looked around and saw Bethany clad in an extremely tight, black leather cat-suit that left absolutely nothing to the imagination. She had added a pair of cat ears and a cute little mask that had long whiskers attached to a little black stubby nose.

"Don't you dare Dotty," threatened Helen as she clapped her hand over Dotty's mouth.

"Whoa…" gurgled Dotty, and as Helen released her hand muttered indignantly

"I wasn't going to say anything."

"Oh yes you were you were going to mention a certain humped animal that lives in the desert and combine it with the word toe," said Helen glaring at Lily, who cottoning on quickly, had started to giggle.

"Well," said Dotty "If you choose to go commando there are certain outfits you shouldn't wear."

"What on earth are you two on about?" asked a confused Maggie and then blushed a vivid red as Lily whispered in her ear.

Following Bethany, were a trio of elderly ladies dressed in identical black and white furry cat onesies. Each of them carrying a collection tin labelled with pictures of cute little kittens. Bethany glided over to their table.

"Bleeding hell," said George, a bit too loudly "So that's why they call it a Camel Toe." Maggie whacked George round the head as he gawped at the obviously knicker-less goddess.

"Hello Hazel," Bethany said to Helen, oblivious to Georges comments "How lovely to see you here, these are my friends," as the introductions were made and everyone shook hands Dotty scrabbled furiously through her large handbag.

"What are you looking for?" Helen asked her as makeup, tissues, Filofax and phone were pulled out of the handbag and flung on the table.

"A packet of Tena pads I shoved in here" whispered Dotty "If this carries on I'm going to wet myself laughing."

"Wait till Selena arrives," laughed Lily "She always has to make an entrance."

A sudden hush swept through the bar as a loud and angry cacophony of car horns came from further along the road. The waiter nearest the entrance looked down the road and clapped his hand to his head swearing loudly in Greek. Slowly into view came a large horse plodding down the middle of the road with his head hung low and his tail swishing angrily in disgust at the weight he had to bear. Sitting sidesaddle on the horse was Selena Warrington-Smyth. She was dressed in a Dalmatian costume and with one hand holding the reins and the other waving graciously, she was nodding from side to side as if bestowing her blessings on the confused holidaymakers.

Following her was a group of both men and women carrying or leading an assortment of dogs, puppies, and goats. Pulling tightly on the reins, Selena brought the poor horse to a halt next to the swearing waiter and instructed her troops to move aside and let the trail of angry taxi drivers and locals drive pass. Helen watched in astonishment as Mavra, holding tightly to a pair of baby goats on leads, came running out of the crowd with a step ladder tucked under her arm. Placing the ladder next to Selena she helped her off the horse and Selena handed the reins to the bemused waiter and swanned into the bar as if she owned it. Placing the step-ladder in the centre of the room, she climbed the three steps and held up her hands to demand silence,

"Good evening ladies and gentlemen," she boomed. "As poor Madeline is no longer with us I feel that. I, as her very best friend and closest of companions, should deliver the opening speech for the 2015 season."

A murmur of disgusted boos and hisses echoed around the bar and those seated at Helen's table grabbed hold of their rattling drinks as an angry Christos leapt from his seat and jumped on top of their table.

"Actually Selena," he roared, holding the Kalvos cup high above his head "I am the only Kalvos here in the bar tonight so I will be doing the honours." As the bar erupted in cheers Selena, glowing red, tossed the floppy ears on her Dalmatian onesie and clambered off the ladder.

"Firstly," started Christos "I would like to officially welcome Madeline's niece Helen to Zakynthos, and I hope you will all go out of your way to make her feel very welcome" another cheer and shouts of "hear, hear" went round the bar. Christos hushed the rowdy crowd and in a more sombre note continued, "as you all know, this year is our first year without our beloved Madeline and we have decided that the Kalvos Cup will forever more be known as the Madeline Kalvos Cup in order to honour the wonderful woman who brought so much, in so many ways, to the people and animals of Zakynthos." Another rousing cheer and a thunder of applause and stamping feet reverberated around the bar and Helen blinked back tears of pride for the aunt she wished she'd known. Christos took a piece of paper out of his pocket and taking a deep breath continued "Madeline knew she would not be with us this year and gave my father this letter to be read out tonight" as a hushed silence fell over the bar Christos unfurled the piece of paper and read out.

"My Dearest friends

I only wish I could be with you all but the only certainty in life is death and to death I must finally succumb. I have been gifted to live to a ripe old age and being able to spend half of my lifetime on this beautiful Island was the greatest gift of all. My only regret is that so many of our beautiful animals will not get the chance to live the long, happy lives they so deserve. My final wish is that each and every one of you, tonight, hold hands, with both your friends and enemies and together, promise to make this the best year ever.

God bless you all

Madeline"

A hushed silence hung in the air as Christos climbed off the table and reached out his hand to Selena, who in turn clutched Lily's hand. One by one everyone in the bar stood up and took the hand of the person next to them, with all eyes on Christos they watched as he slowly raised the Madeline Kalvos Cup and declared "To Madeline, the best year ever." Echoing his words the animal lovers raised their hands and cheered.

"Well done Christos," whispered Lily "You did her proud." Christos nodded and wiped a tear from his eye.

"Ladies and Gentlemen, if you are all ready, may the fundraising commence," declared Christos as he let go of Selena's hand and took a large swig of George's Mythos.

Dotty clutched Helens shoulder as a sudden rush of bodies, eager to get to the exit jostled pass them. The Crazies, swinging their cat's tails and meowing, were the first to hit the street followed rapidly by Don, keeping tight hold of Cynthia and half a dozen pensioners dressed similarly in T-shirts declaring them to be Dogs of Zakynthos Lovers. Selena and her troops marched out of the doors and lined up across the width of the road, completely ignoring the traffic and tourists trying to get past. Taking up a position in front of the line Selena raised her hands for silence, determined to be the centre of attention

"Ladies and Gentlemen" she yelled so loudly that the baby goats bucked and butted their heads in distress. "Go forth into the bars and restaurants of Tsilivi and rattle your tins like you've never rattled them before." The line of fundraisers raised their tins above their heads and shouted "Rattle, Rattle, Rattle," and trotted off down the road.

"Does this happen every week!" yelled Helen over the noise of one of the two brothers blowing a whistle and cranking up the music.

"No!" Lily yelled back "Only the first week then everyone heads off to different resorts and hotels each week!"

Markos had parked his truck up a side road and had stood unnoticed at the back of the bar as his son had stood up to Selena and delivered Madeline's last message. His heart was bursting with pride and despite his intense dislike of Christos' mother, he was grateful that his son had inherited her confidence. Once the crowds dispersed, he made his way over to the table and gathered his son into his arms.

"Dad!" exclaimed Christos, "I thought you were in Athens?"

"The seminar was cancelled" lied Markos "well done son, I'm so proud of you," Helen smiled at the love between father and son and realised sadly that she had never seen William hug the twins like that. Full of the well-known British reserve, William would shake James' hand and kiss Annabelle on the cheek, leaving the hugs down to Helen.

"So what happens now?" asked Helen, watching Selena walk back into the bar and settled down on one of the comfy leather armchairs.

"We all get drunk and watch the chaos continue" laughed Maggie

"No, I didn't mean right now" laughed Helen, who once again had hundreds of questions whizzing around her brain "How did Madeline know who had raised the most each year, did she count it all?"

"No" answered Markos, who had sat himself down next to George. "Each group has their own treasurer, and they would submit the accounts to your Aunt on a monthly basis, along with bank statements." Helen watched a long slow smile appear on Markos' face "Amazingly" he winked, they seem to take it in turns to win each year, I do believe the Crazies are due a win this year."

"You mean it's rigged?" whispered Helen, not quite sure what to make of this information.

"Not exactly rigged" Markos winked again and lowered his voice.

"Let's just say that at the end of the season one of the groups usually receives a rather large anonymous donation that will edge them into the lead."

"Oh, that's…" Helen stopped suddenly as she felt Dotty pinching her arm "Ouch, what was that for?" Dotty rolled her eyes towards Selena, who had, surprising quickly and unnoticed managed to manoeuvre herself to the sofa behind and was attempting to listen in on their conversation.

"Good evening Selena, can I get you a drink?" asked Markos "I was just explaining to Helen how Madeline kept track of all the fundraising."

"Thank you Markos dear," smirked Selena "I would like a glass of Prosecco please, that's if this quaint little bar has actually heard of Prosecco," as Markos headed to the bar Selena's chubby and surprisingly deft fingers tapped out a Facebook status to the world informing them that she was having a "lovely drink with our lovely vet." Shifting into Markos' vacated seat she reached over and clasped Helen's hand "Now Helen dear, as my wonderful friend Madeline is no longer with us," Selena attempted a very fake sniff and wiped an imaginary tear from her eye "I, of course, will be very happy to take on the job of checking all the accounts, I'm sure it's what your dear Aunt would have wanted."

"Oh," Helen wasn't sure how to respond to such a bold statement but was sure that Selena was not the person her Aunt would have recommended. "Thank you, Selena, that's really kind of you, but you will have to discuss that with Markos, I'm sure that sort of thing was all sorted before my Aunt died."

"What was sorted?" asked Markos placing a glass in front of Selena, who took a sip and cringed at the taste.

"I was just explaining to Helen that I would be the perfect person to take over the accounts on behalf of Madeline, after all, we need someone with honesty and integrity."

"No need." Markos answered, "Madeline sorted everything out before she died, she asked Peggy and Alf to oversee everything."

"Peggy!" spluttered Selena "That woman has got the brains of a goldfish, absolutely ridiculous, I won't have it, it's simply not acceptable…" Selena jumped as a hand tapped her on the shoulder, startled she turned to see a fuming Peggy stood there with an armful of puppies.

"For your information Miss Snotty Pants, before we moved to the island I was an accountant for a very successful business in Notting Hill and if you are really interested in the welfare of the animals on this island you might want to head down to Dimitris and rescue Mavra's goats before the chef turns them into a curry."

A livid Selena stood up so suddenly that the small wicker chair she had squeezed herself into remained firmly attached to her rather large bottom. As she swung herself round to insult Peggy, the chair swung along the top of the table knocking the drinks flying and just missing Maggie's head.

"Bleeding hell" shrieked Maggie "You stupid cow, you could have knocked me bleeding head off."

Markos, laughing loudly but ever the gentleman tugged the wicker chair off Selena's bottom and patted her gently on the shoulder.

"Selena," he soothed "Madeline left many instructions and assigned everyone to the roles she thought would suit them most," he patted Selena again on the shoulder. "She wanted you to have the most important role of all as she felt you were the only person who could fulfil it," he continued cryptically.

"Oh," Selena grinned smugly, she was convinced that her name must be the one written in the secret envelope and this information confirmed in her mind that she was indeed set to inherit Madeline's villa. "Whatever Madeline wanted me to do, I will do with all of my heart in memory of my dearest friend." She clutched at her breast and sighed dramatically, as Markos whispered into her ear. "Really? little old me, she wanted me to do that?" Selena puffed her chest out, patted her hair and smirked down at the group. "I would be honoured to organise the Annual Zakynthos Dog Show; now if you will all excuse me, I must go and rescue Mavra and her goats."

"Genius Markos, absolute bleeding genius," guffawed Alf patting Markos on the back "Me and our Peggy have been worrying ourselves stupid over that bleeding dog show, and it's only two weeks away."

"Well to be honest Madeline did suggest we let Selena organise it, she will terrify the local businesses' into sponsoring it, and I know none of us like her, but you've got to admit she is brilliant at organising everybody."

"And she'll be so bloody busy she won't have time to go barging her great big nose into everyone else's affairs" laughed Lily "She might even leave Helen and Dotty alone for five bloody minutes."

"Sorry, did someone say my name?" asked Helen, who was so busy mopping up the alcohol and shattered glass that had tipped into her lap that she hadn't heard Markos and Selena's exchange.

"Oh my god!" exclaimed Dotty, spotting the mess in Helen's lap "Are you okay? It's not cut you has it?"

"No, I don't think so, but it's soaked right through the bandage on my leg and I don't want to move until I've picked all the glass out." Peggy, feeling mortified that she had caused Selena to jump up shoved the puppies into Alf's arms and ran around the table to help out.

"Oh blimey Helen, you're going to have to get that dressing off and changed."

Allowing Dotty and Peggy to remove the rest of the glass and help her up off the sofa Helen was beginning to wonder what exactly she had got herself into when she'd agreed to come to Zakynthos.

Helen closed the lid of the toilet and sat down shivering in just her underwear. She had stripped off her sopping wet dress and passed it under the toilet door to Dotty who taking a quick look had yelled "won't be a minute" and rushed off to god knows where. Looking at the drenched bandage, Helen pulled off the tape that secured it and slowly started to unwind it. Wincing as she peeled back the large dressing, Helen stared in shock at the angry, red wound running the full length of her thigh. The neat black stitches were oozing with pus and in a few places had come apart and left gaping holes. Feeling sick she gripped the sides of the toilet and shook her dizzy head.

"Helen, let me in," yelled Dotty, banging on the cubicle door. Seeing Helen's white face as she eased open the door Dotty gazed down at the horrible wound and gasped. "I think we need a doctor," she said to Peggy, who was stood behind trying to peer over her shoulder.

"I can't magic up a doctor, but I know where I can get a couple of vets," Peggy muttered, racing back out of the toilets and into the bar.

Dotty edged herself around the tight toilet door and held up a beautiful aqua-marine sarong that she had spotted in the souvenir shop across the road.

"I don't know Helen" Dotty pretended to nag "All that gorgeous underwear I give you for free, and you still insist on wearing those grotty granny pants and bra set," pulling Helen up she wrapped and tied the sarong around her so that it resembled a pretty summer dress.

"How on earth do you do that?" asked Helen impressed with the way the sarong fell flatteringly over her body.

"Tricks of the trade," laughed Dotty. "You'd be amazed at the things I can do with a sarong. Right, let's get you back to the bar and work out what we are going to do about that leg." Squeezing themselves back out of the cubicle Helen used one hand to hold the Sarong away from her wound and with the other clung onto Dotty's arm as they headed back to the bar and the comfort of the soft leather couches.

"It's a bleeding good job it's so early in the season!" declared Alf as Markos and Christos bent over Helens leg muttering in Greek to each other. "If it were much later this bar would be heaving with nosy parkers all wanting to gawp at your lovely legs," he guffawed then clamped his mouth shut as Peggy gave him a stern look.

"Can you two speak English please?" Helen begged, "it is my leg you're discussing."

"Sorry Helen," said Christos looking ashamed, "we are just having a bit of a disagreement" he looked at his father and shrugging his shoulders stood up and walked off.

"Yes Helen, sorry" grunted Markos "Christos is newly qualified and has…shall we say certain ethics…he does not think I should dress your wound…because I am a vet, not a doctor" Markos looked at Helen and shrugged his shoulders "It is up to you, I can clean and dress your leg now and take you to Dr. Marouda tomorrow, or we can go to the hospital now?"

"Markos, please just sort it out, I really don't want to end up in the hospital" Helen saw Christos walking back with a large black bag and realised the decision had already been made.

Watching a large family entering the bar and looking inquisitively over Alf and George stood themselves up and with their backs to Helen formed a shield from the prying eyes, realising what they were doing Peggy wandered over to the family with the gorgeous Papa, Jasmine and Smudge nestled in her arms. Lily, quickly cottoning on grabbed the puppy's bottles of milk from Peggy's bag and joined Peggy hoping an overload of puppy cuteness would distract the gawping stares and raise awareness of the strays on the island.

Helen watched as if from afar as Markos and Christos worked

together to clean and redress her wound, she felt strangely detached from the whole experience and let her eyes wander around the bar until suddenly she focussed on Dotty, who was trying very hard to flirt with the hunky waiter. She felt the first gurgle of a giggle rumbling in her stomach and clapped her hand over her mouth trying to suppress the snort that was threatening to escape.

"Christ Helen, sorry, did that hurt?" asked Christos mistaking the strange noises for groans of pain.

"No!" spluttered Helen "look!" allowing the laughter out she pointed over to Dotty, who was completely unaware that her black wig had slipped sideways and clusters of her exotic, blonde extensions were escaping out the side. The poor waiter, rather than flirting back was looking terrified and edging himself back behind the bar.

"Oh lordy" laughed Maggie "Should we tell her?"

"Not before I get a photo" answered Helen, rummaging through her bag for her camera, hearing the laughter Dotty turned, giving Helen the perfect opportunity to snap the photo that she could bribe Dotty with for years to come.

"What's so funny?" asked Dotty wandering back over. Helen held up her camera to show Dotty the picture and laughed even more as Dotty shrieked and dashed off in the direction of the toilets.

With the dressing all done, Helen thanked Markos and Christos and settled back with one eye on the toilet doors, eager to see which version of her best friend would appear?

"I don't think the hopping up and down our hill has really helped matters, Helen," said a concerned Lily. "Things will get much worse tomorrow when everyone arrives; we will be so busy we won't be able to help you much, maybe we should ask Peggy and Alf if you could stay with them for a bit longer."

"Lily, don't worry, I will be fine and besides, Peggy's daughter-in-law arrives tomorrow." Helen looked furtively over at Peggy who was still chatting with the family and Alf who was at the bar with George and lowered her voice. "Peggy and Alf don't know it yet, but their son Jacob has managed to get a couple of weeks off and is coming too but shush it's a big surprise."

"Ah love a duck, how exciting," said Maggie "It's well over a year since she's seen them and Suzanne being in the family way too, Peggy will be crying her eyes out when they turn up" Maggie mopped an emotional tear from her eye and sighed with contentment.

"Hmm, I might have an idea," Markos said mulling the idea over in his head "When I told everyone that Madeline's villa was to be closed up until the will had been sorted I wasn't strictly telling the truth." Markos hung his head in shame and muttered, "sorry Helen."

"What do you mean?" asked Helen with a puzzled frown.

"Madeline wanted you to stay in the villa while you were here, she thought..." Markos looked up at the three women staring at him and blushing continued. "She thought if you stayed there, you would fall in love with Zakynthos quicker but I..." Markos felt too guilty to continue and looked beseechingly at Helen, who reached across and grasped his hand.

"Markos, I get it, it's okay," Helen reassured him. "If I were in your shoes I would want to protect her property from a complete stranger, please don't blame yourself," as Markos gazed gratefully into Helen's smiling eyes Lily and Maggie nudged each other as they recognised all the signs of a budding romance.

"Christos, if you can help me clean the place up tomorrow morning we can move Helen in after lunch," suggested Markos "Christos?" but Christos' eyes were on the vision that was emerging from the toilet doors. Dotty, now minus the wig, had skilfully turned the oversized t-shirt into a raunchy boob tube that barely covered her enormous assets. The tatty denim shorts had been trimmed even shorter and sat snugly over her pert bum, and the cheap shades had been swapped for a designer pair that nestled on top of the gorgeous mane of blonde extensions that tumbled around her shoulders.

"Wow!" breathed Christos "I would!" he grinned then laughed as Maggie smacked him round the head. "Sorry dad, yes, of course, I'll help you, that's if Helen wants to move to the villa."

"What villa?" asked Dotty perching herself on the edge of the sofa "What have I missed?"

"Markos thinks I should move into my aunt's villa." explained Helen "but won't I be even more cut off there? It's quite remote?" Helen loved Lily's little hotel and family and didn't like the thought of being stuck in a remote area, unable to drive.

"Oh Helen, that would be perfect," grinned Dotty "Can I come too, that way I wouldn't have to wear that bloody disguise all the time. I was going to hire one of those sexy jeeps I keep seeing and can run you anywhere you need to go. Is there Wi-Fi at this Villa

Markos"?

Markos laughed at Dotty's excitement and confirmed that the villa did indeed have Wi-Fi and many other mod-cons that would make their stay comfortable.

"And now that my conference has been cancelled" Markos crossed his fingers as he lied again "I have the whole week free to help out where needed and chauffeur Helen around."

Helen laughed as Dotty and Christos high-fived each other, and Maggie and Lily breathed a sigh of relief.

Markos excited at the thought of a whole week with Helen got up to order another round of drinks then turned quickly as he heard his name being called from the doorway. Three little old ladies in their furry cat onesies were helping a limping, weeping and barefooted Bethany into the bar. Assuming poor Bethany must have trodden on something Markos rushed over and lifted her onto the table at the same time wondering if he should start charging the humans who seemed to prefer his services to the doctors. Lifting Bethany's feet up one by one he examined them carefully but apart from a bit of dirt he couldn't find anything that could warrant so much distress.

"Bethany, what on earth is the matter?" he asked the sobbing girl gently

"I...don't...want...to...die" howled Bethany, struggling to get the words out and grabbing frantically at Markos' shirt.

"Martha?" Markos addressed one of the old women, who was scrabbling her hands together and trying very hard not to burst into tears. "What happened?"

"Oh Markos, it was dreadful, we were collecting donations in the Irish bar, and all of a sudden a drunk man grabbed Bethany round the waist and whispered something in her ear, and now she won't stop crying and thinks she's going to die."

"Bethany, what did the man say?" asked Markos firmly

"He said..." Bethany gulped "He said...I've got...the worst c...c...case of...of...c...c...camel toe he's ever seen," as the whole bar erupted into laughter and Dotty went over and gently whispered into the bereft girl's ear nobody noticed Mavra sneak into the bar and shove a thick envelope into Dotty's bag.

CHAPTER 13
A VEILED MUSE

Under strict instructions to remain in her room until someone could drive her down the steep hill, Helen was starting to get bored. She had attempted to check her emails, but the hotel's unreliable Wi-Fi was having a bad day. She had hopped out to the balcony a couple of times and peered over the wall to see Dotty's doors still very firmly closed and her curtains drawn. Helen wasn't surprised as Dotty had continued to down cocktail after cocktail the night before until Markos had unceremoniously plonked her into the back of his pick-up and driven her back to the hotel. Helen laughed as she recalled Dotty sprawled on a pile of blankets singing Rod Stewarts "Da Ya Think I'm Sexy" as they drove the short trip back to the hotel.

Hearing a rapping on the door, Helen eased herself off the bed then watched in astonishment as Puddles trotted over to the door, jumped up and with one paw, pulled down the handle and nudged the door open with his nose.

"Thank you Puddles!" laughed Lily who was stood there with a tray laden with food and a large carafe of hot coffee "You are a clever boy!"

"Wow!" exclaimed Helen "you're not as daft as you look." She ruffled Puddles head as he proudly jumped on the bed to be congratulated.

"Madeline taught him well," sighed Lily "Puddles was the main reason she was able to stay so independent for the last few months. He could load and unload the washing machine; answer the door and fetch anything she asked for," explained Lily "You certainly are one special dog, aren't you boy" she said, putting down the tray and giving the gorgeous dog a big cuddle. "I've brought us breakfast, and don't thank me." Lily waved away Helen's thanks. "To be honest I need a break from the chaos down there, Mum and Dad are running around like blue arsed flies, and Elias brother has just got back, and they are having a full blown argument about god knows what" Lily moved the coffee and plates of poached eggs on toast out to the balcony table and flopped into one of the chairs.

"Oh Lily, I'm sorry" Helen sympathised, hopping to the table and easing herself into the other chair. "Is there anything I can do to help; I feel a bit responsible for the chaos Dotty's photo shoot is causing."

"Christ, no Helen, It's fantastic, what Dotty is doing is amazing and will put our little hotel firmly on the map. Nobody's arriving for another three hours; everything is organised, and the Danish are all cooking their breakfast in their rooms so I can't see what all the bloody fuss is about." Lily turned and laughed as Scraggy cat, who was perched on the wall, hissed and growled at a bemused Puddles.

"I keep meaning to ask what that little lump in Puddles' ear is," said Helen

"A shotgun pellet," grimaced Lily "He had quite a few when Madeline found him. Those bloody hunters don't care what they are shooting at. Puddles either got in the way or was shot deliberately, who knows." Helen shook her head devastated that such cruelty existed.

The comfortable silence that had settled over the two woman as they hungrily devoured the fresh eggs was suddenly shattered by Dotty's balcony doors squeaking open.

"Argh, get off me you stupid cat!" screeched a very hungover Dotty as scraggy cat, who had taken an instant dislike to her blonde extensions, leapt off the dividing wall and launched himself at the offensive hair. Puddles thinking it was an exciting game danced around in circles yapping in his high pitched girly bark then, with one almighty leap jumped over the dividing wall to join in the fun. Lily, with surprising agility, followed the dog over the wall and untangled the cat from Dotty's knotted hair. Plopping the cat over the balcony onto the freshly mown grass she gazed down at Puddles thumping his tail.

"Get him Puddles," she instructed, giggling as the daft dog, who wouldn't hurt a fly, let alone Scraggy cat eagerly jumped over the balcony and chased after the furious cat. "It won't hurt Scraggy to get a taste of his own medicine," she reassured, "It's about time he was put in his place."

"Ouch!" squealed Dotty, pulling at the tufts of hair that were sticking out of her head. "Thank goodness, my hairdressers, arriving this morning," she groaned. "Is that coffee? I need coffee; I've spent the last ten minutes trying to unlock my door, but I can't find the key" she grumbled to Helen and Lily, who knowing full well where the key would be rolled their eyes at each other. "What?" asked Dotty, spotting the look.

"Dotty, are your lights on?" giggled Helen. Dotty squinted through the balcony doors and nodded, confused "On the end of your key is that little white plastic fob…remember?" Helen and Lily chuckled as realisation dawned over Dotty's face, and she trotted off to retrieve the key and fob that slotted into a socket on the wall and controlled the electric.

"She's not the first and certainly won't be the last," sighed Lily. "At least once a week someone 'loses' their keys." Walking into Helens little kitchen she grabbed a mug and poured Dotty a cup of the still hot coffee then gawped as Dotty ambled through Helens door Dotty was clad in a fluffy white robe and sporting a scarf tied so artistically around her head that it not only looked highly fashionable, it hid the messy jumble of hair. "You've got to teach me how to do that," said Lily, impressed "It looks stunning!"

"Believe me, I feel far from stunning" groaned Dotty, waving a thick envelope "I've just found this in my bag, and I can't for the life of me recall anyone handing me an envelope last night."

"Hmm, maybe it's fan mail?" joked Helen. "Seriously though I don't think anyone gave you an envelope last night, how odd." Taking the envelope from Dotty's outstretched hand, she peered at the illegible scrawl on the front "Is that Greek?" she asked Lily, showing her the strange writing.

"Looks like it, wouldn't have a clue what it says though," Lily frowned. "Why don't you just open it and see," she said, handing the letter back to Dotty.

Dotty ripped the top of the envelope open and pulled out a handful of photographs

"Wow, who *is* that?" she breathed "she's beautiful." Dotty showed Helen and Lily the first photo of a young woman posing on a beach. The woman, dressed in a tiny bikini was kneeling in the shallow waves with both hands stretched high above her head. The large, floppy sunhat hid the models eyes, but laughter was clearly etched on her face as the seawater dripped down on her. "There're more photos, look," said Dotty crouching down and laying the photos out on the tiled balcony floor. The three women let their eyes wander over the eye-catching shots that had been taken in bedrooms, beaches and mountains with the model clad in swimwear, underwear and occasionally nothing but a carefully placed sheet protecting her modesty. In each photo, the models identity was cleverly concealed with a variety of strategically placed hats, sunglasses and artistic use of shadows.

"Very mysterious!" said Helen picking up one of the pictures. "Her face is hidden in every single photo, judging by the style and décor I guess these are at least twenty years old." Flipping the photo over Helen studied the tiny, faded writing etched on the back, "I think this is in English, but I can't make it out."

"Give it here," said Dotty and holding the photo at arms-length, she gradually drew it in closer and squinted "Nope, my eyes are as bad as yours Helen, here you have a go Lily" she handed the picture to Lily, who peered closely.

"*1987 Porto Zorro*... I can't make out the word underneath; it looks like the ink's been smudged. Is there any writing on the others?" Lily asked crouching down and turning the pictures over one by one "Here look." She held up another photo; the woman was stood, with her back to the camera, watching the sun rising over a distant mountain. She was dressed in a sheer negligee that left nothing to the imagination. "I would just die to have that figure," breathed Lily enviously "*1988, Kefalonia...*" she read off the back "No way...it can't be!" Lily's mouth dropped open, and she slowly passed the photo to Helen, who gasped as she read the name and sentiment written clearly on the back.

"*Mavra in the morning sun*...Goodness, do you think it's the same Mavra" Helen handed the picture to Dotty and flicked through some of the others, peering closely to see if she could find anything that resembled Peggy and Alf's neighbour "Why on earth would she give you these Dotty?" Dotty shrugged her shoulders and looked at Lily hoping she'd know the answer.

"Hmm...I guess she wants to be one of your models...let me make a couple of phone calls," said Lily mysteriously. She picked up one of the photos and walked off winking at Helen and Dotty's confused faces.

Dotty clutched her throbbing head in her hands as a loud pinging came from her phone. Picking it up Dotty swiped the screen and despite her hangover, a large smile spread across her face as she saw Molly's latest Facebook post.

"Hah" Dotty laughed "seems we've been replaced on the quiz

team." She turned the phone so that Helen could see the picture of Molly and Ian stood up behind a seated Papa and Helens elderly neighbour Hilda. Under the picture, Molly had written: *"Feeling rejected so called in re-enforcements lol."*

"How funny," said Helen, pleased that her father-in-law was having an evening out. "I wonder how they got on."

"Look at Molly's freckles and red nose" declared Dotty "They must be getting a bit of sunshine back home."

"Hmm" agreed Helen "Molly was telling me how much she would love to holiday abroad but with her ginger complexion she just can't cope with the sun, even factor 50 doesn't stop her burning."

"Oh I don't think the sun has anything to do with it" disagreed Dotty "We all know their business hasn't been doing too well and if Ian didn't spend so much time on the golf course and helped Molly out a bit she wouldn't have to struggle so much."

Helen nodded, she didn't know the full extent of her friend's financial struggles, but she had suspected for a while now that things weren't too good, not wanting to be a gossip she changed the subject.

"Anyway, how come you can get onto Facebook when the Wi-Fi's not working?" she asked Dotty.

"It's not the Wi-Fi you silly moo, it's the internet on my phone; you know that Data Roaming thingy?" Dotty waved her phone at Helen.

"But isn't that expensive?" asked Helen "You could end up with a huge bill…What?" she asked as Dotty rolled her eyes upwards in despair.

"You purchase a Data Roaming add-on pack silly; if you're going to be here a month, you really need to get up-to-date with technology Helen." Dotty laughed.

Helen gazed across the rooftops at the beautiful turquoise sea and let Dotty's words sink in.

"A month…well three more weeks on this beautiful island, I'm not even sure I want to spend another week here," she confessed to Dotty "I've been here almost a week and not even been on a beach yet, let alone worked out what Aunt Maddie wanted me to do. Oh, Dotty why did I rush into all this?" Helen looked at her friend and not expecting an answer continued "I'm just a burden to these wonderful people, they all have such busy lives, and now they have to run around after me because of my stupidity, do you think Dr.

Marouda will allow me to fly home?"

Lily, who'd had no luck with the phone calls, had let herself back into Helens room and was listening, appalled, to Helens words. Quietly she let herself back out the room and sent an urgent text to Peggy.

"Helen," said Dotty sternly "Don't be so ridiculous, in less than a week you have saved three puppies, found Puddles, met some wonderful…and err… not so wonderful…people. You have a good idea of what your Aunt was all about and from this afternoon onwards the only person you are going to be a burden to is me, which will make a nice change as it's normally the other way around." Dotty walked into Helen's room and opening the little bedside cabinet pulled out the hotels complimentary notepad and pen and placed it on the table in front of Helen. "Now let's start making one of your famous lists."

"Yes Ma'am" despite herself, Helen laughed and aimed a mock salute at Dotty "Where do I start," she asked picking up the pen.

"Let's go back to the codicil, what are your options?"

"Okay," said Helen and quickly wrote down

1: Fall in love with Zakynthos (within 30 days!) and live here forever.

2: Guess whose name is in the envelope and inherit the villa with no conditions.

3: Let whoever is named inherit the villa and go back to my normal life.

"Right," said Dotty "Now chose one of those options to aim for." Helen mulled over the three options she had written down.

"Okay, number one is totally ridiculous, for one thing, I don't think my Aunt fell in love with the island in thirty days, I think she fell in love with a man. She also had nothing to go back home for. I have a house, children, Papa, friends and my voluntary work, and I can't for the life of me imagine giving all that up to move here permanently."

Dotty picked up the pen and put a line through the first option.

"What about the other two?" she asked Helen, who was still concentrating on the words.

"My head is saying go with number three," said Helen honestly "but my heart is telling me that's not what Maddie would have wanted me to do, why would she go to all this effort of setting up such a strange Codicil when she could have just left the villa to whoever it is in the first place?" Helen thought a bit more then with a twinkle in her eye, grabbed the pen off Dotty and put a line through number three "If I guess wrong then number three will happen anyway," she laughed. "Looks like it's going to be number two, I need to work out whose name is in that envelope."

"Right, no more silly talk of going home then," instructed Dotty. "I'm going to have a quick shower, and while I'm doing that you can start writing a list of everyone you've met so far and whether you think they could be the one named in that envelope." Dotty looked at the wall between their balconies and contemplated trying to clamber over it. Realising she could end up looking rather silly she thought better of it and picked up her keys "See you in ten," she said heading out of the door. Helen smiled to herself as she knew full well that *"see you in ten"* actually meant *"see you in an hour."*

Lily drove up the chalky track to Madeline's villa. The photo of Mavra was on the passenger seat next to her, but that was the last thing on her mind. Overhearing Helen's wish to go home she had panicked and when Peggy had responded to her urgent text with *"Helping Markos clean villa"* She had muttered some excuse to her bemused mum and dad and jumped in the car.

"Peggy…Markos!" she shouted as she jumped out of the car and completely forgetting the photo ran into the villa.

"Goodness me girl," said Peggy "calm yourself down, now what's all this about?" Peggy shoved Lily down onto one of the newly uncovered sofas and patted her knee "Now you just sit yourself there while I put the kettle on. Markos, Christos, Lily's here she shouted, not sure where the men had disappeared to.

Ten minutes later, with coffees all round they sat listening to Lily recounting Helen's words.

"How on earth can she think she's a burden?" asked Peggy "Oh Markos, we've got to do something, we can't let her go home."

Markos agreed, the last thing he intended to do was let Helen Hardy head off back to the UK.

"I don't think Dr. Marouda, once he sees her leg, will agree to her flying for at least a couple of weeks" Markos looked at Christos who having seen the state of Helen's wound the night before, nodded, agreeing wholeheartedly. "But" Markos sighed "That will probably make Helen feel even more of a burden, I think we need to come up with a plan that will make her feel needed, we need to give her something to do while she is recuperating."

"That's a good idea," agreed Peggy "but firstly I think we need to try and look at this objectively. What happens if Helen does go home Markos? Talk us through this wretched Will and codicil again; I'm still struggling to get my head round all the different rumours I've been hearing."

Markos scratched his fingers over his day old growth of stubble as Peggy raised her eyebrows inquiringly at him.

"Okay," he conceded "There is obviously a lot of detail, and I've not read it all properly but in simple terms. Madeline wrote a will that left her whole estate to Helen, but a couple of months later she added the Codicil. In order for Helen to inherit the estate, she must spend thirty days on the island, when those days are up she must decide whether she intends to stay on the island or go back home and give the inheritance up. If she goes back home, then the estate reverts to whoever is named in the envelope but… and this is the interesting bit…if Helen can correctly guess who is named in the envelope, she gets to keep the estate and do whatever she wants with it."

Peggy started giggling; the giggles quickly turned to chuckles then outright laughter as she slapped her thighs in delight.

"I bet old Madeline had a field day planning all this" she chortled "She always did have a bloody wicked sense of humour, and she knew damn well what utter chaos this would cause."

"True Peggy" smiled Markos "She had that wicked gleam in her eye every time she mentioned the will and codicil, and every letter she sent off to England involved me taking her to the post office so that she could post it herself, I bet she's having a good old laugh now."

"Markos," asked Lily "is Helen aware how big Madeline's estate is? Does she know about the olive groves and the winery or the other houses and the shops?

"No" admitted Markos "Madeline left strict instructions that only the villa and land was referred to until Helen has made her decision… whatever that may be" he added ruefully.

"Okay," said Christos who had remained unusually quiet "The way I see it is that Helen's not going anywhere for the next couple of weeks anyway so we can stop worrying about that but making her feel useful is a good idea. I also think it's a huge ask to expect anyone to make that sort of life-changing decision in just thirty days. I think we need to work out exactly whose name is in that envelope and somehow guide Helen towards guessing it correctly."

Peggy, Markos, and Lily slowly nodded in agreement completely unaware that a few miles up the coast Helen and Dotty had reached the same conclusion. Promising to put her thinking cap on and come up with some ideas to keep Helen occupied over the coming weeks Lily thanked Peggy for the tea and headed out the door. Climbing into the car, she spotted the forgotten photo and called Markos and Peggy over.

"I completely forgot about this" she showed them the photo and explained how Dotty had found the envelope in her bag.

"Oh that's definitely Mavra," said Markos "She was quite the beauty back then." Peering more closely at the picture he recognised Porto Zorro "Back in the late-eighties this Australian photographer turned up. He was twice Mavra's age, but she fell hook, line, and sinker for his slimy charm, she followed him all over the islands telling everyone that she was his "muse", but a couple of years later he disappeared overnight and left her heartbroken."

"How sad," said Lily "I guess she wants to model for Dotty's catalogue, but it's a strange way of going about it."

"I'm heading home in a bit," said Peggy "I'll pop in and have a word with Mavra, see if I can get to the bottom of it," promised Peggy

"Thanks Peggy, I did try ringing her earlier, but she wasn't answering, see you all later…bye."

Helen cocked her head to one side and listened carefully, convinced she could hear a soft scratching sound, but unsure where it came from, she hopped to her balcony rail and peered over it looking both ways. Standing completely still she realised the sound had got quieter and guessed it must be coming from inside her room. Fed up with hopping she tried to put her foot on the ground and winced as a red hot pain shot through her thigh. Gritting her teeth, she hobbled to her bed and picked up the crutches that she'd discarded the night before. Standing still, once again, she listened carefully and worked out that the scratching was coming from outside the apartment's door. Grateful for the crutches she swung herself through the little kitchenette and opened the door.

"What on earth…" she stuttered as Puddles trotted into the room with something dangling from his mouth. She watched the dog jump on her bed and carefully place whatever it was gently down on her pillow. He barked once at her, wagged his tail and trotted back out the door.

Quite used to her stray cat bringing her many "undesirable gifts" over the years Helen braced herself for whatever dead animal Puddles had kindly brought her and eased herself over to the bed.

"Oh my goodness!" she breathed as a beautiful but tiny tabby kitten gazed up at her through vivid blue eyes. "Where on earth did you come from?" she picked the little beauty up and snuggled it into her cheek, loving the feel of its baby soft fur nestling against her skin. Settling herself back against the pillows she forgot all about her pain as she closed her eyes and cuddled the kitten. Five minutes later she startled awake as Puddles jumped on the bed and carefully placed a second kitten in her lap.

"Good boy Puddles." Helen patted the dog on his head and laughed as he once again barked, wagged his tail and trotted off.

Twenty minutes later Helen sat there unsure what to do with the five kittens that Puddles had brought one by one into her room and placed into her lap. The beautiful and very clever dog now lay, with his head also in her lap, licking gently at the little kittens and thumping his tail.

"This is such a lovely present Puddles, but I think their mummy will be looking for them by now." Helen ran her hand over the dog's neck and scratched him behind his ears, smiling as the thumping of his tail quickened.

"Hello…hello…can you help?" Helen shouted from her bed as she heard footsteps and someone whistling outside.

"Helen…is okay?" Elias peered through her open door "Ah, gatáki…is okay…yes" Elias peered down at the tiny kittens and shrugged his shoulders "How I help?" he asked.

"Is Lily around Elias?" Helen asked

"Ah…Lily…yes…I no no."

"You no no?" Helen tried to hide her smile at Elias' grasp of the English language.

"Ah…yes…Lily phone, then go…poof go" Elias mimed Lily tapping a message on a phone then threw both hands in the air to demonstrate that Lily had seemingly vanished in a puff of smoke. "I get help…yes. Is okay?" Elias walked out to Helens balcony and started shouting "Georgios, Georgios…ela…ela."

Helen craned her head to peer through the balcony doors and watched as Georgios walked over the grass towards his dad. Watching father and son speak rapidly in Greek accompanied by wildly gesticulating hand movements she wondered if she could ever learn the wonderfully emotive language. Georgios leapt effortlessly over the balcony and stood in her doorway.

"Oh Georgios, can you help?" pleaded Helen "Puddles seems to have brought me five kittens, but I'm sure their mum must be frantically hunting for them." Puddles, hearing his name stood up wriggling with excitement and peering around Georgios in the hope that his friend Fudge was nearby.

"Puddles…good boy…bravo." Georgios made a big fuss of the dog then walked over and picked up one of the kittens. "I have been searching all morning for these kittens Helen; I found their mother on the road by the water park this morning. I think a car had hit her. She is not one of ours, but I could see that she had been feeding babies. Puddles is a clever boy."

"Oh no, poor little things, what can we do?" Helen watched as Georgios expertly picked each kitten up in turn and examined them carefully.

"I think they are between three and four weeks old, they have many, many fleas and probably worms." Georgios shrugged his shoulders the same way his father did "I will go and get some things to help, is that okay?"

"Yes of course…thank you Georgios." Helen waved him away and made a mental note to herself to offer to pay Lily for the extra cleaning the flea-ridden babies had probably caused. Crossing her fingers, she prayed fervently that Puddles had rescued them in time.

Less than ten minutes later Georgios returned with a large cardboard box. Placing it on the bed Helen could see that it was lined with blankets and had an array of different items inside. She watched Georgios gently pull up the scruff of one of the kitten's necks and then slowly released it, seeing Helen's questioning look he explained.

"I am checking for dehydration, if the scruff is slow in going back to normal it is a sign of dehydration. I have to err…how do you say?" Georgios tapped his head, cross with himself for not knowing the word he wanted to use "err...make a choice?" He looked at Helen hoping she understood

"Decide?" Helen offered the word she thought he was looking

for.

"Ah yes, I have to decide to bath or feed kittens now. The fleas are very bad and can cause err…a blood problem…err anaemia, yes flea anaemia. Is very, very dangerous. Yes. I think we bath first."

Helen was gobsmacked at the young lad's knowledge. She watched him head to the little kitchenette and fill a plastic bowl with warm water and seeing him look for somewhere to place it she quickly cleared the bedside table. Georgios squirted what appeared to be some sort of washing up liquid into the bowl and swished the water around until soapy bubbles appeared.

"This is very mild," he explained. "Flea chemicals will hurt the little kittens, they are too young, but this is safe." Georgios lifted all the kittens off of Helens lap and placed them on a towel he laid at the end of the bed, he laughed as Puddles curled himself around the kittens to stop them toddling off the edge. Placing another towel on Helens lap, he picked up one of the kittens and gently placed it in the bowl. With incredibly gentle fingers Georgios massaged the soapy water all over the kitten then ducked it back in the water for a rinse. He handed the kitten to Helen along with a tiny fine-toothed comb. "Now you must comb the fleas out then dry her" he instructed. It had been a very long time since Helen had been the student rather than the teacher but suddenly feeling useful she nodded and very gently started combing the kitten. The two of them worked quietly and quickly together and were both so intent on the tasks they were performing that neither of them heard Lily walking into the apartment.

Lily choked back the tears of pride as she stared dumbstruck at her shy teenage son. She could not believe that he was in Helens room, let alone working so closely with her on what appeared to be a litter of tiny kittens.

"What's going on here then?" she asked, making Helen, Georgios, and a sleeping Puddles jump.

"Lily, your son is just amazing, Puddles brought me these kittens and Georgios…well, I'm lost for words, to be honest. He just knew exactly what to do."

"He's spent a lot of time with Markos," laughed Lily, perching on the bed and picking up one of the kittens. "They look almost big enough to start weaning but we'll double check with Markos when he comes to pick you up." Watching Helen carefully combing one of the kittens an inkling of an idea started to form in her head and picking up her mobile she sent Peggy a quick text *"Think Puddles has found a solution to one of our problems."*

CHAPTER 14
I SPY WITH MY SNOTTY EYE

"To listen to your messages, please press one."

Gerald pressed one and listened for the umpteenth time to the chatty message from Helen. She sounded happy and relaxed, and he was genuinely pleased for her. He gazed down at the River Seine flowing freely below his window and felt strangely detached from the busy hustle and bustle of the Parisian traffic. The small room in the quiet boutique hotel offered him the solitude he craved, and though very basic it would do for a day or two. He knew though that he would have to move on, he knew in his heart that he could no longer keep the dreadful secrets he had be holding on to for so long.

Picking up a scalpel a few days before his hands had been shaking so badly he knew he could not be trusted to continue with the life-saving surgery. He recalled the eyes of his colleagues as he'd dropped the scalpel, pulled off his mask and stepped back from the operating table. Accusing? Sympathetic? Confused? He'd always been amazed by how many emotions could be conveyed with just the eyes and after a lifetime spent in surgical theatres, he had long ago learnt to read them all. What had they seen in his eyes? He wondered. Fear? Regret? Guilt? He suspected the hospitals rumour mill had gone into overdrive and that many different stories were circulating the wards. He walked over to the small oval mirror hanging on the wall and studied his reflection. He looked haggard he thought and old, so old.

He moved to his bed and looked at the map of Europe that was spread open. With his finger, he traced the route he had opted to take, through Switzerland, Italy, and mainland Greece. His finger stopped on the tiny island in the Ionian Sea. Zakynthos. He wished he'd never heard of it; he cursed Helen's aunt; he cursed Percival Boston Jn. He could have kept his secrets, and Helen could have remained in blissful ignorance for the rest of her life. That was no longer an option and the efforts he had gone to, to protect her from the truth, were wasted. He would give her a couple more weeks he decided; he would take his time and stop a day or two here and a day or two there. Two more weeks before he had to admit the truth and shatter her world.

"Helen…Helen…are you there? Can you hear me?" Helen held the phone away from her ear concerned that the booming voice may perforate her eardrums.

"Yes Percival, I can hear you, there's no need to shout."

"Oh, apologies my dear you never know what these long distance lines will be like, now then Helen. Exciting news. I've discovered the identity of the person who paid the cheques into your account."

"Oh," Helen wasn't sure she was ready to hear the news or what she would do with the information. "Go on"

"Well, what I actually mean my dear is that I know the name of the person, but I don't know who she is."

"She?" Helen was confused, she'd assumed it would be a man.

"Does the name Lucinda Markham mean anything to you?" Asked Percival Boston Jr, his voice squeaking with excitement.

Helen repeated the name a few times in her head; it did ring a very faint bell but she couldn't for the life of her think why.

"Percival, I'm sorry, I'm sure I have heard the name before but I don't know where or why? I'm afraid that's not a lot of help to you is it?"

"Worry not my dear lady, I shall continue with the quest. Now then how is everything going over in Zakynthos, are you having a spiffing time?"

"I'm not sure spiffing is the word I would use" laughed Helen wryly, looking at her bandaged leg. "But I've met some wonderful people, and I'm certainly starting to work out what my Aunt was all about, anyway keep me informed Percival."

Helen ended the phone call and mulled over the name. Lucinda Markham. Lucinda, maybe Lucy. How very, very strange she thought. Why on earth would William lend money to this Lucinda person? Looking at her watch, Helen was shocked to see it had gone 11 am. The last thing she could remember before her ringing phone jolted her awake was cuddling the kittens. She guessed the strong painkillers she'd resorted to taking had once again knocked her out.

"Hello, Helen?" hearing the knocking on the door Helen shouted "come in!" and smiled as Markos walked in followed by Dr. Marouda.

"Dr. Marouda is on his way to Alykanas Helen, so he agreed to stop off on his way rather than dragging you over to him."

"Dr. Marouda, how kind of you…I'm sorry I wasn't expecting visitors," Helen, embarrassed, looked around the messy room still full of the kitten's bits and pieces and clothes draped everywhere. Dr. Marouda waved away her apologies and indicated that he wanted to look at her leg.

Helen lay back and tried to distance herself from the pain as the kindly doctor and Markos deftly unwrapped the bandages and conversed once again in the rapid Greek language. Puddles moved to the side of her bed and lifted his paw, gently prodding her arm as if to comfort her. She patted his head, reassuring him that she was fine, and the men weren't here to hurt her.

Dr. Marouda tutted, shook his head and re-bandaged Helens leg. He patted Helen on the shoulder and promised he would see her again soon. Helen watched the two men walk out of the room and listened as they started one of their heated discussions. Puddles didn't like the raised voices and growled deep in his throat.

"It's okay Puddles" Helen reassured him "It will all be okay."

"Dr. Marouda has agreed to try a couple of different antibiotics for the infection," said Markos coming back into her apartment and hovering in the doorway. "He insists that if there is no improvement in a few days you will have to go into hospital, you must rest Helen, please" Markos begged. "I need to check on the kittens Puddles found and then I will take you down to the bar, everyone is down there waiting for Dotty's friends." Markos backed out of the room leaving Helen feeling confused. The concern in Markos' face had worried her, was he not telling her everything? She wondered. Helen limped to the tiny bathroom, splashed her face with cold water and shouted "won't be a minute" to whoever had just opened her door.

"It's only me" came Dotty's voice "I've just seen Markos; I've brought you a frappe."

"What on earth are you doing?" asked Helen as she came out of the bathroom and saw Dotty hiding behind the curtains and trying to peep round the edge.

"I'm being watched…or you're being watched…I'm not sure." Dotty beckoned Helen over "You see that big hotel on the opposite side of the road?" Helen looked to where Dotty was pointing and nodded "Okay, the second floor up and third balcony from the end…keep watching."

"Christ, you're right" agreed Helen as she spotted the bright flashes of a lens reflecting the sun. It wasn't the first time some random independent photographer had tried to snap Dotty, and it probably wouldn't be the last.

"Here I've got some binoculars, but they are all fuzzy, you have a go."

"You just need to adjust them you daft cow" Leaning against Dotty for support Helen put the binoculars to her eyes and twisted the central knob until the balcony opposite came into view.

"Good grief...the sneaky madam!" declared Helen "It's not paparazzi Dotty, it's Selena, and some other woman...look?" she handed the binoculars to Dotty who had a quick look and swore loudly.

"Are you both okay?" asked Markos knocking on Helens door and walking in.

"Quick Markos, come and have a look." Dotty waved him over and showed him where to look.

"Hmm." said Markos "It appears our friend Selena will stop at nothing to glean information," an idea forming, he grinned at both women "How would you ladies feel about giving her something to gossip about?"

Ten minutes later Dotty peered through the binoculars again.

"Yep she's still there, are you ready?" She looked at Helen and giggled at the sight. Helen had slipped her dress and bra straps off her shoulders and wrapped a fluffy white towel around her. Dotty's black wig had been dampened under the tap and placed on her head to look as if she had just stepped from the shower. Markos behind her, had removed his shirt, rolled up his trousers and wrapped another of the towels around his waist. Helen reached for her crutches then stopped.

"She's going to know it's me if I use the crutches." Helen worried "I'm not sure I can walk without limping either."

"No problem" laughed Markos and easily lifted Helen into his arms "It will just look more realistic" Dotty squealed with childlike glee and remained hidden behind the curtains with the binoculars trained on the hotel opposite.

"Ready?" Markos whispered to Helen and carried her out onto the balcony, expecting Markos to place her in a chair Helen felt a bolt of red hot lust curse through her as he sat himself down with her nestled in his lap. Unsure how to react and embarrassed she hid her face in his neck and hoped he would mistake her trembling for laughter. Markos ran his fingers gently over her bare shoulder.

"What's she doing Dotty?" he asked

"She's stood up and come to the edge of her balcony" chortled Dotty "Oh my god, she's going to fall over the edge if she's not careful!"

Markos ran his fingers the length of Helens arm and grasped her hand in his own; he dropped a flutter of kisses on her shoulder. Realising that his lust would soon become obvious to the woman sat in his lap he quickly stood and placed Helen gently in the other chair. Dropping a kiss on her cheek he walked to the balcony and stretched both arms above his head then ran his fingers through his thick curly hair making sure that snotty Selena could be in no doubt that it was him. Turning his back to the obnoxious woman spying on them he leant back against the railings and winked at Dotty.

"I've not had this much fun since my university days," he laughed "What's happening now?"

"She's just picked up her phone." Dotty screamed with laughter "Oh Markos, you are going to be all over Facebook any minute now."

"Oh dear," said Helen, her embarrassment turning to laughter, "I think we better get down to the bar, I can just imagine Lily's confusion when she reads all about the lovely vet having a secret assignation in one of her rooms."

"Oh quick, do something else, she's got a camera, don't let her snap your face though" warned Dotty, crossing her legs and wishing she'd worn one of her Tena pads. Thinking fast Markos dropped onto one knee in front of Helen and grabbed her hand, Helen threw her head back laughing loudly as she imagined the chaos their fun was going to cause.

Down at the bar, Peggy, Maggie and Lily were sat around a table getting more and more frustrated.

"Are you sure it hasn't left Gatwick?" asked Peggy. Lily held up her phone and showed Peggy the live departures displayed on the screen.

"Definitely says delayed" Lily assured Peggy "The Greeks are having one of their four-hour strikes so the planes are not going to take off until they know it can land."

"Bleeding Greeks and their strikes" swore Maggie "I feel sorry for all them poor buggers stuck in the airport."

Lily swiped her phone back to its home screen and noticed there was a notification on the Facebook icon. She clicked the screen and gasped

"What?" rapidly swiping the screen down she lifted her sunglasses on to her head and peered closely. *"So it would appear that the hostess with the mostest, our lovely Lily is encouraging secret trysts at her little hotel"* she read out. *"And just who is the mystery lady that our lovely vet Markos is clearly very close to???"*

"Oh my Lordy Lily, what on earth are you on about?" exclaimed Maggie

"Snotty Selena has just posted those comments on Facebook" Lily explained "Oh Christ there's a photo as well, oh my God Mum, that's definitely one of our rooms…and oh my, do you think that's really Markos?"

"That's not only Markos, that looks very much like Markos is proposing to…" Maggie peered even closer at the picture "Who is that?"

"I don't know, but I'm bleeding well going to find out" Lily shot out of her chair and ran.

Puffing and panting and with hands on hips, Lily stared, flabbergasted at the scene in Helen's room. Dotty was collapsed on the floor; both hands clutched between her legs as she convulsed with laughter. Helen, still wearing Dotty's wig was laying sideways on the bed and with one hand was repeatedly slapping the sheets as she giggled almost hysterically. Markos was perched on the end of the bed with his shoulders heaving as he mopped tears of laughter from his face and tried to control himself.

"What have you done?" she shouted, trying very hard to sound stern but struggling to keep a straight face in front of the trio's infectious laughter.

"I need a wee!" screamed Dotty, scrambling up and still clutching her groin, she hopped with legs crossed to Helen's bathroom.

"Lily…I'm sorry…I can't…breathe…" gasped Helen

"Markos?" questioned Lily "any chance you can control yourself long enough to explain?" Markos took a deep breath and looked at Lily, biting his lip he glanced at Helen and seeing her face, once again burst into loud laughter.

Hearing a beep, Lily looked at the text from her mum *"Snotty's just pulled up"* she read out loud.

"Markos. No!" Lily yelled as Markos stood up and reached to pull the towel off his waist "I don't need to see your..." Lily frowned at the rolled up trousers under the towel and looked towards Helen, who having finally controlled herself was pulling off the towel to reveal a perfectly decent sundress underneath. She glanced at the second text from her mum *"On her way up the steps, we couldn't stop her."*

"Oh Christ, now what do we do?" laughed Lily, starting to see the funny side of it all. "You can explain yourselves later, but right now you need to hide the evidence from Selena." Markos pulled the key fob out of the socket and thrust it into Lily's hand.

"Lock us in and go and pretend you're feeding the chickens, it will take her five minutes to heave her bulk up the hill, if she asks why my car is here, tell her I'm checking on the kittens." Markos gently shoved Lily out of the door and pulled his shirt back on. He raced out to the balcony and quickly cleared the table and pulled Helens towels off the rails "Dotty can you watch from behind the curtains, as soon as Selena reaches the top of the hill and comes round the corner let me know."

"She's stopped," said Dotty "Looks like she's carrying some sort of clipboard, I think she's stopped because she's out of breath." Dotty looked at Helen, who had removed her wig and pulled up her bra and dress straps. "What's the plan?" Helen shrugged her shoulders; she didn't have a clue what Markos had planned and he was still bent over his phone rapidly texting someone.

"Okay, she's off again," said Dotty "She's just reaching the corner now "Oh!" Dotty jumped as Elias, with his finger to his lips stealthily climbed over the balcony rail and dived into the room.

"Is okay?" he said to no one in particular. Markos spoke to him in Greek and pointed to Helen.

"She's out of sight, now what?" Dotty held in a squeal as Markos picked her up and plonked her over the adjoining wall to her own balcony.

"Stay in your room, if anyone knocks answer it and pretend you've been working" instructed Markos "Helen, will you trust Elias? He is going to carry you down to the bar. I am going to climb over the balconies to Lily's apartment, okay?" Helen smiled and nodded, her early morning thoughts of wanting to go home were rapidly vanishing. She felt like a naughty teenager, and her skin was still tingling from Markos fleeting touches and kisses. Her stomach ached from the uncontrollable laughter, and she happily allowed Markos to lift her over the railing and into Elias' arms.

Rather than turning left towards the hill, Elias turned right and carried her over the grass to a narrow set of stone steps that led them down the other side of the rooms below and out to the poolside and bar. As they'd gone down the steps, Helen had watched over Elias' shoulder as Markos had skillfully climbed across the balcony's and scrambled up the bougainvillea-covered trellis to Lily's balcony.

"Lily, Lily, Lily?" Selena's piercing voice got louder and higher pitched with each "Lily" she shouted.

Coming down a small set of steps with a bag of chicken feed in hand, Lily wiped the sweat from her brow and looked at Selena

"Good Morning Selena, can I help you?" she asked calmly hiding how flustered the last five minutes had left her feeling.

"Ah yes, now then I need you to sign up for the dog show, I thought this year you could run the tombola for us?" Selena waved the clipboard in Lily's face, not waiting for an answer she continued "I see Markos' car is here I need to see him too."

"Yes we've rescued some kittens this morning, he's just up in my apartment with Georgios checking them over."

"Really? I thought I saw him on one of your balconies," Selena said accusingly.

"On one of our balcony's?" Lily feigned surprise "You must have been seeing things Selena, why on earth would Markos be on a balcony?"

"So who's staying in these rooms then?" Selena frowned, she knew exactly what she had seen and didn't like this silly woman protecting Markos.

"These rooms? Absolutely no-one…oh no I tell a lie, Ms. Boothroyd is in that one over there." Lily pointed out Dotty's door.

"Good, I need to speak to her about sponsoring the dog show," before Lily could stop her Selena marched over and rapped loudly on Dotty's door.

Lily was surprised when Dotty looking very studious in a pair of black glasses flung open her door.

"Selena, this is a surprise, can I help you?"

"Hmm…yes…could I come in? I'd like to speak to you about our little dog show."

"Of course!" Dotty invited Selena in and winked at Lily, who was scratching her head, wondering how Dotty had got out of a locked room.

Dotty led Selena out to her balcony and invited her to sit down. The hastily placed laptop, diary, and paperwork gave the appearance that Dotty had been hard at work all morning.

"I hope your neighbours haven't been disturbing you," said Selena looking pointedly at Helen's balcony.

"Neighbours? What neighbours? All the other rooms are empty, well at least until all my colleagues get here later." Dotty put her head on the side and looked perplexed "Why did you think I had neighbours Selena?"

"Oh…just making conversation" Selena blushed "Now about the dog show."

Ten minutes later Dotty had not only generously agreed to sponsor the dog show, but she had also agreed to judge the "Waggiest Tail" competition.

"I'll be in touch" she promised Selena as she showed her out of the door.

Markos and Lily were stood outside the apartments fussing over the box of kittens Georgios held.

"Ah Selena, according to Facebook I've been cavorting half naked on a balcony," Markos said, "if I were you I would go and get your eyes tested." He laughed loudly as Selena waddled off tossing her head and muttering under her breath.

Dotty promised she would meet the others down in the bar soon and walked back into her room. She had a very important email to send and had been waiting for the hotels erratic Wi-Fi to start behaving itself.

Hi Molly

I have attached all your boarding passes, and your rooms are all booked. I'm so pleased that you and Ian are coming over and thank you so much for bringing Papa with you. Helen doesn't have a clue, to be honest, I think she has completely forgotten that she turns fifty in a couple of weeks. The weather really isn't that hot, so I'm sure you will cope, and there is plenty of shade to hide in. The lovely friends we have made here are going to organise a barbeque, and the twins are sorting out a video message for her. Can't wait to see you all.

Love
Dotty

Dotty, read through the email and happy with it, hit the send button. She rubbed her hands together in delight; she couldn't wait to see Helens face when her friends and Papa turned up at her surprise birthday party.

"I thought I was going to have a bleeding heart attack when I saw you climbing that trellis Markos," said Maggie pretending to smack him round the head.

"According to Elias, it's not the first time he's done it Apparently when they were kids they were always clambering over the balconies. I'm surprised my twins have never tried it," laughed Lily "I feel sorry for poor Mavra, her poor hearts going to be completely broken when she sees that picture."

"Oh talking of Mavra, she does want to be in Dotty's catalogue, someone told her she would get paid, and she's trying to raise some money for a couple of large dog runs, apparently she doesn't want Selena to find out though."

"Why does she want dog runs for, isn't that cruel?" asked Helen

"No." explained Peggy "It's for the strays that we take off the streets to sterilise. We need more safe places to keep them for a few days while they recover and before we put them back on the streets."

"Goodness, I've got so much to learn about all your work Peggy. If Mavra wants to do it for the dogs I'm sure Dotty will agree; I'll have a word with her."

"I've not even packed yet Markos, I'm so sorry, what with the kittens and everything else going on" Helen raised her eyebrows at the strange morning they'd had "You're not in a rush to get off are you, I can always get a taxi to the villa."

"It's okay Helen, Dotty said she would pack your cases" interrupted Lily

"Huh, I can assure you that despite what Dotty might say there is no way she will be packing any cases, she normally stops in hotels that have maids to do that sort of thing."

"She won't find any bleeding maids in this hotel" laughed Maggie "Oh Lordy Markos your pictures got over three hundred likes and over a hundred comments, quite a debate going on over whether it's you or not." Maggie handed her phone to Markos who grinned wickedly.

"Hah, listen to this one," he said, *"definitely not Markos, his hairs not grey enough."*

"Bleeding cheek," said Lily "Who wrote that?

"Hmm, let me see, someone called *Cheeky Chappie*."

Markos looked confused as Maggie, Lily and Peggy all burst out laughing.

"Oh Markos, you're bloody hopeless when it comes to Facebook *Cheeky Chappie* is your own son Christos" laughed Peggy

"I'll kill him" cursed Markos grinning "Oh no Christos!" Markos slapped his hand against his forehead and swore loudly "Ladies you have to help me, it's Christos' name day, and I completely forgot."

"Good grief, we forgot too," said Peggy "I've got him a present at home."

"Don't panic Markos, I must admit I remembered to get him a gift a couple of days ago, but I completely forgot about it this morning, Poor Christos, he'll think we've all forgotten." Lily closed her eyes in concentration. "Right, we've still got plenty of time. Where's Christos now Markos? And Mum any news on the plane?"

"He's still up at Madeline's villa, I think he'll be there all day" replied Markos.

"Estimated time of departure 10:30 am, that's UK time so 12:30 pm here" Maggie mentally added on the journey time "Should be landing about 3:45 pm so if we add on time for passports, collecting luggage and the taxis I guess it'll be 4:30 pm before they arrive here."

"Well, we've got loads of spare time then. Markos, you can head into town and get Christos a gift, Mum and me can go to Lidl and get some food in and Helen if you don't mind we could all come up to the Villa this evening and throw Christos a nice little party."

All eyes looked at Helen, who in turn looked utterly confused.

"Of course, but I don't understand, what's a name day?"

"I know," said Dotty appearing behind them "It's like a saint's day isn't it? She asked.

"Sort of" laughed Markos "Us Greeks celebrate all of the saints, in fact nearly every day is dedicated to a different saint or martyr. If you were named after one of the saint's then that day becomes your name day, your name day is more important than a birthday, and we celebrate with gifts and special meals. Christos was named after Saint Christoferos and today is his name day."

"How cool is that, we should have name days in England," said Dotty. "Oh and Peggy, don't you go worrying about your Suzanne, all of my team have been having a wonderful time in an executive lounge since early this morning. They are being waited on hand and foot and by the sounds of it have already started their holiday."

"Oh thank goodness" Peggy sighed with relief "I'd best get off home and take over the puppy sitting from Alf, I'll see you all later."

"And we better head to Lidl Mum, bye everyone." Lily pulled her mum out of the chair and set off for the car.

"Well, I'm all packed, and I've packed all Helens bits, so we are ready whenever you are Markos."

"Dotty, there is no way you have packed," said Helen, knowing full well that Dotty was lying "who did you get to pack for you?"

"Hah" giggled Dotty "I gave that little dark haired cleaner twenty euros and a couple of bikinis, she's done a fantastic job and even carried the cases to Markos' truck."

"Well if you ladies will give me half an hour to pick up a gift for Christos I promise I will be all yours…and thank you…it's a long time since I laughed so much" Markos headed off down the road hoping that it would not be long before he held Helen in his arms again.

CHAPTER 15
YOU CAN'T CON NORA

Mavra paced round and round the small table muttering and cursing to herself.

"It is definitely Markos. Yes?" she asked Selena again.

"Yes Mavra, I saw him with my own eyes, he was leaning against the balcony but turned round before I could take a photo.

"Markos he is...how do you say in English...bastard...yes, bastard." Mavra bent down and peered at the photo on Selena's laptop that had been enlarged. "This woman...she is bitch...yes bitch" she stabbed a vicious finger at the woman who was throwing her head back with laughter.

Selena's hastily contrived committee meeting to organise the dog show had descended into a cluster of angry woman disgusted that some stranger had got her filthy claws into their beloved vet. Selena had described exactly what she had seen from her viewpoint over the road and gone on to explain how Lily and Markos had not only lied to her but made fun of her too. Mavra's initial tears of heartbreak had quickly turned to anger.

"Mavra, ladies, calm down." Selena ordered, "Instead of getting angry, we need to get clever and work out who this woman is."

"I know who it is" spat out Mavra "She is a bitch, with her blonde hair and big fake boobies" Mavra tossed her straggly hair and tried to jiggle her own rather flat chest. "I saw her last night...she had a black wig on. I watched from the bar opposite."

"What on earth are you talking about Mavra?" asked Selena

"I watch them last night!" Mavra repeated "She was sat next to Helen Hardy...she had black wig and big clothes, her wig came off and it was that woman...a bitch." Mavra didn't explain why she had been watching them or that she had sneaked the photos into Dotty's bag.

"What woman?" chorused almost everyone sat round the table

"Dorothy Boothroyd...she has stolen my Markos...I spit in her face."

"Are you sure Mavra?" asked Selena staring at the photo again "I suppose it could be her with a wig on and she is staying there," Selena thought back to that morning when Dorothy had answered the door. "Well, ladies, I think we need to find out a lot more about Dorothy Boothroyd and why she has chosen our little island for a photo shoot. Let's get googling."

"Dotty, if you say wow one more time I'm going to smack you," laughed Helen.

"But these views are to die for Helen, can you imagine how fantastic the catalogue is going to look." Dotty had the car window wide open and was snapping picture after picture of the amazing scenes "Christ knows how I'm going to pick just a few locations, it's all so amazing."

"Maybe if you write a list of the sort of places you want, I can help" offered Markos "There are mountains, monasteries, caves, small harbours even windmills" he laughed at Dotty's squeals of delight. "I will show you my favourite chapel," he said, "It is on our way."

Deciding Helen would be very uncomfortable squashed in the truck with Dotty, Markos had left his keys with Elias and borrowed his and Lily's large family car promising to return it the next day. Helen was settled comfortably in the back seat with her leg elevated on soft pillows, and Dotty was seated next to Markos in the front. Puddles had happily jumped in the back and was snoring gently. Markos pointed out a large sign that said, Porto Zorro.

"When you can swim Helen I will take you there. People come from all over the island to cover themselves in the clay. It makes your skin feel very soft. The sea is also very good for snorkelling; do you snorkel?"

"I haven't snorkelled since I was a little girl" laughed Helen "but I can't wait to try it."

A few minutes later Markos swung the car left off the main road and drove them down a smaller road signposted "Agios Nikolaos."

"This is Saint Nicholas Beach" explained Markos "Agios means Saint, you will see the word everywhere here on Zakynthos."

Helen and Dotty were both stunned into silence as the breathtakingly beautiful view opened up below them. To the left of the golden sandy beach, a rocky piece of land jutted out to sea. A tiny white chapel was perched on the rocks, and Helen placed her hand on her chest as she drew in a deep breath at the sheer beauty.

"The Church on The Sea," said Markos as he drove the car right along the sea front and through a set of open gates. Parking right in front of the chapel he turned to Helen and grinned "Want to get out?" he asked and smiled at her excited nods.

The tiny white chapel had a large red central door and two smaller red doors each side. The main door had six panels, each decorated with a large white cross. Helen gazed up at the tall brick arch that surrounded the main door and housed a solitary bell. Markos laughed as Dotty ran over and tried to open the beautifully ornate door.

"Sorry Dotty, you can't get in, it's kept locked but occasionally opened for weddings."

"Well I never intend to get married but if I did it would have to be here" breathed Dotty.

"Markos, Markos" Helen turned and saw a deeply tanned man in just a pair of shorts and flip flops walking towards them. Beside him, a large black dog trotted along wagging his tail and Puddles ran over excitedly barking at the promise of a new friend. Reaching them, the man shook Markos' outstretched hand and smiled at Helen and Dotty.

"Yasou Spiros" turning to Helen, Markos explained that Spiros worked on the beach, hiring out the boats and organising the watersports.

Helen smiled hello and bent down to pet the dog.

"Oh his poor eyes, and he is so thin. Markos look!" The dog's eyes were crusted over with thick yellow scabs and looked incredibly sore and his ribs protruded out of his skinny body.

"He turned up two days ago" explained Spiros "I have been feeding him, but he won't let me near his eyes to clean them" Spiros patted the poor dog "He had a collar and was dragging a chain."

"Kala-azar, I expect," said Markos sadly. "Can you bring him up to the villa later Spiros, I will put him up at the feeding station and get Christos to take some blood. Hopefully, we can help him" Spiros thanked Markos and said goodbye to the ladies as they climbed back in the car.

"What is Kala-azar Markos?" asked Helen, saddened by the sorry state of the dog.

"It is a nasty disease caused by the bite of a sand fly; you may know it as leishmaniosis?" Helen shook her head, never having heard of it. "Sadly, it is common here" Markos continued, "Spiros said the dog had a chain attached. I suspect he was a guard dog and when he became ill he was no longer useful and would have been dumped; people leave the collar and chains on to make it look as if the dog has escaped."

"That's so cruel," said Dotty "Can you help the dog, Markos?

"I can treat it with therapy…special diet and medication… but it cannot be cured; it is a very nasty disease but we have many dogs living with Kala-azar here, we will see." Markos didn't want to tell Helen about the many dogs that died from the horrible and painful disease or how incredibly difficult it was to rehome a dog with a death sentence hanging over its head.

Dotty clutched the dashboard and pressed her nose almost against the windscreen as they climbed the chalky, steep road. Helen managed to keep her eyes open, not wanting to miss Dotty's reaction as the villa came into sight.

"God Helen, you've got to let me "Wow" at that" Dotty flung open the car door and turned a slow circle taking in the villa, the large barn and the seemingly never-ending rows of olive trees that stretched high above them "You didn't tell me it was so gorgeous."

Markos opened the boot and let an excited Puddles jump out; he laughed as the daft dog raced round and round in circles yapping impatiently. He pulled Helens crutches out and opened the car door to help her. Deciding to leave the suitcases, for now, he led them to the villas front door and eased it open.

"I'll stick the kettle on," he said and ambled over to the kitchen.

"It's so clean Markos," said Helen impressed with the shining furniture that was no longer covered in dust. "Have a look round Dotty and decide where you want to sleep I'm going out on the balcony, just wait till you see the views from there."

Helen threw down her crutches and settled herself in her aunt's old wicker rocking chair. It felt like coming home she admitted to herself and despite her protestations to the contrary, a tiny part of her was starting to believe that she could quite happily spend the rest of her life living in this wonderful villa on this beautiful Greek island.

"I can understand why your aunt never left this island Helen. Who wouldn't want to wake up to that view every day?" Dotty leant against the railings and gazed down below "Is that Gerakas beach?" she asked Markos, who was coming out of the patio doors with a tray of freshly brewed coffee and mugs.

"It is but you don't say the G. it is pronounced Yerakas with a Y."

"You will have to teach us some Greek Markos, you make a good teacher," said Helen watching Dotty rummage through her handbag and pull out the small binoculars she'd had that morning. "What are you looking at Dotty?" she asked as Dotty trained the binoculars on the far left of the beach below."

"Just the views," said Dotty airily, Markos started to laugh, and Helen looked at him in confusion.

"Who told you Dotty? Grinning Markos poured the coffees, knowing full well what Dotty was looking for.

"Told her what? Helen narrowed her eyes and frowned at Markos feeling as if she had missed something.

"Ha, the far end of Gerakas beach is unofficially a nudist beach" Markos laughed at Helens shocked face "I bet Maggie told Dotty about it, she's always trying to get George to take her down there."

Helen giggled, not sure she wanted the image of a naked Maggie and George imprinted on her brain. She hugged the mug of coffee to her chest and sighed contentedly. She could feel Markos' eyes on her and turned to see him looking concerned.

"Are you okay Helen? You look very tired and pale" he frowned, worried.

"I probably need to take some more painkillers" Helen admitted, "They make me so tired though Markos and I don't want to waste any more of my time here asleep."

"Right," said Dotty, taking control "You can stop being so stubborn Helen Hardy. Take some painkillers and go and lie down. Markos can show me around the villa and explain how everything works, and I promise I will wake you up in a couple of hours, that way you will feel much better when everyone arrives this evening."

Helen smiled gratefully at her best friend who could be quite bossy when needed. Allowing Markos to help her she grabbed her crutches and swung herself back into the villa.

"Which bedroom did you choose Dotty?" she asked.

"I didn't, they are all beautiful, you choose, and I'll pick from whatever's left."

Remembering her last visit, Helen swung herself through a door on the right and found herself in what she guessed was her aunt's bedroom. The large double bed was placed opposite another set of balcony doors and Helen thought Dotty was right, who wouldn't want to wake up to that view every morning? She was tempted to start rummaging through the cupboards and drawers, but the overwhelming tiredness was too much, and she sank gratefully onto the bed. Snuggling her head into the soft, luxurious pillows, she made Markos promise to wake her in a couple of hours and closed her eyes.

With her Filofax on the kitchen table and pen in hand Dotty listened carefully to Markos's instructions about the air con, cooker, water and Sky TV. Making rapid notes, she laughed when he told her the Wi-Fi password was "Puddles1."

"I'll show you the hot tub, sauna and swimming pool once Helens awake," said Markos and laughed and Dotty's surprised look.

"What did your Uncle do Markos? He certainly made a lot of money."

"My Uncle" exclaimed Markos "Oh no Dotty, this was all Madeline's, she was the one with money. My Uncle ran a shop in the town selling animal and pet food I thought you and Helen knew that."

"Goodness no, Helen honestly thought she would be coming over to find some tiny ramshackle wooden shack on a beach." Dotty mulled this new information over; she remembered reading Madeline's first letter to Helen saying she had *"Gathered my savings and sold my car"* How odd she thought and jotted a note reminding herself to tell Helen.

"Yasou" Christos appeared, shirtless, in the kitchen doorway looking hot and very, very sexy thought Dotty.

"Christos, Xronia Polla, Happy Name Day." Markos hugged his son "I have a gift but later, when everyone is here."

"Is it my name day?" Christos laughed "I wondered what all the Xronia Polla's on Facebook were for" growing up in England he had never really got his head around the whole "name day" thing. "Hi Dotty, how's the head today" He hugged Dotty loving this tiny and vivacious woman who had happily danced on the tables with him the night before.

"Nothing a few coffees and a painkiller didn't sort out," said Dotty grinning wryly "Sit down and I'll get you a drink" Opening the fridge she spotted a bottle of Mythos and handed it to him "Your dad's just going over a few things, and Helen's having a sleep."

"How is Helen?" Christos asked "This whole business must be a huge shock to her, and Peggy said she is fairly recently widowed."

"Hmm" agreed Dotty nodding "William was killed in a car crash eighteen months ago, it was a horrible time for her." Dotty lowered her head remembering the awful time. "The worst bit was that nobody knew what caused the accident. The car came off the road and hit a tree, but the police could find no cause. There were no faults found in the car, he wasn't speeding, the roads were dry. The coroner recorded an open verdict, and I think Helen is still struggling to come to terms with that."

"She must have loved him very much," said Markos thinking of the photo he had found on Google. "What was William like?"

"Oh he didn't approve of me" grimaced Dotty "He tolerated me, but William was quite the prude, almost Victorian in his ways...don't get me wrong Helen loved him dearly but Helen has this wonderfully playful sense of humour...like this morning?" she smiled at Markos "William would have been horrified by our antics...and you've seen her with the dogs and cats...William never allowed animals in the house. He couldn't cope with any mess." Realising she had probably said too much behind her friends back Dotty changed the subject "Anyway Cheeky Chappie, what's with the *"grey hair"* comments on Facebook?" she faked a frown at Christos and laughed as he had the grace to blush.

"Just what were you all playing at this morning...I nearly fell in the swimming pool when I saw that picture Dad...but I managed to enlarge it on the PC, and anyone looking closely enough will spot what I spotted, I know very well that it was Helen wearing your wig Dotty." Christos looked incredibly pleased with himself and grinned smugly at their open mouths.

One of the women sat around Selena's table was fast coming to the same conclusion as Christos, zooming in and out of the grainy photograph, Nora was focusing on the woman's leg. The fluffy white towel that Helen had wrapped around herself had ridden up, and a white bandage was clearly on display.

"Right then ladies, we have five minutes left then we must get down to organising the Dog Show."

Selena's snotty, condescending tone was starting to grate on Nora, and she had been shocked by Mavra's venomous tone and stabbing finger. Nora had been a good friend of Madeline Kalvos and a long-serving member of the Dozies but a stupid argument a couple of years ago with Don had led to her resigning and joining Selena's Lazies. Nora had been rescuing dogs for over eighteen years and needed their support to help with the food and vet's fees. Cynthia's dementia was having a big impact on the Dozies work. Don was too bloody stubborn to give up the reins and let the younger generation take over and turning up at Don's one day, to find Cynthia, alone in the kitchen, feeding chocolate to some small puppies had been the last straw. Nora switched off her IPad and chose to keep quiet. She would sit through the rest of the meeting then go and find Peggy.

"Look what I have found!" Selena's housemaid turned her laptop around and showed the ladies the large photograph on the screen. An intake of shocked breaths echoed round the table as they all stared at the photo of a very glamorous Dorothy Boothroyd arm in arm with Helen Hardy. They were both dressed in stunning designer evening gowns and were laughing gaily into the camera.

"Well, well, well" sneered Selena "So Helen Hardy and Dorothy Boothroyd are not just strangers who met here on Zakynthos this just proves how cunning Helen Hardy really is."

"Bitches" Mavra threw her hands in the air in disgust then muttered sorry when Selena shushed her with a glare.

"Ladies, Ladies" Selena shouted over the angrily chattering women and raised both hands for silence, "I think we all need to double our efforts to keep an eye on Helen Hardy we cannot let a complete stranger waltz into our lives and just help herself to Madeline Kalvos' estate. She needs to be gone before the thirty days are up so the rightful heir, who is named in that envelope, can take Madeline's place."

"Who do you think is named in that envelope Selena?" asked Nora, hoping to cause embarrassment.

"Well…I don't know…but I was, of course, her very best friend so…" Selena shrugged her shoulders feigning humble innocence and the ladies around the table murmured their agreements. Nora bit her lip trying hard not to laugh at the stuck-up cow who honestly didn't have a clue what most people really thought of her.

Markos gazed at the sleeping Helen; her strawberry blonde hair was fanned out on the pillow. One arm hung loosely at her side; the other was stretched above her head. A smile hovered over her pretty and very kissable lips. He was reluctant to wake her; she looked so beautiful. He would be very content to stand and watch her all day. Sighing he steadied his trembling hands and reached over to gently shake her shoulder.

"Helen, Helen," he said softly, not wanting to startle her awake.

Helen was having her favourite dream; she was running along the beach hand in hand with the man whose face she could never quite see. Puddles was running along beside them splashing in and out of the waves that rippled over the hot sand, she could hear someone calling her name but didn't want to let go of the hand that held her so tightly.

"Helen, wake up" Markos sat on the edge of Helens bed and patted her hand "Helen."

"Oh Markos" Helen rubbed her hands across her tired eyes and pushed herself up.

"Oh dear, sorry, what time is it?"

"It's okay it's only 4:00 pm can I get you a drink" Markos wondered yet again why Helen kept staring at his hands.

"Mm that would be lovely, do we have any iced tea in the fridge? I'm really dry."

Helen stretched her arms high above her head and yawned. Looking around the room, she realised that astonishingly, Dotty had unpacked her suitcase and put everything away. Her laptop, notepad, and pen were placed neatly on the bedside table; she reached over to grab the notepad. Opening it, she looked at the list of names she had started to write.

Markos: *Nephew, first choice, would he do the right thing? Lily thinks he would not be able to mediate or placate people.*

Christos: *Great Nephew, maybe too young to take on responsibility, strong ties to England.*

Peggy and Alf: *Best friends, maybe too…*

Helen had been interrupted at that point and remembered thinking that her Aunt may have felt Peggy and Alf were maybe a bit too old and busy to want any more responsibility. Gosh, this was hard thought Helen; how was she supposed to read the mind of a woman she'd not seen for forty years. She was still frowning when Markos carried her drink into the bedroom.

"Okay?" asked Markos seeing the frown "Is it your leg?"

"Gosh no my legs fine" reassured Helen "Sit down Markos" realising there were no chairs she patted the bed trusting him completely.

"Dotty's gone for a lie-down," said Markos, "She said she needed her beauty sleep and was muttering something about a hairdresser and extensions" Helen laughed loudly as he shrugged his shoulders and raised his eyebrows. The only extensions he knew about were the ones on the sides of buildings. "How long have you and Dotty been friends Helen?"

"Oh goodness. I can't remember a time when we weren't friends. We grew up living next door to each other; she may come across as a dizzy blonde, but I couldn't have got through the last eighteen months without her." Helen smiled and looked at the notepad on her lap. "Dotty is the one that gets me to write lists when my head feels as if it's going to explode with too much information." Markos looked at the notepad and spotting his name was intrigued.

"What's this list about then?"

Helen frowned at Markos; he would probably know better than anyone who her aunt would most likely choose, but she was a bit scared of upsetting him. Since his initial intense dislike of her, he had bent over backwards to help her. Deciding to throw caution to the wind she showed him the list.

"Please don't think bad of me Markos but I'm trying to work out whose name is in that dratted envelope" she looked beseechingly at Markos "I want to do right by my aunt and think my best option is to try and guess the name."

Markos grabbed Helens hands in his own and smiled warmly.

"Peggy, Lily, Christos and I came to the same conclusion. How can I help?"

"Thank goodness" breathed Helen "This is what I've jotted down so far, but I could be completely wrong" she showed Markos the list and watched his expressions closely as he read what she'd written. Markos let go of her hands, picked up her pen and firmly crossed his name off the list.

"The only thing I know for sure is that it's not me. Apart from Lily being absolutely right about my inability to mediate," he grimaced "I told Madeline very firmly that I did not want it, and she promised me my name wasn't in there." Helen was surprised, as Markos had been her first and most obvious choice. "I think you are right about Christos" Markos continued. "He is too young, and there's nothing to say he won't decide to head back to the UK" Markos laughed as he read the unfinished notes about Peggy and Alf "Too emotional? Too busy? Too old? Helen blushed as she admitted she had been about to write "too old."

"I feel awful," she said, "they are not all that much older than me, but I just think my aunt would have gone for someone younger."

"I think your right; she would have. There's a few names to add and a couple of people that you haven't met yet, Lily, Bethany, Selena…don't laugh" Markos grinned wickedly at Helens outraged face "We do of course have to consider Selena even if it's only to write down all the obnoxious thoughts we have about her…okay, there's Nora and Denis, who you haven't met yet and finally you."

"Me?" Helen frowned "but that would make no sense at all, why would she go to all the effort of a codicil and then put my name in there?"

"Because your aunt had a very, very wicked sense of humour and would have been wetting herself at the thought of everybody's shocked faces when you opened the envelope."

Helen burst out laughing; she could well imagine the look of horror on Selena's face.

"When your leg is better…or better than it is" Markos grinned as Helen rolled her eyes "I will take you to see Bethany's Cat Haven and take you over to meet Nora and Denis. Nora is our very own "Miss Marple" you will love her, but right now…he grabbed Helens hand again to stop her asking more questions "Right now you need to eat, I'm not the most imaginative cook or anywhere near up to Lily's standards, but I have managed to cobble together some cheese rolls and a Greek salad."

Knowing that the nosey Mavra would be at Selena's for a good couple of hours, Nora drove into the village of Macherado and pulled up outside Peggy and Alf's. Rapping on the open door, she clambered over the piece of wood that was wedged across the doorway to keep the dogs in.

"Peggy, hello" she trilled "Hello you beautiful dogs" she bent down to fuss and cuddle the half a dozen dogs that bounded towards her and laughed at the smaller puppies that were falling over themselves to catch up and join in the fun "Oh you are all so gorgeous." Peggy walked out of the kitchen, wiping her hands on the apron tied around her waist.

"Hello Nora love, what a lovely surprise." Peggy reached out to hug her friend and offered to put the kettle on and make a brew.

"I'd love a good old cup of Yorkshire tea," nodded Nora "I ran out a month ago, and I've been gagging for a cup, I must remember to order some next time our friend drives the dogs over to England."

Settled in the garden with the much-needed cup of tea Nora cocked her head on one side and scrutinised her good friend.

"Now then Peggy, tell me about Helen Hardy, can we trust her or is she a bloody good actress?" Peggy laughed out loud as Nora, as usual, came straight to the point.

"Blimey Nora, don't beat about the bush will you?" Peggy put her tea on the table and pondered how to answer the astute woman. "Right then, I could sit here and tell you that Helen is one of the most wonderful, compassionate and kind people I have ever met…hang on I haven't finished." Peggy held up her hand to stop Nora uttering a sarcastic retort. "I know very well that words won't convince you, but what if I told you that it took less than fifteen minutes for Helen to coax Puddles out of the olive grove and now the daft dog won't leave her side."

"Never!" breathed Nora, who had herself spent hours trying to catch Puddles.

"Cross my heart and hope to die" declared Peggy. "And, she didn't think twice about diving under an evil gorse bush to rescue these little darlings." Peggy pointed out the puppies curled up in a box under the table. "And that was a pretty serious injury she got doing so."

"Hmm, I'm not convinced though," said Nora "what about all those shenanigans this morning with her and Markos on that balcony, you don't have to be a genius to work out that was Helen Hardy in a wig."

"Hah" squealed Peggy, delighted "Nobody ever cons you, Nora, do they? You should be called Agatha bleeding Christie. Well, let me tell you… and you might be surprised to hear this… but it was all Markos' idea; that bloody Selena was spying on Lily's rooms and Dotty…Dorothy Boothroyd…spotted her so Markos thought it would be a good idea to give her something to gossip about."

"Markos?" Nora raised her eyebrows in disbelief. The brooding and sensible Markos she knew would never come up with something like that.

"Oh yes, Helen has had quite an impact on our Markos and between you and me," Peggy gave an exaggerated wink "He is completely besotted with her and if I'm not mistaken the feelings very much mutual. Tell you what Nora, we are having a little do up at Madeline's villa this evening for Christos name day, why don't you and Denis come along and meet Helen, you keep telling us you're the best judge of character on the island."

Nora nodded and agreed. It wouldn't be a bad idea for her to meet Helen first hand and goodness knows her and her husband Denis could certainly do with a night out. She was just about to tell Peggy all about Selena's meeting when the dogs jumped up and bounded excitedly towards Peggy's front door. Peggy turned to see who it was, and her mug of tea slipped out of her hands and smashed onto the patio. Putting both hands to her mouth in complete and utter shock, tears welled up in her eyes at the handsome young man walking towards her.

"Hi Mum, I'm home."

CHAPTER 16
A PARTY IN THE POOL

"Madam, if you would care to accompany me, your chariot awaits" Christos gave a theatrical bow and held out his hand to Helen.

"How kind, young man" Helen stood up on one leg and attempted a curtsy but the momentum set her of balance, and she collapsed back into the wicker chair in a giggling heap. Markos tried to be cross as he grabbed both hands to pull her up but her infectious giggles set him off laughing too. Christos watched his Dad gently ease Helen out of the chair and prayed fervently that she would choose to stay on the island. He had never seen his father so happy and relaxed, and he hadn't been lying when he told them he'd nearly fallen in the pool with shock when he logged into Facebook earlier.

"Are we going somewhere?" asked Dotty, who, for the past hour had been periodically squinting through the binoculars and sketching frantically in a large A4 sketchpad. Helen, quite used to her eccentric behaviour had ignored her, but Markos was curious.

"Are you drawing naked bodies Dotty?" he laughed, peering over to try and sneak a glimpse of her sketches.

"Nope," Dotty slammed shut her sketchpad and tapped the side of her nose "All will be revealed later, and actually I think it's something your gorgeous son might be able to help me with" she winked at Christos who grinned enthusiastically. In the midst of a teenage-like crush on Dotty, he was putty in her hands.

"Whatever your heart desires my lady" smiled Christo "Now follow me we are off on a magical mystery tour."

Walking out of the villa, Dotty squealed and clapped her hands and Helen burst out laughing. Standing proudly on the driveway was the cutest golf buggy she had ever seen. Bright blue and with a canopy stretching over the two rows of swanky leather seats, the buggy was decorated with images of cats and dogs. Sat in the driving seat with his tail thumping and body quivering with excitement Puddles barked at them to hurry up.

"Now I know Puddles is clever, but you're not expecting me to believe he can drive as well?" Helen said.

"No, Madeline never got around to teaching him that" laughed Markos "Puddles in the back" he instructed the dog and helped Helen into one of the back seats. "A few years ago Madeline finally admitted that she was struggling to get up and down to the feeding station, so she had this brought over from the mainland" Markos offered Christos the driving seat and settled himself next to Helen stretching his arm along the seat behind her.

Christos, with Dotty seated next to him, drove the buggy towards the large barn. Seeing the closed up doors Helen asked what was in there.

"Quite a lot," said Markos mysteriously "I'll show you another time."

Helen's curiosity was soon forgotten as they rounded the barn. A large swimming pool appeared in front of them, and Christos eased the buggy to a stop so they could have a good look. At the far end of the swimming pool a row of typical English beach huts stood. Each hut was painted a different colour and Helen was instantly transported back to her childhood holidays in Weymouth. In front of each hut, old fashioned deck chairs were scattered around haphazardly on the pale blue decking.

"The hut on the far left is a sauna, the two in the middle are changing rooms and that one is where we store all the sun loungers and chairs over the winter" Christos explained. Even Dotty was lost for words until she spotted something else.

"Is that the hot tub?" she asked.

A large hot tub was housed under a beautiful rustic gazebo with a pretty red-tiled roof. Helen let her eyes graze over the hot tub and along to the right where a long bar with the same red tiled roof stretched almost the full length of the pool. A huge brick built barbeque at the end closest to them was already lit, and a large pig was turning slowly above the heat on a spit roast.

"Dad asked me what food I wanted tonight for my name day, I was only joking when I asked for a hog roast" laughed Christos "Christ knows where he managed to locate one at such short notice."

Christos reversed the buggy back and swung onto a small dirt track behind the bar. Driving through the olive groves, he pulled up beside a pretty little villa.

"This is one of the guest houses" Markos explained "There are five dotted around the estate. Your Aunt used to hire them out to holidaymakers, but it got too much for her the last couple of years so she had to stop" Helen remained silent and Markos spotting the tears welling gave her a quick hug and instructed Christos to drive on.

"Hold on tight Ladies" Christos yelled, and he swung the buggy right and started climbing a small, very steep track. Dotty shrieked with fear and not thinking Helen clutched Markos' thigh as they struggled up the hill. Markos laughed and pulled Helen closer to him. He pointed out a group of goats tethered loosely under the olive trees and munching the shrubbery.

"I feel as if I'm in Jurassic Park and any moment a large dinosaur is going to jump out in front of us" squeaked Dotty as she held on tightly to the scarf that still covered her distressed hair.

"Helen, you need to stay in the buggy," said Markos quite sternly as a clearing appeared ahead of them "I don't want any of the dogs jumping up at you and catching your leg. Helen nodded and watched Puddles leap off the back of the buggy and race off ahead of them yapping excitedly.

Markos and Christos climbed out and calmed the dozens of dogs and puppies that bounded towards them. Helen and Dotty stared dumbstruck at the sight. Dotted around were sturdy wooden shelters. A long trough full of fresh water and plenty of large stainless steel feeding bowls were placed on the ground. Dog toys littered the floor, and Helen spotted three chemical dog toilets dug into the ground. A huge, black and white, thick coated dog wandered over to the buggy and gently placed his head in Helens lap. She ruffled the thick fur then laughed as a jealous Puddles tried to nudge the bigger dog out of the way.

"This is Teddy" introduced Christos as he came over to pull the large dog off. "He's a Hellenic Sheep Dog. They are used a lot up in the mountains to guard animals and properties. He was one of five puppies that Madeline found tied up in a bin bag in Laganas ten years ago, the only one still alive."

"Has he been here for ten years?" asked Dotty fondling the dog and gazing into his soulful large eyes.

"Madeline put him up here when he was six months old and over the years his natural instincts have led to him guarding and protecting all the dogs that end up here. He really is the leader of the pack."

"Don't they wander off?" asked Helen finally finding her voice.

"The property is huge Helen and apart from the driveway is fully fenced. I suppose they could run off if they wanted but they all seem content to stay here; they have food, water, shelter and plenty of room to roam. The younger ones are often rehomed, but some of the older ones, like Teddy will live out their lives here."

Helen watched Markos walk to a small barn and pull out a large sack of food. He filled all the dishes and laughed as the dogs gathered round and started to munch their food.

"We have about an hour before our guests arrive," said Markos, looking at his watch. "We best head back and start getting ready." He jumped back in the buggy and suggested Helen close her eyes. "If you thought it was steep coming up it's far worse going back down." He put his arm back around her and laughed as she hid her face in his shoulder and clutched tightly onto his shirt.

"Aunty Dotty...Aunty Dotty!" Dotty, perched daintily on one of the bar stools, turned in surprise. She threw her arms wide in delight as a pretty young girl flung herself into them hugging her tightly. Dotty looked at the harassed young woman hurrying behind and mouthed "What's happened?"

"Dotty I'm so sorry, Mum has gone down with shingles and my sister is away, I didn't know what to do so I just managed to grab a last minute seat on the plane for her. I promise she won't get in the way."

Dotty gently pushed the girl away from her and placed both hands on her pretty face, she leant forward and kissed the top of her head.

"Well Brooke, I'm sure we can find you lots of jobs to do, now how much do you charge an hour?" Dotty hugged her goddaughter to her and laughed as Brooke demanded £100 an hour.

Brooke spotted Puddles laying at Helens feet and raced off to hug the dog.

"Hi Helen is this your new dog?" Helen smiled down at the pretty girl with the long brown hair and a spattering of tiny freckles on her nose.

"Hi Brooke, this is Puddles, and yes I suppose he is my new dog" Helen waved at Brookes mum "Hi Carly."

"Do you think Madeline would mind all this?" Helen asked Markos as more and more of Dotty's colleagues strolled into the pool area carrying bottles of wine and crates of beer. It had been Christos idea to invite them all to his name day party, but Helen felt strongly that they were taking advantage of Markos' generosity.

"Madeline would have loved this. The whole reason she had all this built was for people to relax and have fun."

Peggy walked towards Dotty but seeing her in deep conversation with a young woman she turned towards Helen and Markos.

"Helen, this is my son Jacob and daughter-in-law Suzanne. I can't believe Dotty kept it such a surprise; I've been crying all afternoon." Helen shook Jacob and Suzanne's hands and laughed as Christos raced over and hugged Jacob and Suzanne tightly. Long-time childhood friends, Christos had been thrilled when Jacob moved to England, to marry Suzanne.

"Who is the stunner that's talking to Dotty?" Christos asked

"That's my mummy," said Brooke and grinned cheekily at Christos

"Oh," Christos was stumped "Well your mummy is nearly as pretty as you young lady" Brooke stood up and placed her hands on her hips, she cocked her head to one side and slowly ran her eyes over Christos' face.

"Well… Mummy doesn't have a boyfriend, and you look… okay…ish…not as handsome as Harry Styles but I think Mummy will like you" She high fived Christos outstretched hand and knelt back down to fuss puddles.

"Now then," said Alf, walking over with a cardboard box "Would this young lady like to help me feed these pups."

"O.M.G" declared Brooke "They are actually awesome" she picked up Jasmine and cuddled her under her chin, laughing as the tiny pup stuck out her tongue and licked her. Alf encouraged Brooke to sit in one of the chairs and showed her how to hold the bottle and pup.

"Helen, I know it's a huge ask," said Alf but we've had to pick up another four dumped babies this morning, do you think you could manage these three here in the villa with you, Markos will help out, and I've packed enough milk for a week or two."

"Absolutely," said Helen, chuffed to bits "I've been wondering what I'm going to do with myself, they will certainly keep me busy."

"Well, they are on four hourly feeds now so you'll still get a bit of time to yourself."

"Oh dear Alf, you've beaten me to it" Lily walked up to the group holding another cardboard box "I was going to ask Helen if she could cope with the kittens Puddles found this morning. Bethany is full up and with all our new guests I'm going to be too busy to look after them properly."

"Lily, I'm sure we will manage," said Helen taking the box and putting it down near Puddles. She was so busy watching Puddles nuzzle and lick the kittens that she didn't spot the silent winks and high fives that Lily, Peggy, Christos and Markos gave each other.

A while later Helen lazed contentedly on one of the cushioned sun loungers. Puddles was laid across her feet staring devotedly up at her. She watched enviously as Dotty's friends jumped in and out of the pool and splashed a squealing Brooke. Lily and her mum were idling in the hot tub while Christos was flirting outrageously with Brooke's mum.

"Helen, this is Nora and Denis, they were very good friends with Madeline" Peggy introduced her to a couple in their sixties.

"Hello, you old fraud," said Nora. Helen startled, then quickly realised Norah was speaking to Puddles "I had to see this for myself" explained Nora "I spent hours and hours trying to coax this silly dog down out of the olive groves."

"He's a pretty amazing dog," said Helen and told Nora and Denis about the kittens he'd found that morning. "Can I get you a drink?" she offered and tried to push herself off the sun lounger, giggling she admitted defeat and slunk back again "Sorry" she apologised and called to Markos who was leaning against the poolside bar deep in conversation with Elias.

Markos grinned and ran round the pool.

"Helens certainly keeping me on my toes" he laughed and gave Nora a quick hug "Kalispera Denis" He shook Denis hand "I've just lit the patio heaters come on over, and I'll get you a drink" Nora watched in astonishment as Markos bent down and lovingly lifted Helen into his arms and carried her round the pool. My god she thought, Peggy was right.

"Now then," said Nora once they were all seated comfortably under the heaters "Where's your friend Dorothy I need to warn her about something" Puzzled, Markos called Dotty over and introduced her to Nora. The group listened, captivated as Nora relayed the details of Selena's meeting.

"You need to watch your back young lady" Nora wagged a finger at Dotty who was secretly thrilled to be called young "That Mavra has got a very nasty temper, and I wouldn't put it past her to cause your photoshoot or even you some real problems."

"Christ" Markos hung his head in his hands "It's my fault Nora I should have thought things through before we played such a silly joke."

"Don't you worry yourself, Markos, it's about time someone put that Snotty Selena in her place and that Madam Mavra needs to realise once and for all that you are not interested in her." Nora shook her head in dismay at the stupidity of the women. "I think it would be ten times worse if any of them realised it was Helen in the wig" Helen raised her eyebrows in total agreement, Dotty was far better at dealing with angry people than she was. "I'm going to carry on going to their little meetings; that way I should be able to forewarn you of their plans," continued Nora. "And Helen" Nora turned to look at Helen and reached out her hand "Selena and her little gang are determined to chase you off this island before the thirty days are up, so you need to watch your back too."

"Over my dead body." said Markos angrily putting a protective arm around Helen "Whatever that lot have planned, we will be ready and waiting."

"Thank you Markos" Helen took the mug of hot chocolate gratefully and snuggled herself back into the plush sofa. Starting to feel tired she'd said goodnight to everyone, hugged Brooke tightly and asked Markos to help her back to the villa. She wanted to get the puppies and kittens settled before she got too tired and had been thrilled when Markos produced a pop-up playpen from one of the bedrooms and carefully placed the babies in it.

"Oh look, how sweet" Helen murmured as Smudge and Papa toddled to the kittens and curled up with them. Jasmine, needier, clawed the sides and squealed loudly begging to be picked up. Puddles, not liking the noise, bent his head into the playpen and picked Jasmine up, he plopped her into Helens lap and trotted off to the kitchen.

"Oh dear" chuckled Helen stroking the pup, "I think we are going to have to have a word with Puddles, he can't keep dumping animals in my lap."

"I've made myself up a bed in one of the spare rooms," said Markos. "The kittens are weaned and will be fine but Jasmine, Smudge, and Papa are going to need a feed in a few hours, and I don't think Dotty will be in any fit state to help you" Helen smiled gratefully, with the long hours she'd been sleeping, she'd been worried she wouldn't wake up herself.

"Brooke is a wonderful little girl," said Markos "Is Carly related to Dotty?"

"Oh no, Carly was Dotty's first teenage mum." Seeing the questioning look on Markos' face, Helen went on "Just over ten years ago Dotty set up a charity for single teenage mums. Markos, it's just amazing. She has this wonderful old mansion house down in Devon, and the set-up is, as Brooke would say, just awesome," she smiled "The girls go there while they are still pregnant and are looked after and taught how to care for their babies. Once the babies are born they stay there for a year or even two and during the day study for a career. The whole mansion is purpose designed. They have a proper fully staffed nursery for the babies, and the girls can choose from Hair and Beauty, Fashion, Catering, Childcare or Business. They have a working restaurant that is booked out every night and a lovely hair and beauty salon with regular customers. The charity supports the girls into finding full-time jobs and housing when they are qualified and ready to move on."

"That's fantastic," said Markos "So Carly was her first mum then?"

"Yes, Carly soon showed a real talent for fashion and Dotty encouraged her to design and make a teenage swimwear range, it was so good that Dotty added it to her stock and employed Carly as a designer. She has worked her way up over the last ten years and is now Dotty's chief designer. Her mum and sister help out with childcare, but Brooke is like one of the team and often tags along in the holidays. She is such a good girl that she's never been a problem. Dotty is her godmother and absolutely adores her."

"That's such an incredibly selfless thing for Dotty to do" smiled Markos "Her dizzy blonde exterior certainly hides a remarkable woman."

"Hmm" agreed Helen and thought back to 1980 when a tearful fifteen-year-old Dotty had confided in her that she was pregnant. Her disgusted parents had packed her off to hide with a Great Aunt in

Wales and forced her to give her beautiful baby boy up for adoption. With Dotty's parents long dead Helen was the only person in the world who knew her secret and why she did what she did for the young teenage mums.

Christos and Jacob lifted the hot tub cover back on and grabbing bin bags started to clear the empty cans and bottles. Dotty was locked head to head with her location manager looking through all the photo's she had taken and a quietness had settled over the pool area. Most of Dotty's team had headed back to Tsilivi and Peggy, Maggie, Lily, and Nora were huddled under the heaters, the chilly May evening sending shivers through them.

"Go on then Nora, what did you think of Helen?" Peggy asked

"Well, for once I think you're right Peggy" Nora winked to show she was just teasing "Helen is a beautiful woman both on the inside and the outside, and I can't get over how much she looks like Madeline…quite took my breath away when I first saw her…and I nearly keeled over when Markos picked her up; that poor man is head over heels in love; I just hope to God she doesn't go breaking his heart."

"If you ask me Helens pretty smitten with him too," said Lily "but I think she's battling her feelings out of loyalty to her dead husband, changing the subject Nora, Helen turns fifty in a couple of weeks, and we are helping Dotty arrange a surprise party. You and Denis must come."

Selena slammed the phone down in anger; she was absolutely fuming. By all accounts, both Helen Hardy and Dorothy Boothroyd had disappeared. That stupid village cleaner that Lily had temporarily employed was absolutely useless Selena thought. She had paid the woman to collect information for her, and all she could say was that Markos had packed the two women, the dog, and suitcases into a car and driven off. Mavra had been sat opposite Lily's hotel for hours and swore blind that Markos' truck was still parked up the back.

"Philip…Philip, are you listening to me?"

"Yes dear" Selena's downtrodden husband was hidden behind a two-day-old copy of The Sun newspaper catching up with all the football news from back home.

"Are you sure you checked them all?"

"Yes dear" sighed Philip "I went into every bar and every restaurant in Tsilivi, and there was no sign of Markos or Helen Hardy or Dorothy Boothroyd" behind the paper Philip grinned to himself as he'd spent the last couple of hours sat in the Kaliva Pub watching Man Utd play Liverpool.

"I don't know why you insist on reading that dreadful tabloid Philip, make sure you burn it when you've finished, we can't have the maid finding it."

"Yes dear" Philip smiled, knowing full well that as soon as he retired to bed, Selena would snatch up the paper and greedily devour all the gossip.

Selena snatched up her ringing phone and barked "Hello" listening to a voice on the other end she furiously scrubbed Argassi from the list of resorts she had listed in front of her. Her loyal team of devoted followers had spent the last few hours ringing every hotel in the area they'd been given and so far had all come up blank.

"Shush its ringing" Nora put her finger to her lips and hushed the group of grinning people around the table. She pressed the speakerphone icon and waited for Selena to answer.

"Selena, it's Nora, I have some news...yes...yes," Nora held the phone away from her as Selena's high-pitched voice screeched angrily out of the phone. "Selena listen...I have it on very good authority that Markos drove Helen and Dorothy Boothroyd up to St Nicholas Port this evening and put them on the 19:15 ferry to Kefalonia, apparently they are going to be spending a few days there and will be back on Friday...yes...of course...I'll see you tomorrow...bye." Nora turned off her phone and joined in the slow rumble of laughter spreading around the group.

"Oh lordy me," said Maggie "This summer is turning out to be the best fun we've ever had on this island, and let me tell you something if there's the slightest chance that Helen decides to stay on the island then George and me will be selling up and moving here too. We'd certainly be laughing the whole way to our bleeding coffins."

Selena switched off her phone and allowed a slow evil grin to spread across her face. She quickly googled the Ferry timetable. Friday had 08:00 and 17:00 arrivals from Kefalonia. Just to be on the safe side, she checked the sky-hopper timetable and made a note of the times. Come Friday, her ladies, equipped with cameras would be watching every possible entrance back into Zakynthos. If she could get photographic evidence that Helen Hardy had left the island before her thirty days were up, then the sanctimonious madam would have to forfeit her inheritance. Rubbing her hands gleefully and confident she was the one Madeline had named, she mentally started planning what she would do with the wonderful Kalvos estate. Without a doubt, she thought, the very first thing would be to get rid of those disgusting, filthy dogs up at the feeding station. She shuddered at the thought of that huge and horrible Teddy that guarded them all. A bit of poison on some meat would soon sort that problem out; she could always blame it on someone jealous of her inheritance.

CHAPTER 17
SWEET NOTHINGS

Helen crossed her fingers on both hands and wished she had the ability to cross her toes too. Dr. Marouda finished unwrapping the bandage and removed the thick dressing.

"Bravo Helen" he beamed delightedly and patted her arm "Is healed, I take out stitches now…yes?"

Helen let out a huge sigh of relief and nodded, not caring a jot if it hurt. She settled back and let the kindly doctor do his work. She mulled over the last blissful week. She and Markos had settled into a comfortable daily routine of looking after the puppies and kittens and sharing long lazy lunches and delicious evening meals together. Dotty had made one attempt to drive herself down to Tsilivi to meet with her team. After three hours of being horribly lost and a dozen frantic phone calls to Markos had admitted defeat and hired a couple of cars so her team could drive up and down to Madeline's villa to meet with her and plan the photo shoot. Helen had spent many hours idling by the pool while she babysat an excited Brooke. After a couple of days of Carly and Dotty working frantically on Dotty's mysterious new project, Christos, who had long forgotten his crush on Dotty and was besotted with Brooke's gorgeous mum, persuaded Markos to open up one of the little guest villas and let Carly and Brook move in.

Brooke was an absolute delight; her cheeky manner had them laughing all day, and her total love of the puppies and kittens had helped Helen with the daily feeding and cleaning routines. Markos had driven them the short journey down to Gerakas beach and shown them around the Earth, Sea and Sky Turtle Rescue Centre. Helen and Brooke were both fascinated by the work the group did to save the famous turtles. Seeing the long wooden green ramp that led down to the beach, Helen had opted to enjoy a frappe in the large tavern at the top and let Markos take Brooke down to the beach to look at the little wooden structures that protected the Turtles nests. Helen had whiled away the time watching the little Swifts that flew in and out of their small nests that were built under the thatched roof of the taverna. Later that evening she'd commented to Markos how odd she thought it was that a nation, so quick to dump their dogs and cats, showed such indifference to the birds nesting in their restaurants. Markos had laughed and joked that the Greek's were just too lazy to remove the nests.

"Ouch," Helen bit her lip in pain as Dr. Marouda tugged at a particularly tight stitch.

"Sorry," the doctor muttered and sat back on his haunches to give Helen a breather or two. "Ready?" he asked a couple of minutes later and bent back over her leg.

Helen tried to concentrate on something else and thought back to the previous night when after days of Dotty prodding and probing Markos had finally opened up and told them about Christos' mother, Amelia.

A young and newly qualified Markos had fallen in love with the beautiful young backpacker the minute he'd spotted her picking the olives. A whirlwind romance had followed and discovering she was pregnant Markos had done the honourable thing and married her. Four years later Amelia was disillusioned with life. Believing she had signed up for a lifetime of fun, laughter and happiness in the sun she was instead stuck indoors with a young child and a husband who spent too many long hours working in his clinic. Madeline had offered to look after Christos for a few hours a week and encouraged the young girl to get a part time job.

Amelia had found employment in one of the restaurants opposite the port in Zante town. She would watch the luxurious yachts glide in and out of the dockside and dream of a better life. She flirted outrageously with the young and sometimes older and filthy rich men that whiled away their days idyllically hopping from one Greek island to another.

One afternoon Madeline had rung Markos to ask if Amelia was ill as she hadn't dropped Christos off and Markos had raced home to find his wife and son gone. A brief note left on the kitchen table had informed Markos that Amelia had fallen in love with a Sebastian Mandeville and had taken Christos back to England.

Markos had gone on to tell Helen and Dotty how he had travelled to England and tracked Amelia and Christos to the small town of Henley on Thames. A bitter court battle had followed, and Markos had been left with access during the school holidays only. His utter disgust and anger when Amelia and her new husband had packed

Christos off to boarding school at a young age were still very much obvious on Markos' face as he'd told them the story.

"There…done…finished" said Dr. Marouda, pleased with himself and Helen for laying so still.

Helen looked down at the long ugly scar that ran from the top of her thigh to her knee. She ran her fingers down the bumpy ridge and felt the few hollowed out dips where the infection had burst open the stitches. Gingerly taking a few steps she felt no soreness just a weakness caused by not using her leg for a couple of weeks. A few lengths of the pool each morning would soon sort that she thought. Clasping the smiling doctor's hands, she thanked him profusely and when he refused any payment she promised to invite him and his wife for dinner very soon.

The villa was eerily quiet; Markos had gone up to the feeding station to worm, and flea treat all the dogs and being Saturday, Dotty had given her team the weekend off and joined Carly, Christos, and Brooke on a trip to the Tsilivi Waterpark. They had all agreed to meet up at the wonderful Wine and Roses restaurant later that evening.

Realising she could finally swim, Helen checked on the puppies and kittens and finding them all asleep she changed into a bikini and headed towards the pool. Apart from the weakness causing a slight limp she marvelled at the freedom she felt as she walked past the barn and into the pool area. The midday sun was burning brightly, and she raised one of the parasols and threw her towel down on a sun lounger. Dipping her toes in the cold water, she shrieked to herself and giggling, sat on the edge dangling her legs in. Helen had never been able to work out if it was better to edge oneself into the cold water slowly or to dive straight in. Telling herself to be brave she took the plunge and dived off the side. Gasping in shock at the cold, she marvelled at Brooke's ability to spend so much time in the pool. Once her body had grown accustomed to the temperature, she stopped shivering and started swimming up and down the length of the pool. A strong swimmer she easily powered her way through the water and had soon completed thirty lengths. Aware of an ache in her leg she eased herself to a stop and rolled onto her back floating peacefully in the soothing water.

Markos had got back to the villa to find Helen missing, seeing her crutches leaning against the wall an irrational fear spread through him. Shaking his head, he told himself not to be so stupid; Helen knew Dr Marouda was due later that day so she wouldn't have gone far. Double checking each room and the balcony he wondered if Peggy or Lily had popped up and taken her out for coffee. Feeling hot and sweaty after cleaning up the feeding station he decided to have a quick shower then go for a quick swim.

Helen moved to the side of the pool and deep in thought, leant her elbows on the tiled edge. Despite the blissful week, she was battling internally with the emotions that were coursing through her body. If anybody had asked her thirty odd years ago what her ideal man would be like she would have described Markos to a tee. Strong, handsome, kind and compassionate. She knew she was in love, her heart flipped over every time he walked into a room and smiled at her. She longed achingly to give into her feelings and wondered how different her life would or could have been if her Aunt had been brave enough to ask Markos to look for her when they were both at university in London. Her head was filled with guilt; she imagined the faces of her children and Papa if she told them she had fallen in love so soon after Williams's death. James was so laid back he would probably give her a hug and tell her to "go for it" but her hot-headed daughter Annabelle would be livid. She had adored her father and would expect her mother to remain a loyal widow for the rest of her life. Papa, she thought, would wish her well but be deeply saddened by her disloyalty to his son. She had truly loved William, but it was a very different kind of love. How was that possible, she thought, to love two men in such different ways? Her love for William had grown over a long slow courtship; he had never really proposed to her they just seemed to have an unspoken agreement that after university they would marry and settle down to a long happy life. If she was truly honest with herself, she had never felt the flutters of excitement she felt now nor had she ever before shivered with lust as she did in the dark of the night when she lay in bed thinking of Markos. She blushed with embarrassment at her shameless thoughts and wondered if she should confide in Dotty. She didn't always take Dotty's advice but sometimes her best friend could offer her some very wise words.

Markos flung his towel over his shoulder and grabbed a bottle of water from the fridge; he'd rung both Lily and Peggy and had got increasingly worried when both said they hadn't seen Helen. She'd started to wander around without her crutches the last couple of days, and he was worried she'd gone for a walk and got herself lost. He didn't want to appear too controlling though and talked himself into having a quick dip before he went looking.

Rounding the corner of the barn, he spotted Helen deep in thought at the edge of the pool; she was swaying her legs slowly through the water behind her, and he stared, confused at her unbandaged leg. He was so muddled and frustrated at the different signals she had been giving off all week; he didn't think he would ever understand what went through a female's mind. She had happily allowed him to carry her when needed and sat quite comfortably next to him each evening. As soon as he tried to get too close though she would put up an invisible barrier and quickly back off. He didn't know how much longer he could take the flood of emotions he was trying to deal with. He had even secretly looked into selling up and moving over to England when and if Helen chose not to stay on the island.

Helen was starting to shiver and turning to lift herself onto the side she saw Markos watching her. She breathed deeply as clad only in a short pair of swimming shorts his rippling muscles and tanned body were setting off another tingling feeling down below. She desperately wanted to run her fingers through the dark hair on his chest. Dropping her head, she was very aware of the ugly scar running down her leg and wished she could reach her towel to hide it. Mentally she was shocked by this wish; she had never in her life been even remotely bothered by how she appeared to others.

"Helen, your leg, is it healed?" Markos asked as he walked around the pool to join her.

"Yes, Dr. Marouda was early, he took out all the stitches, and I couldn't wait a minute longer to get in the pool" she laughed and tried to lay her arm across her leg hiding the horrible mess.

"What a beautiful scar" smiled Markos, recognising her embarrassment "That's certainly one you should wear with pride considering what you went through to earn it. Now are you getting in or out?"

"Well I was getting out, but I think I was warmer in the water" she laughed

"Best get back in then," said Markos and with a quick shove, he pushed her back in the pool and dived in behind her

"Oh you beast" Helen squealed and placing both hands on Markos' head she ducked him under the water and valiantly tried to hold him down. Far too strong for her Markos burst up out of the water and grabbed her round the waist, he lifted her high above his head and threatened to launch her across the pool. Helen screeched with laughter and threw her legs around his waist to stop him. With her hands on his shoulders, Helen looked down into his gorgeous smiling face and with every instinct in her body telling her to kiss him she flung all thoughts of Annabelle, Papa and anyone else out of her head and lowered her lips to his.

"Christ" breathed Markos into her neck as he clutched Helen tightly to him "Christ Helen" He ran his hands along the legs that were still wrapped around him and felt himself harden with excitement. Helen, feeling his pleasure arched her back and groaned. Not wanting to let go of this woman for even a second Markos carried her to the shallow end of the pool and climbed the steps. Opening the door of one of the beach huts, he gently laid her on the floor and lowered himself beside her. He ran his fingers over her tanned stomach and dropped butterfly kisses on her shoulder and down across her breasts. Helen moaned and ran her fingers through his hair, clutching the back of his head she pulled his mouth towards hers and pressed her body firmly against him. Markos leant up on one elbow and lazily ran a finger over her lips. He trailed it down her neck and eased it under one of her bikini straps, sliding it off her shoulder. He stopped and looked deep into her eyes.

"Are you sure?" he whispered softly.

"No I'm not" trembled Helen "but I've spent my whole life doing what everyone expected me to do, and it's about time I did what I wanted to do."

A while later they lay, content, in each other's arms. Expecting guilt and shame to be flooding through her body Helen only felt pleasure and a peacefulness she'd not felt for a long time. They both laughed as a yapping and scratching came from the door and Puddles attempted to push his nose under a small gap at the bottom.

"What do we do now?" asked Markos

"Get dressed...maybe"

"No, I mean do we tell our friends...do we keep this to ourselves? Half the island thinks I'm having an affair with Dotty" He grinned wryly at the thought.

"Well" Helen sat herself up and pulled her knees to her chest "If we were a lot younger, we would currently be updating our Facebook and Twitter statuses to *"in a relationship"* then every thirty seconds we would be checking to see how many of our friends have congratulated us."

"Thank God I don't do Facebook" he laughed "the clinic has a page and…" Markos raised his eyes at Helen "if you have a page nobody has managed to find it yet."

"Hah, that's because they're not looking for Hellie Castle."

"Hellie Castle" he laughed. "Sounds like a haunted village in deepest darkest Devon."

"I could never risk my students finding my Facebook, some of the pictures of Dotty and me are not what they would expect their serious teacher to be getting up to."

"You are a teacher?" Markos was shocked to realise how little he knew about Helen

"Was" murmured Helen, "I took early retirement when William died."

Seeing a look of sadness cross her face and feeling a hot stab of jealousy Markos grabbed both her hands and pulled her up.

"Fancy skinny dipping" He winked.

Alf pulled up outside Madeline's villa and sighed. He was sure Helen was fine but when Markos hadn't rung back to say he'd found her Peggy had got herself into a right old tizzy and insisted Alf go and help look. He wandered into the villa and took a quick look in all the rooms. Back outside he heard a splashing and laughter coming from the pool and ambled over towards the big barn. A huge grin spread across his face as he rounded the corner and spotted Helen and Markos, locked in a passionate embrace, in the deep end of the pool. "About bleeding time," he thought to himself and quietly turned back to his car "wait till I tell Peggy."

Markos groaned as he saw the dozens of missed calls from Peggy and Lily on his phone. He quickly sent them both messages to say Helen was fine and carried the carafe of coffee out to the balcony. Helen was curled up in her favourite wicker chair feeding Smudge.

"I think we might try the pups on a bit of solid food tomorrow, Helen, then get Peggy and Alf to get their photo's up on social media and find them some homes."

"I wonder if my friend Molly would want one" Helen replied,

"She was talking about getting another rescue dog" Helen wandered over to the playpen and put Smudge back. She chuckled as the sleepy pup with a belly full of milk shoved himself into the heap of sleeping kittens, yawned and fell instantly asleep. "Molly and Ian are my neighbours" she explained as she wandered back out "They might even take a kitten, buy one get one free" she laughed.

Markos reached for Helens hand and pulled her into his lap. She nestled her head against his shoulder and sighed contentedly. For the first time since her plane had landed at the airport, her thoughts were turning to the possibility of spending the rest of her life here. Feeling Markos kissing the top of her head she smiled and pushed herself off his lap.

"I think it's about time you showed me what's in that barn" She grinned and pulled him up. Handed him his coffee and grabbing her own she told Puddles to look after the babies and set off for the barn.

"Oh, I didn't expect that" When Markos opened the large barn doors and flicked on a light switch. Helen had expected to see a huge open space. Instead, there was a narrow central corridor with a series of doors each side. Markos opened the first door on the left and with a flourish waved Helen through the door. She found herself in a spacious fully equipped kitchen. Sunlight streamed through the skylight and highlighted the layers of dust settled on the worktops and utensils. She frowned at Markos, but he placed a finger against her lips and led her to the door opposite the kitchen. Inside was a large lounge. Old but comfy looking sofas and armchairs were dotted around a central coffee table made from her aunt's favoured driftwood. A large television was mounted on the far wall, and a bookshelf full of books and DVD's was placed in one of the corners. Still not explaining Markos led her down the corridor and opening more doors showed her several bedrooms. Some were single, others housed bunk beds. Although very basic they all had storage space and enough room for a comfortable stay. Behind one of the doors was a bathroom with shower and toilet. Still not explaining Markos led her to the very end of the corridor and opened the final door.

"Goodness" breathed Helen "Is this some sort of operating theatre?"

"Well done" laughed Markos "It's a small veterinary clinic, your aunt set this whole thing up many years ago. She would take gap year veterinary and veterinary nursing students here for weeks or even months at a time. They would gain valuable experience volunteering with the dogs and cats. Under supervision, they would round up mostly female but a few male, dogs and cats and sterilise them. They also treated many of the cuts, broken bones, and illnesses that our strays end up with. Your aunt would provide free lodgings for the volunteers, and they had plenty of free time to enjoy the island."

"Her life's work" Helen murmured so quietly that Markos struggled to hear.

"Sorry?"

"Her life's work," Helen said a bit louder "The letters my aunt wrote mentioned her life's work…I've been struggling to work it out…this is it, isn't it?" Helen looked at Markos her eyes shining with wonder "The strays, the feeding station…this…this wonderful volunteer centre. It's her life's work…and the little holiday villas Markos, did she use the income from them to fund all this?"

"Probably" Markos agreed "Helen, I don't know anything about your aunt's finances. Everything was sent over to the solicitors in London…Boston, Boston and something?" Helen nodded, and Markos continued. "I am just a…err…I can't think of the English word…err…someone who looks after estates?"

"Manager? Caretaker?" suggested Helen

"Yes, a caretaker…thank you…I am the caretaker; I send any bills that arrive off to London, and the solicitor pays them out of an executor's account. I don't fully understand it all. The small villas and the barn were closed up a couple of years ago when Madeline could no longer manage, but everything else has just carried on, the food for the dogs is still delivered, the swimming pool man comes once a week to clean it…" Markos shrugged his shoulders and put an arm round Helen "She knew she was going to die and arranged everything" Markos felt a lump forming in his throat as he thought of the day Madeline died. "She made me promise to look after you; she knew you would come" He dashed away the tears tumbling down his cheeks and smiled ruefully at Helen.

"You kept your promise Markos…you've looked after me better than you could ever realise" She reached up on tiptoes and kissed him gently.

Wandering hand in hand back to the Villa Markos pointed out another small track that led off to the right of the olive groves. "I'll take you up there when your leg is strong enough. The views are beautiful."

Puddles greeted them ecstatically, checking the playpen Helen groaned

"Oh, Puddles what have you done? Where are the babies?" Puddles thumped his tail happily and cocked his head to one side "Show me?" Helen instructed and followed Puddles into Dotty's room. Over the last couple of days, Puddles had taken it upon himself to "rescue" the babies from the playpen and place them somewhere else. "Well I can't see them, give me a clue" Helen laughed as the silly dog crouched himself down and wriggled under the bed. Helen lay on the floor and realising she couldn't reach them she shouted for Markos to help.

"I think we'll take Puddles with us when we go out" suggested Markos "Maybe we can leave him at Lily's with Fudge, if he puts the pups or kittens on the bed they could hurt themselves falling off."

"Okay, what time are we leaving?" Markos looked at his watch

"If we leave in the next hour we'll have time to visit Bethany's or…" he winked "we could have a "siesta" and leave in a couple of hours.

"Let's visit Bethany tomorrow" Helen laughed and led Markos to her bedroom.

CHAPTER 18
WINE AND ROSES

Markos was struggling to keep his hands off Helen as they drove down the long coastal road towards Zante Town. With one hand on the steering wheel and one arm around Helens shoulders he was glad he drove an automatic and didn't have to change gear. They both felt like teenagers in the first flush of love. Slowing down as they reached the small bridge over the Smelly River Helen looked at the huge ferries docked in the port and the luxury yachts moored in the harbour and thought of Markos' ex-wife Amelia. Did he still have feelings for her, she wondered? Driving over the bridge, Markos swung a hard left and bypassed the busy town.

Pulling up at a busy junction, a small, filthy child no older than five darted between the cars and tapped on Helens window; she held out her hand begging for money.

"Look straight ahead Helen and ignore her" instructed Markos. Helen held her hand against her mouth in shock.

"Markos, she's tiny, can't we help?"

"No" Markos sounded quite stern "They are gypsies, is that the right English word? If people give money, it only encourages them to keep on doing it."

Helen knew he was right but still felt sorry for the little girl and angry at the adults that probably made her dodge the traffic every day.

"We call them travellers now in England" she explained, "Gypsy is considered offensive and not politically correct."

"Ahh, political correctness hasn't fully reached the Greek islands yet" grinned Markos wryly.

Reaching Tsilivi, Helen moved away from Markos; they had both agreed to keep their secret, for a while at least. Markos' phone rang and switching it to the speaker they both heard Lily's voice.

"Markos, Helen…" Lily was speaking in hushed tones "Not sure how far away you are but don't come to the hotel. Selena and Mavra have turned up and have made themselves at home in the bar."

"Christ that's all we need" groaned Helen

"Take Puddles down to Alexander and Georgios will meet you, everyone is going to leave in dribs and drabs, and we'll meet you at Wine and Roses in a while."

Markos swung the truck down a small side road and headed towards the sea. Slowing down to let one of the horse and carriages pass them he pointed to the right.

"Menir restaurant, I will take you there one evening" Helen smiled with delight at the pretty restaurant, a live Greek band was playing in the corner, and every table was filled with smiling chattering holidaymakers. A waiter smiled and waved at them, and Helen waved back. Reaching the end of the road, Markos turned left and drove along the sea front. He stopped at a tiny marina full of small fishing boats and jumping out walked round to open the door for Helen. A large speed boat was tied up and bobbed gently on the tidal waves. It had rows of seats and was unlike any of the other boats

"That is Captain Spiros' boat *'The best trip on the island'* Markos laughed. "Seriously though it is the best boat trip to do, that boat skips across the water so fast that you get there much quicker than the large boats. Captain Spiros is so knowledgeable about the island and the environment. He will even stop the boat to pick up rubbish from the sea and tell anyone off who dares to disturb the turtle's nests."

"Maybe Brooke would like a trip" suggested Helen "Shall we offer to take her…Oh I forgot…your week off is nearly over" Helen pulled a wry smile, she would miss having Markos around.

"I've decided to take the next two weeks off." Markos hugged Helen tight and dropped a kiss on her head "The whole idea of Christos becoming a junior partner was to give me more time off, it's about time I let him take the reins for a while."

Moving away from the boats, Markos led Helen round the end of the cliff.

"Oh how pretty!" Helen exclaimed. A wooden boardwalk led them around the edge of a small bay. Lanterns were embedded into the cliff and with the sun going down, lit their way. Markos stopped and pointed to a large island looming out of the sea. Helen shivered, the island was shrouded in mist and looked dark and ominous.

"Kefalonia," said Markos

"Really? It looks so close" Helen thought of Captain Corelli and his Mandolin, one of her favourite books.

Puddles suddenly barked and bounded off into the dusk and Markos reassured Helen that he would come back.

"He's probably smelt Fudge" he laughed. They had reached the large hotel that was built into the cliff. The wooden boardwalk led onto a large decked area and a grey floating pontoon undulated in the waves.

"It's beautiful here" Helen sat down at one of the wooden picnic tables and cocked her head, convinced she had just heard a duck, yes, there it was again, a distinctive quacking. Markos laughed as she looked under the table and saw three Mallard ducks pecking in the sand.

"Well, I never!" said Helen laughing along. She reached across the table and took Markos' hands. "I'm certainly enjoying living in the moment" she smiled "seems there's a surprise round every corner."

"Hmm" agreed Markos reaching forward and pushing a lock of her hair off her face "me too it's going to be difficult tonight pretending we are just friends" The ducks squawked and waddled out from under the table as Puddles and Fudge hurled themselves happily against Helens legs. Markos let go of Helens hands and winked "maybe we can play footsie under the table."

"Are you sure it was Helen and Markos?" asked Peggy for the hundredth time.

"Yes, I saw them with me own bleeding eyes, they were in the pool and were wrapped right around each other snogging their faces off." Alf sighed, wondering how many times he was going to have to repeat himself before Peggy believed him.

"Well you just remember what I said, we don't tell anyone, not even Lily. If this gets out, gawd knows what Selena and her gang will do."

The little poolside bar at Lily's hotel was heaving; laughter rang around the tables, and Elias and his brother were rushed off their feet serving drinks to the rowdy crowd. Lily was sat on a barstool keeping a close eye on Selena and Mavra. They were both bristling with disapproval at the near the knuckle jokes that were being bantered back and forth between the tables. Dotty had worked her team hard for the past week, and they were relishing the chance to let their hair down and have some fun. Most of them were heading off to Laganas later for a night of clubbing on the popular strip. Spotting Georgios sneaking Puddles and Fudge along the road and through the back of the hotel Lily yawned loudly and stretched her arms high above her head.

"Oh excuse me," she said "I'm going to head off home and have an early night," she said to her mum and dad loudly enough for Selena and Mavra to hear. She walked over and kissed Maggie and George goodnight.

"Night love," said Maggie "Me and your dad are going to pop down the town we'll probably grab a take away from the chippie on the way back and have an early night too" Lily waved and wandered slowly up the steps. Reaching the top, instead of carrying on up the hill, she ducked down behind the fir trees and watched as her mum and dad waved cheerio and headed out of the hotel. Exactly as Lily guessed she would, Selena pulled out her phone and tapped away quickly. Lily shook her head, tutted and pulled out her own phone.

"It's just as I thought Mum, as soon as you left Selena messaged someone. Can you see anyone following you?"

Maggie looked behind her but just saw lots of tourists wandering slowly down the cobbled paths.

"I don't know Lily; I can't tell."

"Okay, head down to the Two Brothers and have a drink, if anyone's following you they will probably sit at a nearby table" Lily ended the phone call and walked up the hill. She tapped on Dotty's door and when Dotty answered she went in, took the offered glass of wine, and they both settled on the balcony. Five minutes after Lily had made a second phone call they both laughed as Dimitri fired up his little moped and with a terrified Georgios clinging on started racing up and down the steep hill, occasionally he pulled onto the road and drove past the front of the hotel beeping and waving at everyone. Watching through her binoculars, Dotty laughed at Selena and Mavra, both with their hands over their ears and obviously disgusted at the twin's behaviour. After ten minutes Lily stood up.

"Ready?" she asked Dotty.

"Oh absolutely, I can't wait" squeaked an excited Dotty.

The ladies ran to the top of the hill and waited for Dimitris to pull his little moped up beside them. Kissing the twins gratefully Lily grabbed their helmets and gave one to Dotty.

"Oh let me drive it…please" Dotty begged

"No way," said Lily "Get on the back and hold on tight, it's a bloody long time since I drove one of these" Dimitri and Georgios waved them off, one hoping that Selena didn't notice the switch and the other praying that his beloved moped would come back in one piece.

Maggie and George settled themselves on the sofa and laughed as one of the brothers started blowing a whistle and chucking serviettes all over their customers. The music was turned up, and the whole bar joined in the old John Denver song *"Take me home, country road, to the place I belong, West Virginia"* Maggie swung her arms above her head and sang at the top of her voice, she'd always loved a good old sing song. As the song came to an end, a man settled himself opposite them.

"Philip!" greeted George, shaking the man's hand "Not seen you for a while" Selena's husband smiled wearily and ordered a beer from the hovering waiter.

"I'm under strict instructions to follow you wherever you go tonight and report back to the missus" Philip sighed "I was hoping you'd head down to Kaliva so I could watch the footie."

George guffawed loudly; he had met Philip many years ago after they'd both sneaked off to watch football and they often met up to watch and discuss the matches over a pint or two.

"We guessed she was up to something," said Maggie "Why have you got to follow us?"

"To see if you meet up with Ms. Boothroyd or Helen, look she's even given me a little notebook to write it all down" He showed them a reporter's notebook with a pen threaded through the spiral top. "She had her minions posted at the airport, and the port in town all day yesterday waiting to catch them coming back from Kefalonia" Philip shook his head "They all had cameras with telescopic lenses and little flasks and lunchboxes" Philip chuckled with a wicked glint in his eye. "She sent me up to St Nicholas Port."

"And did you stay there all day?" George grinned

"I didn't even go, I sneaked my fishing rods out and spent a lovely day down at Alexander Beach fishing off the rocks" Maggie and George burst out laughing, and George reached over and shook his hand again.

"Philip, how you put up with your wife I just don't know, but you have my greatest sympathy and respect. Now we are heading up to

Wine and Roses for dinner with our Lily, Dotty, Helen, and Markos. I think Christos may be joining us too; now you know where we are going you might as well head off to Kaliva and watch the footie."

"Hang on," said Philip. He picked up his phone and rang his wife. "Selena…yes dear…of course dear… but…Selena, will you let me get a word in edgeways" Philip sighed and held the phone a few inches from his ear. "Selena listen, I've just overheard Lily's mum and dad calling a taxi to take them to Kalamaki, they are meeting that Ms. Boothroyd and Helen at some restaurant there…no dear, I didn't catch the name of the restaurant…yes dear, I know I need to get my ears syringed" Philip put his phone back in his pocket and winked at Maggie and George "That should keep them all busy for a while, how many restaurants are there in Kalamaki?"

Markos and Helen crossed the road and climbed the few steps up to the lovely Wine and Roses restaurant. A very pretty and petite blonde woman greeted them with a kiss on both cheeks, she showed them to a table where Peggy and Alf were already sat browsing through a large menu.

"Helen, no crutches" Peggy clapped her hands with pleasure. Helen took a seat next to her and slid up her skirt to show Peggy the gruesome scar.

"Dr. Marouda took the stitches out today, no more antibiotics and no more painkillers, I even managed a swim today, it was wonderful" Helen frowned as Alf spluttered and coughed into a serviette. Peggy kicked her husband under the table and patted Helen's hand.

"That's wonderful dear; now I have no idea where the others have got to."

"Lily's having a few problems at the hotel, Selena and Mavra have parked their bums at the bar and are watching her every movement" Markos explained how they had met Georgios at the beach. "I think they are trying to work out a way to get everyone here."

"Well Jacob and Suzanne are having a romantic evening bottle feeding the new arrivals" laughed Peggy. "But Christos, Carly, and Brooke are on their way" said Peggy "and Markos I have a feeling you are going to be mending a broken heart when Carly goes home, your Christos is head over heels in love."

He's not the only one thought Markos.

A moped screeched to a halt outside the restaurant, and two figures jumped off, to the delight of the customers inside they took off their helmets, slowly shook out their hair and pulled off a pretty good impression of two of the Charlies Angels. Bowing theatrically, to a round of applause, Lily and Dotty trotted up the steps and hugged the petite blonde lady. Maggie and George, who weren't far behind quickly joined them and soon had the whole table in fits of laughter as they told them what Selena's husband had done.

"Oh dear" giggled Helen "I can just imagine them all hunting round Kalamaki."

"He should have sent them to Laganas," said Markos "I'd pay good money to see Selena working her way down the strip with all those stag and hen parties."

"Who's having a stag party?" shouted Christos who was walking towards the restaurant's side entrance with Brooke balanced on his shoulders and one arm slung loosely around a beaming Carly.

"Never mind" grinned Markos "hurry up and sit down, I'm starving," Brooke asked if she could have a look in the shop next door and Carly had a quick look at the menu, chose their food and taking Brooke's hand wandered off.

With the food ordered and drinks in hand conversation turned to the photo shoot.

"We start shooting down in Keri Lake Monday morning" explained Dotty "and..." Dotty paused dramatically and waited till there was complete silence around the table "I have picked Mavra as my first model." Everyone but Helen was shocked at this news.

"Helen you don't seem surprised at all, did you know?" asked Lily.

"Oh no, but I do know that Dotty likes to keep her friends close and her enemies even closer" explained Helen "You watch your back though Dotty, from what Nora was saying Mavra's got her evil claws firmly poised to scratch your pretty eyes out."

"Talking of evil...look" whispered Dotty with a genuine shudder. A scruffy old man was sidling towards Carly and Brooke, who had just reappeared outside the shop next door. The man was dressed in dirty clothes and a shabby khaki waistcoat. In one hand he held a bunch of colourful, helium-filled balloons shaped in popular cartoon characters. His waistcoat pockets were filled with a multitude of light-up spinners and whirling toys. He walked straight up to Brooke and shoved one of the lights into her hand, pressing the button a bunch of fibre optics started spinning round reflecting lights across the ceiling. The man grinned, and Brooke reared back, terrified. With a few teeth missing his manic grin was evil and probably the cause of many a child's nightmares. The man shoved his hand out towards a shaking Carly and demanded two euros for the toy. Markos and Christos both jumped up and ran out the restaurant. Christos took the toy and shoved it back at the man and Markos dismissed him with an angry word. The man turned nasty, and a torrent of abuse poured from his filthy mouth, and a repulsive spray of spittle rained out through the toothless gaps. Markos firmly chased the man away from the restaurant and reassuring Brooke they returned to the table

. "Street…er…traveller" Markos looked at Helen "Like the girl."

Helen nodded and told the others of the little girl at the junction in town. With peace restored and Brooke placated the table turned to a smartly dressed and smiling man who was wheeling a trolley towards them.

"Lamb Kleftiko" he declared and with a flourish poured brandy over a foil-wrapped parcel on the table. Whipping out a lighter he set fire to the foil and enjoyed the oohs and ahhs as, using tongs, he waved the parcel back and forward through the flames. The blonde woman held up her phone and clicked away, taking selfies of herself with everyone around the table. She tapped her cheek, insisting the men give her a friendly kiss and encouraged them all to get their phones out and pointed out the Wi-Fi code and Facebook page. Dotty eyed her up and down making a mental note to ask her if she'd be interested in modelling for her.

A good two hours later everyone was groaning, their stomachs overfull with the delicious and incredibly large platefuls of food and complimentary desserts. Asking for the bill they laughed as complimentary shots of liquor were brought over to their table.

"Dad?" Christos stood behind his father and put his arms round his neck, giving him a hug. "will you take my car and give Dotty and Brooke a lift back later. I'm going to take Carly into Laganas for a couple of hours." Markos patted his son's hand, it was nice to see him having fun. A slow smile hovered over his lips as an idea popped into his head.

"Son," he said "I'll gladly swap cars, take Dotty and Brooke back and even help babysit Brooke if you take over the judging at the dog show next weekend" everyone laughed at the comical crestfallen look on Christos' face."

"You old rogue dad," he said "you conniving old rogue."

Seeing the seat next to Helen vacant Markos moved around the table and sat down. Leaning across Helen, he started a conversation with Peggy about the progress of the puppies. Under the table, he secretly clasped Helens hand and softly ran his thumb back and forward across her palm.

"Is the dog show that bad then?" asked Dotty "I've agreed to judge the Waggiest Tail."

"On a positive note Dotty, next week you will be inundated with all manner of home-made bribes. There will be cakes, biscuits, sweets and even flowers delivered. And as everyone thinks you're still at our hotel I will have quite a feast" giggled Lily licking her lips "but the week after that everyone but the winner will hate your guts and slag you off over Facebook and Twitter."

"How exciting," said Dotty, who always loved a good Facebook war.

Reaching into her handbag for her share of the bill Lily spotted the three postcards.

"Helen, I forgot, these arrived for you today" She handed Helen the cards, the top one had a pretty picture of the Eiffel Tower lit up at night.

"For me, how odd," flipping the first card over she smiled "Dotty it's from Gerald."

Hi Helen and of course Dotty

I got your voicemail, I'm taking a long earned break and backpacking through Europe, Well, I'm driving my car and stopping in hotels so not quite the backpacking of our university days but still having a wonderful time. If I ever get a good signal, I'll give you a ring.

Speak soon and best wishes
Gerald.

The next two postcards were from Switzerland and Italy and written in a similar jolly tone.

"Thank goodness," said Helen "I was starting to worry about him."

"Who is Gerald?" asked Markos, trying to keep the curt tone out of his voice but very aware he was bristling with a jealous curiosity.

"Gerald was my husband's best friend" explained Helen. "We were worried as Molly, my neighbour, thought he was having some sort of breakdown, seems he's just gone off on a trip."

"Actually" interrupted Dotty with a glint in her eye "He was Helens friend first, in fact, she was courting Gerald when he introduced her to William, she broke the poor man's heart."

"Hardly courting" argued Helen "we had only been on a couple of friendly dates, and we were only eighteen for god's sake." She frowned as she felt Markos snatch his hand away from hers and light up one of Peggy's cigarettes.

Dotty sensing a strange atmosphere turned to Brooke and asked if she wanted to go and look in the shops before they went home. Bored of shopping Brooke threw her arms round Markos; she asked if he'd take her in the Luna Fun Park. Realising he was being both churlish and childish he ruffled Brookes' hair and nodded, smiling at Helen and Dotty he winked.

"Let's go and win a few teddies from the grabbing machine ladies."

A couple of hours later, with Brooke tucked up in a spare bed and Markos gone off for a last check at the feeding station, Helen and Dotty were curled up on the sofa with mugs of hot chocolate. Helen was struggling to keep her eyes open. The large carafes of village wine she had shared were now resulting in a deliciously warm and fuzzy light-headedness.

"Good day then?" asked Dotty biting her lip as she scrutinised her friend.

"Hmm" murmured Helen.

"Good in bed then, is he?"

"Hmm…what!" Helen jerked upright, spilling hot chocolate down her dressing gown. She glared at Dotty, who was raising her eyebrows at her.

"Give over Helen; I've know you my whole life and I damn sure recognise that post-coital sparkle in your eye."

"Haven't got a clue what you're talking about" Helen faked a shocked looked and mopped up the spilt hot chocolate.

"Well unless you and Dr. Marouda sneaked a quickie after he took your stitches out. I'm pretty sure you and Markos had a delightful afternoon" grinned Dotty, who knew her friend too well. She reached over and hugged Helen tight "I'm over the moon for you sweetie, it's about time you had a bit of fun in your life. Now I'm going to curl up with my book and leave you in peace, that way

Markos won't have to sneak into your room in the middle of the night" Dotty stood up and headed towards the door.

"Oh, Dotty" Helen called airily. "The answers yes."

"Yes?" said Dotty confused

"Yes…he's good in bed, very, very good in bed."

Dotty shrieked with laughter and left her friend to wait for the new man in her life to come back.

CHAPTER 19
A GEO WHAT?

Dotty carried the tray of tea and toast out onto the balcony and frowned as Helen rapidly closed the lid of her laptop and glanced round.

"Oh Dotty, it's you, I thought it was Markos."

"Keeping secrets already Helen" Dotty gave her a questioning look "That's not a very healthy start to a relationship."

"I know, your right but as much as my heart is willing me to live out the rest of my life in this idyllic place with a wonderful man, my very sensible brain is telling me to be careful" Helen opened her laptop back up and started typing. "I'm hoping Percival can answer a couple of questions for me."

"Such as?" Dotty asked

"Puddles for one" smiled Helen "Whatever happens and where ever I end up I want him with me but how do I claim legal ownership of a dog or is he officially part of my aunt's estate?" Helen laughed as Dotty shrugged her shoulders.

"And…what happens if, for instance, I decide to stay and then a few months or even a few years down the line I fall out with Markos and want to go home…do I still forfeit the estate?"

"If I remember rightly the codicil said you have to choose to live permanently on the island," said Dotty scrunching her face up in concentration "Did you ever actually read the thing?"

"No, Percival just told me…why?"

"Well," said Dotty, her brow furrowed "Don't you think the wording is a bit odd? Especially for a legal document. Anyone can "Choose" to do something but at a later date "Choose" to do something different…I'm probably not explaining myself properly…"

"No, you are, I get what you're saying," said Helen "any good lawyer could argue that the emphasis is on the choice I make after the thirty days, regardless of if I make a different choice a week later. I'll ask Percival to email me a copy…Madeline Kalvos, by all accounts, was a very astute woman. The codicil has got to be more specific than that."

"Maybe Markos has a copy," Dotty said

"Maybe I have a copy of what?" Markos walked in towelling dry his hair after a brisk morning swim.

"We were talking about the codicil" Dotty saw Helen shaking her head at her and quickly changed what she was going to say "I didn't realise Helen had never actually seen it" Helen mouthed a thank you at Dotty.

"I've got a copy in my office; we can pick it up on our way back from Bethany's" offered Markos "I don't think I read it properly myself" Markos snatched up a piece of Dotty's toast and laughing at her loud protests headed off to change.

"Bethany lives just outside a town called Katastari" Markos explained as they set off, a while later. They had left Dotty on a sun lounger, supervising Brooke in the pool and a very disgruntled Puddles sulking under the olive trees. When Markos told him he couldn't come he had tucked his tail between his legs and slunk off, throwing them both filthy looks.

"Markos," asked Helen, not sure how to approach the ownership of Puddles, she didn't want Markos to think she had already made a decision to go home. "Is there a way I could officially adopt Puddles? I'd hate anyone else to try and make a claim on him…I guess he did belong to someone before Madeline."

"Of course…I hadn't really thought about it" mulled Markos "but it's quite easy, you just need to go online and reregister his microchip under your name, we could always organise him a passport with you as his owner, can't get more official than that"

"A passport, do dogs have passports?" Helen had heard Peggy and Alf mention passports, but her drug addled brain, at the time, hadn't processed the information.

"Yes, back in 2001 some European Union countries introduced the pet travel scheme. The dogs…and cats, of course, …don't have to go into quarantine anymore, it's how we can rehome so many of our strays abroad."

"That's wonderful," said Helen "So how do we get this passport for Puddles?"

"I do it" laughed Markos "It's quite simple, the dogs have to be microchipped, they have to have a rabies vaccination at least three weeks before travelling, and one to three days before travelling need to have been treated for tapeworm, fleas and ticks."

Helen gazed out of the open window, allowing the breeze to cool her. There was so much more to rescuing and rehoming the strays than she had initially thought, but she was a quick learner, and she was thrilled that Puddles would soon be legally hers.

"Are they bee hives Markos?" Helen had noticed more and more of the wooden hives dotted haphazardly under the olive trees.

"Yes, Zakynthos produces an awful lot of honey" Markos glanced at Helen, smiling "You must have heard of Greek yoghurt and honey" Helen playfully slapped his arm and laughed at his sarcasm.

"My friends Molly and Ian produce their own honey. They started a market garden business a few years ago." Helen started giggling. "My husband had an allergy to bee stings and Dotty convinced him that if he ate lots of honey, he would be cured, He bought jars and jars of the stuff from Molly and had Honey on toast, honey cakes, honey and lemon drinks…after a couple of months, Dotty admitted she'd made it all up, and William was not amused" Markos laughed and confessed he could well imagine the irascible Dotty playing such a prank.

"This is Katastari" Markos announced as they pulled up near a magnificent church. The red, white and tan bricks formed a stunning chequered pattern. "Do you want to get out and have a look?"

"Definitely" Helen pulled out her phone and started snapping away. The two tall towers that stood either side of a pillared archway rose high above her. She walked backwards to try and fit it all in the tiny viewfinder and felt Markos grab her as she nearly stumbled over a small brick wall. Laughing she sat on the wall and looked around. A couple dressed in hiking gear nodded good morning, and Helen watched them closely, recognising the small yellow object clasped in the man's hand.

"No way," Helen said to herself. She stood up and watched as the couple reached a cobblestoned wall and glanced furtively around. Markos leant back on the wall and crossed his arms unsure why Helen was so interested in the strange couple who were now scrabbling about near the bottom of the wall. Helen sat back down next to him and kept one eye on the couple as she quickly opened an app on her phone.

"Hah, thought so…Markos do you have a pen on you" Markos wondered if Helen had started taking the painkillers again as she was acting so weirdly. He walked to his truck and pulled a pen from the dashboard, but Helen was already walking off towards the wall. The odd couple walked back past him, once again nodding. Markos nodded back and caught up with Helen, who was also now scrabbling at the bottom of the wall.

"Got it," she said and pulled a small Tupperware box from behind a loose stone. She opened the lid, and Markos watched, even more, confused as she took the pen and scribbled on a tiny piece of paper. Glancing around to check no-one was watching she replaced the box and quickly walked away.

"What was that?" Markos asked, thinking that maybe he was the one going mad.

"A Geocache"

"A Geo...what?"

"Geocaching, it's like a worldwide treasure hunt based on GPS coordinates" Helen was still playing with her phone "Goodness there's another one up there somewhere" Helen pointed higher up the mountains. "Is there another church up there?" she frowned scrolling rapidly through her phone."

"Helen, I don't have a clue what you're talking about" Markos sighed.

"Markos I'm so sorry" Helen always forgot that not everyone knew about one of her former favourite hobbies. She had started Geocaching a few years ago with William and Gerald and occasionally a reluctant Dotty. The excitement, which had been lost when William died, had suddenly reignited itself.

Markos started the car and drove out of Katastari, turning left he heard Helen squeal as they started to climb slowly up the steep and very narrow mountain road.

"You better explain all this Geocaching thing to me and point me in the right direction then." he laughed.

Twenty minutes later Helen was in her element; her Geocaching App had led them high into the mountain and right to the doorstep of the very old Agios Georgios Church. Peering high and low and turning over stones Markos was also having great fun.

"Helen, this is fantastic, I was born on Zakynthos, and I've never been up here. Look at those views" Helen agreed the views over Alykanas and Alykes were truly beautiful. She was secretly thrilled that Markos was still excitedly hunting. William and Gerald would never hunt for more than five minutes before logging a "DNF" *Did not find* and marching on to the next available Geocache.

"I think I've found it" yelled Markos from behind a wall. Helen stumbled across the stones and cheered as she saw Markos stood with another box in his hand. "What's all this?" he asked. The box was filled with small toys, ornaments, coins and a couple of items on keyrings.

"Aye aye captain, we be finding some treasure," Helen said in her best pirate's voice. "The idea is to swap things" she explained "so you take something you like and leave something in return. Those are travel bugs; they often have a target" she picked up a small car on a keyring and showed Markos the laminated note that was attached. "See this one is from Germany and is in a race with another one to see which travels the furthest in a year. They all have trackable codes…look…the idea is to pick the bug up and move it to another cache and log it online."

"Can we find some more?" asked Markos, back in the car and on the way to Bethany's. He had enjoyed the genuine pleasure and sparkle in Helen's eyes as she'd hunted around. He'd also enjoyed the long lingering kiss she'd bestowed on him when he found it.

"Maybe later" she laughed. They pulled up to a large pair of iron gates, and Markos reached out to press a buzzer. "Good grief" exclaimed Helen; it's like something out of Dallas.

"Hello, hello" Bethany walked out to meet them, and Helen bit back a gurgle of laughter. She was dressed in a casual pair of denim shorts and a plain white t-shirt but on her head was a tight 1970's style swimming hat complete with large colourful flowers. Her masses of curly red hair were tucked tightly underneath causing the hat to bulge out in various places. "Here you go" Bethany handed both Helen and Markos what appeared to be disposable plastic shower caps and insisted they put them on. Helen slid her eyes towards Markos, who with a perfectly straight face, slipped the cap over his head.

"Come on Helen, put it on…it stops the bats" he crossed his eyes and sucked in his cheeks making her laugh out loud.

"The bats?"

"Oh yes," said Bethany, "we're starting in the garage and Mummy never let me go in the garage without my swimming hat on, they can get tangled in your hair you know."

"Oh," said Helen, aiming a kick at Markos, who was still pulling faces.

"And if they get tangled in your hair, they might bite you and then you would turn into a vampire" continued Bethany, completely serious.

"Oh," said Helen again, unable to utter anything else. She followed Bethany into a huge and spotlessly clean garage and despite knowing that there was no way a bat was going to nest in there, found herself peering into the corners.

"These are the poorly ones" Bethany showed them the long rows of cages that housed many, many cats and kittens. Helen swallowed down the nauseous feeling that gagged in her throat as she saw the horrific wounds that some of the cats had, missing eyes and limbs and deep gashes and cuts. Markos took her hand as he spotted the tears starting to roll down her face. Moving through a small door at the back of the garage Helen smiled.

"The teenagers!" Bethany laughed as a cat leapt up on her shoulder and purred around her neck. Helen realised they were actually inside a huge netted enclosure, so big that trees were growing inside it. Everywhere she looked were cats, climbing trees, playing with toys and some just snoozing in the sun. Markos sat on a small stone bench and within seconds had cats clambering all over him. Helen couldn't get over how clean everything was. Large litter trays were dotted everywhere, but most were spotlessly clean with fresh litter. Bethany continued to lead them around her cat haven. She showed them the cats with FIV and Feline Aids who lived separately in purpose built areas. Finally, she led them over to a small barn.

"The babies," large playpens, similar to the one she had at the villa were lined up on the floor. Each had litters of tiny kittens no older than four weeks. Scooping a couple up Markos handed one to Helen, who snuggled it under her chin.

"Bethany bottle feeds all these" he explained "She has a team of volunteers who help out, gap year students mainly" He smiled at Helen, and she nodded, understanding that Bethany had a similar set up to the one her aunt once had.

"Thank you for letting me visit Bethany" Helen hugged her tightly.

"You're always very welcome, Madeline helped me set all this up; I do miss her so much." Bethany's lip started trembling, and big fat tears started rolling down her cheeks and onto Helens shoulder. Markos gently pulled Bethany away and led her into the arms of a kindly looking old woman who patted her back and made soothing noises.

"How did Bethany end up here?" Helen had her feet up on the dashboard and one hand on Markos' muscular thigh.

"Her parents bought the land many years ago and built the huge villa. Bethany and her mother would spend every summer here. The year Bethany turned eighteen, her mother just left her here with her cook, her nanny, and a gardener. Neither her mother or father has ever been back."

"You mean they abandoned her?" Helen was shocked "Are her parents still alive?"

"I have no idea. Bethany is a Lady with a capital L her father is...or was...an Earl. Madeline was so angry. She sent her parents a letter and got her curt reply back from their solicitor. To cut a long story short, it turned out that Bethany was considered an embarrassment in their social circle. She is a considerably wealthy woman but is totally unaware of it" Markos clutched the hand that was laid on his thigh "Madeline took her under her wing and helped her set the haven up. It's a good job all this happened before Selena moved here, only a few of us know that she's wealthy and titled, and we keep it very quiet."

Helen closed her eyes and wondered if Bethany was the name in the envelope. She thought it was a good possibility. Despite her obvious innocence, there was absolutely no doubt that she was as passionate about her cats as Madeline had been about her dogs. Then again, she thought, would her aunt leave everything to somebody who had so much already? She still had Nora and Denis to go and see later that week, but currently, Bethany was in her top three.

"Wake up sleepy head, we're back" Markos leaned over and tenderly kissed Helen.

"Mmm...do I have to wake up? I was having such a lovely dream." Helen kissed him back and ran her finger across his lips. "And before you ask, no it wasn't about you I was dancing the night away with Patrick Swayze and John Travolta." Helen squealed as Markos tried to tickle her. She jumped from the car and ran towards the villas door, but Markos was far too quick and hoisted her up over his shoulder in a fireman's lift. Hearing yells and splashes coming from the pool he carried her around the barn.

"Brooke, Helen has just been very rude to me, do you think I should throw her in the pool?" Brooke, who was just about to dive bomb into the pool herself, jumped up and down screeching "yes, yes, yes, do it, do it Markos."

Helen pretended to beat her hands on Markos back and begged Brooke to help her. None of them noticed Dotty sidling up behind them.

"I think you both need to cool off" she laughed and with a hefty shoved pushed them both into the pool. Brooke ran and high-fived Dotty and leapt into the pool on top of them.

"You just wait! Dorothy Boothroyd!" yelled Helen surfacing above the water and playfully splashing Brooke. "Where's Markos?" concerned that Markos didn't surface straight away Helen ducked her head under the water but couldn't see him "Dotty" Helen kept the panic out of her voice and Dotty, worried herself came to the edge of the pool and peered into the water. Only Brooke had noticed Markos swim underwater to the other end, climb out and sneak behind the bar. He winked at Brooke and stealing up behind Dotty; he scooped her up he threw her into the pool.

"Arghh, help" Dotty thrashed her hands up and down and sunk under the water, she struggled upwards and surfacing took a deep gulp of air "help" she gurgled and sunk under again. Flaying under the water, she started to sink deeper.

"Oh God, I thought she could swim" yelled Markos and dived into the water. Ducking under he pulled a gasping Dotty up and supporting her under her chin, swam her to the side and lifted her out. Pulling himself out he knelt down beside her and apologised over and over.

"I'm so, so sorry Dotty, I never should have assumed you could swim, are you sure you're okay? I feel awful."

"And so you should Markos," Dotty said sternly. She stood herself up and put both hands on her hips and glared at him "You could have ruined my extensions" with that said Dotty stepped to the edge of the pool, executed a near perfect dive and carried out some somersaults under the water. Surfacing she laughed at Markos' astonished face and wagged her finger. "Just you remember Mr. Kalvos; nobody gets the better of Dorothy Boothroyd."

Helen and Brooke were still giggling half an hour later. Helen had changed out of her sodden clothes and into a swimsuit, still conscious of her scar she'd tied a pretty sarong round her waist. Puddles had finally forgiven her and was stretched out beside them while Markos was busy lighting the barbeque. Dotty had disappeared with a giggling Carly and a bemused Christos to work on her "secret project" promising "all would be revealed soon."

"Are you and Markos going to get married?" asked Brooke in the matter of fact way of a ten-year-old.

"Why on earth do you ask that?" Helens years as a teacher had taught her to answer an awkward question with another question.

"I think he loves you, he keeps looking at you and smiling, Christos does that to my mummy, do you think my mummy will get married? Maybe I can be a bridesmaid, my friend Milly was a bridesmaid but I didn't like her dress, maybe Auntie Dotty will make me a dress" Helen let Brooke ramble on and thought of the only wedding she'd ever had "*Till death do us part*" she thought sadly.

CHAPTER 20
LET'S FLY, LET'S FLY AWAY

"Let me get this straight," said Helen "This isn't Keri, this is Keri Lake, and the village of Keri is up on top of the mountain."

"Correct," said Dotty "Well to be exact this is Limni Keri, Limni means lake."

"Oh get you Miss Smarty Pants with your local knowledge" teased Helen. Keri Lake was certainly pretty. It was the closest she had been to the beautiful Turtle Island and it was much bigger than she'd thought. Six of the Big Blue's hire boats bobbed on the sea in front of them, and some men were stood in the sea or on the boats.

"Male chauvinist pigs!" exclaimed Dotty for the umpteenth time and the women around the table laughed. The Greek men, who hired them the boats, had insisted, quite rudely, that all the women had to remain on shore while they instructed the men how to drive the boats and gave a safety talk. Dotty had accused the men of thinly disguised misogyny and threatened to cancel the hire, but Christos had patiently talked her down and persuaded her it was just good old fashioned gentlemanly behaviour.

Helen still couldn't get over the amount of people it took to do a photo shoot. There were stylists, make-up artists, hairdressers, photographers and a variety of others milling around the quayside. She looked over to the next table where a young man was holding a light metre next to Mavra, and a pretty young makeup girl was dusting some powder over her face. She had to admit Mavra looked quite beautiful; it had taken Helen a good fifteen minutes to even recognise her. The straggly hair had been dyed a deep mahogany and was littered with thin strands of golden highlights that glistened in the early morning sun. Her hair flowed in big bouncy curls down her back and framed her strikingly attractive, made up, face. Sadly, the scowl was still there and very much aimed at Dotty. Helen prayed fervently that the two women would be on different boats.

Brooke, dressed in a fluffy pink onesie to keep out the morning chill, clambered onto Dotty's lap and moaned.

"I'm tired Aunty Dotty, why did we have to get up so early?"

Dotty snuggled Brooke to her and stroked her hair.

"You'll soon wake up when we get on the boats darling, and you are going to look so pretty in the pictures with Mummy and Christos."

The evening before Dotty had finally revealed her big secret. A very sheepish Christos had paraded up and down the pool in a selection of men's swimwear. Dotty had never before produced any clothing for men but the hours she had spent peering through her binoculars at Gerakas beach had been nothing to do with the nudists at all. Dotty had despaired at the tiny tight speedos favoured by the Italians and groaned at the long baggy and brightly patterned swim shorts the Brits seemed to prefer. With fond memories of both her and Helen drooling over the gorgeous Bjorn Borg. Dotty had taken her inspiration from the early 80's tennis shorts he so effortlessly bounded across the court in. Hating the garish flowers and fluorescent colours of modern swim shorts she had used simple pastels. The overall effect drew the female eye away from the gaudy prints and emphasised toned muscular thighs and tanned six packs. Her plan today was to have Christos, Carly and Brooke posing as a happy family enjoying a boat trip to Keri Caves. Mavra was scheduled to be over at Marithonisi sunbathing and enjoying drinks from the boat bar.

Mavra was staring at Dotty; she felt sickened that her lovely Markos could be fooled by so much fakery. The fake breasts, the fake tan, the fake hair and even the fake nails infuriated her. Terrified of a good telling off she had finally told Selena of her plans to model but far from being angry, Selena was delighted. They still hadn't managed to work out where Helen Hardy was staying or devise a plan to get her off the island. With no proof that Helen had left, earlier in the week, to go to Kefalonia they were starting to get desperate.

Selena was currently secreted in the back of a van parked in the nearby carpark. Philip had yet again managed to disappear so her irritated gardener was acting as chauffeur. She had her binoculars trained on the group of people waiting patiently to get on the boats.

Markos pulled into the carpark in his truck, unaware of Selena's beady eyes trained so closely on him he nodded at the man leant casually against a nearby van, grinding a spent cigarette under a pair of muddy work boots. The man touched his hand to his forehead and climbed back into the driver's seat.

Markos carried a large brown envelope over to one of the tables and handed it to Helen.

"Morning all" he smiled and ruffled Brooke's hair. He glanced over at the next table where a beautiful woman slowly and elegantly rose from her seat; she shrugged off a towelling beach robe to reveal a spectacular figure clad in an exquisite white and gold bikini. The woman glided towards them slowly and stopped beside Markos.

"Kalimera Markos" the woman purred in a deep, throaty voice.

"Mavra…wow…Eisai omorfh" Mavra smiled at Markos and smirked in Dotty's direction. She slowly turned and in the manner of a professional model, sashayed back to her table ensuring Markos got an eyeful of her curvaceous bottom.

"What did you say to her?" asked Dotty thinking that her bikini looked perfect on Mavra's divine body.

"I told her she looked beautiful" Markos was honest "I didn't add that it's a shame the beauty is only skin deep" Helen smiled, she didn't have a jealous bone in her body, and she agreed Mavra did look beautiful.

"Is that the codicil?" she asked, picking up the brown envelope and peeping inside. They had completely forgotten to pick it up the day before so after dropping Helen at Keri Lake Markos had sped back to his office.

"Hmm, we'll take a look later, once everyone's set off."

A shouting from the boats swung everyone into action, and Helen and Markos watched as for the next ten minutes the boats were loaded with equipment, water, and people. They waved as the boats sped off and kept on waving until they became tiny specks on the water.

Selena spat on the lenses and rubbed them dry with the sleeve of her cardigan. Peering through the binoculars again she fiddled with the little focus knob until Helen and Markos loomed so clearly into view that she felt as if she could reach out and touch them. The writing on the piece of paper that they were studying was annoyingly obscured by two large cups of coffee.

"I can't read it without my glasses" admitted Helen "You'll have to read it out to me."

Markos pulled his glasses from his pocket and laughed as Helen wolf whistled. Pulling the codicil towards him, he started to read.

"*I Madeline Kalvos of Villa Elena, Vassilikos, Zakynthos; Greece hereby* *declare this to be the first codicil...*Do you want me to read out the legal bits?"

"No," said Helen "just go to the next bit."

"Okay," Markos scanned the document quickly "Here we go."

"This codicil sets out the criteria Helen Hardy must meet in order to inherit the estate as indicated in the final will and testament...

"Wait" Helen held up her hand "Read that very first line again, something sounds wrong, but I'm not sure what it is."

"This codicil sets out the criteria Helen Hardy must meet..."

"There," said Helen "I'm named as Helen Hardy, but my aunt said she didn't know if I'd married or not and Percival said they had taken ages to find me...it doesn't make sense."

"Maybe your name was inserted after Percival found you" suggested Markos "does seem strange though" Helen frowned and told him to carry on.

"This looks like the bit we need."

"Helen Hardy must spend a minimum of thirty continuous days in Greece. A sum of £60,000 shall be released from the estate to ensure that Helen Hardy has the funds to fulfil this instruction in a comfortable manner. In the event of a close family member suffering a serious illness, injury or death Helen Hardy will be permitted to leave Greece without forfeiting the inheritance. The number of days she has completed will still count towards the thirty days will which recommence upon Helen Hardy's return to Greece.

"Blimey, Madeline certainly thought this through," said Helen as Markos paused to take a breath.

"On, before, but no later than the thirtieth day and in the presence of Markos Kalvos, Percival Boston,"

"This lists half the island" laughed Markos "including Selena" he raised his eyebrows at Helen and continued where the list of names ended.

*"Helen Hardy must state her intention to move permanently to Zakynthos and take up residence in the Villa Elena. If Helen Hardy does not state this intention, then she will be asked to state the identity of the one named in the sealed envelope which is deposited with Boston...*and so on...*If Helen Hardy fails to state the correct name, then the entire inheritance will convert to the said one named in the...*you know the rest" Markos stopped to gauge Helen's reaction.

"That bits all quite clear," she said "it's interesting that she's used the term *"The one named"* as if she's telling us that it is just one person and not a couple" Markos nodded in agreement.

"Oh dear" groaned Markos "This bit's not so good…listen"

"If Helen Hardy states her intention to move permanently to the island of Zakynthos she will inherit the entire estate of Madeline Kalvos. However, if during the ten years following her inheritance she states any intention to relocate or move permanently off the island of Zakynthos she will thereby forfeit all of the said inheritance. In this case, the estate will be sold, and all proceeds will be equally split between the Zakynthos Cat Haven and the Dogs of Zakynthos groups."

"I think that's a big clue" interrupted Helen "why not the person named?" Helens brain was whirring "I think maybe that could indicate that in ten years' time the person named might be too old, not living here or even dead."

"You're right" agreed Markos, who was also thinking hard "That puts Peggy, Alf and Nora firmly back in the picture. There's quite a bit more legal stuff about making the groups having official charity status, then this bit;

"If Helen Hardy correctly identifies the one named in……" Markos skipped all the legal bit *"Then Helen Hardy will inherit the entire estate with no conditions attached."*

Markos took off his glasses and rubbed his eyes. He looked over at Helen, who had her head in her hands.

"I've got to work out who it is" Helen shook her head and sighed, things weren't getting any easier, in fact, they had just got a lot worse.

"Or move here," Markos said softly reaching over to take her hands

"Oh Markos, I can't make that decision in just a few days, I have to think of my children and Papa, besides that, could you imagine what life would be like for the next ten years. Every Tom, Dick, and Harry will be out to make my life hell and Selena will go to untold lengths to take over one or both of the groups and get me off the island" She laced her fingers through his strong hands and smiled at his sad face. "Oh Markos, every fibre of my body wants to stay here, with you, forever." Helen stood up and walked round the table. She pulled Markos up and put her arms around his waist. "I promise you that whatever happens and whatever I decide, you're not getting rid of me that easily." Markos gazed into her eyes and not caring who could see bent his head and kissed her.

Selena nearly toppled over in shock as she watched Helen and

Markos kissing. She scrabbled for her phone to take a photo for Facebook but by the time she'd found it the conniving pair were walking side by side towards his truck. She grabbed a large floppy straw hat and a pair of sunglasses and shook her sleeping gardeners shoulder. Heaving her bulky frame in a most unladylike fashion, she clambered over to the front seat and ordered the man to "Follow that truck."

Markos was worried about Helen; she'd stared glumly out of the truck window for the past ten minutes and refused his offer to stop for some breakfast. Thinking back over the codicil he suddenly realised something and a gem of an idea started to form in his brain.

"Have you got your passport on you, Helen?" He asked

"Hmm…Yes, it should be in my bag, why? Helen checked her handbag and showed him her passport.

"We're going to the airport" he grinned

"Why, have you got some dogs to sort… why do I need my passport for that?"

"Not dogs, I thought we could pop over to Athens."

Helen stared at him; she didn't find that sort of joke funny especially after reading the codicil. She chose to ignore him and resumed looking out the window.

"Helen, the codicil didn't mention leaving Zakynthos, it said you weren't to leave Greece, well Athens is in Greece, and Kefalonia is in Greece. We could go island hopping." Helen looked at him incredulously.

"Oh my god, your right. I've always wanted to see the Parthenon, can we go there and back in a day?" Helen felt her worries drifting away and a nervous excitement take their place.

"Let's go for more than a day; we can use the sky hopper or ferries and go wherever we want."

"Don't be silly" laughed Helen "We have the puppies and kittens to think of and Puddles, we can't just disappear."

"Oh…about them" Markos scrunched up his face and had the grace to look ashamed "Peggy and Bethany will be happy to have them; we may have lied a little bit about them."

"Lied, whatever do you mean?"

"Well Lily overheard you saying you felt like a burden and wanted to go home so we thought we'd find you something to make you feel useful…sorry and Puddles will be fine, he can stop with Fudge for a few days."

Helen started giggling. The giggling turned to full blown laughter, and she struggled to compose herself.

"Oh dear, that's so funny, and it worked a treat" Helen agreed "Shall we head back to the villa and pack an overnight case."

"No" Markos grinned wickedly "Let's go and get some tickets then go straight to the airport, I'll take you shopping in Athens" He pulled Helen towards him, a few days away would hopefully take her mind of the codicil and everything connected to it."

Selena was grateful for the large packed lunch her maid had given her that morning. She'd munched the big cheese rolls greedily while they waited outside the Zakyta Travel Agency. Markos and Helen had disappeared into the shop ten minutes earlier, although Selena couldn't imagine why. Finishing her lunch, she pulled a large camera from its case and attached a telephoto lens. She had sent so many messages and emails from her phone that the battery was running worryingly low.

Helen followed Markos out of the shop and with a quick wave behind her climbed back into the truck. Damn it thought Selena, with a camera to her eye she had been hoping to catch them holding hands. Following the truck, she realised they were heading towards the airport; Selena started to get very excited. There was only one reason you went to a travel agent and then to an airport; Helen was leaving Zakynthos. Selena instructed her driver to park a few cars away from Markos' truck. Wrapping an ugly black mac round her large body, she pulled a walking stick from the back of the van and heaved herself out of the door. Hoping she looked like an old Greek Yia Yia, she stooped over and hobbled behind the duo following them into the departure lounge. Yes, she thought, Helen and Markos had indeed gone straight through the security barriers.

Selena yanked off her hat, sunglasses, and Mac and chucked the walking stick in a nearby bin. Puffing and panting she waddled back to the van and told her fed up driver to find a spot she could see the runway from. Rolling his eyes, he drove a few yards round the corner and pointed to a good spot. Selena had never been a patient person, but there was no way she was going to miss this photo opportunity and finally after forty minutes of waiting she spotted Helen and Markos getting off the bus and walking hand in hand to the Olympic Air plane. Selena took a few snaps of the pair and even managed to get them kissing as they waited to climb the steps to the plane. She quickly switched the camera to video mode and filmed them entering the plane and the large jet taking off and disappearing into the sky.

"Got you," she said out loud "Absolute proof that you left the island Helen Hardy." Selena checked the video was ok and emailed herself a copy, an email would substantiate the date it was filmed.

Peggy and Alf had driven up to collect the pups and didn't recognise the van that was parked in the driveway. Hearing voices near the pool, Peggy shoved Alf in front of her, and they edged round the side of the barn, terrified that they had caught burglars in the process of stealing something. Alf reached the corner and ducked back quickly almost knocking Peggy off her feet.

"Shh" he whispered. "It's Selena and some man." Peggy angrily pushed back her shoulders ready for a fight, but Alf shushed her again and told her to listen. Selena's loud, snotty voice wasn't difficult to distinguish, and they listened open-mouthed as she described exactly what changes she would be making when the villa became hers.

"Those silly common beach huts will have to go, and I think we will install a marble fountain in their place. And that barbeque and hot tub are so outdated they will have to be ripped out. I've seen a wonderful outdoor kitchen that will fit all along that side."

Alf quietly turned his phone to record and hoped it was strong enough to pick up Selena's loud condescending words.

"First thing will be to remove those awful dogs from that feeding station; I quite fancy a large log cabin up there. Hmm, a few nice juicy steaks with some of that poison you've got in the garden shed should do" Selena looked at her gardener who nodded. "It certainly worked a treat on those pesky dogs and cats that kept coming on our land last year."

Alf slapped one hand over Peggy's mouth and grabbing her round the waist dragged her kicking and gagging back to the car. She was so angry he thought he was about to witness a murder on their peaceful island.

"Calm down Peggy" he shouted once she was safely locked in the car.

"Did you hear that bleeding bitch, she wants to kill the dogs, let me out so I can kill the effing cow" Peggy was turning a vivid shade of red and panting so heavily, Alf was convinced she was about to keel over.

"Peggy, stop it, there is no way that Selena is ever going to get her hands on this villa, and you know that."

"Did you hear her slagging of Madeline's beautiful beach huts?"

"Yes and hopefully so did my phone" he held the phone up to show Peggy "Now shut up woman and listen." Alf hoped his stern voice that he rarely had to use would do the trick. It did. Peggy shut up and grabbed his phone and pressed play.

Sadly, they hadn't got the bit about the beach huts, but Selena's threat to the dogs was very loud and very clear. Alf pressed the save button and smiled.

"I think we may have just found the perfect way to get Selena Warrington-Smyth out of our lives for good. Now once you've calmed down we will walk around and politely ask her what she's doing." Alf patted the pocket he'd put his phone in "this little secret is one we will keep for the moment."

"Can I help you Selena" Peggy smiled politely as Selena jumped around looking decidedly guilty.

"Ah Peggy, I was just showing my handyman Madeline's pool area, it is exactly how I would like mine to look, and hopefully he can glean some ideas." Selena didn't even blush as she told the outrageous lie. "As you well know Peggy, Madeline always made me feel very welcome…and well…just between you and me" Selena attempted a wink "Madeline and I had many secret tete-a-tetes to discuss the island's business. Well I'll be off now, good day to you."

Coming down to land at Athens airport Helen and Markos were blissfully unaware of the goings-on back on Zakynthos. They had toasted each other with champagne and were both ready for a few days of rest and relaxation.

CHAPTER 21
BY LAND, BY AIR, BY SEA

Gerald screwed up the piece of paper and threw it angrily on the floor. He walked to the window of his small hotel room in Kyllini and watched the tiny cars driving onto the large orange and white Ferry. The closer he got to Zakynthos the harder it became. He was going to take the coward's way out. He would write Helen a letter. Only it wasn't as simple as that. He'd started so many letters that his floor was littered with the screwed up pieces of paper. How would she ever get over what he needed to tell her? He knew it had to be done; he couldn't keep the secret anymore. He tore a fresh sheet from the hotel's complimentary notepaper and again, picked up the pen.

My Dearest Helen
I am so dreadfully sorry. If I were a brave man, I would tell you to your face. I'm not brave though; I never have been. But then you know better than most what a coward I am. I need to tell you about the day William died. I don't think you will forgive me; I can't forgive myself for the lies I have told and the secrets I have kept I will go to the police when I return home…

Gerald scrunched the paper up; he couldn't do it. He would go to Zakynthos and tell Helen face to face. For the first time in his life, he was going to be brave. Turning on his phone, he sent Dotty a quick reply to her email.

Hi Dotty, I've reached Kyllini. I'll get the ferry over later today. I can't wait to celebrate Helens 50th tomorrow.

Gerald sighed deeply and picked up the Levante Ferries leaflet. The last couple of weeks, touring Europe, had been good, really good but that was all about to change.

Dotty heard her phone ping and reached into her bag.
"Yay, Gerald's on his way. Are you sure you can fit him in Lily?"
"No problem, with you and Helen at the villa we can use those rooms. How about Helen's Papa, will he manage that hill?"
"It's only for one-night Lily; I'm sure Helen will want him to stay at Villa Elena."

Lily cleared the table and wiping the sweat from her brow flopped into a chair. "Phew don't get me wrong Dotty, I love all these guest but it ain't half tiring."

"I don't know," said Maggie "These past few days we've been almost back to normal, Selena and her cronies are so busy organising the dog show they've kept well away, and we've not seen hide nor hare of Dotty's lot. I have missed Helen though" Maggie fussed Puddles who had thoroughly enjoyed his sleep-overs with Fudge "I still think it's a bit bleeding odd though the way she and Markos just disappeared, are you sure there's nothing going on between them."

"Maggie, I've told you over and over" sighed Dotty "They read the codicil and realised that Helen could go anywhere in Greece not just Zakynthos. Markos had business in Athens so offered to take Helen with him. I'm pretty sure that Markos has been cooped up in meetings every day, and Helen has been swanning around Athens with her intellectual nose stuck in a guidebook" Dotty turned away to hide her grin and wondered if her acting was worthy of an Oscar.

"Morning" Peggy walked through the pretty archway with a big smile on her face, she was followed by Suzanne, Jacob and a grumpy looking Alf "Our Alf's got the miseries this morning" laughed Peggy "He wanted to go fishing and got in quite a sulk when I told him he was helping with the planning."

"Oh Alf, sit down, and I'll get you a coffee" laughed Lily.

"Right," said Dotty looking at Suzanne "before we finalise Helen's birthday plans I've got an announcement" Lily forgot the coffee and sat back down. All eyes were on Dotty's excited face.

"I've decided to open Greece's first Dorothy Boothroyd Boutique, here in Zakynthos" Dotty sat back and enjoyed the gasps of surprise. "And" she took Suzanne's hand. "I would very much like you to manage it." Suzanne looked completely shocked and turned straight to Jacob who had a wide grin on his face.

"Dotty spoke to me a couple of days ago," said Jacob "It's completely up to you Suzanne, I can easily get work here" He glanced sideways at his mum who had gone very pale and was holding her breath.

"But the baby, maternity leave, I don't even speak Greek." Suzanne was almost lost for words

"That's all sorted, Carly and Brooke. for some strange reason," Dotty winked "leapt at the chance to spend a few months over here helping you out and Jacob, there will be plenty of work for you designing and decorating the shop and where could you find better babysitters than a pair of doting grandparents."

"Then yes." squeaked Suzanne "yes!" Jacob turned and pulled his weeping mum into his arms.

"We're coming home, mum. We're coming home."

Molly shook Papa's shoulder to wake him; he had slept the whole flight which was probably a good thing, she thought. It had been worse than taking a toddler on holiday. They had lost him three times at Gatwick early that morning and lost count of the number of times he'd walked away and left his hand luggage on a seat. Her nerves were stretched to almost breaking point. Molly had tried every excuse to get out of this trip. Her ginger complexion hated the sun and trusting anyone to look after their little market garden business was way out of her comfort zone. It was only when her mother offered to take charge for a week that she finally succumbed and agreed to the holiday. Hating flying and terrified of the landing she reached across to hold Ian's hand but he snatched it away and turned to look out the window. Molly sighed, this was a make or break holiday. Their seemingly happy marriage was a complete farce. Behind closed doors, their rows had boiled over into fierce and angry resentment. They had agreed on one last attempt, but were both fully aware they would be going back to a rekindled love or a very messy divorce.

Helen leant against the rails letting the wind stream through her hair. The large turtle that swam gracefully below them had drawn most of the passengers out onto the decks of the Ferry and cameras were clicking and whirring all around her as they captured the momentous sight. Markos was stood behind with his chin on her shoulder and his arms wrapped tightly around her waist. Their couple of days had turned into six blissful days and idyllic passion filled nights littered with the sights, smells and sounds of Athens, Mykonos, Santorini and finally Kefalonia. Santorini had been her favourite, the beautiful white houses with their blue domed roofs would be etched in her memory forever. She hadn't wanted their trip to end but the dog show tomorrow was important to her. She knew Madeline would have wanted her to go, and she'd promised Dotty she would be there for moral support while her best friend worked out which dog did indeed have the waggiest tail. Helen had laughingly threatened to enter Puddles but guessed that wasn't fair. They drew slowly into the port at St Nicholas, and both laughed when they spotted Christos with Brooke perched on his shoulders. Brooke was screaming and waving at them. Helen felt the same comforting feeling that she'd always felt when she returned home from a holiday. She smiled up at Markos.

"I think I've made my decision. I need to ring Percival Boston Jr."

Gerald drove down the steep hill and stopped when his Sat Nav told him he had reached his destination. He tapped the dashboard of his classic Mark11 Jaguar.

"You've done us proud old girl," he said fondly. Climbing out of the car he stretched and looked over the hotel's wall. The pool looked very inviting, he thought and so did the bar. Walking through an archway, he heard a familiar squeal.

"Hello Dotty," he said accepting and returning her hug. Dotty was shocked; Gerald had lost so much weight she could feel his ribs protruding under his shirt. She pushed him away and studied his tired and drawn face. The usually immaculate Gerald was dressed in clean but crumpled shorts and a t-shirt.

"Come and have a drink Gerald," said Dotty kindly "Molly and Ian will be here any minute now, and they're bringing Papa, Helen doesn't have a clue, I don't think she's even remembered it's her birthday."

"It's surprisingly good to see you Dotty," said Gerald with a wry grin, their love-hate relationship had survived many years, but Gerald was quite sure it would not survive the bombshell he was soon going to drop. A beeping from the road caused them both to turn, and Dotty squealed again as Molly helped a beaming Papa from the car.

"Papa, you star," said Dotty, thrilled that the octogenarian had managed the journey, and from the look of him exceedingly well.

"Now then young Dotty, how are you? I must say this islands changed a bit since I was last here."

"You've been here before?" Dotty wondered if he was confusing Zakynthos with somewhere else.

"Oh yes, back in 1972, we did a bit of island hopping and spent a few nights in a place called Kalamaki, William was just a young boy then. I must dig out the old photos when Helen gets home."

Dotty reached to hug Molly and Ian and settled them all at a table.

"Helen's Heroes, minus Helen of course" she laughed as they all clinked glasses "I hope to God Merv the Perv doesn't come strolling through the archway.

Maggie leant on the bar studying the group carefully, she'd always been a people watcher and prided herself on her ability to suss people out. Something wasn't quite right with this group. The eminent cardiologist was not the distinguished looking man she'd expected. He was a haggard old man with guilt written all over his face. The ginger woman and her husband had an anger bristling between them that they were both trying hard to hide. Helen's Papa though was quite adorable; from the moment, she shook his hand she wanted to smother him with protective love. Papa was also the only one Puddles was interested in. The daft dog had walked straight over and laid his soppy head in Papas lap. Well, she thought Dogs always were the best judge of character.

"Daphne, where are you girl" Percival Boston Jr waddled up the corridor as fast as his short chubby legs could carry him. "Daphne, we need to book flights to Zakynthos this instant, darling Helen has made her decision, Daphne."

Daphne shoved her copy of "Fifty Shades" under the desk and smiled sweetly at her boss.

"How exciting, when do you want to fly?" she quickly googled flights to Zakynthos.

"We, not me, you're coming too. Tomorrow, no today, oh fiddlesticks I don't know, when's the first flight available?" Percival mopped his brow and leaned over to look at Daphne's computer.

"EasyJet has space tomorrow morning 5:50 am" she read off the screen. Percival visibly shuddered.

"No, no no, they don't even have business class, let alone first class, what else is there" Daphne typed rapidly on the keyboard.

"The only way you can fly business class is to go to Athens then get a flight or ferry across to Zakynthos…nothing available until Wednesday I'm afraid."

"What a damned nuisance" huffed Percival; Daphne leant back in her seat as a large drop of sweat threatened to drop straight off Percival's nose and right into her cleavage. "Okey Dokey, hire a private jet then, 10 am tomorrow and book us into a 5* Hotel for five days. Madeline Kalvos was worth millions; I'm sure the estate can pick up the bill."

Daphne picked up the phone to make arrangements, waiting till Percival had left the office she quickly dialled a number.

"Sweetie, it's Daphne, can you fit me in for the full works this evening…yes, bikini wax, tan, eyelash tint…yes that as well, Oh and manicure and pedicure, you're an angel bye for now, love you." Daphne blew kisses into the phone and wondered how much luggage she could take on a private jet.

"Dotty, you've got to stop texting me, Helen is going to think I'm having an affair" Markos had gone up to the feeding station and by walking around and holding his phone aloft he had finally got a signal. "Everything is in place Dotty. I'm cooking dinner for Helen this evening so she won't want to go out, there is absolutely no chance she will run into her friends. Christos is picking up Puddles tonight, and we will be at the dog show all afternoon tomorrow. I will text you when we are on our way back, and everyone can hide in the beach huts. Okay, see you tomorrow, bye."

CHAPTER 22
AND THE WINNER IS…

"Happy Birthday to you, Happy Birthday to you" Helen opened her eyes and laughed. Brooke was walking towards her with a large choc chip muffin clasped tightly in her hands. One tiny, lit candle was pushed into the centre, and Brooke was holding it at arms-length wary of the flame. "Happy Birthday Helen, Aunty Dotty said to tell you breakfast is served on the balcony."

"Thank you darling." Helen blew out the candle and hugged the charmingly sweet girl "Tell Aunty Dotty I'll be there in a minute" Helen stretched and looked out of the huge bedroom windows, she didn't think she would ever find a more beautiful view to wake up to. She wrapped a gown around her and pulled tight the belt. She picked up her phone to double check the date. She felt quite foolish that she'd totally forgotten it was her birthday.

Helen walked out onto the balcony to smiles and yells of "Happy Birthday" She clapped her hands in delight at the table laden with a sumptuous breakfast buffet. Dotty, Markos, Carly and Christos smiled at her pleasure and Brooke patted the seat next to her.

"I don't know what to say" blushed Helen "I didn't even realise it was my birthday."

"That's just silly," said Brooke to much laughter "Nobody forgets their birthday."

Markos got up and put his arms around Helens neck, kissing her cheek he whispered "Happy Birthday Darling."

"Dad!" exclaimed Christos "Is there something you've not told us" Markos laughed heartily.

"I'm so sorry Christos, we've been so wrapped up in each other I completely forgot to tell you, but yes, I and Helen are very much *"an item"* as you youngsters might say."

"Well go dad, and go Helen" Christos hugged them both, absolutely ecstatic.

"Doh Christos, your soo sloooow" teased Brooke and grinned when Christos stuck his tongue out.

"Present time" cheered Dotty handing Helen a beautifully

wrapped gift "It's a one-off Dotty B special" she laughed. Helen gasped as she opened the paper and pulled out a gorgeous bikini in hues of green and blue that matched the Ionian Sea below her. Aware that Helen was still so conscious of her scar Dotty had created a matching wrap-a-round swim skirt that stopped just below her knees. Helen mouthed a "thank you."

"Now mine" squealed Brooke, who loved giving as much as receiving. Helen gasped at the beautiful photo frame that was covered in exquisite little sea shells. "Aunty Dotty helped me make it last week; it's just like the ones your aunty used to make."

"Brooke darling, it is, you're so clever" Helen wiped a tear from her eye. Carly handed her a cardboard tube, and Helen felt more tears welling as she unrolled a wonderful hand painted a portrait of Puddles.

"The artist in Tsilivi painted him while you were away," said Brooke "and it fits in my frame."

Markos gave her a small flat cardboard box that was tied with a pretty gold ribbon. Unlacing the ribbon and lifting the lid Helen gasped and allowed the tears to flow freely. In a beautiful silver frame was a very old photo of her and Madeline sitting on the beach in Weymouth. Helen couldn't speak for the lump in her throat. She ran her fingers over the picture and laughed as her tears plopped onto the glass.

"There are boxes and boxes of old dusty photo's stored in the loft. Madeline kept this one by her bed and asked me to give it to you when I felt the time was right" explained Markos as he gently wiped the tears from her cheeks. Now then, that was from Madeline, this is from me" Markos wrapped a silver charm bracelet around her wrist, a pretty charm from each of the islands they had visited dangled from the bracelet. "By the time you reach sixty, we will have filled it with a charm from every single one of the Greek islands" Helen lifted each pretty charm in turn and thought ahead to the fun they would have.

"Dotty, Christos… what Markos means is that I've made my decision, I can't imagine spending the rest of my life anywhere but here" She smiled as they all hugged her tightly.

"Helen Hardy" teased Dotty "for once in your life, I do believe you've made the right decision" Helen playfully slapped her best friend and silently agreed.

"One last thing from me," said Christos "Puddles" he called. The clever dog who had been waiting patiently in the kitchen came trotting out with an envelope in his mouth, expecting a card, Helen frowned as she pulled out a small blue booklet. The twelve yellow stars of the European Union formed a circle at the top and in both Greek and English the words "Pet Passport" were etched on the front.

"Puddle's is now officially all yours Helen; I've reregistered his microchip so nobody can deny you legal ownership."

Helen laughed happily, hugging her gorgeous dog. What a wonderful birthday she thought and what a wonderful place to be spending it.

"So you're really going to stay here then?" asked Dotty, they were both hidden in the toilets of the bar that was hosting the dog show. Dotty hadn't been able to move without eager dog owners shoving bribes into her hands.

"I think so" replied Helen, turning the taps on to wash her hands. "I feel so happy here Dotty, Markos and I have talked it over and over. I'm forty-nine…no fifty" Helen smiled wryly as she realised how old she was. "I love Markos and the twins are grown up and will be off doing their own thing, I'm going to rent my house out rather than sell it, so they've always got a home to go back to" Dotty nodded; it was the sensible thing to do.

"It's Papa I worry about most, leaving him will be so hard" Helen sighed "but…the lovely Mr. Boston Jr is on his way though, so there's no going back. I know I've still got a week of the thirty days left, but now I've made my mind up I can't wait to make it all official."

"Well, I think you've found your happy ever after" laughed Dotty "If George Clooney would just hurry up and ask me out, I might find mine" The woman screeched with laughter and headed off to brave the crowds.

Mavra slowly opened the cubicle door. She was quivering with a hot, jealous anger. How dare that Helen Hardy come over here and steal her man. Selena kept on telling her not to worry *"I have proof she left the Island"* but Mavra wasn't interested in the inheritance. Helen Hardy needed to be gone from Markos' life, and she was going to make it happen.

Helen laughed as a tiny Dotty, walked along if front of an

assortment of dogs that were all wagging their tails furiously. A tiny Yorkshire terrier yapped aggressively at a large St Bernard, who, terrified, tried to dive between his owner's legs to the hilarity of the watching crowd. Dotty calmed the dog and owner and carried on down the line. She's good, thought Helen.

"Helen, please could you remove all the daggers from my back" grinned Christos as he flopped down into the seat next to her "I don't think I will ever forgive my dad for this."

Christos had judged Best Working Pedigree and Best Child Handler and was now being ostracised by those that didn't win.

"Dotty looks quite professional, don't you think?" said Helen

"Might be something to do with all the YouTube videos of Crufts she watched last week" Helen shook her head, she had to admit her best friend was quite savvy.

"Watch out, here comes Snotty" Helen shielded her eyes from the sun and saw Selena marching towards her. Helen bit her lip and tried not to laugh at Selena's strange attire. She resembled a tennis umpire. A tight white pencil skirt strained over her colossal hips and was teamed with a bottle green blazer. On her head, a pure white flat cap was perched at a jaunty angle.

"I think Selena's been watching Wimbledon instead of Crufts" snorted Helen.

"Good Morning Helen, how kind of you to come to our little dog show" Selena sneered down her snotty nose. Helen stood up and shook Selena's hand.

"Selena, this is all so wonderful, you really are a very skilled organiser, congratulations." Helen genuinely meant what she said. The small field behind the bar was overflowing with locals and tourists, all eager to have a go on the tombola, raffle, and the many side show stalls dotted around the central ring. Children with their faces painted were sat over in Puppy corner cuddling the furry babies.

"Thank you" Selena was unused to real compliments and struggled to know what to say, she blushed and walked very quickly away.

Helen looked back to the ring where Dotty was calling five of the entrants towards her. A cheer went up as she awarded third place to the St Bernard, who was so excited he dragged his tiny owner right out of the ring and over to the burger bar. Second went to a bouncy

Bichon Frise mix and playing along to the expectant crowd Dotty paused and tapped her fingers against her chin. A huge roar went up as she walked to a small girl who was holding on tightly to a wriggling spaniel puppy.

"Oh very clever" laughed Christos "she's given it to the cutest kid, nobody will dare complain."

"How's it going" Markos joined them and took a seat the other side of Christos, Helen had insisted that they keep their relationship a secret until the formalities with the inheritance were over.

"Wonderful," said Helen "It's a lovely way to spend my birthday" She frowned as Dotty ran towards them waving her phone. With another BAFTA winning performance, Dotty stopped beside them, panting heavily.

"Helen, I'm sorry, I've got to go, there's some stupid row going on up at the photo shoot, I need to go and bang a few silly heads together."

"Dotty, it's fine, you go" interrupted Markos. "Once Helen's finished here I'm going to take her somewhere special for a birthday lunch and a bit of snorkelling."

"I'll need to go and get my swimming stuff then," said Helen then smiled as Markos admitted it was already packed in his truck.

"Where do the funds raised from the dog show go," Helen asked as they walked towards the truck "It's obviously a joint effort."

"That's long been the cause of many arguments," said Markos "Both the Dozies and the Lazies try to claim it. Madeline set a separate account up in the end, and it all goes towards food for the feeding stations and sterilising the strays" Markos glanced at Helen as she climbed in the truck "Just for today Helen, let's put any more talk of dogs…or cats out of our heads and have some fun…It's your birthday…remember"

"What happened here?" Helen asked sadly as they drove through an area devastated by fire. The charred remains of trees stood amongst large swathes of sparse, charcoal littered mountainous terrain.

"One of the forest fires," said Markos "It happens often, some are small, but this was big and lasted a few days. It destroyed much of the forest."

Helen had earlier commented on how lush and green the west side of Zakynthos was compared to the east but this was horrific, she thought, how very sad. Reaching the village of Agios Leon, Helen was convinced Markos was turning into a farmer's drive, but she soon realised they were actually on a tiny and very steep road. She yelped as the road got steeper and Markos expertly navigated the terrifying hairpin bends. The cliffs dropped away right next to her and terrified she closed her eyes and willed the journey to be over. She only opened them when Markos stopped in a small carpark next to a Taverna.

"This is Porto Limniosis" he declared "The most beautiful spot on Zakynthos" Helen agreed. The Taverna was perched on a cliff looking down on a tiny narrow cove. Far below a couple of small boats drifted on the water and tiny figures were snorkelling in and out of the caves eroded into the cliffs.

"Wow, how do we get down there?" asked Helen, expecting a neat set of steps with a handrail. Instead, Markos pointed to a steep, crumbly path that made Helen's stomach tumble with a mixture of fear and excitement.

"Do you want to eat first or snorkel first?" asked Markos and remembering her mother's wise but probably untrue advice to *'Never swim on a full stomach'* Helen pointed to the path and clutched Markos' hand tightly.

After a delightful half hour snorkelling, Helen sat back and allowed the hot afternoon sun to warm her shivering body. She thanked the waitress who brought them a large pizza and salad to share and thanked Markos for bringing her here.

"I've asked Peggy and Alf and Lily and her mum and dad to join us for drinks this evening," said Markos, "I thought it would be nice to have a small birthday celebration."

"That will be lovely" Helen agreed "We could stop at Lidl's on the way back and get some meat for a barbeque."

"Hmm" agreed Markos, knowing full well that the food and drink were already bought and was probably being prepared at that very moment, "I think there's enough food in the freezer" he lied.

Peggy, Maggie, and Lily were indeed all frantically busy cooking up a monster of a feast in Madeline's large kitchen.

"I've ordered a cake from the little bakery in Macherado," said Peggy "Remind me to pick it up when we go home to change" she shouted through to Alf, who was rummaging through Madeline's cupboards looking for firelighters to light the barbeque.

Dotty was having great fun driving Papa, Molly, Ian and Gerald around the estate. Molly oohed over the pretty guest villas and hoped they would be invited to stop in them. Papa was in his element and kept begging Dotty to let him drive. He'd played on his age to bag the front seat and laughed as the others had squashed themselves in the back. Ian and Gerald both seemed to be more impressed with the luxurious golf buggy and were both bemoaning the fact that Zakynthos didn't have a golf course unless of course you counted the Fantasy Mini Golf courses located in Tsilivi and Argassi.

Dotty stopped the buggy by the barn and linking her arm through Papa's led the group round to the pool.

"Oh my God" gasped Molly. "If I were Helen I would happily live here for the rest of my life" Dotty kept her mouth firmly shut, Helen's decision was hers and hers alone to tell them. Papa almost ran to the hot tub and started pressing buttons. He grinned widely as the bubbles burst into life and the jets pulsed ripples of water across the tub.

"I've always wanted a go in one of these things; it'll do my old joints the world of good" He ran his hand through the water "I wish I'd brought my swimming trunks with me."

"No problem," said Dotty and opened one of the beach huts to show them the mixed array of swimwear and towels for guests to use. "Help yourself, Papa; you've got a good couple of hours till Helen arrives."

An hour and a half later Peggy and Alf drove back up to hill to Madeline's villa.

"Stop" yelled Peggy "The cake, you didn't remind me to pick up the bleeding cake Alf" she slapped his arm and pulled out her phone "It's too bloody late to go back I'll have to see if they will deliver it" she made a quick phone call, and huffing and swearing ended the call "They'll bring it up but not until after the shop closes at nine"

"Better late than never," said Alf rubbing his arm and wondering why it was always his fault.

Mavra walked into the bakery to get some fresh rolls for her tea. She admired the beautiful cake that was placed on the counter. Peering closer she read the words iced on the top *"Happy 50th Helen."*

"Is that Helen Hardy's cake?" she asked the young girl behind the counter.

"Yes, Peggy forgot to pick it up. I've promised to run it up to the Villa Elena, but they will have to wait till I've shut the shop" Thinking fast Mavra smiled sweetly at the girl.

"I can take it for you; I've been invited to Helen's party."

"Oh Mavra, that would be so kind thank you." The girl handed Mavra the cake and luckily didn't spot the hate filled glint in the woman's eyes.

Mavra carried the cake over to her pretty little house and placed it carefully out of the dog's reach. She had a few things to do this evening but if she hurried she could make it up to Madeline's by 8:30 pm when her party should be in full swing.

"Shush Papa, you've got to be quiet" whispered Molly. They were all hidden away in one of the beach huts waiting for Helen to arrive and Papa was fidgeting like an excited ten-year-old.

Helen walked arm in arm with Dotty round the corner of the barn and squealed as her new friends cheered and let off party poppers.

"Goodness, who's cooked all this food?" she ran her eyes over the sumptuous feast. "There's enough to feed the five thousand here." She hugged Peggy, Maggie, and Lily and thanked them as they piled presents into her arms. Dotty, laughing, helped her by offloading some of the gifts and suggested they put them on the end of the bar. Leading Helen closer to the beach huts, she helped her pile up the presents and secretly winked at Brooke.

"Can someone help me?" shouted Brooke, rattling one of the beach hut doors "I need to get some cushions out." Helen seeing that she was the closest strolled over and twisted the door knob.

"Argh!" she screamed and jumped back as a figure almost fell out the door.

"Papa…what…Papa…Molly!" Helen screamed again as her friends jumped out shouting "Surprise!" She didn't know what to do, and everyone laughed as she swung round to look at Dotty and swung quickly back to check she wasn't seeing things "How?…what?…Gerald!" Helen flung her arms round her friends and burst into tears of utter joy."

"I can't believe you kept this a secret" she scolded Dotty "Thank you, thank you so much, it's the best birthday present ever." Everyone seemed happy, she thought, Gerald was chatting to George and Alf, and Molly were sipping cocktails and discussing the joys of homemade honey with Peggy. Papa was snoring contentedly in one of the deckchairs and Markos was listening to Ian explain why they should build a golf course on the island.

"Dad, Dad, quick!" Christos ran towards them with an urgency in his voice "Nora's just rang, she thinks some of her pups might have Parvo." Markos groaned

"How many?" he asked grimly and swore when Christos answered "eight."

"Peggy, Alf, we're going to need your help," he smiled apologetically at Helen, who urged him to go quickly, she knew how dangerous Parvovirus was, and her only thoughts were with the pups.

A quietness had settled over the group, and Helen was telling her friends of her trip around the islands when Brooke suddenly grabbed her arm.

"Helen, there's a funny fat man over there, look!" Brooke pointed to the barn where Percival Boston Jr stood. He was dressed in a large Hawaiian shirt and a baggy pair of matching shorts. It was his feet that were causing most of the snorts and giggles from her friends. A pair of white ankle socks pulled halfway up his calves were encased in a pair of good old fashioned brown leather sandals.

"What ho! Helen" said Percival, waddling towards her and waving enthusiastically "I must say this is all jolly spiffing don't you think."

"Percival…and Daphne, Hello, you got here very quick." Helen hugged the man warmly.

"The Private jet, wonderful invention" boomed Percival "Daphne, folders?" he stuck out his hand and took two pink Manilla folders from her and opened the top one.

"We are all set up for Monday morning at 10 am. The delightful hotel we are staying in has given us a conference room, and invitations will be delivered tomorrow to all the people concerned. It's all so exciting" Percival stopped to take a breath and Helen shushed him and offered him a seat and drink.

"Just one other thing," said Percival. He leant forward and said very quietly to Helen "This other folder contains pictures and a bit of info on all the Lucinda Markham's we could find." He gave an exaggerated wink and held a finger to his lips. "When you have a minute have a peep through, see if you recognise anyone."

Helen stretched and yawned, it was only just gone 7:30 pm but she felt hot and sweaty from the busy day and long drive they'd had today.

"Dotty do you think anyone will mind if I go and have a quick shower and wake myself up a bit?"

"Don't be silly; they probably won't even notice" Helen looked round and agreed everyone was either in the pool or the hot tub or in Gerald and Ian's case following their cave man instinct's and grilling thick steaks on the barbeque. Dotty went to join the fun in the hot tub, and Helen stood up just as Ian's phone shrilled a tinny ringtone.

"It's your mum Molly" he shouted towards the pool "Hi Lucinda, how's it going?"

Helen felt the hairs on the back of her neck stand up. Spinning round she looked at Molly, who was groaning as she took the phone from her husband.

"I thought Molly's mum was called Lucy?" Helen said to Ian with a shiver of fear running down her back.

"Everyone calls her Lucy, but her real names Lucinda." Ian frowned wondering why Helen would ask. Helen pictured Molly's mum, just a few years older than herself. A divorcee who lived way beyond her means. Helen thought back to the sweet little waves she would throw over the fence when William was cutting the grass and the pleas for him to help her with her finances. Filled with horror and letting out a tiny moan she snatched up the folders and ran towards the villa. Gerald was the only one who heard the moan and seeing Helen's white face he followed after her.

He found Helen sat at a large kitchen table scrabbling through a pile of paperwork; she barely glanced up as he walked in the door but it was enough for Gerald to see the panic on her face. She stopped suddenly and stared at a photo with some writing underneath. She slowly raised her horror filled eyes to Gerald.

"Lucinda Markham, Molly's mum, my friends mum…what's going on Gerald? Why would William give Molly's mum so much money?"

Gerald gripped the edge of the table, his knuckles white, he swayed as he realised he would have to tell the truth.

"Oh God Helen, not today, not on your birthday" sobbing he sunk into a chair and clutched his head in his hands.

CHAPTER 23
SEPTEMBER 15TH 2013

Gerald parked the dusty old van he'd hired for the day in the layby and watched William walk to the burger van and purchase two coffees. He was quite sure William hadn't spotted him but just in case he opened a copy of The Sun newspaper and held it in front of his face. Five minutes later he peered over his paper as another car pulled up behind Williams. He recognised the car and the woman who got out, and he scowled angrily as she took a quick glance around and walked towards Williams's car. She was carrying a small white box, and Gerald wondered if it was a parting gift. He was close enough to see her lean over and try to kiss William as she climbed in the car and he was close enough to witness the argument that started when William pushed her away. He knew what is was about, he was the cause of it. A few days earlier as they'd reached the ninth hole on the local golf course William had admitted to yet another affair; this one had got totally out of hand though. There had been many short-lived affairs over the course of Williams's marriage that had finished as quickly as they'd started and none had ever threatened Helen's happiness. This affair though had been going on far too long and was far too close to home. Gerald had given William an ultimatum, finish it or he would tell Helen, not just of this affair but of all the affairs he'd had.

When William had tried to end it, things had turned nasty. Eighteen months before the woman had asked William for a large loan and scared of her veiled threats to tell Helen of their affair he'd stupidly leant her a ridiculous amount of money. She'd paid a bit back but recently the repayments had stopped. William had made the call to the woman there and then in front of Gerald, but the woman was having none of it and demanded he talk to her face to face.

Gerald knew they were meeting today. He'd parked the rusty old van close to Helen and William's house and followed William a few miles up the road to the layby. He needed to be sure it was over. He watched the woman angrily throw open the door, climb out and pace up and down. William climbed out and followed her, his hands gesticulating wildly as the row continued. Gerald shuddered as the woman suddenly turned and angrily slapped William round the face and threw her coffee over his smart suit. *"Nothing less than the old fool deserves,"* Gerald thought. William slumped his shoulders and wiped at the coffee with his sleeve. The woman shoved the now empty cup into his hands and pointed to the nearby litter bin. That's odd thought Gerald. While William walked to the bin, the woman quickly opened the back door of his car and placed the small white box on the back seat. Very odd, must be a parting gift he thought.

He watched the woman drive away with a screech of tyres and a rude gesture. Starting the van, he followed William's car down the country road. He peered through the windscreen and slowed as the car started to veer erratically from side to side, then sped up a bit and watched in horror as William took both hands off the steering wheel and frantically started waving his hands above his head. Gerald slammed his hand hard on his horn scared his friend was having a mental breakdown. It was no good. Williams's car veered off the road and slammed into a nearby tree. Gerald ran faster than he'd ever ran. It was too late; there was nothing he could do he thought as he looked down at his friend's lifeless body.

CHAPTER 24
A STING IN THE TALE

Gerald raced round the table to Helen; he was scared; she didn't seem to be breathing.

"Helen, breathe, slow deep breaths" Helen spluttered and gasped a deep breath in and raised wild eyes to Gerald's face. She threw both arms in the air and started to attack him, battering her arms around his face then thumping her fists against his chest. He gripped her arms tightly trying to stop her.

"Why didn't you tell me?" she screamed, struggling to get out of his tight clutches "Why didn't you tell me how he died? Why didn't you tell me about the affairs?" Helen suddenly slumped to the floor, and he pulled her up and held her tightly in his arms soothing the vicious sobs that were convulsing through her body. When the cries of anguish finally petered to quieter sobs, he sat her gently in a chair and watched her closely as her shoulders continued to shudder.

"I think I knew." She stared through red-rimmed eyes at Gerald. "Deep down I think I knew, all the little signs were there. The too long business trips, the scent of another woman's perfume, the receipts in his pockets for gifts I never received." Helen wiped at her eyes and took a few deep breaths trying to calm herself. "I chose to believe his excuses, I chose to ignore it for the twin's sake; I pretended it wasn't happening."

Gerald tried to take her hands, but she snatched them away, still livid at his betrayal.

"How long Gerald" Helen stuttered "How long was he seeing Molly's mum?"

Gerald dropped his head in his hands; he couldn't bear it.

"It wasn't Molly's mum; it wasn't Lucinda" Helen stared at Gerald. The image of a small yellow post-it note swam in her head *"9 am Meeting with G."*

"No" Helen whispered, then let out a strangled cry "No, not her…please, not her. *"Ginge"* Williams nickname for Molly, her neighbour, her friend, her confidant.

"Molly" came a voice from the doorway "It was Molly." Ian stood there, wringing his hands together. Needing the toilet, he'd followed Gerald to the villa and standing outside the kitchen door, had heard it all. An icy fear was now starting to slither from the depths of his stomach. "I found her diary not long after William died. She'd always told me her mum had invested the money for the Market Garden" Ian joined them at the table. "It was a lie, she'd borrowed it from William, but it was mummy dearest who helped her with a couple of the repayments" he spat out sarcastically. "Gerald, the white box, can you describe it?" Gerald nodded and thought hard as he described the little white box that Molly had placed in the back of Williams car.

"I think you'd better call the police." Ian sounded grim "that sounds like the package our honey bees are delivered in…she only had to loosen the lid…" Ian sunk to the floor, shaking his head "The box would have slid off the seat as the car went round a bend…"

"No, no, no" pleaded Helen as she realised what Ian was saying "Nobody would do that, his bee allergy."

"He would have panicked straight away, and tried to bat the bees away" whispered Gerald "It's why he took his hands off the steering wheel and waved them above his head. Oh my god no!"

"Christ Helen, if I'd have known I would have gone to the police straight away." Ian's face crumpled as he thought how horrific Williams last moments must have been. "I've wanted to tell you so many times about the affair, but what was the point, William was dead, why heap more hurt on you."

Helen shivered, she felt sick and tried to swallow back the bile that was pooling into her throat, gagging she rushed to the sink and vomited again and again until she felt her knees shaking. She slid down to the floor and pulled her knees to her chest hugging them tight.

"Don't call the police now" She stared at Gerald. "These people have been so kind to me, they've opened their hearts and their homes, I can't put them through this." Helen stood back up and splashed her face with water. Taking some water from the fridge, she rinsed out her mouth and sat back down at the table. Thinking of Markos, she drew strength from his love and tried to think.

"We'll call the English police tomorrow. Ian I don't ever want to set eyes on Moll…" Helen stopped realizing she was too late. Molly stood in the doorway paralyzed with fear, her usually pale complexion was bleached white.

"I'm sorry…Helen…I didn't mean to kill him…I just wanted to scare…"

A low guttural moan came from Helen as she slowly stood quivering with rage and hatred. She raised her fists to strike the first blow and Gerald leapt and grabbed her round the waist.

"You killed William; you slept with my husband…" Helen screamed and spat at Molly. She raged and grappled against Gerald's strong grip. Molly's frightened face suddenly turned to a sneer.

"Oh, you're so perfect Helen, with your perfect life and your perfect children…want to know the truth?...You're boring Helen. William found you boring; that's why he wanted me. I gave him what he needed, and he loved me."

"Get out…get out…now" Helen snarled then fell limply against Gerald.

Molly spun around and fled from the villa, she ran into the darkness of the night and stumbled as she slithered down the crumbly chalk road.

"Let her go," said Gerald as Ian got up to follow her "the police will soon find her."

"She's my wife." Ian pleaded. "Right now I hate her, but she's Libby's mother. I have to think of Libby" Ian tried to hug Helen, but she shook him off and thinking of the poor sixteen-year-old Libby she nodded and told Ian to go.

Gerald looked at Helen, and she looked right back, she felt sorry for him. The years of hiding the truth to protect her had taken their toll. He looked so old and tired. She took his hands and tried to smile.

"It's okay, I know why you didn't tell me," she said softly. Gerald bent his head "It's why you sorted all his finances and became so controlling isn't it?" Gerald nodded.

"I love you, Helen; I couldn't bear to hurt you. You are always there for me, every time the black dog rears its ugly head you are the only one that can pull me back up."

Gerald stood and leant against the worktop.

"I know you love me Gerald, but we both know it's just the love of a long and deep friendship, like I have for Dotty" Helen stood and hugged him tightly, rubbing his back as a mother would to a child. "I've told you so many times Gerald; you will only be truly happy when you are honest with yourself and everyone else."

"I know" murmured Gerald "he buried his head in her hair "I know."

Mavra walked towards the villa with the cake in her hands. She'd wondered if she should stop and offer help to the strange woman with the vibrant red hair who was rushing down the road. Spotting a man chasing her she'd decided not to interfere. She glanced through the kitchen window and couldn't believe what she was seeing; Helen Hardy was embracing a tall, silver-haired man. It wasn't just a hug; his face was buried in her hair, and she was stroking her arms up and down his back. Mavra carefully balanced the cake in one hand and reached into her back pocket for her phone. Clicking the little camera icon, she snapped three pictures. She filmed a few seconds of the scene in the kitchen then quietly placed the cake on the doorstep. She ran back to the car with her heart thumping and a joyous feeling coursing through her body. As soon as she'd finished helping out at Nora's she would upload the pictures to Facebook. That would wipe the smile off Helen Hardy's face.

Dotty and Helen sat on the balcony and watched the beautiful sunrise. Helen couldn't even raise a smile at the wondrous sight; she just felt numb. The night had been long and difficult. Dotty had been distraught when everyone left, and Helen finally told her what had happened. Papa was unaware of the events of the previous night and was happily snoring in one of the spare bedrooms. Gerald had finally succumbed to sleep an hour ago and was laying on one of the sofas. Dotty had tutted when Helen laid a blanket over him.

"I don't see how you can forgive him," she said, she couldn't even look at the man who had betrayed Helen so deceitfully.

"Dotty, would you have told me if it was you, honestly?" Dotty had sat and thought for a long while.

"No" she finally admitted "I love you too much to hurt you."

Percival and Daphne were still there, somewhere. The lovely man had sat and listened to the full story and taken a firm control of the horrible situation. Daphne had sat, quietly and professionally taking notes and making phone calls. Hoping Ian had found Molly and taken her back to the hotel, Percival had contacted the local police. They'd heard a short while ago that Molly was under arrest and would be escorted onto the plane this end and escorted off by the police already waiting at Gatwick. Markos had not yet returned, and Helen felt guilty that she wanted him to leave the pups and come home to her.

Markos and Christos were exhausted; they had worked through the night to save the pups and were totally unaware of the events at Villa Elena. They were both grateful for the team of volunteers who had turned up to remove and quarantine the dogs and pups that so far seemed unaffected. Nora had sobbed as Denis had closed up the empty dog's quarters and placed a large "No Dogs" sign on the gate. It would be six months before the area could be used again, even after decontamination with bleach and disinfectant. Christos had his feet up on the dashboard and was struggling to keep his eyes open. He felt his phone vibrate and wearily glanced at the Facebook post. At first glance, it looked like a happy picture of two people embracing but the words written above it made him sit up straight and look more closely.

"Happy Birthday to Helen Hardy, who just turned 50. How lovely, she got a very special surprise when her boyfriend turned up from the UK."

Christos groaned as he realised the picture was definitely Helen, and she was definitely wrapped in Gerald's arms. The man seemed to be murmuring sweet nothings into her hair. A second post suddenly appeared. A video. There was no mistaking the way that Helen was lovingly stroking her arms up and down the man's back.

"What is it?" asked Markos looking at his son. Christos debated whether to show his dad the incriminating photo and short video clip then guessed that if he didn't, someone else soon would.

"Pull over Dad" Christos waited until a concerned Markos had stopped the truck then grimly showed him his phone.

Markos jolted as the bottom fell out of his world. For the second time in his life, he'd fallen in love and once again it had been with a conniving two timing bitch. He slammed his hands angrily on the steering wheel and berated himself for being so stupid. He should have trusted his instincts. He hadn't trusted that Gerald from the moment he first met him the night before. His face had been full of guilt.

"I've been a fool…again" Markos started the engine and continued his journey, he would drop Christos off then decide what to do.

Helen and Dotty's phones both started to ping and buzz with messages at the same time. As the island of Zakynthos woke to the dreadful Facebook posts, the rumour mill was alight with gossip. Dotty stared as comments were added so quickly to the post that her phone couldn't keep up. Helen stared at the text message from Lily *"Please tell me this isn't true"* and one from Peggy *"What happened last night?"* She looked at the post that had now been added to Twitter and Instagram and moaned. Gerald, on the sofa, was woken by the constant pings and beeps. He walked out to the balcony and frowned as Dotty and Helen were both rapidly tapping away on their phones. Shaking his head and yawning he made his way to the kitchen thinking that coffee might help whatever was going on.

The fifteen-minute journey had helped calm Markos down. Christos had been the voice of reason as he'd tried to reassure his Dad that Helen wasn't like that, and there was probably a very simple explanation. He drove straight past the villa and dropped Christos next to the little guest villa that Carly and Brooke were staying in. Needing some air and wanting to stretch his legs before he faced Helen, he left the truck where it was and lighting a rare but much-needed cigarette he strolled towards Madeline's villa He was angry with himself for jumping to conclusions, Helen didn't deserve the thoughts he'd had. Helen wasn't anything like Amelia; he thought smiling wryly. Stopping outside the kitchen window to extinguish the cigarette beneath his boot, he glanced through the pane of glass and felt his whole body stiffen. He clenched his fists so tightly that his nails dug into his palms and drew blood. Gerald was in the kitchen, very much making himself at home. He was dressed in the same crumpled clothes he'd had on the night before and it was obvious he'd been there the whole night. Markos gritted his teeth as a blistering anger surged through him. He opened and closed his fists and fought the overwhelming urge to storm in and beat the man senseless. Spinning on one foot, he ran back to his truck and took off. Stopping at the bottom of the hill he pulled out his phone and sent Helen a sarcastic message. *"Good luck with your inheritance, I hope you and Gerald enjoy every minute of it!"*

Helen was tempted to turn her phone off and ignore the constant messages, but she still hadn't heard from Markos, and an icy fear was causing her to shiver uncontrollably. Dotty had tried to calm her. Markos was a sensible man; he wouldn't take any notice of the silly picture or video. Helen wasn't so sure; she had a really bad feeling in the pit of her stomach. She took the fresh mug of coffee from Gerald but kept her eye on her phone. Finally, she saw his name displayed, and she opened the message.

Helen couldn't even cry. She looked at the horizon, and as her eyes drifted to the cliffs at the end of Gerakas beach, she wondered what it would feel like to throw herself off. Devoid of any emotions she numbly went through the routine of showering and dressing herself. Brushing her hair, she idly picked up the half empty packets of the strong painkillers that Dr. Marouda had prescribed. That wouldn't hurt, she thought, it would be just like drifting away. Dotty walked over and took the pills gently from her hand. She took the hairbrush and brushed Helens hair whispering soothing words. Dotty didn't know what to do. She had never seen Helen like this. When William had died there had been tears, and grief filled anger. This was different. Helen was scaring her. The icy hands and the sheer lack of any emotion were frightening to watch. Dotty had tried showing her the funny and loving video the twins had sent for her birthday. Helen had watched without comment then calmly asked how she should tell the twins that their father was a serial adulterer who had been murdered by his mistress. Dotty eased Helen down against the pillows and pulled the duvet over her. She patted the bed for Puddles to jump up and taking the tablets went to ring Peggy.

Across the island, a man on a moped was dropping invitations through people's doors. The thick cream envelopes were eagerly being opened, and phones were busily ringing. Those due to work at 10 am the next day were hastily rearranging their busy schedules. Nobody wanted to miss the moment Helen stated her intentions. Selena was busy double checking the pictures and film that showed Helen leaving the island. Mavra's wonderful Facebook post was just an bonus she thought gleefully.

Mavra was shopping in Zante town; she was trying to find the same Maxi dress that Helen had worn at the dog show. She stopped at the bridal shop and moving so that her reflection seemed to be wearing one of the beautiful gowns she smiled. "I think we will marry at the chapel on the sea," she said aloud to nobody in particular.

Peggy was wringing her hands together. They'd been catching up on much-needed sleep when Dotty had rung and told them the awful things that had happened the night before. That poor, poor girl she thought and that stupid, stupid Markos. Alf had gone to get the dear Dr. Marouda, hoping he could help.

Lily and Maggie were cooking breakfast and keeping a close eye on their phones, waiting for news. Elias and George were combing the island for the missing Markos.

Molly with her head held high and still protesting her innocence, was being escorted onto an EasyJet plane. Ian trailed behind and refused to sit anywhere near her. He needed to get home to their daughter who was blissfully unaware her mum may be spending the next few years in prison.

Papa had woken to the sombre atmosphere that invaded the villa. He listened carefully as Gerald told him the terrible truth about his son. He had allowed himself to shed a few tears then with wisdom that came with his eighty years of age he sat himself on the edge of Helens bed, he stroked her hair and held her hand.

The hours ticked by and still Helen didn't move. The kindly doctor had given her a sedative but each time Dotty checked Helen was still awake and staring out of the large window and rhythmically stroking Puddles head. Christos had woken and joined the search for his father, Carly, sensibly, had taken Brooke to the beach. As dusk started to settle over Zakynthos Helen rose from her bed and moved to her aunt's favourite chair on the balcony. She could hear the quiet chatter in the kitchen as she rocked back and forth and knew they were all concerned about her, but she was alright. Her mind was firmly focussed on the name in the envelope. Percival had tried to insist she cancel the meeting; she still had six days to make a decision, but Helen had shaken her head. At 10 am on Monday morning, Helen would be there, ready to state her intentions.

The chance to live here, happily, with Markos was gone. She knew she could explain the photo and a few simple words about Gerald would reassure Markos, but she wouldn't betray a confidence and besides all that Markos had hurt her deeply. He hadn't trusted her; he hadn't even come back to talk to her. Helen stroked Puddles ears and felt the little shotgun pellet lodged in his ear. This was real unconditional love she thought, the love between her and her dog and the only love she needed. She thought of Bethany and her cats and Nora, Peggy, Alf and Lily, all dear, sweet, caring people who truly deserved the inheritance. Christos? She wondered, was he too young? Puddles lifted his paw onto her lap and whimpered.

"I know Puddles, it's tough, I think I have to choose between Christos and Bethany" Puddles just thumped his tail, and she smiled down at the soppy dog. "They are both young, they both fit the clues in the codicil, but which one? Oh, Puddles if only you could talk" A thought popped into her head and for the first time in twenty-four hours a smile hovered around her lips. She walked back into her room and re-read all the letters from her Aunt. She picked up the codicil and ran her finger across the words. "I know who it is," She said to herself "I know who it is."

CHAPTER 25
THE LOGIC OF A CHILD

Markos unzipped the sleeping bag and shivered in the cold morning sun. The little stone shepherds hut did little to keep the chilly mountain air out, and he quickly lit the small gas camping stove. Taking a pan to a nearby spring, he scooped up some water and placed it on the stove. He needed a coffee before he did anything else. Hearing the chug of a motorbike he groaned. Elias, he thought, only his oldest and best friend would guess where he was. He dug in his rucksack for another tin mug. Elias climbed off the bike and looked at his old friend, his red-rimmed eyes and pale face told of a night of pure anguish. He hugged Markos tightly and accepted the coffee. He handed Markos the cream envelope and watched as the vet read the invitation then silently held it to the little gas flame till the ashes blew away on the breeze. Elias started to speak; he told Markos a tale of a wonderful woman who had been so betrayed by the man who was her husband. He told of the ginger haired woman who had murdered the man. He told of the man's best friend who had finally told Helen the truth and had held her as she'd wept in his arms. Lastly, he told of Helen's decision to try and guess who was named in the secret, sealed envelope.

Markos felt his heart shattering as he thought of the horrors he'd left Helen to deal with on her own. The shame and remorse welled to a crescendo of tears, and he fell into his friend's arms and sobbed for the love he'd thrown away. Elias looked at his watch; it was only 8:30 am. There was still time to make it. He shook his friend's shoulders roughly and shouted at him. Turning off the gas stove, he pulled Markos up and led him to the bike. Markos' truck was parked at the bottom of the mountain, and when they reached it they lifted the bike into the back, and Elias climbed behind the wheel.

Helen paced the hotel room starting to doubt her thoughts. The night before she'd been convinced she was right but a fitful sleep had left her wondering. The tired faces of her friends had been shocked when she'd marched, fully dressed into the kitchen that morning. She had used her stern teacher's voice and briskly hurried them all to get ready. They'd arrived at the hotel in town an hour early but so had many other people and inside she'd shivered as she felt the many hate-filled eyes glaring her way. Holding her head high and with nothing to be ashamed of she'd allowed Daphne to lead her and her friends to a large executive suite where breakfast and coffee were provided. Helen looked over to Brooke, who was playing Minecraft on the hotels Xbox. She sat down beside the young girl.

"I think I need your help Brooke?" Brooke looked up at her with shining eyes. "I have to work out a secret, do you think you can help?" Brooke nodded excitedly and listened carefully. "My Aunt Madeline wrote a name down on a piece of paper and hid it in an envelope." Helen smiled at the concentration on Brookes' face "Well, this name would be the person that my aunt loved and trusted most in the whole world, and I have to guess who it is."

"Oh that's easy," said Brooke. Helen tapped her ear and smiled as Brooke quickly whispered a name.

"That's exactly what I thought" smiled Helen, she was always in awe of children's simple logic. While adults would mull over and analyse things for hours, a child would just state the obvious.

"Are we all ready?" Daphne held the door open and ushered the small group through. Helen gripped Dotty's hand and tried to calm the butterflies in her stomach. They were led through a side door, and Helen blanched at the rows of people seated in the conference room. Percival was stood alone at the front, and he invited Helen to sit in a lonely chair next to him. She sat and with her hands nestled in her lap she bowed her head. Puddles trotted up beside her and settled at her feet. He thumped his tail a few times grateful for the sausages Brooke had sneaked his way.

"Ahem, hush please" Percival held his hand up for silence. "In order to meet the exact terms of the codicil I need to check that everyone invited is present. When Daphne reads your name out, please raise your hand" Daphne slowly read out the names listed in alphabetical order and people raised their hands and answered yes. When she shouted "Markos Kalvos" a silence descended and everyone glanced nervously around. Daphne repeated the name and Helen's head shot up as a quiet "yes" came from the back of the room. Markos was stood with Elias; his pleading eyes met Helen's, but she dropped her head needing to remain calm until this whole silly business was over.

"Jolly good" boomed Percival "We shall begin. Helen if you would like to stand up and declare your intentions."

"Hold on, hold on" Selena Warrington-Smyth stood and walked to the front of the room. She raised her hand for silence "I wish to declare the codicil null and void. I have absolute proof that Helen Hardy did not remain on Zakynthos so therefore did not fulfil the instructions" Selena nodded to Mavra, who switched on the overhead projector and fiddled with the attached laptop. The gathered group gasped and excited chattering spread through the room as a photo of Helen and Markos kissing filled the screen in front of them. A short film of them climbing the steps of the plane and taking off followed. Selena sniffed and thrust her mighty bosoms out thrilled at the reaction she'd got.

"Quiet, please quiet" Percival flapped his hands up and down trying with little effect to regain order in the room. Dotty marched up to the front and shouted "Shut up" and waited for everyone to settle before she smiled at Percival and suggested he continue.

"Ah, right erm Helen did you leave Zakynthos?"

"Yes," Helen answered honestly "We went to Athens, Mykonos, Santorini…"

"And Kefalonia," said Markos loudly. He locked his eyes on Helen's as he walked up the side of the room. They smiled at each other as they remembered the wonderful six days and nights. Markos stood behind Helen and placed his hand on her shoulder.

"Selena" Markos looked at the snotty woman "The codicil clearly states that Helen must remain in Greece, it does not mention Zakynthos. I can confirm that at no point did Helen leave Greece" Selena turned white and stared at the faces all looking accusingly at her. Peggy, bristling with anger grabbed Alf's phone and marched to the laptop, grateful that Jacob had shown her what to do she pulled a wire from her pocket and deftly connected the phone and pressed play. Selena's snotty and condescending voice echoed around the room describing how she would poison the dogs at Madeline's feeding station and how it would not be the first time she had poisoned the poor strays. The room erupted into utter chaos as Peggy sat back down and Alf patted her on the back. Mavra walked over and slapped Selena round the face and spat at her back as the woman ducked her head and wobbled towards the door but her usually meek, and mild husband stood firmly in her way.

"Oh no you don't" Philip yelled "This meeting can't finish if you leave the room" George saw her eyeing up the other side door and took up a firm stance in front of it. He winked at Philip and looked forward to their next beer together.

Eventually, calm was restored, and Percival mopped his sweaty brow and continued.

"We have ascertained that Helen Hardy has not broken the terms of the codicil" he paused for a breath and smiled kindly at Helen "Now then Helen can you inform us of your intentions" Helen reached up and gripped the hand that was still reassuringly on her shoulder.

"I intend to guess the person who is named in the sealed envelope" you could easily have heard a pin drop in the silence that followed the initial gasps. Markos gripped her shoulder tighter, with him there, he had hoped she would change her mind, but he wasn't going to abandon her now.

Daphne handed Helen a whiteboard and pen and Percival held up the sealed envelope to show that the seal was still intact. Markos looking over her shoulder frowned then grimaced and shook his head in dismay as she slowly wrote a name. Percival thoroughly enjoying the theatrics, took the whiteboard and handed it to Daphne who held it hidden against her chest. He opened the envelope and pulled out a single sheet of paper. Practicing earlier they both knew what to do. The jolly fat solicitor looked at Daphne and counted "One…two…three" and they turned the whiteboard and paper for all to see. The same name was written twice, once on the paper and once on the whiteboard. The shocked silence was broken by Christos as he climbed on his chair and whooped.

Helen looked down at the dog that was still happily at her feet. "Good boy Puddles" she whispered "good boy" The daft dog just thumped his tail he didn't have a clue why everyone was clapping and cheering and not being cleverer enough to read didn't realise his name was the one that Madeline had tearfully written so many months ago.

Hours later Gerald stood in the kitchen and shook Markos' hand.

"Markos, I'm happy for you and Helen. I love her deeply but only as a friend. I could never love a woman in the way you think" Gerald gulped and for only the second time in his life uttered the words "I'm gay." He felt a huge weight lift from his shoulders as Markos patted his arm and merely shrugged in a non-judgemental way. Dotty shook her head "*I bloody knew it*" she thought. She'd been telling Helen for years, but Helen had always vehemently denied it. Helen just smiled, many, many years in the early eighties when the horror of Aids first started to shock the nation, Gerald had uttered the same words to her. His future as a cardiologist hung in the balance, the thought of a homosexual surgeon would terrify any patients. She had kept his secret and never told a soul.

Helen settled in the rocking chair with Puddles at her feet. She opened the letter that Percival had given her and started to read.

Darling Helen

If you're reading this, then you've decided to stay on the island, or you've guessed the right name. I hope you chose to guess, and I pray you got it right. Only a true dog lover and someone worthy to take my place would know that Puddles was the one. I also knew that Puddles would find a new owner and dogs are the best judge of character aren't they? Whoever he chose would be the right one to guard and manage his inheritance.

I've been quite naughty haven't I? You see when I was first told I was going to die, many months before I told anyone else I started to look for you. The wonderful Percival tracked you down. He told me of your life as a teacher. He showed me photos of you, gosh you look so much like me, how funny. Your twins are beautiful James and Annabelle, such lovely names. Your husband, William, it broke my heart to find out he'd died and in such tragic circumstances. I'm so sorry my dear. Don't tell poor Percival off for his lie's he was only doing as I asked.

I wish I had a crystal ball, so I could peer into the future and see what happens but who knows if there is life after death I will surely be watching. I pray every night that you do the right thing. Your father hated me for what I did; I hope you don't hold the same hate in your heart.

I have a silly dream sometimes, a happy dream, though. I dream I am sitting on my balcony watching down below as you and Markos walk hand in hand along the beach with Puddles racing happily beside you. Silly I know.

I love you Helen, whatever you decide I will always love you. Goodbye, my dear.

You're loving Aunt Madeline

Helen kissed the letter and held it close to her heart. The silent tears flowed freely down her cheeks. The next few weeks would be hard. She would have to tell the twins about their father and she still had so many questions about her father and Madeline. It could all wait a while though she thought. With Puddles and Markos and her new friends by her side she could be strong. Helen looked up at the handsome man who had walked out to join her and took hold of his strong, tanned hands. She smiled as she thought of the thirty days it had taken Madeline to fall in love.

"I fell in love too" she whispered.

EPILOGUE
OCTOBER 1ST 2015

Helen sat in the white wicker rocking chair with Puddles at her feet. She stroked the tiny puppy in her lap and smiled as it burped, contended with the full belly of the bottled milk. Helen gazed over at the turquoise hues of the Ionian Sea and felt totally at peace. She rocked gently back and forth. She had finally got her head around the vastness of her aunt's estate, the winery and the shop and properties in the town had come as a huge shock to her. The assets added to much more than a million and Helen was determined to do nothing but good with her inheritance. The plans to reopen the barn next spring were already underway.

The last few months had been hard. She'd flown to some remote island in the Indian Ocean to tell the twins face to face the truth behind their father's death. The pain was still etched on her face when she returned alone. She'd encouraged them to continue their travels and keep far away from the horrors of Molly's court case. Molly had finally pleaded guilty to manslaughter and was serving her sentence in some women's prison in Yorkshire. Ian had sold the house and business and disappeared with their daughter Libby.

Papa was loving being an honorary Greek, he had refused to leave Helen and still stubbornly independent, had happily moved into one of the guest villas.

Carly and Brooke were in another one. They were all amazed at how quickly Brooke was picking up the Greek language. The pretty young girl had refused Helen's offer to home-tutor her and had enrolled at the nearby village school.

Suzanne was putting her feet up during the last month of her pregnancy and between feeding the many pups, Peggy was happily knitting far too many baby clothes.

Selena had disappeared, Philip was still on the island, he had no idea where his wife had gone, and he didn't care. His new 50-inch Smart television was permanently tuned to Sky Sports, and he was finally enjoying his retirement.

Mavra had chosen to hide away in her little house and was rarely seen. She had changed her vets, and Markos no longer had to hide in his little operating theatre.

Maggie and George had said a tearful goodbye with promises to look more seriously at moving to Zakynthos permanently.

Gerald had returned a few weeks ago and stayed in one of Helens guest villas. He had shyly introduced Helen to his new partner Simon, a lovely man.

And Dotty, the lovely Dotty was currently hidden in Helen's bedroom. Markos had picked her up early that morning, and Helen didn't have a clue. She peeped round the edge of the curtains and told Markos to hurry up before she once again wet herself with excitement. Dotty smothered a squeal as Markos gave Puddles the little box and told him to take it to Helen. She watched as Markos followed the dog out and dropped to one knee beside Helen and she clapped her hands with glee as Helen opened the box and gasped, nodded through her tears and allowed Markos to place the beautiful diamond ring on her finger. Helen threw her arms around Markos, kissing him deeply. Dotty thought she'd give them a few minutes, well maybe a few seconds. She dropped the curtain and raced out to congratulate her best friend, already mentally designing a one-off Grecian wedding dress.

The End

ABOUT THE AUTHOR

Netty Morgan is a happily married Mum to four wonderful grown-up children and "Nanny" to three gorgeous Grandchildren. Netty lives in Berkshire with her husband, cats, and dogs. Taking early retirement from a career in teaching, Netty finally had the time to fulfil her lifelong wish to write a novel.

Two of Netty's biggest passions are the beautiful Greek island of Zakynthos and the stray dogs and cats that relentlessly roam the streets. Going through the process of adopting two dogs and a kitten Netty has made many special friends who live on Zakynthos and devote themselves to rescuing, fostering and rehoming the strays.

Facebook:
https://www.facebook.com/profile.php?id=100011532543519

Puddles of Love: https://www.facebook.com/Puddles-of-Love-by-Netty-Morgan-1679371255648793/?fref=ts

Email: nettymorganauthor@gmail.com